CROSSES TO BEAR

A MACDUFF BROOKS NOVEL

M. W. GORDON

Crosses to Bear
 Published in the United States by Swift Creeks Press

swiftcreekspress@gmail.com
www.swiftcreekspress.com

SWIFT CREEKS PRESS EDITION, NOVEMBER 2012

Mill Creek, Paradise Valley, and the areas around Livingston, Bozeman, Emigrant, Jackson Hole, St. Augustine, and Gainesville are real places, hopefully described accurately but used fictionally in this novel. This is a work of fiction, and the characters are either the product of the author's imagination or are used fictionally. Any resemblance to actual persons, living or dead, or to actual events or locales is unintentional and coincidental.

Library of Congress Cataloging-in-Publication Data
Gordon, M.W.
Crosses to Bear/ M.W. Gordon

ISBN-13 978-0-9848723-2-9

Printed in the United States of America

For Buff, Beth, Huntly and Patty, Brittany, Garrett, Kendall, Stephen, and Ellie

ACKNOWLEDGMENTS

This book was written with the encouragement of family, friends, and the many readers of the first of the Macduff Brooks novels: *Deadly Drifts.*

Particular thanks go to Roy Hunt, Johnnie Irby, Jeffrey Harrison, Marilyn Henderson, and my editor Iris Rose Hart.

PROLOGUE

Elsbeth Brooks looked up from the manuscript, removed her new reading glasses, and stared out from her small cottage over the turquoise undulations of Pine Island Sound bordering Captiva Island, Florida. She was oblivious to eight brown pelicans that had caught an uplift, and moved silently with rigid wings along the high tide mark. Four glided in a ragged line stretching off to the left from the leader, three to the right—a kind of missing pelican formation. She closed and set the yellowing, frayed-edged manuscript on the table beside her and sipped from a glass of ice tea—the ice long melted as she had been captivated by the three hundred pages her dad Macduff had written years ago. It was the second manuscript he had sent to her in the past year.

The first had confirmed the obvious: her dad and Wuff had survived the shooting on Osprey *during the float from Deadman's Bar to Moose. She had wondered as a teen why Wuff—the family sheltie—had a slight limp that increasingly bothered her in her twilight years. Elsbeth had never known that on that same float Lucinda Lang had been shot several times, was critically injured, and for two weeks had been in a coma in a Salt Lake City hospital.*

For years, Elsbeth had tried every tactic she could think of to convince her dad to move to Captiva and spend his remaining years with her. He had turned ninety-one last month, and she worried about his isolation living alone in his log cabin on Mill Creek in Paradise Valley, Montana. Milly, the daughter of his long-time housekeeper, Mavis, often looked in on him and increasingly had to make up excuses for doing so, such as bringing mail from the post office or dropping off some special meal Milly had tried and cooked "too much of" for her own family's needs.

Last month Elsbeth finished transferring the title to Macduff's land south of St. Augustine on which his winter cottage had sat—a gift to the National Conservancy. Macduff's occasional helper, Jen, had passed away three years earlier. Jen's son Tom handled the legal work for the land transfer. He was a prominent attorney in St. Augustine whom her dad had mentored for many years. Tom had always suspected that Macduff had some legal training, but Macduff never told Tom about Maxwell Hunt. Elsbeth thought she would let Tom read her dad's two manuscripts, but only after Macduff passed on to wherever loving fathers go.

Tears flowed freely as Elsbeth reread the parts about Lucinda.

CROSSES TO BEAR

THE SECOND MANUSCRIPT

1

AT PRECISELY FIVE P.M. one hazy, humid mid-July evening, on a day I hadn't guided fly fishing clients, I heard an oboe begin to play the plaintive theme for the duck in Prokofiev's *Peter and the Wolf*. Prokofiev must have disliked the oboe: His duck was quickly eaten by the wolf, and the oboe is heard no more. But the duck's plea I was hearing was the ringtone on my cell phone.

I knew it was five p.m. when the call came because I was setting a dinner bowl on the tiny Oriental rug, serving as Wuff's dining mat, in a corner of the kitchen of my log cabin forty miles north of Yellowstone National Park. My place is not far from the ubiquitous blinking traffic light at Emigrant. Most Montanans do not favor traffic lights. Even though the light at Emigrant only blinks, rarely slowing the occasional vehicle, some locals think the signal is an unnecessary government intrusion.

Ever since my rescued sheltie, Wuff, recovered from being shot in my drift boat *Osprey*, she has been obsessed with the idea that living with me means her next meal may be her last and that she's *entitled* to special treatment. I was shot on that same float three times more than Wuff was, and no one's giving *me* any special treatment. Wuff expects her meals to be served promptly. Once she tolerated leaving me a ten minute window on the far sides of six a.m. and five p.m., but since the shooting her meals have become due at *exactly* those times. Earlier service is appreciated, but any slight delay causes an annoying, nasal whine, followed by physical prodding with her long nose.

I picked up my cell phone, a replacement for the phone that was shot on that float. "Macduff here."

A Spanish accented voice from what sounded like a confident, assertive Mexican woman asked with interrogating authority, "You Meester Macdoof Brucks?"

"Close," I answered.

"You speek Spanish, no?"

"Not in America." I keep deceiving myself that English remains the official language in the United States. But I also keep believing that enforcing such an abstract notion is a losing battle considering the capricious and fatuous herds we send to Washington and our state capitals.

"You the Meester Brucks who take people catch feesh?"

"I try."

"I am VictoriaGlorianaGonzalezMontoyaCaranza," she said without pause, making it sound like a Mexico City law firm. "You call me Veeky."

"Thanks . . . Veeky."

"I want you know *my* beezness ees now do all you shuttle beezness. Start mañana."

"Julie Conyers does my shuttle service. I'm very happy with her. But thank you. Maybe if she isn't available I could call you sometime."

"You no comprendo, Meester Brucks. *I* now do you beezness. Julie no can do it no more."

"Veeky, Julie hasn't told me she and her partners have sold their business. I talked to her this morning. She's doing a shuttle for me tomorrow."

Julie's business—the Shuttle Gals—formed about five years ago. They're a reliable and efficient quintet and the choice of many Yellowstone River fly fishing guides. For a fee—thirty-five dollars this summer—they pick up my SUV and trailer where I've launched my drift boat and drop them off downstream where I plan to take the boat out after a day's float.

During the fishing season they may do as many as thirty shuttles a day. With decent weather they take in about a $1,000 a day. That translates into $30,000 a month because during the season they work every day. After expenses it means nearly $5,000 a month for each of the women and maybe twice that for Julie, who organizes the service and manages the scheduling and bookkeeping. The gals take pride in their service and welcome the extra income.

Julie's a single, lesbian mom with a nine-year-old son, George. Lucy Denver's married to a finish carpenter. Marge Atwood's living off-and-on with a fly fishing and hunting guide, and Olga Smits and Pam Snyder are partners who went through a civil ceremony in San Francisco and, despite Montana law, hold themselves out as *married.* They are all the best of friends, and I had no idea they were even contemplating selling their business.

"*I* do you shuttle mañana," the Montoya woman continued. "Same arrangements, but cost now sixty dollars. Cash only. In advance. See you mañana, Macdoof."

More than a little confused, I poured a glass of Spanish Rioja, a Montecillo *Crianza*, drew a deep breath of its fruity aroma, took two sips, and called Julie. I interrupted her preparing dinner for George.

"Julie, I just finished a strange call from a Vicky something, who said she's taking over all your shuttles. Starting *tomorrow*. I didn't know you and the other Shuttle Gals were selling out. You're too young to retire and I'll miss you."

"*Damn!* Macduff, we're not selling to that obnoxious, loco fat little Chihuahua. She showed up at my door yesterday and announced that she was taking over all the shuttle services in the valley. *Starting* with the Shuttle Gals. Can you believe it? . . . *Announced!* I told her where to go. She asked me if I knew who her brother was. I said I hoped not. She said that he was Roberto Montoya of Ciudad Juarez in Mexico and that he was *muy importante* . . . a real VIP in that *hell-hole, cesspool, drug-infested* border town."

"Julie!" I interrupted, "calm down! I've never heard you this angry. Forget her."

"I met that creep two months ago. We rented a hot tub room at the Valley Spa to talk about the business and have fun. We hung a sign on the door that said: 'Reserved-Private.' Montoya barged in anyway, stripped, jumped in our tub like a tsunami, and began telling us how rich and important she and her brother are. We sort of politely asked her to leave. She started swearing at us in Spanish. At least it sounded like swearing the way she said whatever she said."

"Julie, let me do some checking. I'll call you back in a bit, after your dinner. . . . Say hello to George for me." I hung up, topped off my *Crianza*, and went through my week's pile of *The New York Times*. I was looking for an article I'd read a day or two ago. Reading the *Times* in Montana is often like reading science fiction—*not one* of the articles bears any resemblance to your own life. One of the *Times'* recent feature stories was about drug-related violence bleeding across the uncontrolled border between Mexico's Ciudad Juarez and the U.S.'s El Paso.

Downstairs in my "music room," entered by a stairway hidden behind a bookcase that swings out as a door, I turned on my computer, went on the *Times'* website, and typed in "Roberto Montoya Ciudad Juarez Mexico." The results were worse than watching *Texas Chainsaw Massacre.*

A dozen articles linked Montoya to the Juarez drug cartel. More than *linked*, he had seized the role of cartel *jefe* in the past year by repulsively brutal killings. He heads the *Olmecas,* one of two competing Ciudad Juarez and El Paso cartels that control drugs.

Two months ago Montoya and other *Olmecas* crossed the border to El Paso, drove to an exclusive gated residential community, and walked into a *Cinco de Mayo* holiday backyard garden party at a home Montoya mistakenly thought was owned by the head of the other cartel—the *Caimans*—alligators. The *Olmecas* machine-gunned everyone present, killing thirty-two, including eight women and seventeen children. Three dozen police arrived, suspiciously too late to do any good. Fourteen of those police resigned from the El Paso police force the next day.

One brief year-old piece in the *Times*, buried in a discussion of high-end U.S. house sales to Mexican drug lords, noted that Roberto Montoya had bought a four-million-dollar home in Jackson Hole, Wyoming. It's in a gated community in Teton Pines near the ski slopes; the same gated community where former Vice-President Cheney owns a home. Montoya lives only three houses away from the Cheney McMansion. It's rumored that one morning Cheney, in a rush to get to the golf course, saw Montoya jogging, stopped the car, rolled down the window, and tried to hire him as a gardener.

Further searching disclosed that Montoya had a sister Victoria. She'd been married to the Saltillo drug cartel boss who was brutally murdered a year ago in a turf war with the Tijuana cartel. What remained of him was found impaled on the spikes of a giant Sago cactus below a "Bienvenidos a México" billboard ten miles south of the border at Mexicale. There's always hope for good Mexicans that the cartel members will keep knocking off each other like the U.S. mafia used to do.

The article also told about Victoria being in trouble in Ciudad Juarez, where she manages the protection racket for her brother—extorting weekly payments from small businesses to assure that organized crime wouldn't bother them. Not surprisingly, the organized crime that wouldn't bother them was her brother's cartel.

The protection racket was one of the *Olmecas* cartel's businesses, but it was threatened by the *Caimans*. They had put a price on Victoria Montoya's head two months earlier, soon after their leader's spouse was murdered and dumped in the Rio Grande. The slain spouse's sister, Teresa Tormenta, overseer of the *Caimans'* youth gang, the *Alacranes*—scorpions—had made one unsuccessful attempt on Victoria Montoya's life. Roberto was less concerned about the hatred between Victoria and Teresa than he was about the thought that his sister's disputes would disrupt one of the most lucrative parts of his cartel's businesses.

The most disturbing part of the *Times'* articles disclosed the cartels' increasing use of youth gangs as training grounds for careers with the cartels. Members had life expectancies no better than Mexican soldiers had while serving under Santa Anna a century-and-a-half earlier.

The gangs were made up mostly of homeless youths, often as young as ten or eleven. They'd proven to be unrepentive, callous killers who without the slightest remorse disposed of anyone they were ordered to kill. By the time a gang member turned sixteen, he (and in many cases—she) had killed as many as twenty or thirty people. Their brutality confirmed, members "graduated" to being assassins for the cartels, however short that new career might be.

Victoria Montoya formed her own youth gang in Ciudad Juarez to collect the protection payments. It took the name *Cascabelas*—rattlesnakes—and had become the most ruthless border-city youth gang.

To avoid questioning after her husband's murder and the death of the *Caimans'* leader's spouse, and further urged by Roberto who was at times scared of his sister, Victoria moved to the United States. Not as an illegal. She was a U.S. citizen by birth.

Her mother, a Mexican citizen who once operated a small laundry in a village outside Chihuahua, had never married. But she gave birth to seven children, including Victoria and Roberto, the only two who shared the same father. Except when Roberto was born—in Mexico—each time her eighth month of pregnancy arrived, Victoria's mother hired a coyote who snuck her over the border. She showed up on the doorstep of one of El Paso's public hospitals. *She* got free maternity care. Each new baby got U.S. citizenship. The El Paso hospital got stuck with the bills.

When I tried a separate online search under *Victoria* Montoya, I discovered she'd bought a large ranch in Paradise Valley from an American movie star. The celeb had overpaid for the ranch, moved in for a decade, tired of the isolation (and even more from the lack of local adulation—not to mention the absence of any nearby rehab centers), and relocated to another celebrity-favored hot spot.

Victoria Montoya's ranch was only six or seven miles from my Mill Creek cabin. I'd heard rumors about her place. Literally in the middle of one night, her imported, illegal Mexican workers had torn down a large classic log ranch-house that was on the National Register of Historic Places. She'd replaced it with a concrete block copy of Tara from *Gone with the Wind.* She thought of herself as Scarlett O'Hara and even dressed the part. Displeased neighbors were calling the house *Casa Mala*—Bad House.

≈

Later that evening I called Julie back, having given her time to digest her dinner. I told her what I had learned about Roberto and his family. "Has Victoria threatened you?" I asked. "Did she try to get your shuttle service to pay weekly amounts for protection?"

"*Nothing* about protection. She was threatening only by her manner, swearing, and *announcing* she was taking over our business. She never said she would *do* anything to me. I think she believes we'll give in to her."

"Julie, let's hope she's bluffing. Anyway, I'll see you at the Emigrant ramp tomorrow morning if you're there to do my shuttle by eight. We'll see what happens. If I were you, I'd be careful. The Mexican drug cartels aren't people to fool around with."

"OK, Macduff. Thanks. You're a love!"

I savored the last sip of wine and called Victoria Montoya. Without giving her a chance to interrupt, I said, "Ms. Montoya, this is Macduff Brooks. I've talked with Julie Conyers. She hasn't sold her business to you. She will continue to do my shuttles. Including tomorrow."

"I *took* her beezness!" she screamed into the phone. "I no pay her *nothin'!*"

"Another thing, Ms. Montoya. I searched you and your brother on the internet. I don't want anything to do with either of you. *Stay away* from my shuttle people. And don't call me again."

"You sumbeech, Macdoof. Nobody talk this way with Victoria Montoya. I ask 'bout you, too. I know lots. You got sick girlfriend in Hanover, Indiana. Lives with Mother. Pearson Avenida. Numero 47. You give me trouble I send man there with beeg gun. I *love* think 'bout him shove barrel in girlfriend's mouth and pull trigger. Shoot brains all over bedroom. No more sick!"

I could hear her laughing.

"You like that, Macdoof?"

I *didn't* like that, but I didn't say anything more. I hung up, opened the door in my bookcase, went downstairs to my music room, and cleaned and loaded a 9mm Glock.

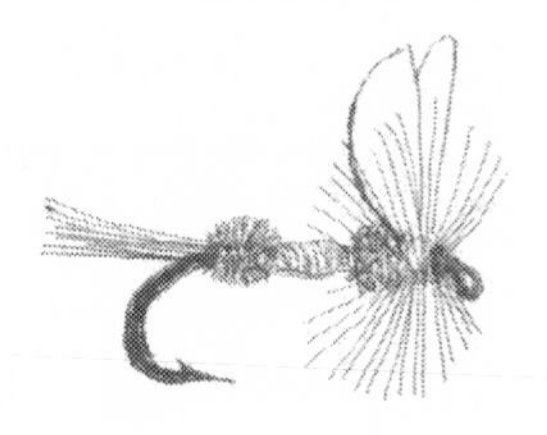

2

ROBERTO MONTOYA sat in a Ciudad Juarez cantina sipping a margarita. He was about to order *fajitas de pollo* for lunch. He always sat in the room's darkest corner at a table with his back to the wall. He had more enemies than he liked to count.

At forty-seven he appeared ten years younger. He enjoyed joking that taking years off other people's lives added a few to his own. Montoya was short, chunky, and had no uncommon facial features by which one might remember him.

His black hair was swept back and glistening as though it had been sprayed with Armor All. He had removed his Italian double-breasted suit jacket, carefully folding and placing it on a chair across from him. On the edge of the chair next to him, underneath the local newspaper, he set a Beretta Cougar .45 ACP pistol. This model held 8 + 1 cartridges, two less than the .357's 10+1. Montoya preferred the stopping power of the larger .45 caliber.

He was wearing one of the white, silk dress-shirts that he bought in three-dozen batches when a tailor from Kowloon, Hong Kong, made his annual visit to Mexico. Montoya's silk tie tastefully combined the Mexican flag's green, red, and white colors. Tasseled Mephisto shoes were being polished by a shoeless, diminutive twelve-year-old boy who hadn't seen the inside of a school room for four years. Hanging around the cantina shining shoes, he earned more than his drunken father.

Montoya's cell phone began playing *Guadalajara* by a Oaxacan mariachi group. The screen showed the call to be from his sister Victoria in Montana. He hesitated a moment, wondering what she wanted this time, then put the phone to his ear and said, "*Hola, hermana.*"

"Roberto, ees Veeky."

"Como estas Vicky. . . how are things in Montana? Tell me in *English* Vicky. You need to practice. Your English is *terrible.*"

"Me Ingles ees stupendious! But *I* no so good, Roberto. *Nobody* like me here. I here one whole year! I *try* meet people. No so good. I go church. I go town picnics. I go everything where people ees. No so good. Three months ago, I go hot springs spa. Meet five women who have stupid little beezness moving feeshing boat trailers. They *ignore* me. I do real nice invitations for beeg party in me casa last month. Beeg mariachi band. Beeg marimba. Beeg fireworks. Beeg piñatas. Mucho cerveza. Mucho ron. I sen invitation everybody een theese crummy valle. NOBODY come! Last week I go local women's club. Nobody talk wit me. All beetches! I like to keel them! I buy at stores in Emigrant—I get ignored. I don't get *nobody work* for me. I pay good. *Nobody want work!* You know I gotta bring illegals from Juarez to work my house."

"Be *patient,* Vicky. Take a course in English. You'll meet some new people there, maybe from Mexico."

"I no need that. I speek good. Good as you."

"No, Vicky, you don't."

"No need speek good English. Soon Spanish ees *only* language here."

“Not as soon as you think, hermana. *Believe* me. Try to be nice. . . . Talk to you next week.” Roberto hung up, signaled to the waiter, and asked for another Margarita. A double. Light on the salt.

Victoria Montoya put down her phone and cried loudly. Her tears mixed with words that made her illegal Mexican maid cross herself repeatedly and slip quietly out of the room.

“I feex them beetches,” Victoria said loudly, pouring a large glass of rum that Roberto had made at a Monterrey factory he had “purchased.”

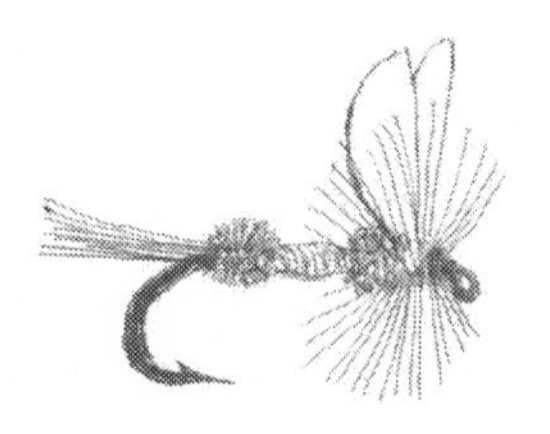

3

THE NEXT MORNING AT 6:30 I hooked up the trailer that carries my plastic drift boat. I use my wooden drift boat, *Osprey,* only for clients whom I personally know *and* who respect wood. *Osprey* is a 16' Guide model designed by Jason Cajune, the young owner of Montana Boat Builders. His boatshop is a long cast from the Yellowstone River on Pine Mountain Road a few miles north of my Mill Creek cabin.

I built *Osprey* the year I moved to Montana. I had to repair it after the shoot-out on the Snake River in Jackson Hole last fall. Its mahogany, ash, and oak surfaces gleam again under another newly applied eight layers of Bristol Finish.

I've never floated with today's clients, a couple from Maine who are combining business and vacation. Maine makes me think of Kath Salisbury and her husband Park. Three of my floats over the past four years involved Park Salisbury, a duplicitous investor from Newport Beach, California. Kath was a likable gal from Bar Harbor, Maine, who came slowly to acknowledge that she was in a destructive, dead-end relationship. That understanding came on the float when she accompanied Park.

That was four years ago in this same plastic boat on the Deadman's Bar to Moose section of the Snake River in Jackson Hole, Wyoming. Halfway down that float, while we were wade fishing after lunch, Park caught and clubbed to death a Snake River Fine-Spotted cutthroat trout, a small-spotted *variation* of the Yellowstone cutthroat. Killing the trout broke the law and was contrary to both the Jackson fly shop's rules and my own.

Park and I swapped angry words. I pushed off with Kath in my drift boat, leaving him stumbling along the bank screaming at me, his hairpiece floating in the current beyond his reach. He had to walk out, a four-hour hike through prickly berry bushes along the river. When Kath and I reached the takeout at Moose, she didn't wait for him. She flew east to her parents' home in Maine and filed for divorce. I drove north to my home in Montana and filled a glass with Gentleman Jack.

≈

Almost to the day a year later, I was floating an upper section of the same river—Pacific Creek to Deadman's Bar—when my client and long-time friend, retired foreign service ambassador Ander Eckstrum, was shot and killed by a sniper hidden on the shore. Jackson police thought the shooting was linked to a problem Ander had with some radical Muslims because of comments he made when he was ambassador at Khartoum in the Sudan. I thought the bullet might have been meant for me, fired by an old adversary from Guatemala, Juan Pablo Herzog. I also thought that Herzog had tried to bomb my Montana cabin a year later. But on both occasions the bad guy proved to be Park Salisbury.

The year following the bombing attempt, he succeeded in killing both Kath and her fiancée while they were hiking in

Maine's Acadia National Park. Three days later, wearing a clever disguise as an unknown, first-time client from Oregon, floating with me again on the Deadman's Bar to Moose section, Salisbury tried to dispose of me, my companion Lucinda Lang, and my devoted canine sidekick—Wuff.

Salisbury succeeded in shooting all three of us. Wuff and I survived. Lucinda spent two weeks in a coma. When she came out of it, she had severe amnesia which she currently struggles to overcome at her Indiana family home.

Fortunately, Salisbury was shredded by shots from Lucinda's Glock pistol, from several Teton County Sheriff's Office snipers, and . . . though late . . . from my Glock. The shots were followed by an epic finale that concluded with Salisbury impaled on a splintered tree limb when I intentionally crashed my boat into a huge strainer—a thirty-foot-high pyramid of dead trees contributed to annually by the spring runoffs.

Who actually killed Salisbury? As in Agatha Christie's *Murder on the Orient Express* who-dunnit, a whole bunch of people "did it." And a tree.

≈

After yesterday's initial call from Victoria Montoya and our less pleasant follow-up conversation, I had a premonition about today's drift. My heightened concern was enough to cause me to add one final item to my boat gear for the day: a new, loaded .357 Glock from my music room.

The *music room* is a hidden basement below my Mill Creek log cabin. It's where I store some special weapons, work at my computer and communications center, and play my oboe and English horn. Why the wind instruments are in a below ground room is the easiest of the three to explain—the soundproofing diminishes the likelihood of any neighbors complaining about my ruining some of the world's most endearing music literature.

My Glock is a masterpiece of polymer and metal. It fits easily into the right zippered side-pocket of my Simms burnt-orange-panel guide jacket. It's the same jacket that saved my life last year—a Kevlar-lined custom edition. Huntly Byng, the Teton County Sheriff's Office's chief homicide investigator and a personal friend, said I need quicker access to my gun on floats. But a shoulder holster wouldn't convey confidence to my fishing clients. I could hang it from a retractor on my vest, but that's already filled with flotant, nippers, a hemostat, and a diamond hook hone.

More to the point, I'm not much of a fast draw. I didn't get my old 9mm Glock out quickly enough to save Lucinda from several shots by Salisbury or to save Wuff from a ricocheting bullet. She recovered, but on cold mornings she begins the day with a slight limp. It's remarkable that anyone wants to float with me—man or dog. I don't like the thought that I've become more tourist attraction than professional fly fishing guide.

≈

I left my cabin early enough to fortify my scarred body with some oatmeal, excessively covered with light-brown sugar. Plus somewhere more than three mugs of coffee. All at the Howlin' Hounds Café in Emigrant, my favorite Paradise Valley breakfast hangout next to Angler's West Flyfishing Outfitters where I'd arranged to meet my clients at 8:30. I parked my boat in front of the large café windows to keep an eye on it.

Sipping coffee, I noticed a thirtyish woman looking over my boat. Although physically attractive, she tried everything possible to project counterculture. Frizzy, black hair was tied back with a handful of variously colored rubber bands. A tinted, iridescent-green forelock drooped in front of her left eye. The tress was an aberration that could serve a better purpose tied on a #16 hook to give a little oomph to a Lime Trude fly.

Her eyes projected a cool, clear Montana sky-blue, but embedded deeply inside circles of thick, black mascara. They were like looking down into a Maya *cenote* in the Yucatán. A half-dozen Cheerio-size silver hoops were aligned along the top curl of each repeatedly pierced ear. A couple of smaller hoops intruded on one eyebrow, and several more dangled from her lower lip.

A small, round-cut, putative diamond protruded from the right side of her nose. When she opened her mouth, three tiny metal barbells emerged along the top of her tongue. Special sirens must go off when she passes through airport metal detectors. Maybe she likes being searched by TSA patters.

Black-on-black was her dress for the day. Tight black jeans. Black leather belt, needed mainly to support waist-encircling thick metal chains. A black vest opened over a black T-shirt with large silkscreened initials. I could see only "AR."

One colorful item, other than the rubber bands and hair lock, was an awareness plastic bracelet, mimicking the pink ones people wear to support cures for breast cancer or purple to stop global warming. Or bright red to promote a drug free week. (I wonder if Roberto Montoya ever wears a bright red bracelet?) The woman's bracelet had alternating green, red, and white bands. I knew what they meant. And realized that the "AR" on her T-shirt was the middle part of PARA—People Against Recreational Angling.

Some fishing guides believe the last "A" means *Anglers* more than *Angling*. These radical members of PETA have broken off to form a group militantly focused on fish *rights* rather than animal *welfare*. PETA—People for the Ethical Treatment of Animals, known disparagingly by critics as People Eating Tasty Animals—was meeting nearby at Chico Hot Springs. Yesterday its more humorous and silly members had clashed with the militant PARA folk.

Finished with breakfast, I went outside. The young woman was leaning against my boat.

"This a fishing boat?" she asked.

"Yep."

"Commercial or recreational?"

"For me a little of both—it's partly the way I make my living."

"You gotta stop!"

"I have a license."

"Doesn't matter."

"Sorry if you don't like it. . . . I have other things to do." I turned to go away. She followed. Her metal jingled.

"You fishing today?" she called over my shoulder.

"Yep," I answered, without looking at her.

"Where?"

"In the river."

"Smart ass. *Where*?"

My usually generous patience sometimes comes to a dead halt. This was one of those times. Turning to face her, I stared at her agitated eyes and quietly but firmly said, "Where I can find the most fish. And where I can *eat, wear, experiment on, or use them for entertainment.*" That's in PETA's motto—I thought she might like to know that I knew it.

Swearing, she yanked the chain from around her waist and raised her arm behind her to take a good swing at my drift boat. She didn't see Park County Sheriff's Deputy Ken Rangley approaching behind her.

Ken and I first met when he stopped me a few miles north of Emigrant the evening I arrived in Paradise Valley five years ago. I was driving forty-five mph at dusk without my lights on, mesmerized by the receding sun over the Gallatin Range to the west. He didn't give me a ticket, but he did suggest that I might want to drive a little faster and use my lights. Since then we've become friends and often fish together.

Ken grabbed the woman's arm as it came forward, which upset her balance. She and her chains tumbled to the ground.

"Helga Markel," Ken said calmly, removing his hat as though there were some lady present, "I told you yesterday, when you were thrown out of the meeting at Chico Hot Springs, that you *can't* solve your differences by using that chain. This time you don't go free."

I interceded; the kinder side of my patience had returned. "Ken, I was a little testy reminding her of the PETA motto. It got her excited."

Ken nodded at me and asked her, "Where you headed?"

"Missoula," she said. "There's a law professor at UM who supports PARA. I called him last night after we were tossed out of the PETA meeting. He wants me to talk to his Animal Rights Law seminar Monday."

"What on earth are they teaching in law school?" Ken pondered aloud. After he paused a moment he added, "Get in your car right now and head north. I don't want to see you around here again—GO!"

She went glumly, gunned her Honda Element adorned with PARA and other counter-culture stickers. As she shot through the blinking red light and sped north, she rolled down the window and tossed Ken a bird.

"That's strange," Ken said quietly, watching her disappear. "I would have thought that *tossing* a bird was against PARA principles."

"Only if you consider the toss *entertainment*," I replied.

≈

Helga Markel fumed and swore as she sped north on 89 from Emigrant. She thought out loud: "I have to do something risky and outrageous to show those wimps at PETA that PARA knows how to stop recreational angling. Something that will gain *national* attention. Even at the cost of a life. . . . If only I'd been born a few decades earlier, I would have been part of the Weathermen movement."

Markel idolized Kathy Boudin, who lingered in prison for two decades after the 1981 Brinks Robbery by remnants of the Weathermen resulted in several deaths. "*Weathermen* knew how to gain attention," she thought. On her cell phone she dialed a Missoula number. A man's voice answered.

"Hello?"

"Professor Plaxler, it's Helga."

"I told you yesterday to use my cell phone, *not* this number. It's my law school office. Calls come in through a system where they're forwarded to a central office, *and recorded!* Call me back on my cell phone." Plaxler hung up. His cell phone rang twenty seconds later.

"Professor?"

"Where are you?"

"Still in Paradise Valley."

"I thought you and your PARA friends were coming to Missoula?"

"Not yet. There's an opportunity for us here I can't let go."

"Tell me about it."

"I was driving from Chico and saw a fishing boat parked at Emigrant. I was going to trash it when the owner came out and ridiculed me. Then a cop showed up. He grabbed me and threatened me."

"Were you arrested?"

"Nope, the cop was going to, but the wimp who owned the boat said he provoked me by his comments about PETA and PARA. So the cop told me to scram. I flipped him a bird as I drove off."

"Not too smart, Helga. PARA isn't helped by that kind of action. . . . *Why* did you call me?"

"I want to teach the guy who owns that boat a lesson. He's guiding on the Yellowstone today. He leaves his SUV and trailer where he puts the boat in. I thought I might wreck it or back it into the river or something, after he leaves on the float. We've gotta stop this elitist fishing."

"That's not the way to stop it. At our seminar we'll talk about what we can do to stop recreational angling. See you Monday."

"I may see you before then . . . Your wife in town this weekend?"

"She's at a physical therapists' conference in Philadelphia. She'll be back Monday."

"I *will* see you before Monday. Bye."

Helga abruptly turned her car off 89 at Pine Creek Road and doubled back south on East River Road. When she passed the fenced trash collection area at the corner of the road to the

Chico Hot Springs resort, she noticed several eight- to ten-foot wooden beams piled there for disposal.

She had an idea. But she'd need help. She turned toward the Chico resort where some PARA colleagues were packing to leave. Hopefully, the most anarchistic of them, George Tucker, hadn't left yet. He'd love her idea. And he drove an old school bus filled with tools. Including a chain saw.

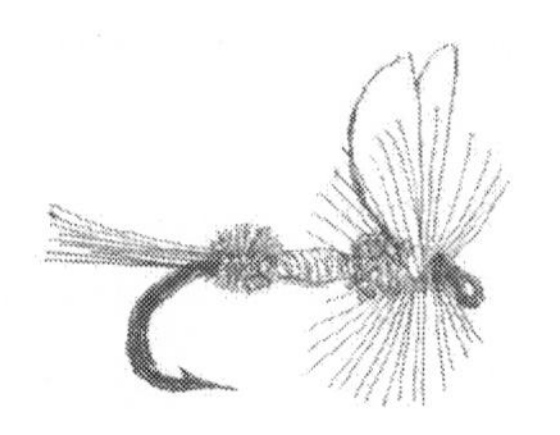

4

KEN RANGLEY DEPARTED EMIGRANT heading south in response to a call. Glancing in his rear view mirror, he was pleased to watch Markel's car disappear north. Hopefully, she'd disperse her anxieties in Missoula.

My clients for the day arrived—Cassie and Viktor Burzynski. Together we crossed 89 down to the launching site on the Yellowstone, barely out of sight of Emigrant's diminutive commercial area. Julie Conyers arrived ten minutes later. Her Shuttle Gals partners dropped her off and continued north in their van to do other shuttles. After I launch my boat, Julie will drive my SUV and trailer downstream to the Loch Leven takeout, where she left her car. Then she'll join the other gals and do more shuttles.

"I guess Victoria Montoya has more bark than bite, Julie. She said she'd be here today to take over your shuttle."

"I'm still mad. So mad I've borrowed my dad's .45 Smith & Wesson to carry."

"If you have a shoot-out, *please* somewhere other than from *my* SUV!"

"If I see that Mexican bitch, I'll put your SUV in four-wheel drive and leave her as road kill."

Julie is one of the calmest, sweetest, and most mild-mannered ladies one could know. The Montoya woman had riled her pretty good yesterday; I was relieved the float would begin without incident. After being paid for the shuttle, Julie stayed with me while I backed my drift boat into the river.

Julie's tall and trim; her olive skin glows from her time outdoors. Her large, clear blue-green eyes are disarming and draw attention when she looks at you. She did just that and asked, "Macduff, *when* are *you* going to ask me to marry you?"

"This isn't the first time we've had *that* conversation, Julie. You *aren't* going to marry a *straight* guy. You were married once and he beat the daylights out of you. You're a *lesbian.* You don't like guys!"

"I could make an exception for you," she said.

"Would I have to have a sex change?"

"We could talk about that."

"Go home and take care of that great boy of yours." Julie's exceptional—I've often wished she were the sister I never had. Raising her son George, running the shuttle service in the summer, teaching history at a Bozeman private secondary school in the winter—she deserves someone to live with who'd treasure her. I sometimes doubt that she's a lesbian. Maybe she's living that role to keep guys from hitting on her while she does her own selection. I wish I weren't part of *that* process.

≈

The Burzynskis are living in Maine, but only for another year, while Viktor finishes a dam removal project. He's a civil engineer. Cassie's an OR nurse and easily finds work wherever they live. Their permanent home is near Washington, D.C. Neither has ever fly fished; they've come to Livingston for a conference.

Online Cassie had read that the Yellowstone River is a fluid jewel meandering through Paradise Valley between the Absaroka and Gallatin ranges and then through downtown Livingston. Matson Rogers operates the Angler's West Flyfishing Outfitters shop in Emigrant that booked the float. He knows I like guiding people new to fly fishing. Wading a stream or floating a river is my favorite way to spend a day that passes for working. Catching fish is a plus, but I enjoy even more helping others catch their first fish, especially rising to a dry fly.

I started with Cassie and Viktor discussing reasons for catch and release and using barbless hooks, at least until we're using tiny #20 or smaller flies. At #20 I have trouble knowing whether I've flattened the nearly invisible barb. Barbless hooks mean fewer fish landed, but more survivors. At least that's the side of the debate I think makes the better sense.

We spent about thirty minutes on some grass by the parking area practicing roll casts, followed with standard casts, and finally mending. I start with the roll cast because it's easy . . . only a half cast . . . and less intimidating than starting with full casts with tight loops. Plus, the roll cast is useful in a drift boat where someone else in the boat is exactly in line with a back cast.

I don't like to teach by telling a novice a lot of "don'ts"—like "don't break your wrist" or "don't make such wide loops" or "don't drop your tip so much." It makes more sense to be positive and try to explain the "do" rather than the "don't do."

"Cassie. Viktor. The roll cast is good when you don't have room to back-cast. Because of bushes, sometimes a high bank, or even a person behind you. It's a kind of flip cast. Start with the rod tip straight up—twelve o'clock—and then bring the tip back a little, to about one o'clock. Hold the line with your left hand between where it comes from the reel and the first rod guide. Control the line with your thumb and forefinger. Pull enough line from the reel to pile some loose line on the ground in front of you, about the length from your rod tip—if it were pointed toward your target—to where you want the fly to land. Better a bit more since you're not trying to hit a trout on the head.

"Think of having the fly land a few feet upstream from where you believe the trout is lying, so the fly floats into its feeding lane. The line you'll have in the water is going to have some resistance from the water when you do the cast. Make sense?"

"Yeah," Viktor answered. "If I don't provide some tension with this line but try to cast, nothing will happen." He tried to thrust the rod tip forward and little did happen.

"Right! With the line here on the ground or in the boat piled on the floor or deck in front of you, there isn't enough resistance to bend and load the rod when you do the cast. *You* have to provide that resistance by holding the line firm with your left hand. When you start the forward motion of the rod, its tip is held back a bit because you're holding the line taut."

Viktor and Cassie both tried and sent a line out about fifteen feet. "What you need to add is when the rod tip moves forward your left hand should pull or haul down and away from you. The taut line causes the rod to bend or *load*. That forward motion is quick, but not a long arc—only from about one o'clock to eleven o'clock. *Maybe* as far forward as ten o'clock, but you don't want to throw the line *down*."

"Why not?" asked Cassie. "I want the fly to land in the river."

"Remember that the line follows the tip. Thrust out and not down or the line will drop onto the water too soon. If you don't have sufficient *thrust* forward, you won't cast the line because the rod won't bend and load."

They both tried again, but their forward thrust slowed down as they reached eleven o'clock. "Even though you're thrusting forward, at eleven o'clock you *must* come to a quick stop. That makes the rod-tip bend forward, throwing the line toward your target.

"In the roll cast you're making a large loop in the line and throwing that loop through the line so it unrolls right to the fly. You might have done that with a piece of rope as a kid. You laid the rope out in front of you and then did what we're doing with a roll cast, but without a rod. You flipped the rope forward, came to an abrupt stop, and watched the loop in the line actually run along the length of the rope."

Their next casts were pretty good roll casts, enough to get their flies twenty-five to thirty feet away from the drift boat.

We shifted our casting to the drift boat, and, as the day unfolded, the Burzynskis seemed pleased. They both caught a few Yellowstone River native cutthroats, some rainbows and cutbows, the latter a cutthroat-rainbow hybrid. Cassie was enthralled with the beauty of the cutthroat. Viktor liked learning a new skill, but he seemed more attentive to the river's course than to its native fish.

"What is it about Paradise Valley that makes it so revered?" Viktor asked. "It *is* physically magnificent. There must be more to the mix that makes it so magical."

"People have tried to describe this valley for decades," I answered, "usually without doing it full justice. It starts with the two parallel mountain ranges: Gallatin to the west and Absaroka to the east. No dominant peaks like in the Grand Tetons, but there's no doubt about the Gallatin and Absaroka being *mountains*. When I lived in Connecticut as a kid, my dad often talked about going *over* Avon Mountain driving home west from Hartford. *Mountain!* It was more like a speed bump. The Gallatin and Absaroka are what I call *mountains*. Add the Yellowstone River, the largest undammed, free-flowing river in the country, and you have a magical paradise.

"The river changes from its origin as a tiny creek in Yellowstone Park in Montana, flows through Yellowstone Lake, then rapids and meadows and canyons, finally leaving the park and meandering through this valley. The Crow Indians lived here for 200 years before the fur trappers arrived—the most famous probably was Jim Bridger—moving up and down the valley in the 1800s. Ultimately, the land became used for agriculture and cattle ranching, but that's giving way to large tracts owned privately by people who want the land preserved. Give me time, Viktor, and I'll talk about this valley until you scream 'enough!'"

Viktor's attentiveness was momentarily distracted. He seemed concerned about something, looking off behind me toward the Gallatin Range. "I hate to sound worried" he said, "but do you see the dark clouds moving in from the southwest?"

"Been watching them," I replied. "The southwest is generally where our thunderstorms come from. The one you've been watching should pass us to the west, slipping along the Gallatin ridges. Shouldn't be a problem."

"What about lightning?" Cassie asked.

"We watch it *carefully*. There's not much to do when it comes, but put on rain-gear and pray a little. I don't like rowing to shore under trees. If lightning gets close, we stop fishing, set our rods aside, and cover-up with rain gear. And wait." Golfers say even God *can't* hit a two iron. I know He *can* hit a graphite fly rod."

During lunch on a gravel bar, half-way along the float, I asked Viktor about the Livingston conference he'd come to attend.

"I've been retained by the Food and Water Resources Protection Association. They want some advice. I work on dams. For the past two years I've been helping remove one from a river in northwest Maine."

"What does the *Association* do?" I asked. "There're no dams on the Yellowstone to remove. It isn't the longest freestone or undammed river in the lower forty-eight because people haven't tried to build dams here. Fortunately for the valley, they've all failed."

"That may change," said Viktor. "FWRPA wants to *assure* that Paradise Valley remains an agriculturally productive part of Montana. Local farmers and ranchers sell a lot to other states and abroad. To keep increasing sales means access to new supplies of irrigation water."

"A huge amount of irrigation water is already taken from the Yellowstone," I countered, trying not to be argumentative. "Not the result of high dams, but by means of a bunch of diversion dams. The largest must be the Intake Diversion Dam in eastern Montana near Glendive. It sends about half of the Yellowstone's flow into what becomes a couple of hundred miles of lateral canals, which, in turn, feed some five hundred farms. There are some much smaller diversion dams in Paradise Valley, especially on the creeks that feed into the Yellowstone. There'd be a lot more water in the Yellowstone from side creeks, like Mill Creek where I live, if the flow wasn't diverted for agriculture before it reaches the Yellowstone. There has to be a balance. We need the food, but I wonder how Americans will feel when Montana farmers want to divert even more water to feed China and India."

"There's no assurance year-to-year there'll be enough water," Viktor countered, "because there's no *storage* on the Yellowstone. What the group I'm going to speak to wants is a new dam on the Yellowstone for water storage."

"*A new dam! Where?*"

"Preferably either a couple of miles upstream of Livingston or a mile downstream of Emigrant."

"That means we'd be having this lunch underwater."

"No. We would have gone close to Livingston and fished in the tailwaters produced by the dam. Could be great fishing, like below the Palisades Dam on the South Fork of the Snake in Idaho, or the Flaming Gorge Dam on the Green in Utah, or the Navaho Dam on the San Juan in New Mexico. After the conference I'm going to visit those three dams."

Tailwater is the part of a river *below* a dam. The Yellowstone's called a *freestone* river—there are *no* dams. "Viktor, I guess you asked for this float to see what the river is like and to imagine how a dam would change it. I assume you've been filled in on the history of dam building attempts on the Yellowstone."

"I know the late 1950s Bureau of Reclamation Yellowstone River Basin Study identified five possible sites for a new dam."

"You're right, but the efforts to build any dam stalled in the 1960s," I countered.

"I know. But they were renewed a decade later by the lobbying efforts of energy interests. Especially Montana coal mining interests." He had done some homework.

"The state legislature responded with the Montana Water Use Act," I noted. "That shifted the focus from challenging any dam building to assuring that the Yellowstone wasn't depleted."

"The FWRPA's plan isn't to divert the water; it's to store it to assure its available for the country's needs."

Ignoring him, I continued, "After that Montana act was passed, the state Department of Natural Resources granted the state Fish, Wildlife and Park Service water reservations for the Yellowstone and hundreds of tributaries. That ended the dam debate. I think the matter's closed."

He smiled as though I were a naive child. "The act only postponed people realizing the benefits of a dam. Can you imagine all the recreation a dam in Paradise Valley would bring? Power boats, PWCs, float planes, parasails, and—my favorite—airboats."

I was too agitated for further debate. And I needed to learn more about both the history of proposed dams on the Yellowstone and about this FWRPA. I have a hunch it's a front for coal-mining interests. China's more interested in Montana's coal than in its beef or agricultural produce. There are parts of Southeast Montana where coal veins run forty feet thick and are easily strip mined. Southeast Montana was once a shoreline of huge inland seas that left thousand foot deep deposits of sand, mud, and peat. Given time—measured in millions of years—it became coal.

Paradise Valley fortunately missed out on the evolution of coal—the Absaroka and Gallatin ranges are volcanic. Even though Southeast Montana is far from Southwest Montana and Paradise Valley, letting coal interests run the state—including support from the governor's office—implants a mindset of seeing nature primarily as an extractable resource. Coal mining means carbon dioxide and methane releases, plus heavy metals as mining waste products. The mining creates a huge demand for water. The impact would extend to this valley.

Extraction of natural resources has run rampant in Montana since prospectors and miners arrived. Copper, silver, and gold mining dominated, but production of those metals ultimately shifted to cheaper places. Nevertheless, mining is demand driven, and when the prices of those products move higher, schemes for what are invariably alleged to be safe, non-polluting mines pop up like Phoenix rising from the ashes. For coal miners, regardless of the consequent pollution, talking about *energy demand* is the name of the game.

My anxiety level was soaring. If I couldn't get my focus back to fly fishing, this was going to be a poorly remembered day.

"Enjoy the Yellowstone today as a freestone river, Viktor—tomorrow's another day." I wanted to add: "Leave the building of new dams to the politicians." But that might be the worst possible choice.

≈

We'd owned this section of the river for the day—not another boat in sight. Likely due to the poor weather forecast. But we'd done well. Cassie and Viktor both gained a sense of accomplishment with their newly acquired casting skills.

Our takeout was to be at the Loch Leven ramp on the east side of the river.

"Time to pack up," I suggested. "The bend ahead is a couple of hundred yards before our takeout point. I hate to end a good day, but if we pass Loch Leven it's three more miles to the next takeout. And my SUV and trailer will be at Loch Leven. Take a couple of more casts and bring your rods in."

"This river is *extraordinarily* gorgeous," declared Cassie. "I can't believe we've been floating for nearly *seven* hours."

They were good clients, aside from Viktor's comments about a new dam. They took advice well, laughed at their mistakes, and kidded each other. I hoped they might return another time. Repeat clients help reduce the gamble of spending a long day with unattractive people. Plus repeats are a measure of being a good guide.

"Viktor and I talked a little after lunch when you were getting the boat ready for the afternoon. We want to float with you again. Could you take us next summer, maybe float a different section of the Yellowstone?"

"Sure. Let me know your dates. Next time we'll use my wooden drift boat, *Osprey*. The one you said you saw outside the fly shop in Emigrant."

"Why didn't we use it today?" Cassie asked.

"I don't use it for first-time clients I don't know," I answered.

"Don't you want to impress clients so they'll come back?"

"I want to know they'll respect a *wooden* boat. You obviously do. Many repeat clients still go out in this plastic boat. Some show up wearing wading boots with metal cleats. Others insist on smoking and set lighted cigarettes or cigars on the casting deck. *Osprey's* casting deck is varnished mahogany."

"But since *they* haven't pleased you, why do you even take them on another float?"

"I struggle with deciding where to draw the line. It does seem a little inconsistent. But this *is* my living. There's a big gap between people like you two and the *three percenters*. You get wood. Those in the gap get plastic. The three percenters stay home."

"Who's a three percenter?" asked Viktor.

There was just enough time before we reached the takeout to tell them about Park Salisbury, my client from hell. I told them about only the first float when I made Salisbury walk, not about the subsequent two drifts and shootings. And not about his attempt to blow up my cabin.

"I'm glad we're nearly to the takeout," Cassie quipped. "I don't want to walk five miles if you get mad at *me!*"

"Don't worry—so far my only three percenters have been men."

"Thanks a lot," murmured Viktor.

When we turned the final bend, I was surprised and curious to see my red SUV backed to the water's edge at the Loch Leven ramp. My trailer was almost entirely underwater. Julie never did that before. She left it carefully parked a hundred feet away from the ramp. I rowed the boat in on the downstream side of the trailer, so we wouldn't float into it. As we came close, Cassie, sitting in the front seat, screamed, "There's a *face* under the water!"

Pulling the anchor release, I stepped out. Six inches below the water's surface, the open-eyes of Julie Conyers stared upward. The water's depth magnified her large eyes, bulging from a lifeless face. Her mouth was open. Two tiny fish swam out. Cassie and Viktor were standing in my drift boat, staring at the body. Cassie was trembling. Victor's mouth was agape. None of us could believe what transfixed us—Julie Conyers' naked body had been crucified on a large, crudely made wooden cross that was tied to my drift boat trailer. Large nails penetrated her feet and hands. A foot-wide green, red, and white sash tied her waist to the cross. What magnified the horror was mutilation—her breasts had been cut away from her chest.

Helping the Burzynskis out of my boat, I led them to a spot to sit out of sight of the ramp. I've added two more clients who think floating with me spells danger.

I also called Ken Rangley. I wanted to move the SUV and pull the trailer from the water, but not tamper with any evidence Ken would want to see.

Ken answered. "Have a good float today after that bratty PARA gal left?"

"I'm at the Loch Leven takeout. Julie Conyers' dead *body* is splayed across my trailer. She's *underwater*."

"What! I don't believe it! On my way as you talk. I'm at Albertson's, south of town. . . . Are you sure she's dead?"

"She can't be alive. No bubbles. Tiny fish are swimming in and out of her mouth. Her face is only a few inches under. Her hands and feet are nailed to a big wooden cross tied to my trailer. A colored sash is around her waist. And her breasts have been cut out!"

"Oh, Jeez! Leave her there. *Don't* move the trailer. I'm ten minutes away." He arrived in eight.

I'd used a small camera to take several photos before Ken skidded into the parking area. All the others on the camera disc were of fish from the Yellowstone. They were photographed and gently returned alive to their world. Julie wouldn't have that chance.

Ken took more photos. He'd called the Park County Sheriff's Office from his car. The homicide investigation people arrived twenty minutes after Ken. Once they looked at the ramp area and the photos, and took more of their own including video, they had me slowly pull the trailer out of the river. It wasn't a pleasant task. When the trailer with Julie's body was clear of the river, I went behind the restroom and gave up a good lunch.

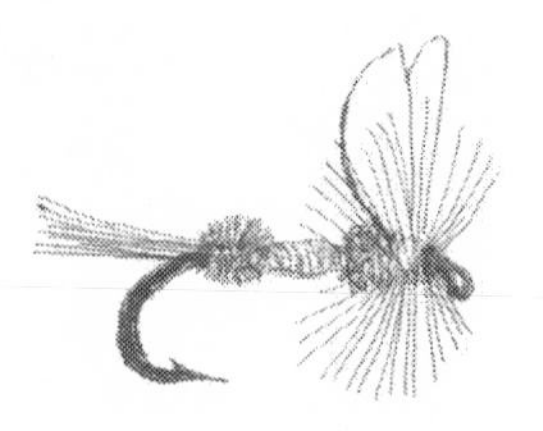

5

THE PARK COUNTY SHERIFF'S OFFICE'S homicide division deputies from Livingston asked Cassie and Viktor a score of questions, helped them fill out a report form, and wrote down their contact information. A deputy drove them to Emigrant to pick up their car. They departed confused and distraught; what had been a dramatic first day of fly fishing had the ending of a Shakespearean tragedy. I watched them leave, wondering if they would ever set foot in a drift boat again. Much less book a float with me next season.

I faced a lengthier questioning than the Burzynskis. This wasn't the first time I've had to answer questions from investigating police after a drift. When the inquiry had been in Jackson Hole after Ander Eckstrum's killing on *Osprey*, I expected and prayed it would be the last. Some prayers get misplaced.

Leading the initial investigation was the Park County Sheriff's Office's number two homicide detective, Erin Giffin. I know Erin; she's a half-inch on the high side of five feet and a pound or two on the low side of a hundred pounds. She's a diminutive beauty—looks like a tiny J.M.Barrie garden fairie you want to pick up and hug.

Erin comes across as exceptionally bright. Her brain must count for half her weight. PhD in philosophy and Master's in forensic sciences from UC Davis. Co-author of a new textbook on forensic pathology. When she's working, or engaged as a *kendoka* in her pastime—*kendo*, the Japanese martial art of sword fighting—she wears her long, auburn hair in a French knot that adds three inches to her height. When she's dressed to go out, she wears her hair long, touching her shoulders. Either way, she turns heads. All this, and Erin's about to turn 35.

"Hey, Macduffy," Erin said quietly to me. "How many bodies in your boat does this make?"

I'm not thrilled about her calling me Macduffy, but I'm not about to call her on it.

"Hi, *Kendoka*—she's not *in* my boat. Different trailer. Different boat—I didn't use *Osprey* today. Different jurisdiction—first body on *your* turf. Different state. Different river."

"More of your distinctions without a difference. You should have been a lawyer, Macduffy. . . . You need *me* for protection. Why don't you hire me to sit in the back seat of your boat? I'll bring my real sword, not the practice bamboo *shinai*."

"I couldn't keep an eye on you sitting behind me. You might fall through the rear drain plug and drown."

"That'd add another notch to your boat."

"A *small* notch." Erin's the most unself-conscious vertically-challenged person I know. "I'd miss you and you know it, Erin."

She leads a Park County program for people who've adjusted poorly after losing loved ones in tragedies. I became part of her group last year when I went spiraling down into a black alcohol-induced abyss of self-pity. It was soon after my lady friend, Lucinda Lang, was shot on my drift boat on the float that's now called the "shootout on the Snake."

Before that float, Lucinda, piece-by-piece over a four-year period, had mostly extracted me from an earlier bout of depression over the death of my wife, El. Erin helped me realize I can't help Lucinda by killing myself.

After I was released from the same Salt Lake City hospital where Lucinda lay comatose after the shooting, I went straight to her room and spent every day at her side. When she came out of the coma, she stared at me, with no idea who I was. I tried for days to help her remember, until the consequences of grief caught up with me and I slipped into oblivion, falling in an unconscious heap beside her hospital bed. I hadn't been caring for my own needs. I'd shed twenty pounds, without the agony of a diet.

After a day of pumping me full of unnamed intravenous fluids, Lucinda's doctor physically escorted me to the hospital entrance, put me in a cab, and told the driver: "Airport." The doctor dropped a ticket in my lap for Bozeman and said I didn't need to stay because Lucinda didn't know who I was or even that I had been with her the previous day. Amid tears, I said, "She may not know me, *but I know who she is.*"

Back in my cabin on Mill Creek, I didn't improve; I wasn't eating and deteriorated again. Mavis, my neighbor, occasional dog-sitter, and house-watcher, became worried when I hadn't answered the phone or knocks on my cabin door for three weeks. She could hear Wuff whining through the door. She called the hospital in Salt Lake City. A nurse told her I hadn't called about Lucinda in over a week. Mavis next called Paula Pajioli, knowing that she was a friend but unaware that she was my confident as well as my local contact for the CIA and responsible for any problems in Montana.

Paula was in Livingston visiting her friend Erin Giffin. They rushed to Mill Creek. Met by Mavis, when they opened the cabin, they found me semi-conscious on a fouled bed, emaciated, and near death from a virus I may have picked up in the hospital.

When medics loaded me into their emergency van, I heard Erin say to Paula, "My God, he's a mess. He won't make it to the hospital. But he doesn't seem to want to. Maybe he's thinks he's spent all the time on this planet he was allocated. His dog has more determination; she's survived on her supply of dog food."

That was how I first met Erin. Her stinging words, repeated to me later by Paula, made me mad. I was determined to prove her wrong. Once I recovered enough, Paula nudged me into Erin's program. A determined nudge that wasn't subject to debate.

I became the program's best behaved pupil, partly because Erin brought me back to the beauty of being alive, especially in Paradise Valley. But mainly because she scared the hell out of me. *No* wasn't an acceptable response to any demand or suggestion Erin made. I'd list her program's degree of difficulty just behind becoming a Team Six member of the Navy Seals. Erin was a master of intimidation, humiliation, and tough love.

After the first group session, I made Erin a folding, portable eighteen-inch-high platform that she could stand on behind a podium. I gave it to her and said, "I heard you but never saw you the first evening of your program because you were hidden behind the podium. All I saw was a hand and part of an arm occasionally thrust out to one side or the other of the podium." That's when the name Macduffy began.

When I said, "I'd miss you and you know it," as she was beginning her questioning about Julie's murder, she responded, "Macduffy, while your brain's functioning so cleverly, tell me everything that happened today. *From the top. Everything!*"

"OK." I told her what I could remember. Even though I was experienced in post-murder questioning, after Ander's shooting and the finale with Park, I knew what she was thinking: "He's no Hercule Poirot."

"*Who* might have done this? Anybody come to mind?" she asked after we finished with *what* happened.

"Because of some peculiar conversations within the past twenty-four hours alone, I can think of three people, or the organizations they're connected with, who might want to make some contrary statement about fishing on the river. But murder is beyond making a statement, and it doesn't mean any one of them killed Julie."

I told Erin all I knew about Victoria and Roberto Montoya. Erin had visited and questioned Victoria earlier in the month when a neighbor complained about her dogs.

"Other than Victoria Montoya, no one I know *specifically* disliked Julie," I said. "I think Montoya disliked *all* the Shuttle Gals because they rebuffed her. But I've learned from my troubles on the Snake that the target isn't always who you might first assume. And I learned today . . . Ken can tell you more . . . that some people don't accept recreational fishing. But that doesn't mean murder is the way they'll try to stop fishing."

I told Erin all I knew about PETA, PARA, and my confrontation with Helga Markel.

"Also I learned today that there are some new interests emerging that want to build a high dam that would flood much of Paradise Valley. It's been attempted several times in the past century. The last effort was stopped partly because of the opposition of concerned local people like the late Dan Bailey, fly fishing icon and outfitter/guide from Livingston."

I told Erin all I knew about the dam proposal, my conversations with my client Viktor, and my unsupported suspicion that Montana coal interests might be involved.

"And of course, Erin, you probably knew Julie was a lesbian and very outspoken about gay and lesbian rights. In fact, two other Shuttle Gals are lesbians. Not only partners, but they went to California and were married. That made a lot of people mad. But murder? I don't think so."

I told Erin all I knew about Julie and the discrimination she and the other two gay Shuttle Gals had experienced.

"Your mind actually has the capacity to occasionally function rationally, Macduffy. A lot better than when we found you hanging off the bed in your cabin. You've had a long, busy day. When I'm through here in another hour, let's go to dinner. I can tell you need to get away from this. Me, too."

"You treating, *Kendoka*?"

"Depends on what you order."

"Bison sirloin, wild rice, and mixed vegetables. OK?"

"I can do that."

"And a nice red wine."

"*You* can do that."

"I'll throw in dessert," I said. "You're not big enough to eat more than a spoonful."

"Try me. . . . Follow me to my office in Livingston. I'll drive us to Ted's Montana Grill in Bozeman. I've never been there."

"Got something against bison, other than they're taller than you?"

"My dinner offer's rescindable, if it isn't accepted on *my* clearly expressed terms."

"Did you go to law school—now *you* sound like a lawyer?"

"In between my Master's and PhD. UM law school at Missoula. Never took a bar exam, went straight to the PhD."

"You're over-educated."

"Probably. I bet you are, too."

"I finished grammar school." Strangely, I had never been asked about my education by anyone in Montana or by my few new friends in Florida. I didn't want to lie to Erin. I don't like lying because it's addictive, and she's likely to see through me if I try to deceive her.

"Did you start guiding right out of sixth grade?"

"Nope—went through high school and college. Back East. Played soccer. Drank beer. Drove fast. Chased coeds. All the things guys go to college for."

"Take *any* courses? . . . I don't believe the chasing women part. Macduffy—I know some things you don't know I know. Remember, Paula Pajioli and I went into your cabin when you were delirious. I know Paula works for the federal government, but I've never gotten her to talk about what she does. I suspect FBI or something like that. I'd think CIA, but that's international.

"Paula knows an unusual amount about you. She was very protective of you when we were in your cabin; she tried to control where I went and what I looked at. There was a bookcase, pulled out slightly, near the back sitting room. I peeked in. Stairs led to a basement. While Paula cleaned you up before the medics arrived, Wuff squeezed by the bookcase and went down the stairs. I followed. I saw a music stand and woodwinds.

"There were some complex music scores on the stand, including scribbling and notations as though whoever was playing was making some minor changes. Not many can make Vivaldi sound better. There was also sophisticated computer equipment. Copier, printer, two desk-top computers, four monitors.

Plus several small black-metal boxes I couldn't identify. Two desk phones, one with a lock. There were guns, including a sniper rifle. Remember, I deal with forensics. The Chey-Tac is a very specific weapon. And you have Glocks and a Sig. Upstairs, along with the rifles by the doors and your bed, I saw the .44 magnum pistol in the drawer in the table beside your bed—Paula and I were looking for pill bottles. Thought you might have overdosed. And—shall I go on?"

"We do have a lot to talk about at dinner," I said. I wondered what she might have asked Paula about me after the medics had left with me. And how much Paula had really told her.

6

THAT EVENING ERIN AND I SAT at an outside table among planted pots at Ted's Montana Grill in Bozeman. It shares the ground floor of the Baxter Hotel with the Bacchus Pub, which has a touch of medieval Europe with carved and painted heads of monks lining the walls and ceiling center beam.

A large electric "Hotel Baxter" sign adorns the roof. Its lighted when nearby Bridger Bowl has two inches of new "cold smoke," the fresh powder snow that often piles up on the ski slopes when not a flake has fallen in town.

The Baxter is one of those striking buildings that exist in almost every small-town urban landscape, rising several stories above the town's norm. These buildings have served as the lodging and dining centers for generations of visitors, even as many town centers became decimated by new suburban malls. Bozeman retains a vibrant downtown—one of America's main-street jewels. The Baxter is the lustrous, center diamond of that jewel.

Once the sun disappeared behind the town's brick and stone fabric, the evening quickly chilled. I offered Erin my guide jacket. She wrapped it around her shoulders. The jacket's bottom draped nearly to the brick terrace floor.

"It looks like a cape on you. Extra-large on extra-small."

"I hope you cleaned the blood off from last year's shootout," she commented, looking at the repaired bullet holes in the front.

"The Simms folks in Bozeman did that and never sent me a bill. Park Salisbury's bullets went through the outer orange panel, but not through the next layer—Kevlar." The jacket was a special order gift from Huntly Byng, friend and head detective for the Teton County Sheriff's Office in Jackson, Wyoming. He thought I needed a bullet-proof vest *whenever* I floated the Snake River.

My companion, Lucinda, had a jacket that mirrored mine in all but size, and the two shots from Salisbury that hit her in the chest only bruised her. A third shot, catching her above the jacket in the neck, caused a serious loss of blood, put her in the coma, and left her with yet-to-be-determined consequences.

I didn't want to think about that day on the Snake. I had to focus on a more immediate problem—Julie's death. But for now I wanted to enjoy my dinner with Erin. She's paying for most of it.

Erin sat across from me, looking bigger than she is, but attractively elfin.

"No French knot in your hair, Erin? A sign of relaxing?"

"I left my sword at home. No kendo tonight."

"Save that for Victoria Montoya."

"I dislike her," she said abruptly. "Between you and me, she's a bitch. And maybe a killer. It was foolish to tie a red, green, and white sash to Julie's waist. They're the national colors of Mexico. . . . We're looking for Montoya. She wasn't at home a couple of hours ago when Ken went to question her about her whereabouts today. Her maid said she'd left quickly about three p.m., carrying a small suitcase. With her were two

Mexicans. Probably bodyguards. Probably illegals. We think they might be headed for Ciudad Juarez. Her brother Roberto keeps a private jet at the Jackson Hole airport. We've asked the Wyoming Teton County Sheriff's Office to hold them if they show up. You know the detective I talked to in Jackson—Huntly Byng."

"I know him well. Heads homicide. Good man. We . . . " My cell phone rang . . . I'd forgotten to turn it off. I started to tap the mute button, but noticed the call was from Indiana.

"You all right?" Erin asked. "You look upset."

"I'm sorry. I think I should take this. . . . Stay here. You know as much about Lucinda as anyone. I talked to her Indiana doctor a week ago. He confirmed that she was in good physical health, but was disappointed with her slow progress with the amnesia."

I'd flipped on the cell phone speaker. The cool air had driven the other diners inside.

"Mr. Brooks? It's Rosa Lipsius."

Rosa is a therapist. She's helping Lucinda face the amnesia. "This is Macduff. Something about Lucinda?"

"It is, Mr. Brooks. This afternoon Lucinda began askin' for her husband *Maxwell.* She thinks her name is *El,* and that she and Maxwell live in *Florida.* Do you know why Lucinda's havin' such memories? Her mother's havin' fits and blames you. It's pretty hectic, not good for Lucinda."

I shouldn't have turned on the cell phone speaker. Erin doesn't know anything about Maxwell Hunt. My thinking was fuzzy. The news wasn't what I'd been expecting, and I didn't know how to react. With more emotion than reason, I thought Lucinda was ready to come back to her ranch near my Mill Creek cabin and even think about returning to her job in Manhattan. Now I needed something plausible to say that would satisfy Rosa's curiosity while not telling Erin any more than she knows.

After a moment of confused mental gymnastics, trying to sort out the safest response, I managed to utter, "Lucinda knew about the death of a couple named El and Maxwell. Whenever Lucinda and I discussed the dangers of drift boat fishing, we talked about their tragic accident on the Snake River fifteen years ago. I know that story troubled her. I often mentioned I didn't want to take any risks when she was floating with me. . . . I'm going to leave here immediately for Indiana. Thanks for calling." I snapped the phone shut and turned to Erin.

"I'm sorry. I *have* to go. I need to get her out of there. I need to see her. I. . . . " Erin moved closer until our shoulders touched and grabbed my hands. Hers were soft and distracting.

"*Macduff,* you're not yourself. We're going to the airport. You can catch the late flight to Minneapolis, stay at an airport hotel, and go to Indiana on the first morning flight. . . . Are you going because you need to see Lucinda or to do some damage control about two people named El and Maxwell? You can tell me more about *them* when you're back."

That's not what I needed to discuss. Erin knows more than I thought. It wasn't the time to give an impromptu fumbling explanation.

"Thanks. You're right. I'm in no shape to drive to Mill Creek for a few hours' rest and come back to the Bozeman airport in the morning. I hate to abandon our dinner. Can you keep my SUV, call Mavis and ask her to take care of Wuff, and give me a rain check on another dinner—my treat? . . . I don't look forward to dealing with Mrs. Elizabeth Parker-Smith Lang."

"I know, Macduff. But she *is* Lucinda's mother. If I were her and knew only what little she knows about you, I'd be protective. Far *more* than she is."

After sitting up all night in the Minneapolis airport, in plastic chairs designed by someone who never travels—there was a convention in town that had absorbed all the rooms—I took the first morning flight to Louisville, Kentucky, rented a car, crossed the Ohio River into Indiana, and drove to Hanover. Without a thought that I was still in the clothes I wore on the tragic float the day before, I went directly to Lucinda's family home—a middle-class house in a middle-class neighborhood in a middle-class suburb.

≈

When Lucinda had emerged from the coma last fall after the shooting, her mother and two siblings insisted she be flown from Salt Lake City to her family home. They were immediate family. I was, in their collective view, no more than a fishing bum who had pursued their Lucinda for four years—making no commitments, offering no future, and placing Lucinda at risk twice. First, two years ago when my cabin was rigged to be bombed, and second, last year when she was shot three times while fishing with me.

I can't argue with her family's blaming me for her injury. But her mother, who was the daughter of a prominent, knighted English High Court judge—The Honorable Sir Henry Parker-Smith—had never taken to the idea that her successful investment-advisor daughter, owner of a magnificent ranch in Montana and a small but exclusive apartment in New York City, could be attracted to a fly fishing guide with a deeply hidden and suspect background.

When our paths crossed unexpectedly several times in Salt Lake City during Lucinda's hospitalization, I suffered through Mrs. Lang's eternal litany of dangers to which I had exposed her daughter. More troubling is that I completely agreed.

For an agonizing five minutes I stood before Lucinda's front door without knocking. When I gathered some courage and knocked, the door opened, only partly, revealing an immaculately coiffured, gray scowler.

"You're a fright, Mr. Brooks. You look contemptible! I presume you're here to speak *briefly* with *my* Lucinda," Mrs. Lang said, surveying me from head to toe, her carefully preserved British Oxbridge accent adjusted by Mid-West sensibility and spoken through pursed lips. She knew damn well why I was there. I wanted to say "Why the hell else would I be in Indiana?" But I didn't.

"Rosa called me last evening, Mrs. Lang, and said Lucinda was not making sense yesterday. And that my being with her might help."

"She certainly *wasn't* making sense. She thinks her name is El, and she's married to a Maxwell Hunt. And they live in *Florida!* Of all places . . . *that horrid swamp!" Nodding at me, she went on,* "I trust *you* have a very appropriate explanation. Lucinda has suffered enough because of you. First, when she was with you when your cabin nearly blew-up and again when she was shot on the river. And you probably had something to do with that terrorist threat in New York City, when she had to flee to her friend's house in Connecticut."

I'd disclosed much of my life as Maxwell Hunt to Lucinda. I'm sure she hadn't passed any details or any thoughts about the planned terrorist attack in Manhattan to topple the Chrysler and Empire State buildings. What Mrs. Lang doesn't know—

yet—is that El was killed while she was floating with me. And that yesterday Julie Conyers died shuttling my boat.

"Lucinda and Wuff saved my life at the cabin and on the river. You know that," I said, more plea than statement.

"*You* should have been saving *her* life. Like her grandfather Sir Henry, and her father, saved their countries from the Nazis. You don't seem very capable of even taking care of yourself. . . . Oh, well! I guess it's best you come in and see Lucinda for a few minutes—and no more!"

Mrs. Lang escorted me upstairs to Lucinda's bedroom, watching me as though I'd come to steal the family jewels and silver. The house looked like a Laura Ashley showroom. Lucinda had joked to me about her mother insisting that her daughter grow up a proper English lady. As we entered the bedroom, Lucinda woke from a light sleep, turned her head slightly to look at me, and exclaimed, "*Maxwell!*" Mrs. Lang abruptly left.

I wanted to jump in bed and hold Lucinda. I opted to gently take her hands. A slight squeeze told me more than words, communicating what her mother couldn't comprehend. For a moment her pallid face showed the enchanting Cheshire cat grin that I first saw nearly four years ago when she opened the door of her ranch welcoming me to Thanksgiving dinner.

"Maxwell, when are we going home to Florida?" She waited for my answer. When it wasn't quickly forthcoming, she rested her head back on the pillow, closed her eyes, and drifted off.

Rosa had quietly joined us and stood by the door. Hearing Lucinda's comment, she whispered, "She's bound to be fuzzy in her thinkin', Mr. Brooks. The doctors don't believe she's suffered any brain damage. She has a form of retrograde amnesia where she can't recall identities or much of her life before the trauma. It'll take time; the effects can be long lastin'."

I knew that. Lucinda may have what her doctor described as bilaterally damaged hippocampus, causing a lack of spatial coherence—meaning she may mix different events when she either re-experiences the past or imagines the future. But she's a very strong and determined woman. I looked down at her; she was as captivating as ever. But some of her appearance was deception. Smoke and mirrors from her mother applying cosmetics. Keeping up appearances. Stiff upper lip and all that. I sat in a chair next to her bed and soon fell asleep. I had been up since six a.m., Montana time. The previous day.

Awakening two hours later, I quietly slipped out of the house and went to the old hotel in town where I've stayed on my previous visits. When I looked in the bathroom mirror, I understood Mrs. Lang's dilemma. I hadn't shaved and still wore the clothes from yesterday's float. They smelled a curious mix of the PARA woman's horrid hair gel, Yellowstone River water, Ted's Montana Grill cooking odors, and Delta's infamous stale cabin air.

A quick trip for incidental toiletries, underwear, a pair of khakis, a blue-checked shirt, and walking shoes helped me prepare to face Mrs. Lang. I finished dressing just as Rosa called and said it was a good time to come over. Mrs. Lang had left for a church affair and wouldn't return for another three hours.

Lucinda looked the same. "Maxwell, I'm too weak to talk much. But I can listen. Tell me what's happened."

"I'll try, Lucinda."

"Why did you call me Lucinda?"

"What should I call you?"

"El, of course. As you always do, Maxwell."

Rosa motioned me to step out of the room.

"Mr. Brooks, the cure for amnesia includes patience and understandin'. We're workin' with her on memory loss. It would help if you stayed another day. She's lookin' better today with you here."

I stayed two more days, Mrs. Lang notwithstanding. Lucinda and I talked when she wasn't sleeping. But I tired her, and sleep came often. She ate well and looked better each day. I held off further confusing her by correcting her thinking she's El and I'm Maxwell. Previously, she didn't have any identity at all. There's some irony in that it took several years for me not to feel like Maxwell, and it was principally Lucinda who helped me become Macduff. Now *she's* calling me Maxwell!

Preparing to leave on the third day, Mrs. Lang came bursting into Lucinda's bedroom and thrust a newspaper in my face. "Mr. Brooks, I want you out of here. Right now. And forever!" Lucinda was shocked; her mother rarely raised her voice. When she talked to me, it was always with a moderate voice, although it made me feel I was receiving acupuncture.

"You killed *another* woman!" She had the local paper opened to a piece about the death of Julie Conyers. A death described as caused by crucifixion had made the news even in Hanover, Indiana.

I looked at Lucinda. She was staring at me. "*Mac!*" she exclaimed. The shock had stopped her focus on Maxwell and El. She acknowledged me as Mac, even though it was the nickname she used only when she was troubled.

Rosa grabbed my arm and pulled me from the room. "It's best you leave. She's had enough for now. But she's makin' progress. She may be partly shocked out of amnesia. I'll be in touch."

7

ERIN HAD LEFT MY SUV at the Bozeman airport. There was a note: "Hope Lucinda's better. Give me a call. And remember, in case *you* have amnesia, that you owe me a *whole* dinner. Including wine!"

Ninety minutes later I was sitting on my porch at Mill Creek. Wuff at my side and Gentleman Jack in my hand. One glass a day—max. Just in case there's a call from Indiana and I have to leave quickly. I started to call Erin, to thank her for arranging with Mavis to take Wuff, but I noticed I'd turned off my cell phone when I arrived in Indiana.

There were fourteen incoming messages, eight from area code 406. That doesn't say much; 406 is the only area code for the entire state of Montana. Florida has seventeen area codes and another one seems to be added every month, keeping pace as the retirees flow in legally from the north and economic refugees flow in illegally from the south. I assumed most of the calls were from Erin and called her.

"Hi, Macduffy, how's Lucinda?"

"Progressing," I replied, avoiding explaining any more about her confusion with names and places.

"I have a bunch of calls from a 406 number. It's not yours, but close." I gave her the number.

"That's Shaw's number. *Chief* Detective James W. Shaw the Fourth! Better known as Jimbo. My boss. You're not going to enjoy being questioned by him."

"I'll survive it. Huntly Byng and a brace of FBI agents intensively questioned me in Jackson about Ander Eckstrum's death on my boat. And again last year after the shootout with Salisbury."

"But Shaw *dislikes* you."

"I don't know why; we've never met. What's his problem?"

"You're in better shape. He's jealous. Jimbo claims he weighs the same as when he 'played' football for Alabama, but his weight's more fat than muscle and mostly wrapped around his middle. . . . I suspect his dislike for you is deeper than looks."

"Does he dislike fishing? That'd be strange for Park County."

"He hunts. I don't think he fishes. Never said anything *negative* to me about fishing."

"Tell me about him."

"Montana native. Big jock at Bozeman High School. All-State football. Never dated the same girl twice; I think because they never said 'yes' again. Turned down in-state scholarship offers from Montana State and Montana and went to *Alabama* to play. Told his Alabama teammates, mostly Southern boys, that his name was James Shaw the Fourth. They nicknamed him Jimbo, which he never liked but which stuck, even when he returned here. He sat on the bench at Alabama for four years. Talks about Alabama football as though he'd been a star. Truth is he *never* played a single down in a game. He was fodder at practices for the starters. . . . He's really pretty smart, Macduffy, and he wants you to know it by badgering you. He doesn't like playing second string. He had enough of that at Alabama."

"Actually, Erin, the bench is third or fourth string; second stringers get to play. . . . What's *your* relationship with Jimbo?"

"*None.* Shaw's divorced. Three marriages in seven years. Problems with mentally abusing his spouses. Last divorce was final last week. He hasn't gotten over her leaving him six months ago and moving in with the women's basketball coach of a small college in Billings. I should also say 'the *woman* who is the women's basketball coach!' Now he's on the prowl again."

"Hitting on you?"

"Yeah. I told him anytime he wants, we'll do some kendo together. With real swords. I could slice off some of his fat."

"Anything else, Erin? Something you were hoping I wouldn't ask about?"

"Maybe. . . . Shaw thinks I'm interested in you, and he doesn't like the way you've been in the press a lot. From building your wooden drift boat a few years ago, to adopting your rescued sheltie, to the shootout on the Snake last year. Even about Julie Conyers' killing a few days ago. I think he's jealous of the press attention you get."

"Thanks for the warning. I assume I'm not a suspect, but I'm going to want a lawyer when I talk to Shaw. Any recommendations?"

"Without question—the best criminal defense attorney in the area is Wanda Groves in Bozeman. She's a UM law grad who finished with the highest GPA in two decades. She's been practicing for a dozen years and has had run-ins with Shaw on several occasions. I saw her yesterday at a lecture at MSU in Bozeman. We talked a bit about Julie's death. Nothing significant—in case she became involved. We did talk about you. I said I thought you might have issues with Jimbo Shaw. So she won't be surprised to hear from you."

After we finished, I noticed I'd had *another* call from Shaw's number at the sheriff's office while Erin and I were talking. I called the number.

A male voice answered and gave a loud and forceful, "Yo?"

"Macduff Brooks returning your call. Who is this, please?"

"This is *Chief* Detective James W. Shaw the Fourth—Park County Sheriff's Office. Where the hell have you been the last three days? I want questions answered."

"I've been out of town on personal business. I gave an extensive statement to Erin Giffin the day of Julie's death."

"I've read it. That was *four* days ago. There's a lot more I want to question you about. Erin's not the chief detective. I am!"

"I understand. What do you want to know?"

"Lots. For starters, where you lived and what you did before you moved to Montana five years ago."

"You writing an article about me for *Gentleman's Quarterly*?"

"I *heard* you were a wise guy."

"I graduated valedictorian of my pre-kindergarten class."

"*Damn it!* I want to know where you were between preschool and Montana."

"Out and about."

"*Where* out and *where* about?"

"Am I a suspect in Julie Conyers' death?"

"You're damn right you are."

"Then talk to my attorney . . . Wanda Groves. I think you know her." She wasn't my lawyer yet, but I hoped she would be ten minutes after I finished talking with Shaw.

"Why the hell have you retained *her*? We have some good attorneys right here in Livingston."

"I'm sure there are. I might remind you, Detective, that a suspect has the right to choose his own counsel, even if it's a lawyer who's made some deputies look bad."

"She never made *me* look bad. I beat her every time we met."

"Like the *Corcoran* case?"

"You get your butt in here this afternoon, or I'll send a half-dozen squad cars after you, and we'll drag you here in cuffs and leg irons."

"Wanda will call you." I hung up.

A judge had publicly rebuked Shaw in the *Corcoran* case a year ago for tampering with and destroying evidence, ruling a mistrial. The case involved charges Shaw had likely made up against the owner of a gay bar in Bozeman. On advice of the County Attorney, the case wasn't retried.

I called Wanda Groves. Her secretary put me through quickly.

"Hello, Macduff. Erin Giffin told me you were likely to call. Jimbo Shaw causing trouble?"

I repeated my conversation with Shaw.

"Don't go today. I'll call him and set up a time for tomorrow. We'll go together."

"Could I take you to lunch in Livingston before we meet with Shaw? There're some baggage I carry you need to know about."

"From what I hear that could take more than a lunch. You're rumored to be an exceptionally private guy. But Erin and Judge Amy Becker both say you're a diamond that's not as rough as you want us all to think. The way you've stood by Lucinda Lang and the way you treat Wuff are much talked about."

"Sure. Some treatment! Lucinda was shot three times and in a coma for two weeks. Now she has amnesia. Wuff was shot and has a limp when it's cold. By the time I fired my Glock, it was mostly over."

"We'll talk about it at lunch. Second Street Bistro at noon?"

"Closed at lunch. LBG?"

"Livingston Bar and Grill? Just plain closed."

"Park Place Tavern?"

"Fine, noon tomorrow."

≈

Wuff and I relaxed for a couple of hours that afternoon on my cabin's rear porch, overlooking Mill Creek. It was an eighty something sunny summer day, but we were in the shade in line with a cool breeze from the west that funneled up the creek and spilled onto my porch, dropping the temperature to the mid-seventies. Thankfully, the spring runoff that makes Mill Creek a truculent challenge in May and June, and sometimes into mid-July, had passed.

On days like this, I often fish the Mill Creek portion that flows through my land. Using a 7' 4-weight bamboo rod, I catch small cutthroats that remind me there's a complex, living world beneath the shallow creek's deceptive surface. There's another 7' bamboo rod I'd like to see used here again—one I made for Lucinda for Christmas a few years ago. It's been languishing in a corner near the fireplace at her ranch a mile or so up Mill Creek Road. Activity's been subdued at her ranch—no one knows what the future has in store. She has a manager and a couple of loyal hands keeping up the grounds and the few cattle and horses. Mavis, the neighbor we share as a housekeeper, takes care of Lucinda's ranch house.

Detective Shaw wants to know about my life before I moved to Montana five years ago. Erin knows more about me than I'm comfortable with. Meanwhile, Lucinda thought I'm Maxwell and she's El, my wife who died in the drift boat accident on the Snake some fifteen years ago. And Lucinda may still think we live in Gainesville, Florida. It's all a bit confusing.

Tomorrow, I'll have to bring Wanda into my past as well as my present. I'm a little hesitant; if I'm not careful, I'm going to risk having my old nemeses, Juan Pablo Herzog and Abdul Khaliq Isfahani, discover I'm alive and hurry here to settle the score. If scars count as points, Herzog's ahead in the game, as my time in Guatemala proves. But he'd like to run up the score.

Isfahani is another matter. My unsuccessful attempt to assassinate him left him with a disfigured face; he won't hesitate to take revenge if offered. But I don't think he knows I was the shooter.

≈

I made two more calls. First was to Amy Becker, the Bozeman judge who four years ago asked if I might like to rescue Wuff. I wanted to check on Wanda Groves. Amy said Wanda is tight-lipped about her clients and is the lawyer she'd retain if in trouble.

The second call was to Dan Wilson in D.C. He works for the CIA, that elusive entity variously known as the *company* or the *agency* or for its location—Langley. A few years ago, he led me through the procedures under the federal protection program that provides new identities to compromised government agents. That program changed my life after twenty years as law professor Maxwell W. Hunt at the University of Florida law college. I became Macduff Brooks, fly fishing guide in Paradise Valley, Montana.

Dan and I talk every month or two; I consider him a friend as well as an advisor. Maxwell Hunt was the first law professor who acted as an *agent of convenience* for the agency and ended up in serious trouble. Such agents collect information as innocuous as public opinion and as potentially consequential as transmitting foreign policy influencing information from foreign contacts.

I moonlighted as one of those agents, becoming increasingly reckless after El died, until I was severely beaten in a ninth-floor hotel room in Guatemala City. The assailants, Herzog and Isfahani, were surprised by CIA agents from our embassy. They hurriedly carried me off and flew me to Washington where the State Department announced I had died from a fatal stroke. The stroke and death were cover for the new identity Dan Wilson orchestrated to change me to Macduff Brooks.

After telling Dan about what had happened to Julie and about the demands I faced from Detective Shaw, Dan said, "If things get difficult, we can intervene and get Shaw out of the picture. But that creates other problems I won't trouble you with. . . . I'm pulling up on my screen the file on Wanda Groves. She represented some Montana State University students a half dozen years ago who were charged by the Department of Justice with violating travel to Cuba rules. They became part of a witch hunt by some vindictive Florida congressional reps. Thank God the students weren't enrolled in state universities in Florida!

"Wanda Groves was investigated and came out with a stellar confirmation of professionalism and integrity. You're in good hands. Tell her as much as you think she needs to know;

she's *not* going to compromise you. She'd go to jail first. . . . By the way, how's Lucinda?"

"Pretty good news. She's beginning to recognize some names and places. Not always the right names and places. She thinks she's El. And calls me Maxwell Hunt!"

"My God! She's more of a threat than Shaw is. Want us to take care of *her*?"

"I hope you're joking. We're using more traditional methods of curing her amnesia. Everyone attending to her is being told by the doctors she's assumed a new make-believe identity as a result of her trauma."

"Send her to us. We'll put her through the IIPA program."

"I'll come, too. New names and we'll live in Monaco!"

"And be a fly fishing guide on French canals?"

"I doubt there's anything living in French canals. I could be a blackjack dealer in a casino. Lucinda can launder hedge funds for New York banks."

"Keep up your sense of humor; it makes me feel we can work out problems. And you do cause them. How many notches on *Osprey's* rail?"

"Always room for you, Dan. . . . I mean fishing with me, not as a notch."

"Of course, you do! Call me soon." He hung up.

When I checked my e-mail there was a message from Wanda. We would meet with Shaw at the Park County Sheriff's Office tomorrow after lunch.

No sheriff's office squad cars arrived at my cabin that afternoon. Even though I left the gate open for them and had a chilled bottle of Spanish Miguel Torres Fransola waiting, along with cheese and crackers.

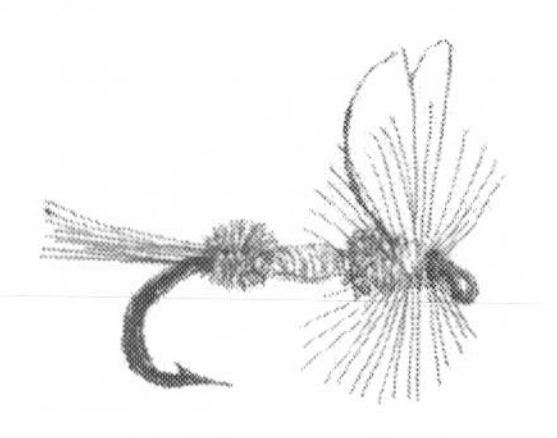

8

WANDA ARRIVED FOR LUNCH at ten minutes past noon the next day in her gleaming, polished black Hummer. I'd arrived ten minutes before noon and was sipping a Moose Drool draft beer. She ordered unsweetened ice tea and a raw spinach salad. I was tempted to ask if they served lobster tail, but wondered what kind of lobster lived within five hundred miles of Livingston. I ordered a bison burger. Bison live almost within sight.

Since she wasn't going into court and didn't dress to please Chief Detective James W. Shaw, Wanda was in designer jeans and an attractive elbow-length burnt-orange cachet-cardigan with a shawl collar. This was the first time we'd met, although I'd seen her photo in the *Bozeman News* occasionally, usually involving a case, but sometimes relating to work for one of her favorite charities. She was average height, average weight, average looks, and immediately overwhelmingly charming. I imagine she lassoes juries and leads them wherever she wants them to go.

"So *you're* Macduff Brooks! The only photo I've seen of you was several years ago in the *News* when you were building your boat. You had a nice butt."

"Flattery will get you nowhere with me, counselor. . . . My butt hasn't changed. . . . Oh! Maybe a few bullet scars. I wish Detective Shaw were as complimentary."

Wanda had seen the photo in the Bozeman paper of me hanging over the side of *Osprey,* working on the interior with only my backside showing. I wanted it that way—I'd only been in Montana a few months and was photo-shy because of my new identity.

"Jimbo Shaw's the last person on earth who'll compliment your butt. He's homophobic, an intricate and ambiguous person. If he likes you, he'll do anything for you. If he doesn't—look out! In your case I'm afraid it's: 'look out.' He'll use all the tools of his trade to make your life hell."

"What do we do?"

"I'll control what he gets from you. He's investigating the murder of Julie Conyers, not your life. He's known to use questioning to accumulate information about people he wants to know about for reasons unrelated to his questioning. I've been through this before. Let me handle it. Don't answer any question until I nod or intervene."

"Your call."

"Any chance you have any law in your background? Criminal justice courses in college? Involvement in litigation, especially criminal cases?"

"I need to fill you in on the time before I came to Montana five years ago. For some reason Shaw wants to know about those years. I want you to listen for the next half-hour. I won't have to tell you what compromising my identity would mean. And I don't believe there's a chance in the world that, if my identity were compromised, it would be traceable to you."

It took longer than a half-hour. By the time I finished, we had ten minutes before we were due at Shaw's nearby office.

Wanda suggested we arrive a few minutes late. . . . Shaw said to be there promptly at one.

"I know what you told me needs to stay private," Wanda stated assuringly. "Telling me helps make my work that much easier."

Shaw was ready for us. When we walked into his office at 1:12, he never got up. Instead he spun around and tilted his chair as far back as it would go without ejecting him. He looked at us and with dramatic deliberation lifted his left arm, pulled up his sleeve a few inches, stared at his watch, and turned his stare to us. Without a word telling us that one o'clock *means* one o'clock.

He sported a flat crew-cut haircut, showed a ruddy complexion, and was tall and heavy. Mostly heavy. Probably went three hundred pounds when he sat on the Alabama bench, munching whatever one does to add pounds to compete with the three hundred and *fifty* pounders. Shaw hadn't gained any weight since football days, but it had moved and shifted his center of gravity visibly lower.

Like Erin, as a detective he didn't wear a police uniform. He was neat and crisp in triple-XL clothes that exude "Western." Polished Tony Lama boots, sharply creased tan moleskin pants, presumably held up by a belt that disappeared under his stomach when he dressed in the morning, and a pressed deep-red plaid shirt with four pearl buttons on each cuff. Plus Western yokes and spade-flap pockets.

Shaw wanted us to use an interrogation room that was undoubtedly wired. Wanda didn't complain. She whispered to me that it would help us were Shaw to later lie about what transpired.

"Brooks, let's start with the question I asked you on the telephone. Tell me about what you did *before* you moved to

Montana." His manner was guarded politeness. It was probably because of Wanda. He wasn't afraid of *me*.

Wanda interceded, "Jimbo, you know better than to ask that kind of question. My client is here solely in connection with your investigation of the murder of Julie Conyers. You know that Mr. Brooks, on the day of the murder, left the Emigrant launch around 8:30 in the morning in his drift boat, rowing two clients you've questioned—Cassie and Viktor Burzynski. You also know they've filed a complaint about your allegedly intimidating and unprofessional conduct during their questioning. Julie Conyers was at the Emigrant ramp when my client and the Burzynskis set off on the river. Mr. Brooks was with them the entire day—never out of their sight—until they reached the Loch Leven ramp where Julie was found dead. Are you serious about thinking of my client as the murderer?"

"Everyone is a suspect until they prove themselves otherwise," said Shaw.

"Is everyone guilty until they prove their innocence?" Wanda asked.

"As far as I'm concerned, establishing innocence is your job, Wanda, not mine. Now let's get back to my question—where was Brooks before he moved here?"

Wanda turned to me. "Don't answer that." She looked back at Shaw. "What's bothering you so much about my client's life before five years ago? You can check any records you like—police reports, FBI. You have access. He has *no* prior record."

"Brooks has no prior *history*. I've tried and drawn a blank. It's never happened before. It's as though Brooks has no past before he moved here. The first thing I know is that he flew to Bozeman from Washington by way of Denver, on May seventh, five years ago. The D.C. police have no record of him.

I've checked *every* state—nothing. The FBI says they've never heard of him. I want to know *where* he was and *who* he was."

"My client will answer any questions *relevant* to Julie's death. We aren't letting you go on another witch hunt. Any *appropriate* questions?"

"When I get Brooks on the stand, he'll have to answer *my* questions."

"No. He'll have to answer questions from *me,* if I decide to have him testify, and from the county prosecutor on cross-examination. I doubt that Will Collins, the prosecutor, will defer questioning to you. Anything more, *Jimbo*?"

"There will be—*damn sure,*" Shaw said, obviously mad at coming in second once again. Then he added, "Brooks, we have a complaint about you from Victoria Montoya. I'll be following up on that, after we finish the Julie Conyers investigation. Anything you want to comment on regarding Montoya?"

"Detective Shaw," I said, "when you're ready to discuss Montoya, call Wanda. I doubt you even know where Montoya is."

As we walked to our cars, I asked Wanda, "How did Shaw get to be head detective? I'm impressed with the only other members of the sheriff's staff I've met—Erin and Ken."

"Like some people are bootmakers to the King, Jimbo is a bootlicker to the sheriff. He puts in lots of hours helping at re-election time, and our sheriff has been in office six terms—twenty-some years. Jimbo can retire in another few years on a nice pension. It's strange because the sheriff is a good man, generally well liked, and he doesn't need Jimbo's help at election time."

"There must be something else," I commented.

"There must be," Wanda confirmed.

9

MY CELLPHONE RANG while I was washing *Osprey* at the Emigrant car wash. I'd been fishing Henry's Fork in Idaho with a friend from guide school days. I try *always* to use a pressure hose after floating a "foreign" river, meaning anything other than the Yellowstone in Paradise Valley.

The New Zealand mud snail and other trout habitat invaders have been establishing new homes in U.S. rivers. I do what I can to avoid carrying one of those creatures to a different river to establish a new home. Maybe it's a waste of my time. Sooner or later the folks in Washington will hear of the mud snail, rename it the American mud snail, and place it on the endangered species list, giving it entry rights along with such other unwanted traffic as the African python.

It was a familiar voice on my phone.

"It's Huntly Byng in Jackson. Got a minute?"

Byng is the Teton County Sheriff's Department head of homicide investigations. We met four years ago when Ander Eckstrum was shot in my drift boat on the Snake two hundred yards upriver of Deadman's Bar in Jackson Hole. Ander's daughter Kris was the third person in the boat. It was concussive for a sixteen-year-old to watch her father's head explode as a .30-30 bullet struck Ander an inch above his left eye. He was sitting and casting a dozen feet from her.

Kris was considering going to college in the West, becoming a guide, and ultimately buying into an outfitter's business. But the killing of her dad, a former Foreign Service officer who had been in Skull and Bones at Yale, soured her on settling in Jackson Hole.

Since then she's followed her dad's footsteps to Yale, was tapped for Skull and Bones, and is headed for a Foreign Service career. I see her nearly every year when she's home in Jackson between terms or on vacation. She's never gone back on the Snake or any other river. Her widowed mother has remained in Jackson. *Her* trauma has endured, and she hasn't remarried.

"What am I getting myself into this time, Huntly?"

"I need a favor," said Byng.

"The last time someone called me from Jackson to ask a favor, it was Bruce Samson from his outfitter store. He urged me to take a client who turned out to be Park Salisbury. You know the rest."

"I do. Still have your Kevlar-lined Simms jacket?"

"Yep. But I'm not wearing it. Should I put it on before you tell me about the favor?"

"No. But keep it accessible. What I need is for you to take a special guy floating next week here on the Snake. Deadman's Bar to Moose. You know that float."

"That's the section where Salisbury shot the hell out of me, as well as Lucinda and Wuff, before he was killed—maybe by a tree."

"Give Lucinda *some* credit for the kill."

"OK. And your guys as well. Some fireworks! I haven't fired a weapon since that day. I'm not especially accurate with my Glock."

"Don't waste your time with little pistols. Get a rifle, so you can lie down and take your time shooting."

"I doubt I'd be any better." Byng didn't know about my background with rifles. Especially my attempted assassination of Isfahani, which left him alive but with a face that would sink a thousand ships. I wasn't about to tell Byng.

"Tell me about this 'special' guy you want me to take on a float."

"You know my work with disabled and disadvantaged kids. This person's a disabled vet. Ever heard of Project Healing Waters?"

"Of course. It's unique. I'm on the list to work with PHW here and did one float for them two years ago, but none since then. Apparently, there's enough mayhem on my boat without putting stress on combat wounded vets who've *really* been through tough times."

"We'll gamble on you. The float's Tuesday. There'll be twenty-five vets with us and a blue ribbon group of guides participating. The vet you'll take is Juan Santander."

"Huntly, one question—is he Guatemalan?"

"That's a strange question for *you* to ask. He's neither. His family emigrated from Spain. They came over to Florida with Pedro Menendez in 1565. Part of the first settlement in what's now St. Augustine, Florida. Seventeen or eighteen generations later, some family, including his parents, still live near there. You have a place in Florida, don't you?"

"I do. A cottage on the salt marshes, twenty miles south of St. Augustine. . . . Tell me more about Santander."

"Quite a story. Public schools. Soccer star in high school. No men's soccer team at UF, where football rules, so he took a scholarship to Notre Dame. All-American. Number four academically. Won a Rhodes and went to Oxford for two years.

Came back and began law school at Stanford. But he walked away after a year and joined the Navy. Remember that football player, Tillman? He gave up pro football to serve, and was killed in Iraq. Santander had read about Tillman and decided *he* owed his country a couple of years. He made the Seal/UDT program. Then the elite Team Six. On a mission having particulars that remain in locked files, he was badly torn up. Lost his right leg from the knee down, his right hand at the wrist, and his right eye."

"Prosthetics?"

"Yes. He runs 5Ks with an artificial leg."

"Sounds well adjusted."

"Unfortunately, he's not."

"Any idea why? . . . Huntly, I think I know who you're talking about."

"I thought you'd realize it sooner. Your memory is worse than your shooting."

"He's Cassie and Ander Eckstrum's nephew—I think his mom was an Eckstrum who married a Santander who was an ambassador."

"Right. His dad was ambassador to three countries, including France and Spain. Still interested?"

"More like being excited to meet him."

"Maybe not. He's had a rough time. Became addicted to pain killers in the VA hospital. Got out and went downhill fast—more drugs and then drinking. He's reclusive, irritable, and agreed to join the program only because his aunt Cassie Eckstrum badgered him into participating. He's been staying in Jackson with Cassie."

"Huntly, I'm only worried about people who might shoot me. I'm not worried about Juan Santander."

"You'll do fine. We're to meet Monday for dinner at the Gun Barrel. At six. See you there."

≈

Wuff remained at Mill Creek with my neighbor Mavis. I drove south through Yellowstone Park, my first time in the park and Jackson Hole since the shooting. I was early. Driving through Grand Teton raised my spirits, until I pulled off at the rest stop along Highway 89 where Ansel Adams took his classic photo of the silvery Snake River below Grand Teton.

Sitting on the stone wall watching a tiny drift boat glide through a riffle hundreds of yards below, I had visions of El's death. Then, thinking about the final shoot out with Salisbury overwhelmed me. The smell of conifers on the slope in front of me became the acrid stench of gunpowder, and the cry of a gliding bald eagle became the screams of El.

I began to hyperventilate—the eighty-eight degrees of a cumulus clouded day didn't help. My breathing was labored; I was expelling too much carbon dioxide. It was a panic attack in lay terms, *metabolic acidosis* in medic-speak. My blood's pH value was accelerating, turning alkaline, constricting blood vessels to my brain and generally screwing up my nervous system.

A woman saw me, came over, and asked if she could help. Said she was nurse from Jackson. I couldn't get out a full sentence and nodded my head, scattering a mixture of perspiration and tears, spotting her light-blue denim dress. She sat down by my side on the wall and took my hand. I was glad no one else was there. And glad she was.

The presence of a caring human took effect. My senses and speech returned. She sensed some causative grief, but didn't ask questions. She soon left with a pat on my shoulder, mentioning her name was Mary. I thought it might have been Florence . . . as in Nightingale.

My maudlin episode caused a quarter-hour late-arrival at the Gun Barrel. I left my drift boat in a safe, far corner of the parking lot and walked toward the front door.

Huntly Byng came rushing out the door behind a guy a good six inches beyond six feet tall. Trim build. It wasn't until I was ten feet from them that I noticed the guy had a limp, a prosthetic right hand, and a right eye that didn't move with his left. Distracted by my arrival, Byng turned to speak to me, allowing the big fellow freedom to spin and grab Byng in a bear hug. I thought they were fooling around until Byng yelled, "Juan, let me go, you damned fool. I told you not to show up drunk again."

It had to be Juan Santander—my disabled vet client for the float the next day. He threw Byng to the ground and fell on top of him. I'm no street fighter, especially when the opponent is a Navy Seal, present or former. My guns were all at Mill Creek. I assumed I wouldn't need them in the midst of a couple of dozen certified heroes. If I jumped on top of the two, I'd soon be on the bottom. I took out a red Sharpie felt pen, removed the cap that was about the size of a gun barrel, and pressed it against Santander's right temple, figuring his having only the left eye he couldn't see the pen.

I said, quietly but firmly, "You best hear this, CFB. Let the officer go and put your hands behind you, or I'll blow a hole through your head so the bullet will come out your good eye."

Why it worked was beyond me, but welcome. He put his hands behind his back, and I shoved him off Byng, who I expected to jump up and have his gun in Santander's face in two seconds. He didn't. He did the jumping up part, but his gun remained holstered. I was standing with the two parts of the red Sharpie in my hand. When Santander saw them, he burst out laughing.

"Juan, meet Macduff Brooks, your guide tomorrow," said Byng.

"Hi, Macduff. Think you can handle me in the boat?" He had a huge smile that a three-week-old beard didn't begin to hide. He was a little unsteady and smelled like he'd showered in Moose Drool.

"Because you've got a prosthetic leg, Santander, I may have to tie you to your seat. *You* get extra—a chain and lock."

"What if we capsize?"

"You're a Seal. You figure it out. If you can't, I do burials at sea."

"Hey, Huntly. You said Macduff was a nice guy."

"Not when you cross him. The last guy who gave him trouble may still be hanging from a tree limb that pierced his chest on a float on the Snake last year."

Santander turned and looked at me wide-eyed. No more smile. Head cocked a little. Not a word for a couple of minutes, and then he said, "*You're* the guy Cassie told me about. Didn't you lose *another* client last week on the Yellowstone?"

"Nope. Someone used my trailer to deposit a dead body. *Nothing* happened on my boat."

"So I'm safe, as long as I'm *in* your boat?"

"Maybe not. I've lost two clients floating. One a really good guy, your uncle Ander. The other was worse than bad."

"I'm taking Juan home to Cassie," interjected Byng. "See you tomorrow. Go in and meet the other guys. And one gal—a super Army sergeant—Lucie Yee. She lost an arm and gained a Distinguished Service Cross."

"Not a fair exchange, Huntly," I said. "Can I trade a Navy Seal for her?"

"Wait a minute, guys," Santander said. "*That's* not fair. I got one of those medals, too."

"Yea, but I bet she's prettier, and she won't grab me in a bear hug and throw me down."

"Don't you *wish*, Macdoof. . . .Sir!""

10

NEXT MORNING WE ALL GATHERED EARLY at Moose for breakfast at the teepee. . . . Ambient and anxious to start the fishing. The food was heavy on bad cholesterol and light on good nutrition.

An hour later the half-dozen boats starting their floats at Deadman's Bar had rigged up, finished with a few casting basics on shore, and shoved off at about ten minute intervals. I rowed *Osprey;* Santander was in front. I was the only one without a second person fishing from the rear seat; no one else would go with Santander after the incident at the Gun Barrel.

"You cast pretty good with that fly rod strapped to your prosthesis, Santander. You fished before?"

"Yea, with Ander when I was a kid. Sometimes with Kris. And some spin casting back home in Florida along the intracoastal. Maybe I cast better now. No wrist to break!"

"Good attitude. Let's try an attractor—something big and bright. Left to us by the Brits, an escape from Victorian drabness," I said as he snapped off his small elk-hair caddis dry fly with a poor back cast. "Nothing's rising yet, but an attractor might bring one up along the west bank." I didn't want to do anything for him that he could manage, but tying a fly on a 4X tippet seemed a little too much to expect. I grabbed his tippet and threaded it through the hook's eye.

"What do you think you're doing? *I* can do that." He slipped the rod from its rig, set the rod down, grabbed the fly and tippet from me with his left hand, pulled the tippet out of the eye, and clamped the fly in his right prosthesis, which had a poly-looking forefinger and thumb he could squeeze. Then he slipped the tippet through with his left hand, used his finger to push the tip around five times, poked the end through, and pulled it tight with his teeth.

"Hell, I might as well go home. You don't need me, Santander."

He re-attached the rod to his arm, flipped the line off to the side, began to toss lengthening casts toward the near bank, looked over his shoulder at me with a smirk, and said, "Macduff, call me Juan. You sound like my lieutenant when you call me Santander."

"Another time I might have been."

"Jarhead? Squid? Grunt?" he asked.

"Squid."

"Canoe U?" asked Santander, using slang common to the Naval Academy.

"Nope. Newport Officer Candidate School. A ninety day wonder."

"My God, only ninety days to become an officer and a gentleman! . . .Sea going?"

"Yep."

"*Monitor* or *Merrimac*?"

"Little newer. Tin cans."

"Well, Macdoof—*Sir*. It's gonna be hard to salute with this rod in my hand."

"No salutes on this ship, Juan. And call me Mac. . . . Why not watch your fly? You've had three takes so far. *Lift!*" I yelled as the fourth strike gulped the orange-bodied attractor that had disappeared into the corner of the mouth of an eccentrically red-slashed seventeen-inch Snake River cutthroat. A few minutes later it was in my boat net.

"Good fish, Juan."

"You had the boat in a pretty good spot."

The compliment was welcome. A major part of a guide's work is placement of the drift boat so that fish are within the client's casting ability.

The morning passed as what we'd call a "happy" ship in the Navy. Juan caught a half-dozen trout and a few of the inevitable intruding, but certified and legitimate, Snake River resident whitefish. A couple of times Juan's concentration shifted to somewhere else, perhaps far away in the hot desert of Iraq or the ragged mountains of Afghanistan. I didn't ask.

An hour after lunch, we drifted near the remains of the Bar B-C dude ranch, decaying along the west bank from government neglect. A thirty-something nerdy looking guy, wearing glasses that he kept pushing up on his nose, pulled a small, yellow kayak into the water along the western shore.

He and a boy about five climbed in. His lady companion handed him a cooler he placed behind him. With her was a tiny girl, at the most three. The guy lifted the boy to the front, pushed off with the paddle, reached behind him, and took a beer from the cooler.

It wasn't an encouraging sight. The river ahead was filled with strainers and sweepers from the spring snow melt, and neither man nor boy wore a life vest.

"Should he be doing that?" asked Juan.

"Kayaks are allowed, Juan, but life vests like ours are required. Even for Seals! This is a treacherous stretch of the Snake. We'll keep an eye on them."

Fishing became less our focus as we watched the man consume four beers and increasingly ignore the boy's climbing about the kayak. He moved forward and sat on the front of the bow, one foot dragging on each side. Well out of reach of the man.

"Juan, I'm staying near them. I've got to tell the guy to put the kid further back and lend him two of my life jackets."

Before I could say another word, Juan slipped out of his jacket and was ready to toss it to the man, who now had our uninvited and unwelcome attention.

"I'm doin' fine. I don't need no help," he called in our direction, a little slur in his speech.

"You're putting this jacket on the boy, or I'm taking him in the boat," called Juan, with intimidating force that didn't faze the man.

"Stay off," he called. "I can handle this. . . . Want a couple of brews?"

Closing to a boat length, the man reached around behind him to grab another beer just as the boy turned to hear what we were saying. Their weight shifted to the same side. The kayak rolled over. The man struggled to hang on; he didn't appear to be a swimmer. The boy disappeared. The current was moving, and we were approaching some deep holes.

Before I could do anything more, Juan suddenly slid over the side without a splash and went under. I thought he'd fallen, but I saw his left leg kick strongly as he vanished. We reached the kayak, and I grabbed a line from its bow. The man was hanging on, yelling for the boy. His glasses were gone, and he was disoriented.

There was no sign of the boy or Juan. I pulled the man into the stern of the drift boat and tied the line from the kayak to *Osprey's* transom. Nearly two minutes passed while I was trying to recall how long one could stay underwater. A minute later and three feet in front of my right oar tip, Juan and the boy exploded through the surface like leaping dolphins.

Juan tossed the boy into the front of the boat at my feet, pulled himself over the gunnel, and immediately began CPR in the cramped space. Within seconds the boy began to cough and spume water, then cough some more and gag—and then give a welcome sob. I passed him back to his dad, who held him tightly.

"You don't deserve him," I said to the man. "Get his clothes off. Open the locker under your seat. Take out the dry bag; it has extra clothes. Large and baggy, but dry and warm."

Within twenty minutes the boy was laughing again. His dad wasn't. He was half in shock, half drunk. He didn't utter a word—just held on to the boy tightly, avoiding Juan's stare.

Juan had been wordless, but that suddenly changed. "You don't deserve to be a dad, dude. It's dangerous enough even to be on this river with the boy, but adding no life jackets for either of you and letting him sit on the bow out of your reach, while you guzzle brew, make you unfit to be alive. If I'd been Mac, I would have whacked you with an oar and left you to drown. You're a poor excuse for an adult. You're lucky Mac's between us."

Not a word came from the man. He was smart enough to realize that Juan said a lot less than he could have, probably in deference to the boy.

By the time we approached the takeout at Moose, Juan had the boy in front with him and was teaching him how to cast.

The boy asked, “You don’t have a real hand. And one eye’s funny. What happened to you?”

“Jimmy, don’t ask those questions,” said his dad.

“I had an accident, Jimmy,” said Juan. And nothing more.

After Juan and I unrigged and strapped *Osprey* on the trailer, I went to make sure the boy and his dad were OK. The woman and little girl were the man’s wife and daughter and had been waiting for them at the Moose takeout. They didn’t know anything about the incident, and it didn’t appear the father was going to tell them much.

When they’d left, I noticed Juan sitting on my trailer fender and drinking a beer. There were already three empty cans next to him. He was staring at Grand Teton, transfixed by its magnificence or not knowing it was there—lost in a private world he hadn’t dealt with close to the way he’d saved the boy.

“Juan, you OK?” I asked, not sure what effect the beer already had.

“I could’ve killed that guy, Mac. It was all I could do not to grab him and snap his neck. If the boy had drowned, I know I would have killed him. You got any more beer?”

“You don’t need any more, Juan. Where can I drop you?”

Before I could move, Juan got up, shoved past me, opened the rear deck of my SUV, flipped up the cooler’s top, and brought out four bottles of strong Montana pale ale. I grabbed two from him and then realized he was on the edge of a razor-sharp fence and could go either way.

One way was after me, and I knew I wouldn’t fare well. I had to have him choose the other path and quickly said, “Two are for me. Thanks, Juan.” I opened one of the beers, took a sip, and looked at Juan. “Let’s sit and finish these and then be on our way. I have a long drive home to Montana tomorrow.”

Juan looked at me. His false eye staring off to the side while his good left eye ripped through me with an intensity that made me shudder.

"Cold, Mac?" he asked. In an instant his demeanor changed. "Take my jacket."

He emptied the last quarter of his bottle on the ground and placed the second back in my cooler. Then grabbed an iced tea.

"This was a day with a lot of ups and downs. I don't handle that too well."

"Don't you realize what you did? You saved a kid's life. I was certain he was *gone*. His dad couldn't help him. I didn't do a damned thing. Can you believe my first thought when you went over was 'can Juan swim?' Really smart thinking—'Can a Navy Seal swim?'"

"I haven't been in the water since my injuries. I didn't know if I *could* still swim."

"Like a dolphin. . . . Want to fish again sometime?"

"I was going to ask. I want to work on some ideas I thought about today, to attach my right arm stub to the rod better. Also, I want a left-hand wind reel, not the right-hand wind I used today. I'm not used to cranking a reel left handed. . . . And I'll work on knots."

"My fault you had a right-hand wind. Call when you're free. I'm headed east to Indiana sometime soon, but I don't know exactly when."

I hadn't mentioned Lucinda or my Florida winter cottage. But we had talked about St. Augustine, the origin of Juan's deep roots in America. I made one blunder. It was the first time I've talked to anyone other than Lucinda about the Navy. Macduff Brooks was never in the Navy, much less on destroyers. Maxwell Hunt was. I'll have to do some thinking about how to weave that into the fictional past of Macduff I'm slowly creating.

At breakfast in Jackson the next morning, I was badgered by inane questions from a fledgling, local newspaper reporter, who didn't have a clue about floating the Snake, about the day's events, or about Juan's lifesaving swim.

On the drive to Mill Creek, I began to think about my own need to save another—how I might help Lucinda with her memory lapses, her difficult decisions about her future, and her need to do some more damage control with her mother. I don't know much about my own future. And I'm often confused answering questions about my past.

11

THREE WEEKS LATER, during unexpectedly high humidity for a Montana August, Rosa Lipsius called from Indiana.

"Lucinda's progressin' favorably, Mr. Brooks. It would be a good time for you to visit. There are troublin' issues with both her mother's doctor and lawyer."

Two days later, irritable after my Delta flights to Indiana took more time than travel by a 19th-century steam locomotive, Rosa met me at the door. Mrs. Lang learned I was coming, and when she heard the doorbell excused herself from the dinner table and went upstairs to her room. She was likely rehearsing the berating I received every time we talked.

Lucinda was nearly finished with dinner. I was astonished at the improvement of her color. Even better, her engaging smile was back. She was about to start her dessert—a delicious looking *flan de vanilla* she protected when she saw me.

"May I have a bite of your dessert?" I asked.

"It's fattening. Luke warm. Unhealthy. Mostly calories and lots of bad cholesterol."

"Looks delicious."

"*I* need it to gain back my weight."

"That's unfair. You're playing on my sympathies."

"There's *flan* for you in the icebox in the kitchen."

"Icebox? Haven't refrigerators made it to Indiana yet?"

"I have amnesia. I remember only way back. My grandparents had an icebox."

"When are you planning to join the present?"

"When you learn not to ask for my dessert."

She looked up, smiled, and said, "Here's my spoon." She gave me the *smaller* of the two spoons on her tray. I remembered a similar time at Moose when we joked about her eating my dessert. It was hard to speak. The best I could do was: "You look wonderful, El."

"*Maxwell*, I'm *not* El. I'm *Lucinda*. . . . Are we married, Maxwell?"

"No."

"That means we've been living in sin."

"It depends on how much you remember about what we've done."

"I think we *must* be married. Dr. Kent called yesterday from Salt Lake City to check on me and asked about you. She said you sat in a chair in my hospital room for two weeks without leaving the room, and nearly killed yourself because you hardly ate or slept. She said you looked like a homeless vagrant and they had to force you to leave. You wouldn't do that if we weren't married?"

"You saved my life. And I nearly caused your death. You also saved Wuff."

"*Wuff!* I remember! That's *my* dog. She's a sheltie. Did you bring her?"

"She's in Montana. She's fine. Waiting for you." I didn't want to upset her by correcting her about who owns Wuff. Maybe we should ask Wuff, but I might not like the answer.

Lucinda was pleased with herself. The mention of Wuff brought back "dog" and "female" and "sheltie." She was building a memory bank at the rapid pace young children learn.

I decided to test her memory, and said, "Lucinda, my name isn't Maxwell, just as your name isn't El."

"What *is* your name?"

"It's Macduff."

"Macduff?"

"Yes. Macduff Brooks."

"But my name's not Lucinda Brooks? Or Lucinda Hunt?"

"That's right. It's Lucinda *Lang*."

"Lucinda *L*. Lang," she corrected. "This is my family's house."

"That's right. This is where you were born and raised."

"But don't we have an apartment in New York?"

"It's *your* apartment. A very nice one."

"Do you live in New York, too?"

"No, I live in Montana, very near where you also spend part of the year."

"But you also live in Florida, Macduff. In Gainesville."

"Not in Gainesville, but in a small cottage. . . ."

She interrupted. "On a beautiful salt marsh twenty miles south of St. Augustine!"

"Perfect! You're doing great."

"Macduff, you exhaust me with all these questions. Were you ever a teacher?"

Rosa and I helped Lucinda from the table to her bedroom. I sat in a chair beside her bed. She fell asleep quickly. It took me a few seconds longer. I was tired from the flights and drive.

I woke an hour later. Rosa had touched my arm and thought I should leave. Mrs. Lang was not pleased I had come and had been giving Rosa trouble in the kitchen. She and I went to the front porch and spent an hour talking about Mrs. Lang's problems with the doctor and the lawyer.

"What worries me most, Mr. Brooks, is that Dr. West, Lucinda's doctor, is givin' her large doses of some drugs every time she shows some improvement with her memory. The drugs cause her to forget more!"

"What's West giving her?"

"I know she's takin' some statins, such as Lipitor. *I've* used that for high cholesterol. He's also givin' her a lot of Valium, which I thought was for anxiety and actually may *cause* amnesia. But the last straw was when I found him givin' her Viagra. Viagra, Mr. Brooks! I looked it up online and learned erectile dysfunction drugs may *cause* amnesia. What does all this mean?"

"I don't know, but I'm going to find out. I want you to watch everything she takes. Call Dr. Kent in Salt Lake City. She was Lucinda's doctor when she was taken to Salt Lake City after the shooting. And get Dr. Kent's approval before you administer anything. Don't tell Dr. West."

The next morning I went back to see Lucinda before I flew home to Montana. She was in the dining room having breakfast.

"Eggs Benedict?" I asked.

"Eggs jumbled," she said.

"You mean scrambled?"

"Whatever. Like my brain. So how are you this fine morning—Professor Macduff Brooks of Montana and Florida?"

"Professor?"

"Weren't you a professor?"

If I told her "no," I would not only be lying, but also be harming her progress. She's uncertain enough about facts without my telling her that something she correctly remembered *isn't* correct.

"I was a professor once. I'll tell you why later, but it's best you don't refer to me as a professor."

"OK. . . . When're we going home?"

"I'll ask Dr. West when he arrives."

West is a general practitioner. He alludes to knowing about amnesia. I have doubts that have become more justified since Rosa told me about the medications he's been administering.

When West arrived, his first question was difficult to answer. "Your past is unclear to us, Mr. Brooks. Lucinda's beginning to remember things about you that apparently you don't want discussed. I talked with Dr. Kent in Salt Lake City late yesterday. She brought up the admissions records on her computer. She was on duty twenty-one years ago when a Maxwell Hunt of Gainesville, Florida, was airlifted to the Salt Lake City hospital. Maxwell had been injured in an accident in a drift boat on the Snake River. He was a law professor. His wife was killed. Her name was El. Until a couple of weeks ago, Lucinda thought she was El and you were Maxwell Hunt. What should I believe?"

I told him as little as possible, trying to convince him that El and Maxwell were indeed two people, but that I had apparently used their tragic story so often in front of Lucinda when we floated with clients that she thought she and I were El and Maxwell. I'm not sure either Dr. West or Dr. Kent likes me. I appreciate how protective Dr. Kent had been about Lucinda, but I'm not sure about Dr. West. I don't want him to become suspicious, either of what I once was or of what I know about medicines he's been giving Lucinda.

"Dr. West, I'd like to take Lucinda to Montana and help her through her long-term recovery."

"She needs professional therapy. And it can only be done properly here . . . under my care."

"Couldn't she get the therapy in Montana?"

"In Bozeman, possibly. But not what I can provide for her. However, there's another problem. It's Mrs. Lang. She adamantly refuses to let Lucinda leave and threatens to get an injunction if you force it. I have to recommend that Lucinda remain here, if only to avoid the trauma that might arise if she tries to leave. You may visit occasionally, but best for very brief periods."

I was confused how to play my role and thought it best to agree with Dr. West. But I'd do some investigating on my own, as soon as I reached Montana. I hated to say goodbye and leave Lucinda in his hands. When I walked into her room to say goodbye and have a last hug, she was sitting in the slanting sun beams coming through the window blinds. She'd put on a sleeveless, deeply scooped cami in her favorite burgundy.

"Your *trapeziuses* are still beautiful!"

"Macduff! You said that once before. On a porch . . . where we were having dinner . . . in Florida. . . . Your neighbor from Gainesville and her friend sat at the table behind us. You avoided her and even though we were in deep evening shade, you put on your sunglasses"

"And you said I could search for something," I added, thrilled at her recollection.

"My *illiopses!* And you *did* when we got back to the cottage!" She then saw Rosa step from behind me. They both blushed.

"There'll be time soon enough for you both to do some more searchin'," Rosa commented, and left us.

≈

Home at my cabin on Mill Creek, I started to inquire about the effect of drugs on amnesia. I didn't like what I learned. I also contacted clients booked for the remainder of the season and arranged for other guides to substitute so I would have four days twice a month in Indiana. The clients were cordial, but after the death of Julie Conyers, they may have welcomed my calls as a way of avoiding making their own calls to cancel floats. They did understand my wish to spend time helping Lucinda.

A week later, I watched the sun set one evening—a glass of Gentleman Jack in one hand and Wuff's grooming brush in the other. I looked at the creek and the forest and wondered why my life had turned so unruly. If it hadn't, I'd be in my law school office discussing complex international law questions with bright students. As my mind drifted to those days, my cell phone rang. From Indiana!

It was Lucinda, her first call since I left.

"I feel *so* much better. I'm not taking all that medicine. Rosa throws it out after Dr. West leaves it. I don't understand."

"Do what Rosa says."

"I've been able to sort out my past—it seems mostly *our* past—much better than before. I have a question."

"OK."

"Did you shoot a man in Guatemala?"

"Yes . . . I did," I said, before I realized where this might take me. I tried to remind her about Abdul Khaliq Isfahani's attempt to destroy the Chrysler and Empire State buildings, but didn't go into her accidentally coming across me practicing with my CheyTac sniper rifle near my cabin, weeks before my unsuccessful attempt to assassinate Isfahani in the western highlands of Guatemala. At times, Lucinda seemed to know more than she wanted to discuss about my life as Maxwell and the dangers she'd shared being with me in Montana and Wyoming. Especially the attempt Park Salisbury had made to bomb my cabin and the final shootout on the Snake River.

"Why was Isfahani in Guatemala? His name isn't Hispanic. . . . Wait! I remember you telling me about a Guatemalan named Jose Pablo. . . . No—but similar. *Juan* Pablo! Wasn't he a terrible person who tried to kill you?"

She was ready to restore her memory of the dark side of my life—the most evil man I ever encountered in my moonlighting assignments for the CIA.

"Juan Pablo Herzog was a brilliant Guatemalan student of Maxwell Hunt. He studied at the University of Florida at the same time as Isfahani. Until the day Salisbury attempted to kill us, Herzog was the main suspect in killing Ander Eckstrum two years earlier and attempting to bomb my cabin. I hope Herzog is finally out of our lives."

≈

I didn't tell her that I often wake abruptly at night in a chilled sweat from a nightmare that Herzog is far from being out of our lives.

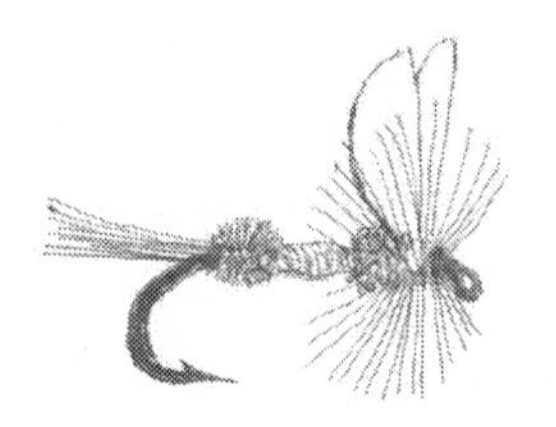

12

WHILE I WAS DEALING with Lucinda and her mother in Indiana, six hundred miles south an impeccably dressed and groomed gentleman, appearing taller than he was because of his carriage, walked unannounced into the walnut-paneled office of Hobart Perry, much admired dean of the University of Florida law college in Gainesville. He was on the telephone, and the intrusion was unexpected. Visitors rarely made it past his secretary, Donna, without her assurance that the dean was available and aware of their arrival. Dean Perry was finishing an encouraging conversation with a loyal alumnus whose family had contributed millions to the law school over the past two decades.

≈

"Walter, your recent contribution brings us within a million of making it the most successful fund raising campaign ever. We can always count on you for. . . . Sorry, someone I wasn't expecting walked into my office. I'll get back to you."

"I'm sorry," Donna said as she protectively tried to step between the intruder and the dean.

"That's all right, Donna. I'll call Walter back. . . . Is there something I might help you with, Mr. . . ?" Dean Perry asked the stranger, rising from his desk chair and extending his hand.

"I apologize sincerely for interrupting Decano. I feel confident you will excuse my rude entry. I have come to fund the creation of a professorship."

"Please sit. . . . Coffee?. . . Are you one of our graduates?"

"Strangely, I'm not a coffee drinker, though my family is extensively involved in its growth and production. Nor am I a law graduate. But I am a graduate of this fine university. My name is Juan Pablo Herzog. Nearly twenty years ago, I matriculated here in Gainesville and received a degree in agricultural engineering."

"What brings you to the law school rather than to our agricultural college?"

"Every student should have the experience of studying with a teacher who has a lasting influence on the student's life. I benefitted from that kind of experience, but not in my agricultural college. It was in a course at the Center for Latin American Studies, taught partly by Professor Maxwell W. Hunt of this law college."

"I never knew Professor Hunt. He died tragically of a stroke shortly before I became dean."

"It was a loss I have grieved over since his untimely death. I wish I could have been present when he died . . . to console him in his last moments."

"You and Professor Hunt became friends?"

"Yes, I spent many wonderful evenings at his home with a small group of students. An Iranian-born student and I were the most frequent visitors to his home. Professor Hunt had lost his wife in a tragic accident several years earlier. He missed her terribly, referring to her often. With her absence he directed even more of his attention to his students. During my last year he even had us to his home for Thanksgiving dinner, which he personally cooked. I was unable to go home that vacation because of forthcoming examinations. My home is Guatemala. . . . Dean Perry, tell me please about endowing a chair."

"There are various options. One is. . . ."

"May we begin with the most prestigious position?"

"We have one chair funded with a grant of two million dollars. Half was donated by an alumnus; the remainder was provided by the state under a matching program."

Juan Pablo Herzog opened his briefcase and took out his checkbook. He sat and began to write, looking up for a moment to ask, "How should I make out the check?"

"The University of Florida Foundation is the center that administers gifts. Excuse me if I seem a little surprised. It's unusual for a non-law graduate to walk in and immediately write a check. "

"Of course. . . . Here is my check."

Dean Perry looked at the check. His eyes widened; he slumped back in his chair. "Mr. Herzog, this is for four million dollars! That's an *extraordinary* gift. . . . But, I see it's dated two months from now?"

I have two requests, Decano. The money is to be for a single chair in the name of Professor Maxwell W. Hunt. A chair in international law. No restrictions on the area within that field. Nor will I ever make any requests or suggestions regarding who should be appointed to the chair."

"That request should create no problems, Mr. Herzog. I don't know what to say. I'd like to call our president and inform him of your generosity. I know he'll want to thank you in person."

"Please, let us wait for two months, when an announcement might be arranged with more planning. I do have a second request. . . . According to my understanding, Professor Hunt died of a stroke in Washington, D.C."

"That's correct. He was attending a law association meeting. He suffered a massive stroke that was quite unexpected in view of his age and apparent good health."

"But there doesn't seem to have been a burial here in Gainesville," Herzog responded. "The *Gainesville Gazette* announced his death, but no further announcements of internment were published. I wonder why he wasn't buried here in Gainesville, where he spent a very happy decade with his wife El before she died. My staff in Guatemala City checked the death records both here and D.C. There is no record of his death in either location. Isn't that strange?"

"I don't have any knowledge of the details of his death, Mr. Herzog. I didn't assume the deanship until later. If I recall correctly, the ashes of Professor Hunt's wife were scattered on the river where his wife died. In Wyoming. Hunt may have wished the same rather than burial here. I'll ask one of my associate deans to look into your questions."

"Wouldn't it be embarrassing to have a chair established and filled in his memory, and then learn he didn't die of a stroke?"

"Indeed, it would be most embarrassing. Do you have *any* reason to suspect that a stroke might not have been the cause of Professor Hunt's death, Mr. Herzog?"

"No. That is why I have dated the check two months from now. I would like to have a detailed report from you within that time, assuring me that Professor Hunt indeed died and is not living in luxury in Monaco or Rio on stolen funds!"

"That is hardly the case, I'm sure. But I will make inquiries. There's nothing I'm aware of in Professor Hunt's record to suggest he did anything unlawful."

"Dean Perry, your records should show that Professor Hunt made numerous trips to my country before his death. He had just returned from Guatemala to the U.S. when the alleged stroke occurred in Washington. His final CV on the law school website indicated he was to present lectures at the law school of Francisco Marroquin and the Chamber of Commerce. He never gave those lectures. Local contacts in Guatemala have told me he was in my country working with the CIA mission at the American embassy."

"That's astounding! I have no knowledge that Professor Hunt, or any of our faculty, ever worked for the CIA when they were abroad. Actually, I'm not sure I would know if they were engaged in such activities. But I will investigate, in view both of your request and my concern that one of our faculty might have been conducting activities abroad other than representing the university and the law school."

"My dear Dean Perry, that is most kind of you. I look forward to receiving your report, so that the creation and endowment of the chair may be announced. If you will permit, my plane is at the Gainesville airport, and I must return directly to Guatemala City."

Once Herzog had left the law building, Dean Perry asked his secretary to bring him the file of Professor Hunt, which Perry had never reviewed. He also asked his new senior associate dean, Gloria Martinez, to come to his office, where he repeated the conversation with Herzog from his memory and the few notes he had scribbled. The scribbles were mostly numbers with dollar signs.

"I'd like you to prepare the report. You're Guatemalan, aren't you, Gloria?"

"Yes," Ms. Martinez related. "I was born in Guatemala and lived there until I came here to undergraduate school. You have no reason to know that Herzog is one of the most powerful men in Guatemala. He has aspirations to become President. But there is a dark side to him, consisting of allegations that have never been disproven."

"We need to keep this under wraps, Gloria. We might not be able to provide Mr. Herzog with a report he finds adequate, or we might find information that demands rejection of his request. It would be embarrassing to announce the gift and later have to retract it."

When Ms. Martinez left to begin her investigation, Dean Perry, scanning through Professor Hunt's file, thought: "There is a thread that runs through a large percentage of the foreign countries Professor Hunt visited. Not only Guatemala. Numerous parts of Yugoslavia just before it broke apart after Tito died, the Sudan on the eve of its downfall, Paraguay as President Stroessner's government was collapsing, and ongoing problems with leftist rebels in Nicaragua and Panama. Each of the countries was relatively unstable at the time Hunt visited—perfect locations for engaging in activities for the embassy, and especially the local CIA mission."

Forty minutes later, standing by the side of a private jet refueled and ready for departure at the Gainesville airport, Herzog dialed a number on his cell phone. A voice answered and said only, "Yes, here."

Herzog spoke softly into the cell phone, "Abdul, the final chapter has begun."

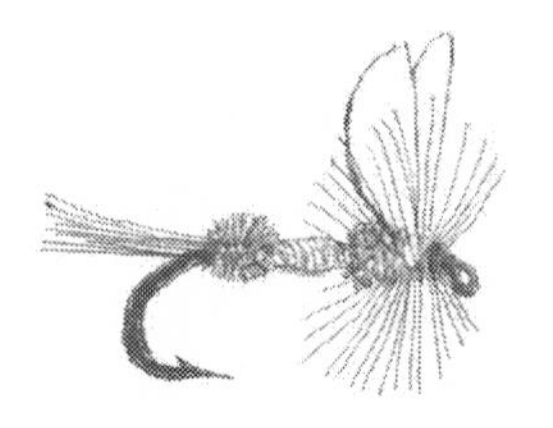

13

WUFF AND I WALK EVERY DAY, usually starting across a footbridge I've built over Mill Creek. Then west along Mill Creek Road, beyond the gravel road onto macadam that marks the change from forest to valley. We never walk far up the road in the opposite direction because I don't want to pass Lucinda's ranch.

Intermittent phone conversations with Lucinda haven't reached the brief time of her life spent on vacation at Arrogate Ranch, about a mile upstream from my cabin. It's the magnificent spread where we first met. She hasn't asked me about her ranch or about her career as an investment broker in Manhattan. I don't plan to initiate discussing that part of her life. When she's ready, she'll ask.

≈

At the Howlin' Hounds for breakfast early one September morning, after walking Wuff, Ken Rangely walked in unexpectedly and joined me. When we finished, he asked to talk outside, away from others having breakfast. The tables at the Howlin'

Hounds are close to one another. Conversations are easily overheard. But that's part of the charm of the place.

"Your update on Lucinda sounds encouraging. You must be doing something right."

"Day-to-day. Sometimes she seems to be remembering things I've forgotten, and then a major regression sets in. It's frustrating for us both."

"When I left the house this morning, Sarah asked . . . again . . . 'When's Macduff going to marry Lucinda?'"

"Did you tell your wife when, Ken?"

"That means *you* don't know?"

"How can I do it? I can't take advantage of her when she still has the effects of the shooting. It's unfair. Her decision made one day might be forgotten the next. And her mother might kill me."

"I understand, but are you certain her injury isn't an excuse for you not to think about it? You managed to avoid it for a long time before her injury."

"That's unfair. . . . Let me share something that can't go further. OK?"

"Fine. Shoot."

"When Park Salisbury shot us on *Osprey,* one bullet hit a small black velvet-covered box in my outside jacket pocket. The bullet demolished the box and struck a ring inside, twisting the setting and dislodging an emerald-cut diamond which apparently landed in the river. It was lost. And not insured. I have the box and the setting. . . . I was going to offer Lucinda the ring that evening."

"She'll understand that you decided to ask her before the injury and, despite what happened, you still want to marry her."

"It's a little more complex. She's convinced we're already married, but she's often in another world. If she doesn't understand, she might believe I feel obligated to marry her because I nearly caused her death."

"From what I hear, *your* choosing the Snake River channel you took saved you both when you impaled Salisbury on the tree. And saved Wuff."

"I fired my Glock *after* both Lucinda and Byng's snipers fired. I think Salisbury was dead by the time I shot him and rowed him into the tree limb."

"Believe what you want, but I think you should at least propose and be engaged. You don't have to rush the wedding date."

"I thought you wanted to talk about Julie Conyers, not plan my social life?"

"Sometimes you face the right direction, but you need a push. . . . I do want to talk about Julie. In detail. But not now. Can you take some time in the next few days and spend part of a day with me? I'm helping Erin. Jimbo's shifted a lot of the investigation to her, because he'd prefer not to deal with you. He says your mind functions like a lawyer's. Can you believe that? Erin asked me for help. She says she has trouble when she's talking about Julie being so brutally murdered, nailed through her feet and wrists to the wooden cross. And especially her breasts being cut out."

"Was Julie sexually assaulted?" I asked.

"Repeatedly," Ken answered. "We don't want this in the press, but we have DNA from three different males who had sex with her."

Julie was admired by nearly everyone who knew her. I feel the same anger as I did about Isfahani when I shot him—I'd have no reservations about killing Julie's assailant.

"What can I say? Or do to help?"

“Walk me through your history knowing Julie. I’ve learned you provided the money for the Shuttle Gals to buy their two vans.”

“Purely a business arrangement.”

“Nonsense. A no interest loan—pay me back when you can—isn’t *normal* business.”

“She paid me the full amount within two years.” This was going nowhere. I had to shift the focus. “What do you think about floating with me? You know I haven’t floated since the murder. It’s been a couple of months. I need to get back on the river. With a friend. Would you go tomorrow on a half-day float? You don’t have to fish, just sit in the front seat facing me, and we’ll talk.”

“Fine, but I’ll bring a rod. I haven’t fished in months. I hear it’s been better than average.”

“Hoppers are everywhere. We’ll hit the banks. Let’s meet here tomorrow at 7:30, have breakfast, and be on the river by 8:30 at Mallard’s Rest.”

14

THE FOLLOWING MORNING, after feeding Wuff, I hooked up *Osprey* and drove to the Howlin' Hounds Café. Ken was reading the Livingston newspaper and sipping coffee.

"Can we switch *Osprey's* trailer and use your truck?" I asked. "My SUV is crying for an oil change. Mavis said she'd drive to Livingston to have it done and do some shopping."

"*Of course.* I'll follow you back to your cabin when we finish breakfast."

Launching *Osprey* an hour later, I rowed us out to merge with a sparse mist that was tracing the flow of the river. Ken asked, "Who's doing your shuttle? If *anyone* will still work for you!"

"I've met with each of the Shuttle Gals. They'll *all* work for me. They didn't think it was their service that was being attacked, but that someone was specifically targeting Julie. I reminded them all of Victoria Montoya and warned she might go after any one of them, even though she'd only talked with Julie. And I told them about Helga Markel and her association with PARA." I didn't mention my coal and dam interest theory; I couldn't picture Viktor Burzynski as a murderer.

"So, who's doing the shuttle today?"

"Olga Smits, one of Julie's partners. Like Julie, she's a lesbian. Her partner is Pam Snyder, another of the Shuttle Gals. They 'married' in California. . . . Are you pursuing the possibility that the killer is homophobic? Maybe a radical group . . . or an individual who hates the whole gay and lesbian culture?"

"Jimbo hasn't mentioned that," Ken replied. "But Erin has. Remember the murder of a student named Shepard at the University of Wyoming about a dozen years ago? He was targeted because he was gay. The two scumbags who murdered him escaped the death penalty. Shepard's funeral was picketed by anti-gay church members carrying signs saying 'God Hates Fags' and 'Matt Shepard rots in Hell.' It remains an explosive issue. We *have* to pursue it."

"How could Julie's death have happened, Ken? The wooden beams she was nailed to were 4x6s—nearly seven feet long. Victoria Montoya couldn't have done it alone."

"You can buy 4x6 eight-footers at any lumber company. We've checked. In the month before her death, the Home Depot in Bozeman sold over seven hundred of the same size to more than a hundred different buyers. They're commonly used for fence end-posts. We're tracing each beam purchase, but we have a dozen other stores in Livingston and Bozeman where similar beams could have been bought. The rope that tied the two beams was common rope from any hardware. What wasn't common were the nails through her feet and hands. They were black iron-forged nails, about ten inches long. We don't know where they came from. They could be from Mexico; they look hand forged. And we don't know where the sash came from bearing the Mexican flag colors— green, red, and white."

"Wood usually has a small barcode tag stapled near one end. Any chance one was on one of the beams?" I questioned.

"Don't we wish! We even looked for staple holes. But wood was cut off the ends of the two beams. The tags, if there were any, had to be on the waste parts."

"Could the wood have been stolen from a job site?. . . But I guess a couple of 4x6 beams might not even go missing."

"That's something we'll check. You can understand how much time it takes to investigate. We're a small force. There aren't many murders in Park County."

"Had Julie received any hate mail or phone calls?"

"We're sorting through both at Julie's house. And her e-mail. Her son George is staying with her parents. He's only nine. Julie didn't have a companion. It helps when there's a spouse or companion who the victim might have talked to about threats or fears."

"Did Victoria Montoya ever threaten Julie?"

"Not that we know about. No record yet of helpful phone calls. No mail—regular or e-mail—at least not that we've discovered."

"I'm not any help."

"You may be . . . on a different matter. It's Erin. She's acting strangely about this killing. I can't pinpoint any one incident, but her personality shifts when we talk about the case. Erin respects you, Macduff. A lot. Has she talked to you about the killing?"

"I haven't talked to Erin regularly, mainly due to my flying to Indiana to see Lucinda every couple of weeks. Truthfully, if Lucinda hadn't survived, I might view Erin differently. She's got to be on the area's 'most eligible' lists."

"At the top. She's attractive and a whiz professionally. She doesn't think the PARA gal Markel was involved. More intuition than anything. She's never met Markel. We'll probably bring Markel in for questioning. *If* we can find her. The last we knew she was in Missoula."

"Erin's probably right. I don't think Markel had enough time. She confronted you and me about eight that morning and left heading north in a car too small to carry even one beam. How could she have decided to kill one of the Shuttle Gals, gotten the beams and rope and nails, and done the killing? . . . We *saw* Julie doing the shuttle soon after I launched with my clients. When Markel confronted us, I don't think she knew any details about the float, much less the shuttle."

"How'd you schedule the shuttle? Telephone? E-mail?"

"This one was e-mail. I sent Julie a list of several shuttles we'd arranged, just as a confirmation."

"Did it include dates and places to pick up and drop off the trailer?"

"Yep. All that. . . . Important?"

"Maybe. E-mail can be accessed by a hacker. I don't know much about it, but we'll follow-up. Another thing, we took Julie's prints from your SUV. That would be from when she moved the SUV and trailer."

"Soon after Julie dropped my SUV and trailer at Loch Leven, her van should have arrived to pick her up for another shuttle."

"It did. She did some other shuttles that morning and was finished a little after noon. The gals split up at Carter Bridge, where they left cars and went their own ways. We lose Julie there. You found her body on the trailer about 5:20. You called me at 5:27."

"So your thoughts on where or how Julie was killed are all speculation?"

"Unfortunately, that's correct. She wasn't murdered doing your shuttle, but the killer used your trailer to display her body.

We don't know *where* she was killed. In a basement, a garage, a house, in her car?"

"Was she nailed to the beams on my trailer alive and then killed? Maybe by drowning?"

"Think, Mac. It's unlikely anyone would pull a trailer on a public road with a body splayed on a cross tied to the trailer. Of course, they could throw a tarp over the body, but that's not what happened. There were no tire marks suggesting your SUV and trailer were moved from where they were parked other than down to the water. We don't think the killer, or killers, intercepted or took Julie alive to Loch Leven and killed her there. There's too much openness and the possibility of someone arriving at the takeout and seeing the killers in the act."

"Meaning she was dead and her body was taken to the Loch Leven area and nailed to the beams that had been tied to the trailer?"

"Yes. She'd been dead for a couple of hours when you arrived. Whoever placed her on the trailer probably did so between 3:30 and an hour before you arrived. They might have watched you from the highway. Or the Mill Creek Road bridge. We think they wanted *you* to find her, not some third party stopping at the Loch Leven ramp. Several orange cones blocked the ramp's entrance when we arrived after your call."

"How do *you* think Julie was killed, Ken?"

"Someone abducted her after she left the Carter Bridge ramp when the Shuttle Gals broke up for the day. Julie's car was at her house, so they must have waited until she got home. Her son George was at an after-school soccer practice. Julie's house is partly secluded. There was no sign of a struggle in the house. She probably never went inside. I think someone was waiting for her in her yard. And I think it was someone she knew."

"Why do you think that?"

"Partly hunch. She has two dogs. They're kept outside in a pen. They bark only when strangers arrive. Neighbors sometimes hear them. We asked the neighbors but they recalled no noise from Julie's direction. The closest neighbor was working in his yard all afternoon and never heard a bark. Julie may have gotten into another car voluntarily."

"That points to Victoria Montoya," I proposed. "Julie didn't like her, but she didn't fear her."

"That's why Shaw is so certain Montoya did it. Likely directing some of her Ciudad Juarez gang members. And using the green, red, and white sash—Mexico's colors."

"Then Montoya and the men took Julie from her property, killed her somewhere, and took her body to Loch Leven?"

"Exactly."

"And the men raped her? In front of Montoya?"

"I think so. A reward by Montoya for the gang members' help. Julie was raped repeatedly, and at some time strangled. We think she was raped by three different people. Then came the finale. Cutting off her breasts. That was done with a very sharp thin blade."

"That seems to let Helga Markel off."

"Unless Markel had accomplices . . . Julie wasn't an angler. PARA is after those who do the fishing more directly."

"Would that include me?" I asked.

"You're closer to those who fish than the shuttle people. But you don't fish when you're with your clients, do you?"

"I give instruction. I carry spare rods. And I fish other times when I'm not guiding."

"Be careful, Mac."

"Unless you have an important follow-up question, there's something that needs our attention."

"Lunch? A beer?"

"Nope. Turn around. We're heading toward rising fish. Thirty yards ahead off the east bank. Got a fly on?'

"No. Any suggestions?"

"I don't see a hatch. But something's on the surface. It could be hoppers. Sun's high. Bright on the water. We don't need bright attractors. Put on a hopper with a red bottom. About a #10. I'm slowing us down so I can tie on a Blue Dun—a #14.

"Last night I was looking through a book my grandfather passed on to me—Ray Bergman's *Trout.* Published in 1938. Granddad used the color plates and descriptions to tie his flies. A bookmark at one of the plates illustrated dry flies: Coachmans and Cahills. The bookmark had 'try Blue Dun 10, 12, 14, 18' scribbled by granddad on the back. I'm trying the size he circled—a #14. I tied a couple last night."

Shifting *Osprey's* stern slightly to the right, I back rowed so the current would push us closer to the bank. When we were thirty feet off, I slowed our drift and straightened the boat. Ken made two false casts and dropped his hopper twenty-five feet ahead of the boat and six feet upstream from where three decent trout were anxiously sipping something or pushing something around on the surface. Could there be that many grasshoppers on the water?

When the current took Ken's fly into the middle of the feeding area, two trout raced for it. The first to the fly hit it head on with an open mouth, wasted no time heading for the bank and then streaked upstream past us, pulling a sweeping curl in and spraying droplets from the floating line. Ken's rod tip was too low, and when the line came taut, his 5X tippet broke. It was the weakest part of the backing-to line-to tippet-to fly.

"Damn, what did I do wrong?"

"Your chances would have been better if you'd brought your gun and shot the fish as it came past. Your rod tip was too low—pointed right at the fish. Keep it high. Let it bend and absorb the pressure. Your tippet's a 5X. That's three- to four-pound test. From what I could see, you lost at least a four-pounder. Take my rod. There's another trout rising off the bank. See if the Blue Dun works."

It did. Ken dropped the fly two feet from a rise and exactly where the next break of the surface would likely come. The Blue Dun disappeared beneath the surface, sucked under by a feeding trout that never broke the surface film. This time Ken kept the rod tip up, and a few minutes later a fourteen-inch cutthroat was in the net.

"Your grandfather would be amazed that his note scribbled more than a half-century ago would produce a trout today. . . . Where'd he fish?"

The answer to that might lead to difficult further questions. But Maxwell Hunt's father and grandparents could be a good fictional surrogate family for me.

"Mostly New England streams. Seven to 8' foot bamboo rod. Hardy reel that clicked and whined on a run, silk line, cotton mesh net. Plus a wicker creel with leather trim to carry home one or two fish for dinner. Granddad would come home and complain how crowded the streams were getting and how there seemed to be fewer and smaller fish than when *his* father and grandfather fished.

"My grandfather began fishing with silk lines. Just before he died, I remember him trying new ones made from nylon and Dacron. Each cast a little differently. Dacron's specific gravity is heavier than silk's and nylon's lighter." Maybe I'd thrown

Ken off what might be troublesome additional questions about my earlier years.

"Aren't we close to the Pine Creek takeout?" Ken asked.

"We are. We've floated less than four miles, but we played around McDonald's Creek for an hour. It was worth it. . . . We should be seeing the Pine Creek Bridge any minute."

I don't like the Pine Creek ramp area, but it was a good takeout after our short run. Ken took apart both our rods. . . . Setting the second rod in its cloth bag, he glanced ahead and said, "Does something look out of place ahead? There's a trailer backed into the river. Damn! It has to be *your* trailer. It's hooked up to what looks like *my* pickup."

"I don't like the looks of this. Call your office and tell them to stay on the line. We'll be at the ramp in three minutes."

"That *is* my truck! . . . My God, there's a bare foot bobbing in the water. The body is attached to a cross on your trailer. Just like Julie!"

"See any vehicles leaving the area?"

"No, and we haven't seen another boat on the river. It's a weekday, and we started early. Most folks are working."

We drifted along the western riverbank and passed under the bridge. It looked as though Julie Conyers' killer had struck a second time.

Ken was out of *Osprey* in two feet of water, splashing in strides to the trailer. He called back, "It's a *woman.* All but the one foot is underwater. Eyes open. Breasts gone. Nailed to two tied cross beams. One nail through a foot must have come loose. There's a green, red, and white sash tied around her waist, just like with Julie. We've got a Mexican serial killer on our hands. Got your camera?"

I gave him my small camera. Only two nights ago, I'd deleted the photos of Julie Conyers taken under the same circumstances. The photos had been transferred to the sheriff's office files, and the camera was returned a week ago.

Ken told the office dispatcher to hurry. He turned and said, "Erin's on her way. I left my cell phone on—she heard our conversation. Shaw shouldn't be far behind."

But nothing could be done except start a new murder investigation. Julie's Shuttle Gals partner, Olga Smits, wouldn't be doing any more shuttles.

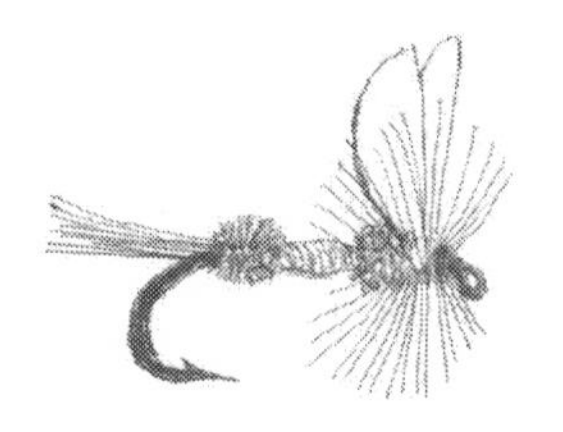

15

ERIN ARRIVED IN TWENTY MINUTES; Shaw, five minutes behind her.

"What the hell were you doing on the river, Brooks?" Shaw demanded menacingly as he approached. "You've killed *another* person!"

"Jimbo, stop it!" Ken interceded. "Macduff didn't kill Julie, and he didn't kill this gal—Olga Smits." Ken was no match physically for Jimbo, but he was in his face.

"She's dead on *his* trailer, *Deputy* Rangley. That's enough for me to bring him in."

"Then you have to bring me in, too. It's *my* truck that's pulling that trailer. Mac and I have been together since breakfast. *Back off, Jimbo!*"

"*I'm* chief detective, Rangley. What I say goes. Brooks, I'm impounding your boat and trailer. You stay here. I'll have some questions for you, after I deal with Rangley."

"Just a minute, Shaw. You can take the trailer for examination. But you don't get my boat. The boat wasn't involved in the murder."

"Don't tell me what I can take, Brooks. I said wait here until I've talked to Rangley."

"That should give me enough time to call Wanda Groves," I answered, pulling out my phone.

"Not until I've questioned you, Brooks."

"I'll make a statement to Erin or Ken, but not a word to you, Shaw, unless Wanda is here and approves. Take it or leave it."

"Erin," Shaw called, "get over here and get a statement from your toy boy." Shaw and Rangley walked away.

Erin, furious, came over. "I apologize for Shaw," she said. "He's in one of his bad funks. Ignore him."

"I was hoping to see some kendo. Watch you cut him down to your size."

She looked at me with a wry grin and quietly said, "Don't think I haven't wanted to do that a hundred times over."

There was nothing for me to hide. I'd been with Ken the whole time. Erin took my statement. Shaw looked over at us occasionally and glared. When we were through, he and Ken walked over.

"Rangley," said Shaw, showing his confusion and anger with the three of us, "take the boat to the compound. I'll deal with it later. You'll get it back in a month or two, Brooks."

"Jimbo," Ken responded, "that boat's the way Macduff makes his living. As he said, it's the trailer you need, not the boat. If you take that boat, I'll take you before the Park County Commission."

"I *own* that commission," Shaw boasted. "I paid for most of their campaigns."

"I think you'll be surprised that you didn't buy a single vote on the *new* commission," Ken commented.

Erin leaned her head toward me and whispered quietly, "Shaw did put a lot of money into the campaigns of the commissioners. The truth is he gave money to *all* the candidates, thinking he was buying the full commission. They all thought he was a fool. Shaw is proof that 'a fool and his money are soon parted.' The candidates did a neat job of parting Shaw from a good bit of his money."

"Shaw," I said, "you can take the boat as long as Ken tows it. And I want it back *next* week."

≈

When Ken and I reached my cabin, I noticed Mavis had put a bottle of Gentleman Jack and a glass on the porch. Ken had called ahead and said we were coming and it might be a good idea to have a drink waiting.

"I'd offer you a drink, but I know you're heading back to the investigation. Rain check?"

"As soon as I have a moment, I'll be back to cash in. Sorry about the day. I'll keep an eye on *Osprey*. Jimbo Shaw won't put a scratch on your boat."

"Before you leave, I want to call Lucy Denver—while *you* listen. She's one of the Shuttle Gals."

I dialed Lucy. She was sobbing when she answered. "It's on TV, Mac. I can't believe it. First Julie. And now Olga!"

"I'm finished floating for the season, Lucy. I'm not emotionally prepared to go back on the river. You may want to rethink doing any more shuttles for a while, certainly not for me. Pam's the one I'm most worried about. She's the third lesbian member of your shuttle group. *If* the killer's after lesbians, Pam's at risk, but you and Marge aren't. I'm going to call Pam and Marge."

"Thanks. I hope this is solved by next season. We need the income, and we like working with the local guides. Including you."

I called Pam and Marge. They agreed it'd be best not to do shuttles in the few remaining weeks of the season. It would be a loss to all of us—what was left of September and much of October were busy times.

After Ken's truck disappeared down my drive, I called Julie Conyers' brother Rich to tell him about Olga's death. He's a granite cutter who had an accident on the job. The company keeps him employed, but he doesn't earn much. I had already told him I'd set up a college trust fund for Julie's son, George. When he's ready for college, there'll be enough to cover costs at Montana or Montana State.

My season's over. Maybe my career as a guide. I was committed to two remaining late October floats in Jackson Hole on the Snake. . . . As I set down the first of I don't remember how many Gentleman Jack's I consumed before the night was over, the Jackson outfitter called. Olga's murder was on TV. He said the two clients I was booked to guide already had called and canceled. Several local guides had suggested he not use me anymore.

I needed time to think. I had to remain for a couple of weeks during the initial investigation, but after that I'd hit the road with Wuff and lose myself in the salt marshes of Florida for the winter. I'd stop on my way at Lucinda's in Indiana. I needed her cheerful nature to help me. Maybe Ken's suggestion about giving her the ring wasn't off base.

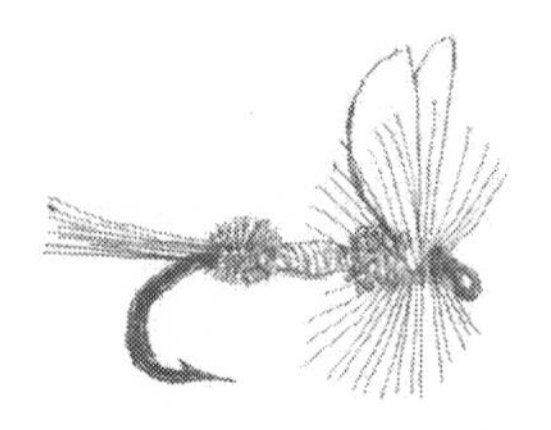

16

ALL WEEK FOLLOWING OLGA'S MURDER, especially following the unpleasant questioning by Shaw, I brooded in my music room, the basement chamber in my log cabin where I keep hidden my most lethal weapons. It was a good space for brooding, among the Chey-Tac, Glocks, and Sig-Sauers.

In stark contrast to some of the chamber's surreptitious, weapons-induced overtones, at the room's opposite end a soft, pastel-brown Persian Kerman Oriental rug covered part of the hickory flooring. On the Kerman sat an unpretentious, wooden, armless straight-back chair, a music stand, and a rack holding an oboe and an English horn. I play them solely for my own repose.

While my life seemed to be moving along at an ominous *basso profundo*, with conclusive movements yet to be written, I tried to disburden myself by working on the lilting opening *larghetto,* and following *allegro,* to Cimarosa's Oboe Concerto in C minor.

I had played it many times, and the familiar sounds brought my troubled mind back to earth from the events of the previous week. My fingers flashed along the silver keys in the runs of the *allegro,* and soon I was far distant, no longer sitting in the middle of *Osprey* on the Yellowstone watching Olga's crucified body suddenly appear on my trailer. I was transported to San Vidal's Church in Venice where I was guest oboe soloist for *Interpreti Veneziani*, my favorite chamber ensemble.

Usually I stopped after Cimarosa's *allegro*, but today I continued slowly through the *Siciliana* and did not halt until the ultimate bars of the final *allegro giusto* were finished. I imagined thunderous applause, but when my eyes opened there was only one face in the audience—on the far wall was the drawing of Abdul Khaliq Isfahani that I had used for target practice before my unsuccessful attempt to kill the Islamic terrorist two years earlier.

≈

As my emotions restored me to the reality of place, my cell phone interrupted the distraction with Isfahani. The phone's screen told me it was from detective James Shaw. I hesitated, wondering whether I would answer. It was unlikely to be a pleasant conversation.

"This is Macduff," I responded guardedly.

"James Shaw speaking. I'd like to talk to you. No interrogation. No threats. I've been way off-base the past few months, and I apologize."

"What had caused this turnabout?" I wondered. Yesterday, he was ready to let me languish in a jail cell. Now he sounds markedly human.

"Detective Shaw, I'll come in any time and talk. When's convenient?" Shaw's change of tone was remarkable. Whether it was sincere, time would unravel. But I need to see Julie's and Olga's murders settled without the acrimony of our last encounters. Maybe the Sheriff or even some Park County commissioners had talked to Shaw. Whatever the reason, I have to meet him at least halfway.

"I'd like to bring your boat to you. I need to keep the trailer another week. I'll help you put *Osprey* on some sawhorses. Could we talk at your place?"

"Tomorrow's fine. I'm doing some work on my plastic boat. I'll leave the gate open. Come any time you wish."

"If it's OK, I'll be there first thing in the morning. Around nine."

≈

When Shaw arrived the next morning, I was fitting a new anchor hanger on the transom of my plastic drift boat. If not installed carefully, a swinging thirty-pound anchor with a dozen protruding three-inch prongs—like a WWII mine—becomes a sledge hammer in rough water—the spikes devouring the transom. If a drift boat anchor were attached to a five-foot pole by a foot-and-a-half foot chain, it would look like what Mel Gibson used in *Braveheart* to discourage northern incursions by the hated English legions against the Scots.

Hearing a vehicle approach towing a trailer, I walked out of the garage to greet Shaw and prayed he wasn't arriving with a pair of dueling pistols.

Osprey looked better than good, not a touch of dirt. There were wet spots suggesting Shaw had stopped at the car wash in Emigrant and carefully used the pressure cleaning hose.

"Can I back this into your garage?" Shaw asked. We easily slid *Osprey* from his trailer onto a pair of wide sawhorses. It's an awkward job for one.

"Let's sit on the porch?" I offered. Shaw smiled and nodded. He followed me into the cabin, where I poured coffee I'd made from carefully hoarded Antigua coffee beans. I had always bought several bags at the airport before leaving Guatemala. But during my last departure, after the beating by Juan Pablo Herzog, I was carried to a private plane and came home with new scars and no coffee. I looked at the rich, dark liquid as I handed a cup to Shaw and wondered if the beans might have come from one of Herzog's coffee *fincas*.

Shaw commented generously on how livable my log cabin appeared. I didn't know much about his private life and, as we sat on the porch and enjoyed Guatemala's finest, I tried to focus our conversation on noncontroversial issues. But I knew the questions were to come. It didn't take long.

"Is this the front door that was wired with explosives a few years ago, when that guy was after you?"

"The very same." I showed him how Lucinda and I'd discovered the rigged bombs and how Park Salisbury had gotten in by removing a vent on the roof. His detective instincts made him curious, and he asked intelligent, precise questions.

"But you never thought it might be Salisbury who was after you?" Shaw inquired, as we returned to the porch with our coffee.

"I didn't. When my client Ander Eckstrum was shot on the float on the Snake, I thought the shooter might have been after me, but I couldn't accept that version. Maybe I should have built upon my intuition and reached a conclusion before it was thrown at me on the last drift. I'm no Sherlock Holmes. Or Wyatt Earp. You've probably heard through the grapevine that on that float I was the last to get my gun out and the last to fire."

"At least *you* got in the game. You've probably heard I never played in even one game at Alabama."

"But I bet you wouldn't trade those years playing on a great team, even if the playing came on the practice field."

"Wouldn't trade a minute. . . . Can I give you my take on the two Shuttle Gals murders and ask what you think?"

"Sure, let's refill the coffee and stay on the porch—it's too nice a fall day to waste inside." Plus, I had no intention of letting him discover my music room.

"There's no killer positively identified—yet. I have some ideas," Shaw noted. "With Olga's death, we're looking more broadly than solely at Victoria Montoya and Helga Markel. Because both Olga and Julie were lesbians, Erin's thinking the killer might be someone who is pathologically anti-gays. She believes the removal of their breasts is consistent with that: the killer wanted to mutilate an identity that made them women. But I have doubts about making this another Matthew Shepard case—you know about that death a few years ago in Wyoming?"

"I do. What makes you believe it wasn't someone who disliked homosexuals, like the Shepard case?"

"Olga Smits *wasn't* scheduled to do the shuttle. It was to be done by Lucy Denver, one of the two straight Shuttle Gals."

"How do you know that?"

"Maybe I shouldn't tell you . . . but I will. Julie Conyers had done all the booking and scheduling. After she died the women were a little disorganized. Lucy got them together, and they decided to keep doing shuttles—a gutsy decision. She agreed to take over Julie's work. When you called about a shuttle, I think you called Marge Atwood."

"I did. She was the first name I looked at on my Shuttle Gals list. I didn't know Lucy had taken over the scheduling;

Marge made no mention of that. She simply said *someone* would be there in the morning to do my shuttle. The four gals remaining after Julie's death and I had talked earlier, leading to my decision not to do any more floats on the Yellowstone this season. But floating with Ken wasn't a commercial float; it was just two friends fishing and talking."

"Marge called Lucy, who agreed to do the shuttle for your float with Ken. But Lucy woke up with flu the next morning. She called Olga and asked her to fill in. No one else knew about the substitution, even Marge and the fifth of the Shuttle Gals, Pam Snyder."

"This all makes sense. I'm sorry I've misjudged you."

"Call me Jimbo, please. Don't worry about misjudging me. Now let me share with you what *I* think should be the focus. I'm increasingly convinced Victoria Montoya killed *both* Julie and Olga, with the help of some of Roberto or Victoria Montoya's loyal gang killers. The same color sash—green, red, and white—was used on each. Those are Mexico's colors."

"Jimbo, the last I heard was that Victoria left her ranch with a bag the day of Julie's killing and was believed to be on her way to Ciudad Juarez. I haven't heard that she returned."

"She didn't *return* to Montana. I don't believe she ever left the valley. I'm certain her Mexican hands covered for her. She's got a big place, with lots of room to hide comfortably as long as she didn't leave the property. We initially kept a watch on her house . . . for nearly a month. We concluded she was in Mexico and not returning. But she was here all along."

"How did you know?"

"She became tired of hiding. She changed her appearance, wore a wig, and two days before Olga was killed, Victoria was stopped by one of our deputies for shoplifting a watch at the Montana Watch Company in Livingston. In her big 350 Ford were a dozen 4x6 eight-foot beams. The same kind used in Julie's murder. She told our deputy they were to finish a fence line on her property. She'd been doing a lot of fencing . . . and adding a lot of 'No Trespassing' signs."

"That was *two* days before Olga was killed? Why didn't you arrest Montoya? Before or certainly after Olga was killed. At least hold her for the shoplifting charge."

"Tried to. We wanted to get some DNA from her. But she has highly paid lawyers. The most we were able to do was take her passport, so she couldn't leave the country."

"Which passport?"

"What do you mean? She has an *American* passport. She's a U.S. citizen."

"She's most certainly *also* a Mexican citizen. The U.S. has never fully dealt with dual citizenship. Thousands of U.S. citizens and legal residents are also citizens of another country and carry a second passport. That's especially true with Mexico."

"That may answer why we haven't located her since Olga's murder. She could go home using her Mexican passport."

"Another thing, her brother owns a plane. With his political connections he probably doesn't bother with U.S. or Mexican customs when he flies back and forth. He likely uses private airfields."

"When we find Victoria, we'll arrest her, Mac. At least get some DNA samples to see if they match what we've found on the beams and trailer. We also have DNA samples from the three men who raped Julie. We took the DNA from her body."

"Does DNA evidence get washed off, like from a drift boat trailer? Or from the wooden beams? Or from Julie or Olga?"

"DNA's not indestructible. Underwater, where there's a current, it's just a matter of time before it washes away."

"Has your office pursued the PARA girl, Helga Markel? I gather you no longer believe she was involved?"

"I don't. She was leaving the county after she talked to you and Ken. She didn't have time after she met you to buy beams, nails, and rope—*and* kill Julie that same afternoon."

"I guess you're right." But I wasn't as convinced as Shaw was about Montoya. Maybe he's right. I didn't know of any evidence that pointed to Helga Markel as much as it might to Montoya. Especially the sash.

"Do you know where Markel was at the time of *Olga's* murder?" I asked.

"No, but we're looking for her. I'd like to question her. But I really want to bring in Montoya. She must be hiding, if she hasn't left the area in the last forty-eight hours. The motive's there: she hated all the Shuttle Gals. Not just the lesbian ones. I'm concerned she isn't finished with whatever it is she intends. She might go after another of the Shuttle Gals."

He paused and looked at me for answers he didn't have. I didn't have them either. What he said made sense. I agree that Markel didn't kill Julie Conyers. But she might have used Julie's death as a springboard to kill another gal, any one of them, gay or not, and cast the blame on Montoya.

"You've been generous with your time," Shaw said. "And thoughtful not to rehash my lousy behavior. I hope we have enough to hold the Montoya woman—if we can find her."

Shaw left me with a lot to contemplate. I remain unconvinced that Victoria Montoya should be the exclusive focus for Olga's death. I've never been face-to-face with Montoya. But I have with Markel, and there's something about her that makes me more mistrustful of her doing spontaneous killings than I was after the phone conversations with Montoya. Maybe if Shaw isn't going to follow-up on Markel, I might do it myself.

I wish I could call my old friend on the law faculty at Missoula and ask him about his colleague, Professor Henry Plaxler IV. He's the law professor Markel was headed to see when she left Ken Rangley and me at Emigrant the morning of the day Julie was killed.

17

PROFESSOR HENRY PLAXLER IV was a third generation Montanan whose wealthy ancestors had moved to the Bitterroot area of the state during the depression of the 1930s.

His great-grandfather, Heinrich, was thirty-five when he emigrated from Germany to Minnesota in 1873. Tragically, his wife and children died in an influenza epidemic. Throwing himself into his work and using his industrious talents brought him considerable wealth. He remarried a Minnesota woman of German ancestry who gave birth to twins in 1894, on father Heinrich's fifty-sixth birthday. One of the twins, Klaus, graduated from the University of Minnesota and entered his father's business. Brother Henry II, the eldest by three minutes, chose to attend West Point. He graduated with the class of 1916 and by late summer was immersed in the grime and filth of trench warfare in France.

Lieutenant Henry Plaxler II led a squad across no-man's land to the German trenches, where he and his soldiers killed fourteen German soldiers before reinforcements arrived and gassed Plaxler and his squad. They had left their gas masks in their trench to make room to carry additional ammunition. Pinned down, Plaxler and one remaining corporal shot two

Germans and ripped off their masks and put them on. Their lungs burned as they struggled back toward their trenches.

Plaxler's corporal was shot in the leg while trying to crawl beneath barbed wire. Plaxler dragged him across seventy yards of horrendous, ear-shattering fire. It seemed the entire German army was determined to prevent the two from reaching their line.

When they made it to their trench, Plaxler was carefully lowering the corporal into the arms of his comrades when a German bullet hit the back of Plaxler's head, expanded, and blew most of his face onto the soldiers in the trench who were helping them.

The irony of the episode was twofold. First, Heinrich had fled Prussia with his family to avoid conscription; Henry II died fighting descendants of those fellow Germans who had not fled. Second, were it to be known, the German who shot Henry II in the head was his second cousin.

Grieved from hearing of Henry II's death, Heinrich suffered a stroke and died at the Minneapolis railroad station when he saw the casket lifted off the train that carried his son home for burial. To honor his late brother and father, Klaus changed his own first name to Henry. His only child, Henry III, joined the family business.

Wary of federal government policies Henry II sold the business shortly before the Wall Street crash in 1929. Discouraged and saddened by the social conditions generated by the depression that followed, Henry II moved his family and wealth west to Montana, where he invested heavily in cheap land and began to ranch.

Henry III adored his father. But Henry III would largely ignore his own sole child, Henry IV, who was born at the end of World War II.

While his grandfather Henry II had immersed himself in college in the works of men such as Plato and St. Augustine, Henry IV moved to San Francisco's Haight-Ashbury district and immersed himself in the works of counterculture outcasts such as Jerry Rubin and Allen Ginsberg. Henry IV became part of the radical Weathermen group that bombed and killed, but money for lawyers and a clever mind kept him free from the charges that sent most of that group into hiding in Canada.

Like many of the beat generation, Henry IV matured and decided to face, if not rejoin, mainstream society. His father relented modestly enough from earlier vows of disinheritance to pay for his son's education. Henry IV graduated first in his class at Cal Davis, which might refute that he had fully returned to mainstream society. Three years later he finished close to the top of his law class at Hastings in San Francisco.

During the brief tenure of a University of Montana law school dean who was determined to "liberalize" the face of the institution, Henry IV was hired to teach federal and state constitutional and administrative law. Mirroring the practice at so many American law schools, after writing the required number of law review articles—few of which were likely ever to be read by anyone other than the promotion and tenure committee—he received tenure and full professor status. He soon cajoled his way out of teaching those basic courses to teach Natural Resources Law, Mining Law, and Oil & Gas Law.

Learning that his courses actually focused on animal rights, nationalization of natural resources, and the transition of the market economy to statism, two-dozen Montana ranchers, farmers, and mine owners attempted to have him removed from his position. The ouster didn't succeed, but Plaxler was denied teaching any further primary courses and assigned a couple of seminars and various administrative duties. He was allowed to have one of the seminars focus on animal rights, although it was called Resources Protection. His schedule left him plentiful time for legal advisement to groups such as PA-RA, of which he was the founding director. Unless he had an heir—his wife proved to be barren—the Plaxler family saga would come to an end with his death. Many who knew Plaxler were not displeased with that possible eventuality.

≈

Professor Plaxler met Helga Markel at the inaugural PARA conference in Missoula. She was immediately attracted to him when she learned that he had been part of the Weathermen movement. Because many think Montana is the premier trout fishing location in the Lower 48, PARA decided to attack every form of recreational fishing, from the smallest streams to the largest lakes. The Yellowstone River was a natural target.

Plaxler preferred that PARA not take on the outstanding trout fisheries in the Missoula area. He had enough trouble without raising the ire of dozens of fly fishing enthusiasts, male and female, who were studying or working at the university. It was reputed to attract faculty who were less interested in the prospects of teaching in Missoula than in prospecting in the myriad local streams and rivers harboring large numbers of trout. A specific target of PARA was the Gallatin River, partly because Plaxler didn't much like Bozeman or Montana State University.

On the Monday after Julie Conyers' death, Helga Markel was a guest speaker at Plaxler's Resources Protection seminar. Because selected law classes were taped and placed online, Erin Giffin had come across the class presentation in a general search, trying to locate Markel. Both Detective Shaw and Ken

Rangley listened to the tapes, and Erin privately forwarded the recording to me.

A student at the seminar asked this question: "Do you think the woman crucified and strapped to a drift boat trailer on the Yellowstone River last week received justifiable punishment for her participation in recreational angling?"

"Personally, I have no trouble with her death," responded Markel. "She got what she deserved."

"Wasn't that a little excessive? . . . At least one website is suggesting that she was raped repeatedly and her breasts cut out," the student replied.

"It closed down the river," Markel answered. "There wasn't a single float the next day. I expect there haven't been many since and I'll bet there've been a lot of cancellations of future floats. One or two more incidents like that could close down the river."

"Was PARA involved with her killing?" inquired another student.

"Of course not!" Helga loudly claimed, as though the question were outrageous. "We're a peaceful organization. But if other activist groups take extreme measures that happen to further *our* goals—I'm not upset."

Another student, trying to divert Markel's emotional comments to legal analysis, asked, "Professor Plaxler, what do you believe is the boundary between lawful and unlawful protest actions?"

"Legitimacy is a subjective matter," Plaxler replied. "In traditional criminal law, self-defense is legitimate action. That may take the form of defending your own life or that of someone about to be killed by another. Should there be any difference if you see another person about to kill your child or your cherished pet dog? Or one of your domestic animals? If killing a wolf pack that is about to eat one of your bison is permitted, what about killing a hunter who is poaching and about to kill that same bison? Carry that further, to saving the life of *any* animal, including fish, and it may all come within the boundaries of justifiable homicide."

"And the rape and mutilation of the woman in Paradise Valley are to be measured on a 'justifiable' scale?"

"That's absurd. You're not listening," said Plaxler. "Killing Julie Conyers was an act directly undertaken to save fish. Raping and mutilating her should be punished severely. Assuming she was dead when she was raped, what could be gained from the rape and mutilation? The intended act was done. A murderer who then rapes or mutilates changes the act from one with purpose to the most abhorrent level of bestiality."

"Thus," the student inquired, "if she hadn't been raped and mutilated, and you knew who killed her, you'd honor them at a PARA conference?"

Plaxler shook his head but with a slight grin. "No. That would be like honoring some of the Weathermen after they justifiably killed Brinks guards. To be effective the group members had to remain hidden or have effective counsel."

"You mean the Weathermen hadn't committed murder?"

"It should be considered justifiable homicide."

That afternoon, eight students in the seminar asked the dean to undertake an investigation to determine whether or not Professor Plaxler was fit to remain on the faculty. After extensive inquiries, the dean terminated the position. Disgraced former Professor Henry Plaxler IV soon left Missoula with Helga Markel, leaving behind his even more barren wife.

≈

I made a note to ask Erin or Ken if anyone knows exactly where Professor Plaxler IV and Helga Markel went when they left Missoula.

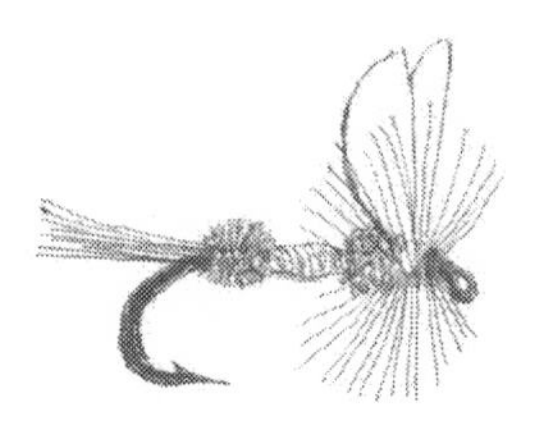

18

A HALF HOUR ON THE FAR SIDE OF MIDNIGHT, the week following Olga's murder, a lone figure walked across the barren, frosted surface of Victoria Montoya's ranch. Under an October new moon that draped a black veil over the landscape the figure headed toward the house that had become known as *Casa Mala.* Clothed in black and carrying only a backpack, the figure climbed the rail fence that encircled the residence and continued to the rear corner of one of several outbuildings. Shining a small flashlight into the building, the figure assumed it to be a workshop for ranch maintenance projects.

As the figure crouched and began to reach into the backpack, an exterior light came on by the main house's rear door. It opened. A man and a woman exited and walked toward the outbuildings, talking in low voices the black-clad figure could not comprehend. The figure remained in a frozen crouch, watching the two.

Both were carrying tools in one hand and what appeared to be a beer bottle in the other. Reaching the building's large double-doors, one slid open a small side door, and both disappeared inside. A single dim florescent light came on, allowing the figure outside to watch the two set their bottles on the workbench and return tools they were carrying to a pegboard on the wall. Exiting, only the man took his bottle. The two returned to the house.

The figure waited twenty minutes but saw no evidence that either person might return to the workshop. After putting on vinyl gloves, the lone figure entered by the same door using only the small flashlight. The far end of the workshop was filled with various power tools. In a wood storage section, timbers of various sizes were neatly stacked, including a half-dozen eight-foot 4x6 beams.

Near a table saw the figure stopped and knelt on the floor. Although the shop had been kept clean—no footprints were evident that might have been left in sawdust—the figure noticed a small fragment of wood about three inches long that had lodged in a corner foot of the saw. The figure picked up the fragment, looked at it carefully, and placed it in a plastic bag.

On the way back toward the door, the figure saw the beer bottle that the woman had left and beside it a set of keys. The figure took the bottle and placed it in a second plastic bag. Both bags were put in the backpack. The keys on the table were left untouched.

Leaving the workshop, the figure returned to the side of the building and extracted from the backpack what appeared to be a notebook computer. A small satellite dish on a tripod, connected to the computer, was directed toward a lighted window on the Montoya house where the two people had been silhouetted since they returned from the outbuildings. The black-clad figure put on headphones, plugged them into the unit, and began to listen.

"Roberto, I *no* go with you to Mexico. I no yet complete here."

"Victoria, the police are bound to come and search here. They have every reason to arrest you."

"I no do *nothing*, Roberto. Just happy two them beetches are dead."

"I don't believe you, Vicky. Are you swearing to me that you were not involved?"

"On the grave of our madre, Roberto. *I* no keel them."

"Where were you when the second woman was murdered?"

"I at cabin of no good hombre Brooks. I going burn down cabin. But hear big dog barking inside. You know I scared of dogs. I left pronto. Come back here. No leave house."

"Vicky, I *have* to go to Ciudad Juarez. Either come with me now or take your chances."

"OK, Roberto. I go. But come back pronto."

The figure listened and watched for another half hour, until the man and woman left the house and disappeared on the far side. A few minutes later, a black Mercedes SUV drove down the ranch road toward the entrance gate. After waiting at the corner of the workshop for a few minutes, to be assured that no further persons had stirred in the house, the figure walked carefully to the other outbuildings, curious about their function.

Shining a flashlight through one window, the figure saw that the building was arranged like a dormitory. There were bunk beds for nearly a dozen people. All but three had no mattresses or blankets. The three in use were neatly made up with pillows and heavy blankets. A guitar lay on one bed; several soccer balls hung in a net from a bed post. In the corner of the room was a table with a computer. Beside it were dozens of computer games.

The figure turned off the flashlight and moved swiftly back across the land, the temperature dropping and causing the figure's breath to fog. In a few minutes no trace of the visit marred the night landscape.

19

GLORIA MARTINEZ, ASSOCIATE DEAN at the University of Florida Law College, following Dean Perry's instructions, spent long workdays and weekends during September and October investigating the death of Professor Maxwell Hunt and preparing a draft report.

Dean Perry was busy with the fundraising campaign; the two had not met to discuss the progress of the report which Herzog had strangely requested—a verification that Professor Hunt truly died of a stroke, as had been publically reported.

But this morning, after Dean Perry arrived and finished a first cup of coffee, he called Gloria to his office to update him on the report. The four-million-dollar check written by Herzog lay tauntingly before him on his desk, predated the middle of November—less than two weeks away.

Gloria sat down in one of the two deeply cushioned arm chairs that Dean Perry preferred to use with most visitors to avoid any appearance of "talking down" from his desk.

"How's the report progressing? I assume you're finding information that confirms Hunt's stroke and subsequent death?"

"Unfortunately, I've come up against some barriers," she responded.

"You know what the gift means to us. What barriers?"

"Maxwell Hunt's body seems to have disappeared. Our records show he was approved to spend law school funds to travel to Washington, D.C., to attend and speak at the annual meeting of the American Society of International Law. The records don't include *any* indication or approval of travel to Guatemala from D.C. Hunt reserved a room at the Army and Navy Club for four nights, Friday through Tuesday. But he stayed only Friday night even though the meeting continued to Sunday. He planned to remain in D.C. to discuss a writing project with a co-author at the George Washington Law School.

"Hunt was never approved by us to leave the country. He should have requested our approval to assure he had medical coverage. It appears he went to Guatemala on Saturday after presenting his lecture in D.C. He canceled the remaining three nights at the club. I assume he flew to Guatemala on a commercial flight from Dulles.

"Even with the help of one of our graduates serving in the Senate, we at first lost track of him. There was no record of a passenger named Maxwell Hunt flying on any airline serving Guatemala that Saturday. *But,* our senator called in some favors to find out that Maxwell Hunt did fly to Guatemala—under a *different name and using a diplomatic passport!* At that point we reach a dead end. We can't find anything more."

"Do we know what he was doing in Guatemala?"

"Some. I went to Guatemala two weeks ago to see my parents. I tried to learn more."

"Any success?"

"Yes. I have a friend who teaches at Francisco Marroquin, the leading law school in Guatemala City. She told me Professor Hunt was scheduled to speak at the law school on Monday. He never appeared. But several students who did show up were killed when a bomb went off in the lecture room where Hunt was to speak. I learned that another bomb went off that afternoon at the Cámara de Comercio—the Guatemalan Chamber of Commerce. Two employees were killed. Hunt was to speak at the Chamber that afternoon. The bombing deaths made the newspapers, but Hunt was never mentioned."

"Any thoughts about *why* he might have been in Guatemala to give two *public* lectures, traveling under a different name with a diplomatic passport? Surely he must have been doing something for the U.S. government if he had a diplomatic passport?"

"The rumors point to one person, Dean Perry, whose name is familiar to you and who may have been involved—Juan Pablo Herzog. He was in Guatemala at the time along with a friend—Abdul Khaliq Isfahani. Also a former student here, Isfahani was implicated in the attempt to destroy the Chrysler and Empire State buildings three years ago. But he was never indicted.

"Isfahani was to fly one of the bomb-carrying suicide planes, but he had been shot in the face and nearly killed in Guatemala the week before. The newspapers reported that he was shot by a sniper, believed to have been the most notorious assassin for Israel's Mossad. The sniper's name was Ben Roth."

"My God, Gloria! What are we getting into? Is there more?"

"Much more. I had trouble finding out where Hunt stayed while he was in Guatemala. Through other friends, I discovered he was at the Camino Real. He was given the entire ninth floor, which purportedly was blocked off and guarded while he was in Guatemala."

"What do you mean by 'purportedly'?"

"Sunday night, three men broke into the room and severely beat Hunt. They may have killed him. Our government apparently tried to cover it up by announcing his death of a stroke. But I have doubts. I suspect that he, or his body, was carried down a service elevator or staircase to a U.S. embassy vehicle and taken somewhere for medical help. Or worse . . . disposal.

"That's where my knowledge of Hunt's whereabouts comes to an end. I went to the U.S. embassy and asked questions. I was rudely rebuffed and even warned that I should discontinue my inquiries."

"How is this connected to the announcement that he suffered a stroke in D.C.? I recall that came from the State Department."

"It did. We overlooked the fact that perhaps it ought to have come from the international law association, if Hunt suffered the alleged stroke at the conference, or from the Army and Navy Club, if it occurred at the club. But State Department people came to the law school the following week. I can't trace any of them. My hunch is that they were from the CIA."

"Have you thought of talking to our dean at the time?"

"I called Dean Stein. He was very close-mouthed about it. Remember, he was fired by the president here not long after the incident."

"Professor Hunt's file shows he frequently lectured abroad for the State Department through the AmPart program. Many faculty throughout the country have done that. Any evidence that Hunt was engaged in any CIA activities?"

"Partly speculation. It's common knowledge in Guatemala that the CIA has a mission at the embassy that's very influential. It goes back a long time; Guatemala was used to plan part of the CIA's disastrous Bay of Pigs invasion in Cuba. People often comment that the CIA mission head is effectively above the ambassador in authority. Perhaps not *apparent* authority so much as *actual* power. I'm persuaded Hunt was in Guatemala helping the CIA on some investigation. I believe that it may have involved Herzog."

"Why that link, Gloria?"

"Hunt knew more about Herzog's time studying here at UF than anyone at the CIA mission. He may have done nothing more than provide information about Herzog to the CIA mission. Our administration in Washington doesn't like Herzog, but he represents powerful business and political interests that have kept leftist groups from assuming power. It's a yin-yang situation. The U.S. would like him out of the way. But it needs him to preserve public order in Guatemala."

"Could Hunt have been in Guatemala to engage in any more dangerous activity?"

"Hunt was a skilled marksman in college and the Navy. There are rumors in Guatemala that he was neither killed by Herzog nor died of a stroke, but was alive a few years later, disguised as Israel's Ben Roth, and shot Abdul Khaliq Isfahani in the Guatemalan mountains."

"Gloria, can you *imagine* the reaction if it became public that one of our professors was a paid assassin for the CIA while employed by the State of Florida?"

"Not too favorable. But Isfahani was shot a few years *after* Hunt was reported dead, not while he was teaching. . . . I'm not quite through. We haven't discussed what happened to Hunt. I think he was brought back to D.C. by our government. Very likely on a U.S. government jet. At the very least he was seriously injured. Had he died, there would have been no reason not to turn the body over to be buried here in Gainesville. I don't think he died."

"*You think he's alive?*"

"Yes."

"Where is he?"

"Living somewhere using a new identity. I learned that there's a program under the International Identities Protection Act—a kind of witness protection program—that provides a new identity and location for compromised government foreign agents."

"Would Hunt have been placed in the program because he was in danger of Herzog killing him?"

"I believe so. He was also in danger of Isfahani. Furthermore, the CIA may have had plans for him using his new identity."

"What do you recommend we do?"

"Dean Perry! You only asked for a report! But if I were in your position, I would reject the gift. Herzog is trying to buy information so he can track down Hunt . . . or whoever he now is. I have no doubt that if Herzog finds Hunt he will be killed without a further thought."

"I agree. Can we reject the gift by informing Herzog that we have been unable to complete a satisfactory report?"

"Perhaps that would tip him off that we discovered what you and I have been talking about. It might confirm to him that we think Hunt is alive."

"You've collected enough information that might satisfy Herzog in exchange for the gift. But with his connections couldn't he have discovered the same information?"

"Possibly. If so, we would be providing a concurrence. And a death sentence for Hunt, however he is now called. *If* Herzog finds him."

The phone lighted, telling Dean Perry his secretary Donna wanted him. She knew he was engaged in a conversation with

Associate Dean Martinez about the projected gift, but thought he should take the call. Donna's judgment usually proved correct. The call was from Tim Cox, publisher of the local *Gainesville Gazette.*

"Dean Perry, a graduate of UF law from Tampa, who wishes to remain unnamed, called me this morning and said a former UF student from Guatemala is going to give four million for a chair to honor the law professor who died of a stroke in D.C. four to five years ago—a Maxwell Hunt." Dean Perry switched on the phone speaker so Gloria could hear. "Is it true, and will you be sending us some information? It's front page news."

"If we get that kind of gift, Tim, you'll be among the first to hear. But you know that for every rumored gift many never are finalized. People make demands we can't agree to."

"Having problems with this one?"

"We are doing what is routine, checking to see if the donor carries some baggage. I'll tell you when I know more."

"Thanks," concluded Cox.

"I'm afraid our inquiry has shifted to damage control, Gloria. Let's sit on what to do for the next week. I want to give this matter some thought. You've done a terrific job."

≈

Three days later the *Tampa News Journal* published the following article:

The University of Florida law college, currently engaged in the final months of a fundraising campaign that is only a few million short of its $45 million goal, is reportedly in a dilemma over an apparent offer from a UF alumnus to donate $4 million for a chair to be named in honor of the late Professor Maxwell Hunt. Hunt was reported to have suffered a fatal *stroke in D.C. five years ago while attending the annual meeting of the American Society of International Law.*

The $4 million gift has been offered by Juan Pablo Herzog, a controversial Guatemalan businessman with presidential aspirations. Herzog befriended Professor Hunt when Herzog was a student at UF. What is holding up the donation is an unusual request by the donor for more detailed information about Hunt's death.

There is some doubt that Hunt actually suffered a stroke. The law school has been investigating Hunt's alleged death but apparently is not satisfied that it can fulfill the donor's wishes.

Dean Perry called Gloria immediately after reading the article. "We need to respond to the article. But there's another new matter. Yesterday, after the *Tampa News Journal* hit the streets, I had a call from Senator Georges in D.C. He's our senior senator and one of our law alums, but not the person you talked to asking for Professor Hunt's travel information. He asked that any information referring to Herzog that we plan to make public first be cleared with his office. Georges said it involves *national security*. I've talked to UF President Killingsworth. I'm to meet with him this afternoon. We'll have a conference call with Senator Georges. Keep whatever information you have about Herzog and Hunt locked up."

Perspiring noticeably on his French-blue, white-cuffed shirt, Dean Perry climbed the one flight to the third-floor faculty lounge, where he hoped he might find a faculty member to have coffee with and talk about something less stressful, such as how to avoid sitting in the president's box at Saturday's predictably boring football game against Western South Dakota State. He wondered if he ought to have remained a simple professor of family law in Oregon. Dealing with a faculty member who might have been a CIA assassin wasn't what he had in mind when he accepted the law college deanship.

20

MY GUIDING SEASON WAS OVER. Not because I hadn't floated *every* one of my Yellowstone River *clients* safely to the takeout ramps. This season I did sixty-four floats, with ninety-two people in the boat. *All* ninety-two arrived safely at the takeout. But this was the first season I lost shuttle service women.

I don't keep track of fish caught, but I awaken at night seeing the human tragedy of those two drifts posted in large numbers on an imaginary scoreboard, above what I hoped would be my field of dreams. Add the deaths from floats on the Snake River and I wonder if my decisions made in D.C., after my beating in Guatemala, hadn't unfairly traded my likely end at the hands of Herzog and Isfahani for the deaths of a number of innocent people.

The more I thought about Julie and Olga, the more I knew it was time to head to Florida . . . for the time being . . . leaving behind some tragic images. With some reluctance I convinced myself I should go by way of Indiana and face head-on another who wants my scalp—Mrs. Elizabeth Parker-Smith Lang. At least I'd avoid crossing the more southern wastelands of Texas, Oklahoma, or Kansas, and having to choose which cultural illusions I might speed past.

Going by way of Indiana, I could spend Thanksgiving with Lucinda, however determined her mother is to suppress such hope. With luck and deception I could squeeze in some time with Lucinda when Mrs. Lang's attention is diverted to other holiday matters. I also need to resolve whether Dr. West prescribed inappropriate drugs for Lucinda's amnesia. With Rosa Lipsius' help, Lucinda has not taken another pill West gave her, and her recovery has been extraordinary. It seems time to face all the issues and try to get Lucinda away from Indiana.

≈

Sitting at the small desk in my cabin bedroom, I watched a cold wind push hard on the cottonwoods along Mill Creek, failing to cause the slightest rattle of my special windows. I was working out feasible times to leave Mill Creek, stop at Dan Bailey's in Livingston to overdose on fly tying supplies for the winter, and find accommodations along the route that would accept Wuff's elevated demands.

My thoughts were beginning to coalesce when they were shattered by the unique ring of one of the phones in my music room. That doesn't happen often because it's a special line only to Dan Wilson's office at Langley. Dan more frequently calls on my cell phone to chat as friends. When he uses my music room phone, it's not to chat. I opened the hidden stairwell door in the bookcase and two steps at a time went down and picked up the phone.

"Hello, Dan?"

"You'll understand as we talk why I wanted this to be secure. You in your music room?"

"Standing at my desk. Go ahead."

"Open up your computer. I'm forwarding an article I scanned from the Tampa newspaper this morning."

The article came up, and I read it through quickly. Then a second time, hoping it didn't say what I'd read the first time. But it did. The back of my neck began tingling. The sensation spread down each limb, at the least reaffirming that blood indeed reaches the tips of toes and fingers. There must be a better way to test circulation. My legs weakened, and I dropped into my chair. "I don't want to believe this article. Herzog does *not* believe I'm dead!"

"Not quite. He doesn't believe *Maxwell Hunt* died. But he doesn't know what happened to him."

"He's smart enough to know about the protection program. Any chance he can access your records about my identity change and our communications over the past five years?"

"No. Fewer than a dozen people here know your new name and where you moved to. They were the agents at the table when we worked through your new identity."

"All Herzog needs is for any *one* of them to talk."

"True, but he doesn't know their names. No transcript was made of those meetings. All our people used different names. You may remember names like Smith and Johnson and Collins. All pretty common."

"Yeah. So's *Wilson*! How's the UF dean going to deal with this? Should we worry about him cooperating?"

"We've checked on him. He's a good man. Keeps secrets as far as we can judge. Wants what's best for the law school and university. He doesn't want to help some ambitious investigative reporter harm the university."

"The dean must have information Herzog would welcome."

"He does. Herzog asked him to undertake an investigation confirming Maxwell Hunt's death. The dean assigned a bright, young, associate dean—a woman born in Guatemala—to undertake the report. Her parents live in Guatemala. Fortunately for us, they've expressed no fondness for Herzog."

"Is the dean likely to circulate the report?"

"No, I've talked to him and to the university president. The report is under lock and key. Tomorrow, the president and dean are to meet with Herzog. They will graciously and regretfully decline the gift."

"Herzog will press them to learn the details of the rejection, Dan. Four million is a lot of money for the law college to turn down. It sounds to me as though the dean and his associate concluded that Maxwell Hunt didn't die."

"Not necessarily," Wilson replied. "They don't *know* for certain that he survived. But, I suspect they have doubts about his death. The dean and president will want to bury the fact that a prominent law professor, while employed by the State of Florida, traveled widely for the State Department and was involved with the CIA.

"Your CV when you were Maxwell Hunt disclosed the countries you visited. In many there was social turmoil and political unrest. Meaning the local CIA mission was active. We're convinced the dean and president intend to inform Herzog that university policy prohibits accepting *any* gift that includes conditions, including preparing a special report about a person to be honored by naming an endowed chair."

"Will Herzog believe them?" I asked. "He may win either way. He keeps the four million; plus, he has reason to believe the law college discovered information about Hunt the university doesn't want released to the public—that Hunt was working for us and he didn't die. If he didn't die, the press may demand to know where he is."

"I agree. I'll be talking with the dean after they meet with Juan Pablo. I'll call you—probably tomorrow night."

"Thanks."

After absorbing the disturbing news from Dan, I went upstairs, opened a kitchen cabinet, and took out a glass. A large glass. And the only bottle of Gentleman Jack I could find in the cabin. The bottle held enough for one double—not a drop more. I emptied the dusky, aromatic bronze liquid over some ice, added a splash of bitters, went back to my music room, and put on an Edith Piaf CD. She sang *Tu es partout,* as she had in 1943 in *Montmartre Sur Seine* . . . softly in French that I translated as I listened and sipped my drink.

We loved each other so tenderly, but you left me. I see you everywhere and dream of being in your arms again, hearing you whisper things which make me close my eyes.

≈

I closed *my* misting eyes and thought of El. And of Lucinda. The drink didn't hold back the tears. My life was coming apart—again.

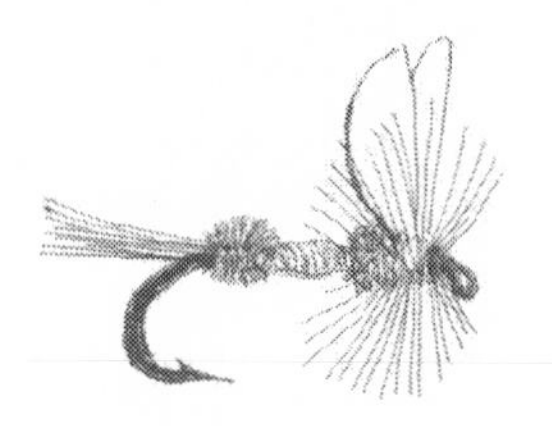

21

A LONG BLACK LINCOLN LIMOUSINE arrived at the law school and parked diagonally across three spaces reserved for faculty. Two Hispanic-appearing men . . . beneath broad brimmed black hats . . . were first to exit from the front seats, wearing tailored black suits and black shirts with high round collars and no ties. Neither wore sunglasses, making their focused, piercing black eyes all the more ominous. Each suit showed a similar, slight bulge below the left arm. Several students on their way to class saw them and changed their routes to avoid coming closer.

After scanning the law school grounds, one of the men leaned over at the left rear car window, which slowly opened no more than two inches. The man spoke briefly at the dark window slit and then opened the door.

Juan Pablo Herzog stepped out, dressed as usual in a recently pressed tailored suit and a crisp white linen shirt. His tie showed alternating orange and blue stripes, the colors of the university. Tiny, fierce alligator caricatures were embroidered among the stripes. . . . There was no indication Herzog was carrying a gun.

The taller man remained standing next to the car while the second man walked toward the building a half-step behind

Herzog, scanning the area until they reached the elevator. When it arrived, they boarded. Herzog's man firmly told three students laden with law books to take the stairs. Herzog and his aide exited the elevator at the second floor, outside the dean's office.

President Killingsworth had arrived a half-hour earlier, parking his familiar 1957 Ford pickup he'd restored on weekends in a space marked "Reserved for State Utility Vehicles," a euphemism for those with authority. No one had accompanied the president. His well-fitted, traditional double-breasted suit showed no bulge under either arm. Killingsworth had led an unsuccessful fight with the Florida legislature and the NRA to ban weapons on campus.

When Herzog walked into the dean's office, again ignoring the dean's secretary, she made no effort to stop him. Dean Perry rose to introduce Herzog to Killingsworth.

Herzog had expected to meet only with Dean Perry, receive a report about Maxwell Hunt, and instruct the dean to cash the check. He didn't anticipate having the university president present.

"Sr. Herzog," Dean Perry said, leading him by the elbow to meet President Killingsworth, "let me introduce our president—Alfred Killingsworth. President Killingsworth, this is Juan Pablo Herzog. Please sit, gentlemen."

Herzog spoke the first words, largely ignoring the president and looking directly at the dean. "I have been looking forward to reading your report on Professor Hunt, Dean Perry. And, of course, to setting the date for the announcement of my gift."

Herzog apparently had not read the Tampa newspaper article. He expected Dean Perry to hand him the requested report, believing money was as persuasive in the U.S. as in Guatemala.

"Mr. Herzog," responded Killingsworth, removing his glasses, slowly folding them, and placing them in the breast pocket of his suit coat, "I think we ought to be frank. The university regrets that it is unable to accept your gift."

Visibly irritated, Herzog adjusted his position in his seat, moving to sit rigidly on the front edge, which brought him closer to the president. "I don't understand. I am giving four million dollars. That is the largest donation to endow a chair ever made at this university—law college or otherwise. I've placed no conditions on the gift. It may be used for *any* area of international law. I retain no rights even to *suggest* persons to fill the chair. I simply wish to honor my dear friend and late professor, Maxwell Hunt."

"Mr. Herzog," continued Killingsworth, "let me explain our policy. We cannot even *begin* to undertake the kind of report you requested. I apologize. I learned of your request only two weeks ago. But I assure you Professor Hunt had an impeccable record during his two decades here. I've made sufficient inquiries to confirm that he indeed died of a stroke in D.C. It would be an invasion of privacy and contrary to state law to publically disclose what you've asked."

"I am not the public," said Herzog. "How can the privacy of a *deceased* person be invaded? It's quite obvious that you have information you do not wish to share with me."

"Universities are under increasingly protective state and federal laws which prevent releasing personal information about members of the academic community, Mr. Herzog. We take our obligations seriously. I'm very sorry about having to reject your gift."

"Will you accept my gift if I withdraw my request for the report?"

It was a difficult question to answer and stunned the dean. He worried that no matter how he answered, it might inform Herzog of something he wanted to know. "Sr. Herzog," Dean Perry offered, diverting Herzog's intense staring at the president, "the University Foundation Board met and decided that the gift should not be accepted. We can't alter that. I think the matter must be considered closed."

"Did the board decide to reject my gift because of the report? If so, they might wish to reconsider in view of the withdrawal of my request for the report. Is that not so?"

"Our foundation board meetings are not public," said Killingsworth, visibly exasperated. "I cannot speak to what was discussed. I am truly sorry, Mr. Herzog."

"Who did you talk to when you were working on the report," Herzog asked in a tone that evidenced a slight rise in intensity and sharpness.

"I shouldn't say anything further, but we briefly talked to people in D.C., as well as here," offered Killingsworth, returning to his customary gentle manner, "including members of the American Society of International Law, where Professor Hunt spoke. Nothing suggests that he did *not* die of a stroke, as announced at the time. The matter is closed as far as we're concerned."

"*I wish to see your report!* I think I'm entitled to see the facts surrounding Maxwell's death." Herzog's hands were squeezing the arms of his chair, his knuckles white as his face reddened.

"There is *no* report," interjected Dean Perry, who rose and placed himself between the president and Herzog. He appeared on the verge of letting his anger reach an unpredictable level. Dean Perry had been warned by Associate Dean Martinez that it was unwise to engage in combative dialogue with Herzog. "President Killingsworth," said Dean Perry, "I know you have a meeting shortly. I'll be happy to walk Sr. Herzog down to his car."

"That won't be necessary," said Herzog. "*But I tell you both,* I do not take this kind of treatment easily. If you read the papers, you know I am considered the leading prospect to head my country. You'll be hearing from me." With that he rose and quickly left, his aide remaining close by his side. At the car Herzog said nothing. The two men with him dared not speak.

In the dean's office the mood was suspicious. Killingsworth turned to Perry, "Hobart, do you think we should expect trouble from him?"

"Mr. President, I do. . . . I'm certain Herzog's aide was carrying a gun under his suit coat. Herzog is unpredictable and threatening. . . . His presence made me think of the last session of the legislature. Aren't you and I now allowed to carry concealed weapons on the campus?"

"Yes, we are, Hobart. But you know how I feel about that." As Killingsworth walked to the door, he turned and, showing his sense of humor that was much admired on the campus, quipped, "Why don't we try to cash his check?"

"If we do," responded Dean Perry, "we'd best use the first hundred thousand to arm and barricade the law college. And also your office, Mr. President."

≈

Four days later, a bomb destroyed President Killingsworth's cherished pickup truck while it was parked in his reserved space in the Tigert Hall lot. He was at work in the building, heard the explosion, and watched fire consume his vehicle. No one was injured. It was the first time any such horrendous act had occurred in the century-plus history of the state's much beloved flagship university.

The next day, outside Guatemala City on the mountain road to Antigua, the parents of Associate Dean Gloria Martinez were both killed when their car went off the road and plummeted into a deep ravine. Dean Martinez immediately resigned her position and went into hiding.

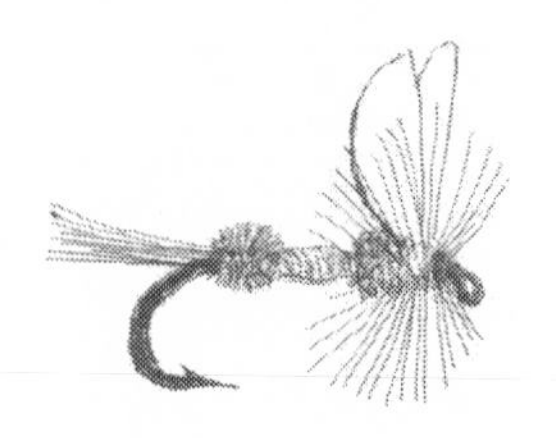

22

THE ONLINE *GAINESVILLE GAZETTE* ARTICLE about the bombing of the university president's vehicle was e-mailed to me by Dan Wilson. I was immediately sure it was the work of Herzog although the article mentioned solely that the matter was "under investigation." I read it again. My concern heightened. My cell phone broke the silence of the Montana afternoon. Not unexpectedly, it was Dan Wilson in D.C.

"I hope you've read the article I forwarded about the bombing. What do you think?"

"Herzog's *modus operandi*—retaliation. How did your phone conversation go with the dean and president after they met with Herzog?"

"The public hasn't been told any details by the university. At a press briefing in Gainesville, that same reporter from the *Tampa News Journal* directly confronted the president about whether the bombing was related to rejecting Herzog's gift. The president disavowed any such link and suggested it was a symbolic bombing against the university administration, rather than him personally. He mentioned how much adverse reaction there had been from the faculty-union to proposals to abolish tenure and hire more adjuncts. He assumes the bombing was the work of some UF faculty union radical. The FBI has been investigating the bombing; we're in touch with them. Most likely, the bombing news will soon move to the back pages of the papers since the UF football team is again in the running for the national title. You know SEC football is the dog that wags the university's tail. . . . We're tracking Herzog. As we expected, he was in Guatemala when the bombing occurred."

"I'm leaving for Florida within a week. I need to get away. But I have to talk to the Park County detectives before I leave. The head investigator, James Shaw, feels pretty certain that the Mexican woman, Victoria Montoya, did *both* Shuttle Gals killings. Other deputies have reservations about Olga Smits' death. The fishing season's over for me—I won't book any floats or shuttles until next spring . . . if then."

"*Please* stay out of Gainesville if you do come east. You don't want to encounter Herzog by some foolish act on your part, when your melancholia over being a law professor obscures your occasionally rational decisions."

"Thanks for your confidence! I have *no* plans to go to Gainesville. I want to sit on my porch on the salt marsh and vegetate for four months. I wish Lucinda could be there with me."

"We'll be talking. Let me know when you depart for Florida. My best to Lucinda."

≈

I called Erin Giffin at the Park County Sheriff's Office.

"Hi, Macduffy. What's up?" she asked.

"I'd like to go to Florida soon, maybe a couple of days before Thanksgiving. Any reason I need to stay?"

"I was going to call you. Jimbo's asked me to take over the investigation while he works on the sheriff's re-election campaign. Sound familiar? Ken's going to help me. . . . Can we have lunch and talk? I'm interested in your thoughts on whether we're likely to face similar problems next season."

"Can we do it soon?"

"Wednesday, two days from now, OK?"

"Good. Where?"

"You owe me a meal. What if I have some eatery here in Livingston make up a lunch, and Ken and I bring it to your place. You pay for it. Then I'll call us even. Deal?"

"You coming with a kimono and your kendo sword?"

"Nope, with my Glock and Taser. See you Wednesday, Macduffy."

"Deal." Some woman! Wish she could meet Lucinda. What a pair they'd make!

≈

Sharply at noon Wednesday Erin and Ken walked in with lunch and asked, "You off to Florida tomorrow?"

"I am."

"Going to stop in Indiana?" asked Erin.

"Yep. Rosa Lipsius, Lucinda's helper and therapist, says she's improving rapidly, and may be able to travel soon."

"OK, you two," said Ken, "this is a Wednesday. That means a *work* day."

"Sorry," I said. "Anything to avoid discussing rape and mutilation. What's new?"

"Nothing I can share. But I can tell you Erin and I have what we think is reasonably convincing evidence Victoria Montoya killed Julie Conyers. It doesn't help one way or the other with Olga Smits, however. Jimbo remains convinced that Montoya killed them both and isn't interested in spending any more time on the matter. He wants to see the sheriff re-elected, meaning that Shaw's job and pension are protected."

"Do either of you believe another shuttle murder might happen?" I asked.

"*Might* happen—possibly. . . . *Will* happen—no idea," responded Erin, her face showing a grimacing dismay. "Ken and I both think there's no good answer. But it's November, and the crappy weather's here early. Some snow and sleet. Nobody's floating. As far as another shuttle death *this* year, I think there won't be one for the logical reason that there won't be many floats until spring. But I have some other thoughts about next year."

"Share them?"

"That requires thinking about the motive of the killer or killers. Montoya wanted to kill one of the Shuttle Gals. She'd been rebuffed by nearly everybody in the Valley. But especially by women. And doubly so . . . in her mind . . . by the Shuttle Gals. *If* she did the second murder, I think she may try to kill all five. That's *three more,* Mac. That would turn our Paradise Valley fly fishing world upside down and affect Yellowstone River floats for who knows how long."

"Agreed," I offered. "But, if Victoria Montoya is mentally unstable, she becomes an intolerable burden to her brother Roberto. Remember, he has a private retreat not far from here in Jackson Hole. He doesn't want to lose his retreat, and he doesn't want the Montoya name tarnished. If Victoria proves to be a serial killer, it may spill over to Jackson Hole. I suspect she's fled to Mexico. If she becomes a threat to Roberto, he's vicious enough to put her away. . . . Permanently!"

Ken, quietly contemplative, intervened, "Why don't we pass on Montoya. She might want to kill more of the Shuttle Gals. But she's out of the country . . . as far as we know. I suggest we hold her on the wanted list and hope she tries to re-enter the country. Mexico won't extradite her to the U.S. because of our capital punishment laws. If she doesn't re-enter voluntarily, the shuttle killings may stop. If she's behind them."

"That leaves Helga Markel to talk about," Erin interjected. "*If* she killed Olga, and even Julie, what would be *her* reason for killing more of the Shuttle Gals?"

"I think *at most* Markel killed Olga," I answered. "I don't buy into her killing Julie, but I think she got the idea of *how* to kill Olga from Julie's murder. If Markel killed Olga, I see no reason she won't *kill* again. But not necessarily another of the Shuttle Gals. Remember, she's hates *recreational angling*, not the Shuttle Gals as individuals.

"One murder should have been enough to make a statement and maybe scare off some shuttle services. But there are dozens of other targets where she isn't known. She might be more likely to kill some wading angler in Oregon than to strike here again. Or kill a guide. Again, probably not here. She wants PARA's focus to be on *angling,* not any specific geography such as Paradise Valley."

"But," Ken observed, "she's linked to that former law professor at Missoula. That could keep her in Montana. But they left Missoula, and most likely Montana, about the time Olga was killed. If Jimbo Shaw hadn't scratched Markel as a suspect, we might have started a nation-wide search for her. We simply don't know where she is."

"Thanksgiving's close," noted Erin. "The holidays through the first of the year are likely to slow down the investigation. It'll likely be mid-January before we know Markel's location. Macduffy will probably be gone until April. There'll be a few boats back on the Yellowstone in the spring for a few weeks, until the snow melt starts the water flowing too fast for drift boat fishing. That'll last until possibly half-way through July. If we have a serial killer, we could see another shuttle murder in April. No sooner. . . .Ken, what do you think?"

"There are problems linking Victoria with Olga's death. I understand Jimbo's view that there's only one killer of both women. That means a serial killer who's either after gay women—maybe only those involved with shuttle services—or specifically the Shuttle Gals, gay or straight.

"In any event, we need to warn the remaining three Shuttle Gals of the danger. Even better—meet with them as a group. I suggest we plan to follow the first few shuttles by the gals next spring.

"We have enough deputies to assign a couple to each take-out ramp on the river, at least between Emigrant and Carter Bridge. Of course, that's assuming the Shuttle Gals are going to keep the business operating. . . . I don't think we've seen the last of the killings."

Erin turned to me. "Macduffy?"

"I'm closer to Ken than Jimbo in thinking about Montoya," I answered. "But *maybe* she did both or at least *arranged* for both. She had a motive. Maybe there's something in her head we can't imagine that impels her to act. She has a history of brutal violence in Mexico. I'm not sure Markel is anywhere nearly as violent a person. She's a lot of talk. But there may be others in PARA willing to carry out a killing. What I'm more troubled with is that, although Julie was raped by *three* different men, Olga wasn't raped. Why? If there is another killing, my first question would be whether a rape was involved. Answered 'yes' and I pursue Montoya. Answered 'no' and I go after Markel. . . . I'm also troubled by the green, red, and white sash used in each of the killings. Why would *Markel* have used Mexico's colors?"

"Macduffy, that's enough for now," interjected Erin, "We can be in touch wherever you are—here or Florida. . . . Now, a little surprise. Lunch is in the kitchen. It needs warming up. You do have an oven?"

I have a microwave and a rarely used small oven. Take your pick. What's for lunch?"

"You'll love it. Alaskan wild salmon over pan-roasted spiced cauliflower with peas."

"What did the salmon do to deserve that?"

"You've never seen a vegetable you didn't mistrust," Erin said exasperated. "You'd live on bison if you could. You need someone to cook for you."

Erin held my attention with the menu. But I could see beyond her into the cabin's rear sitting room, off of which is my tiny kitchen I find intimidating. I looked at the oven and wondered why it scares me more than staring at a Glock.

The solid, paneled rear door is between the kitchen and the large glass window that overlooks Mill Creek. I remembered hearing a car motor while Ken was answering Erin's question. The sound was close enough to be a vehicle driven nearly to the house.

I'd left my gate open for my guests. Strangers not infrequently drive in when the gate is open, turning around as soon as they see the house, especially when cars are present. But something more drew my attention to that door.

A board creaked on the rear porch. Someone *was* there. My occasional housekeeper, Mavis, was away visiting family. No one else was expected. I watched as the doorknob began to turn slowly. Rising, I lifted down the loaded .44 magnum Henry rifle from over the front door, and hustled the few steps to face the back door, cocking the lever action to thrust a cartridge into the chamber.

Three feet in front of me, the door was opening slowly. I took off the safety, pointed the gun at the opening door, and waited, feeling like I did before I pulled the trigger and shot Isfahani in Guatemala. I welcome the chance to do the same with Herzog or have another shot at Isfahani. It will take the slightest pressure on the trigger I have adjusted for an easy shot.

Absorbed in preparing lunch, Erin saw me, dropped the salmon on the floor and lunged at me screaming, "Jeeze, Macduffy, you'll *kill* her! What's wrong with you?" Erin knocked the barrel up as the gun went off, sending the heavy .44 bullet into the main cross-beam above the door.

The concussion caused the door to swing open. Standing in the open door, a small carry-on in her left hand, a bottle of wine in the right, and a look of disbelief on her face—was Lucinda.

Erin grabbed my rifle. Trembling, I grabbed Lucinda. A long embrace of dampened faces followed, devoid of embarrassment in the company of friends.

"Were you going to shoot me?" Lucinda asked, as if she really didn't know the answer.

"Who on earth did you think was at the door?" Erin demanded.

"I lost it. I don't know what happened, but I was sure it was Juan Pablo. . . . " I caught myself before I said anything more.

Erin and Ken looked at me strangely. They didn't know about the trouble at the university in Gainesville. Ken said, "Juan Pablo? Who's Juan Pablo? Is there someone by that name involved with Victoria Montoya? Are you holding something back on us?"

"No. It's from another dark corner of my past. Nothing to do with the Shuttle Gals murders." Erin and Ken stared at me, neither able to understand what had happened. But Lucinda was safe.

A diverting bark came from my bedroom. Ken opened the door and Wuff ran out and hurtled into Lucinda's arms. A reunion of survivors of floating with me.

"Oh! Wuff. You remember me. I guess we share being shot on *Osprey*."

I thought: "And you came close to being shot again two minutes ago. By me." I didn't really know the answer to her question: "Were you going to shoot me, Macduff?"

≈

It took a half-hour to return the atmosphere to what Lucinda's arrival was intended . . . joy in having her back at Mill Creek.

"Have you escaped from Indiana?" I asked.

"Over Dr. West's and my mother's objections. But at the urging of both Rosa and Dr. Kent in Salt Lake City, I slipped out. Only for the holiday. I'm being recalled the week after."

"I hate to see you and your mother having difficulty, but I'm not surprised she didn't approve."

"She's not pleased. She thinks I'll be killed if I'm with you. We have to find a way to convince her I'm not going to be another notch on *Osprey*."

"Maybe not on *Osprey*," I thought, "but maybe on my Henry rifle if I can't get my act together."

"Lucinda, who am I?" I asked, to nudge the conversation away from Juan Pablo, Henry rifles, and Mrs. Parker-Smith Lang.

"You're the guy I met sitting on his butt in front of my door at Thanksgiving, five years ago."

"Remember my name?"

"Macduff Brooks. Also known as Mac, Macduffy, and I understand the Spanish version is Macdoof."

"How did you get here? Did Erin and Ken know about this? You know Ken, but you've never met Erin?"

Lucinda turned to Erin, and they hugged warmly. "Hi, Erin Giffin. Thanks for saving me from Macduff," she said, nodding to me. "Macduff, this *is* the first time we've met, but Erin's the one you can thank for my being here. She called Rosa and said you were miserable, impossible to be around, and that if I could visit, she'd make sure you followed Dr. Kent's orders. Your lawyer, Wanda, met me at the airport and drove me here. She had to go on to a court hearing."

≈

"We met at a Thanksgiving when we were the *only* two present. Let's have Thanksgiving this year at the same place—your ranch house, Lucinda—but with all of us. Erin, Ken and his family, and Wanda? Of course, Mavis and her family." A whine came from next to Lucinda's feet. "OK Wuff, you can come, too."

"How about asking Veeky?" Lucinda said, her face showing the old familiar Cheshire cat grin.

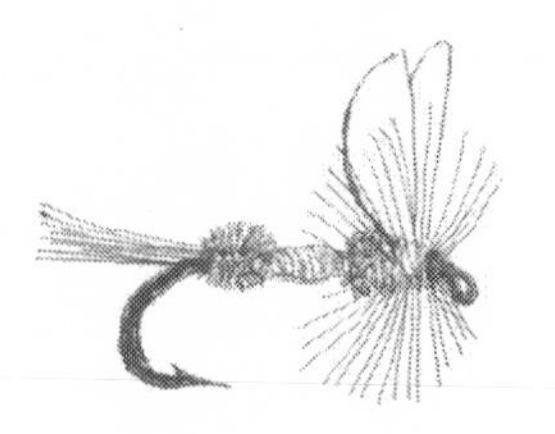

23

THANKSGIVING WAS TRULY A TIME OF THANKS. In the days running up to the holiday, much of Lucinda's memory returned, like a Maine sea-fog swarming across the land and leaving life-giving moisture. There were a few unwelcome but expected days when she didn't make noticeable progress, offsetting only nominally the more common days when I marveled at the results of her remarkable determination.

Sometimes names or events that she remembered for the first time became lost again. Her therapist, Rosa, had explained that memory variations aren't unusual with amnesia and full recovery is measured more in years than months. Patience is an important part of the cure, but clearly after love and understanding.

Lucinda seems to retain what I tell her about *our* past, the area she appears most desirous of reviving. Fortunately for her progress, we go back only four years.

We've ignored the gaps in my earlier life that I've never filled in for her. She thinks they're part of her amnesia, not my reluctance to fully open my past to her. She wants to know about my life before becoming Macduff; she thinks that's part of her amnesia. I'm not always certain about what I had told her about Maxwell Hunt before the shooting, making her progress as confusing to me as it is to her.

We stayed at my cabin except for Thanksgiving dinner and a few brief visits at her ranch lodge. She's more comfortable in the smaller spaces of my cabin where she isn't far from me. We can deal with her ranch in time. She's also beginning to remember *her* life before we met but can't fit it into the present. She doesn't believe she could have been so successful and gained such considerable wealth as a New York investment broker. We have some large gaps to fill.

Sunday dawn ended the frigid, snow-laden Thanksgiving weekend, opening with the sun's return as a warm front moved north from Mexico. At our first breakfast out together—at our favorite Howlin' Hounds Café in Emigrant—Lucinda asked, "Take me on Passage Creek Trail? It's warm today. I'll take a camera."

"Sure," I said. "The leaves are off the trees. The sun should make it through the canopy. The walk could become muddy with a quick thaw after freezing weather and snow. But why not go? We can always turn back."

We packed a lunch, and I took a 7' bamboo rod. I couldn't find the Wyoming fishing regulations—what was listed online was in such fine print I couldn't decipher it. But the Yellowstone River is open to fishing year round and, by my often misty logic and deductive reasoning, I assumed that "open for fishing" rule applied to its tributaries, including Mill Creek. I had never fished this late in the year; we were only a few days short of the first of December. A warm day might bring some small trout to the surface, so I tucked a few #18 and #20 dry flies onto the small fleece square on my jacket.

Leaving my SUV at the trailhead, a few miles up the gravel road from my cabin, we crossed Mill Creek and began the gradual ascent on Passage Creek Trail.

Lucinda didn't speak for the first ten minutes of our hike. But her eyes were as wide open as her mouth was closed. Suddenly she stopped, looked at me, and exclaimed, "Wow! This is beautiful! There aren't many leaves on the deciduous trees, but there are hundreds of pines draped with snow. It shimmers when it melts and slips off the branches. . . . Nobody's here but us. Pretty special."

She had brought a camera. Not her large format, inverted image, wooden folding camera with the hood. Not even the modern digital camera that's replaced her old, clumsy Nikons and Canons with their interchangeable lenses and cassettes of film. She carried only a modest digital camera with a 20x optical telephoto, which she adjusted to control depth of field and give an effect of drawing everything close together. Lucinda has a talent for photo composition that begs for time for full expression. I think her camera could be as much an asset as my patience in helping her progress. But I've noticed she has trouble concentrating for more than short spells.

Placing her camera in her jacket pocket, its Kevlar lining hopefully not needed on Passage Creek, she said, "Want to fish?"

"Fine. We're almost to a small pool on the creek."

"I brought a couple of flies, too. Let *me* tie on a fly. What knot should I use?"

"Maybe a surgeon's knot, in view of our past year," I suggested.

"Or a blood knot! . . . Don't remind me! . . . I'm using an improved clench knot. Through the eye and about seven wraps, then back through the loop close to the eye and through the loop I just made. Did I do it right?"

"Wait and see. If it holds, it was right. If it slips, it was lousy."

"Is that how you teach knots? I don't know how you get *any* clients."

"I may not get any more. My last two floats were canceled, and it wasn't because of my knot teaching."

"I know. I'm sorry . . . my Royal Coachman fly came from that old metal pipe tobacco can that was on your fly tying table. The one you told me held flies you tied as a teen. They're so old I hope they don't come apart."

"They're antiques. Like me. Treat them with due respect."

Her fly landed in the center of the pool, caught an eddy, and began to spin in the vortex. We watched as the head of an eight-inch cutthroat rose and nudged the fly—and disappeared back into the safety of the lower darkness. Another came close but also turned away. "Lucinda, was there anything else in that can where you found the fly?"

"A few old moth-ball pieces."

"How would you like to be about to take a bite of a chocolate-chip cookie and have the stench of moth-balls flood your nostrils?"

"Not so good. . . . I'll take off the fly and try something else."

"Wait a second," I said. "The current may dissolve whatever residue of the moth-ball is on the fly." As I finished the sentence, another cutthroat rose with no reluctance to take the fly. In her excitement Lucinda flipped the fish from the creek fifteen feet behind us into a stand of pines. I found it cushioned in a patch of fresh snow and returned it quickly to the stream, where it rushed from my grasp with a new tale to tell its friends."

"What was it? A cutthroat?"

"A flying fish. Rare in these parts. That's quite a back cast you have. I didn't teach you that!"

"You're jealous! . . . My first catch of the year! But that doesn't say much—it's nearly December. I may not catch another fish this year. I'll remember this one."

"You *are* through for the year, unless you catch another today. There's bad weather coming this way from the northwest. We'd best head east soon and keep ahead of it. You don't need another fish; that was a beautiful seven-inch native cutthroat. The colors are a little less intense than those of summer, somewhat of a winter coat. But it had the trademark red slash."

"Are these *Yellowstone* cutthroats?" she asked. "They're in a creek off the Yellowstone River."

"They are. What we call the Yellowstone cutthroat were first found in the part of the river that flows through the park. They're thought to have come up Wyoming's Snake River and into Pacific Creek, south of the park. You know Pacific Creek; it joins the Snake just above Pacific Creek Landing, where we've started floats down to Deadman's Bar.

"When the water was unusually high, probably centuries ago, the fish may have gotten into Atlantic Creek on the east side of the Continental Divide and ended up over the divide in the Yellowstone River. The biggest population has traditionally inhabited the nine-mile stretch between Yellowstone Lake and the Upper Falls north of Lamar Valley, but the cutthroats are being decimated by the invasive lake trout.

"This one you caught looks like a true Yellowstone cutthroat. The body's a coppery gold, with variations into mauve and indigo. It has the trademark orange-red jaw slashes, and the spots aren't very big. They sparsely dot the head but increase to such density at the tail that they appear to run out of room for any more.

"A hatchery was built on Yellowstone Lake around 1900, and the young cutthroat trout were introduced throughout the West. That resulted in cross-breeding with rainbow trout to create what we call cutbows. The other kind of cutthroat we see in Western Montana is the Westslope. That's in Lewis and Clark country. Drawing on my extensive Latin, all the cutthroats here are *Oncorhynchus clarki*, named for William Clark. The Westslope also honors Meriwether Lewis, named *Oncorhynchus clarki lewisi.*"

"How many different cutthroat varieties are there? Don't name them all please. I defer to your Latin skills, even if limited to a few fish and legal terms."

"Maybe twenty, but it changes as new species are found, sometimes in remote mountain lakes or streams, and as current variations are reclassified. . . . OK, enough *ichthyology* for one day. Sometime we'll talk about a bunch of other trout, especially the only one imported from Europe—our wonderful brown trout. *And* don't forget brook trout, which aren't trout at all but *char*. Enough?"

"*Enough,*" she said.

"Of course—*Parva leves capiunt animas*—small things occupy light minds."

"What's 'the truth finally comes out' in Latin?"

"I wouldn't tell you—if I knew."

"Are you up to climbing above the falls?" she asked.

As we walked Lucinda showed me some of the photographs she had taken on our walk along the trail.

"You have talent. Do you think of photographing professionally?"

"All the time."

"Why not do it?"

"I'm not ready. I'll tell you when I think I am. . . . I'll need your support."

I liked that idea. "Say the word. . . . A more mundane matter—do you think we can leave soon? You said you were recalled. Your mother will be livid if we delay much longer."

"I'm ready. How long a trip?"

"Three days to Indiana. After you dismiss Dr. West, another two to Florida. Has your firm in Manhattan talked to you about returning to work?"

"You know I have a year's leave. They've told me I can extend that. I don't know for how long. I'd like us to talk about it, but I need to deal first with my mother and what I think has been bad medical and legal advice."

≈

The drive across the Dakotas and on to Indiana was easy, much due to having Lucinda next to me in the front seat. Wuff sat in the back and whined. Especially when we were still driving at her five p.m. dinner time.

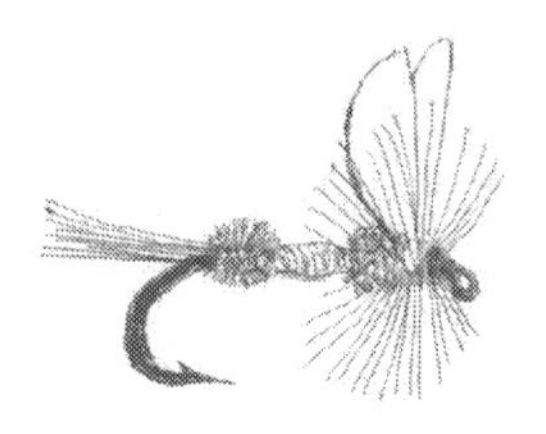

24

TO MINIMIZE CONFLICTS WITH MRS. LANG, I deposited Lucinda on her front porch and drove off. Wuff and I checked into a motel and, after a couple of hours, I reluctantly went off to face whatever Mrs. Parker-Smith Lang would throw at me. It took only ten seconds after her front door opened for her to greet me with a declaration that I had a meeting the following day at nine a.m. at *her* attorney's office. She wouldn't tell me what was to be discussed.

Mrs. Lang's attorney arrived at his office the following morning at ten. I'd arrived four minutes before nine, without breakfast. From the looks of his secretary, she was a major expense. There wasn't much to her dress, but there was a lot of her, which unfolded as she leaned over and handed me a cup of coffee.

When her boss finally entered his office, he said "hello" to her, looked at me condescendingly, entered his office, and closed the door. Twenty minutes later I heard him say to his secretary on the intercom: "Send him in. It shouldn't take more than ten minutes to instruct him about his rights and be rid of him."

I entered and approached his desk as close as I could without being overcome by his cologne. He looked at me sharply and pronounced with senatorial temper, "Mr. Brooks, I am Attorney Leonard Jackson. I am personal counsel to Mrs. Parker-Smith Lang."

He wore a three-piece suit. It should have been a size larger and the vest three inches longer. A white shirt bulged like a cresting wave and separated the bottom of his vest from the top of his belt. His high blow-dried hair and two-inch heels were intended to alter what genes had limited. He still fell short of six feet by a good four inches. I remembered seeing his picture on several billboards entering town, advertising purported legal skills in about every specialty I could recall.

Having absorbed as much of him as I could take on an empty stomach, I asked, "Are you also *Lucinda's* attorney? Lucinda's interests are quite different from her mother's."

"I *am* Lucinda's attorney as well, by virtue of the fact that she is incapacitated and under her mother's care."

"That doesn't sound fully accurate. By what measure is Lucinda incapacitated?"

"Mrs. Lang and I made that determination in consultation with Dr. West and her new physician, Dr. Henry. As of last evening, she is confined to her bed and unable to have any visitors. You qualify as a visitor, however unwelcome."

"Has a court appointed Mrs. Lang as Lucinda's guardian *ad litem?*"

"Are you a lawyer, Mr. Brooks?"

"No, I am not." That *is* true. Maxwell Hunt was a lawyer, affirmed by admission to the Connecticut Bar, but a qualification that Macduff Brooks did not assume.

"Then I suggest you not interfere. Mrs. Lang, as Lucinda's mother, is her natural guardian."

"Lucinda is not a minor. Has a *court* determined her competency?"

"That is unnecessary. The physician I retained, Dr. Lucifer Henry, issued a certificate of incompetency."

"Did Dr. Henry personally evaluate Lucinda?"

"That was not necessary; I told him all he needed to know. Dr. Henry has replaced Dr. West."

"Are you aware that Lucinda is not a resident of Indiana? She officially resides in New York, where she owns an apartment, has her driver's license, voting registration, and pays city and state taxes."

"But Lucinda is *in* Indiana. By her presence here, she is subject to Indiana law."

"Attorney Jackson, I appreciate what you've told me. I intend to recommend to Lucinda that she retain an attorney to represent her own interests, separate from those of her mother."

"That will not be necessary . . . or possible. . . . I am Lucinda's attorney."

"If I *were* a lawyer, I'm sure I'd be able to explain to you why that is total nonsense. I've heard enough from you. You'll hear from *Lucinda's* attorney, if not the State Attorney's office. Goodbye."

As I rose to leave, Jackson called in a waiting process-server who stuffed papers into my hands and said, "Mr. Brooks, these papers include a local court order prohibiting you from having any contact with Lucinda Lang, and the complaint in a lawsuit filed against you yesterday on behalf of Mrs. Lang for causing Lucinda's injuries. It requests damages in excess of ten million dollars."

Disgusted at the inability of Indiana to regulate its physicians and attorneys, I checked out of my motel room. While waiting for my bill, my cell phone rang—it was from a number I didn't know, not Lucinda's land-line.

"Hello."

"It's Lucinda. I'm on a cell phone my mother doesn't know I have. I've been put in my room and told I can't leave. My new doctor, Lucifer something, said I'll be moved soon to a rest home where they can better care for me. I'm scared, Mac. I don't like Leonard Jackson. My mother hired him after seeing his picture on billboards and hearing his slick TV ads. He's actually been *dating* her. She's older than his father! Why didn't you come right back to the house? I would have gone with you."

"I should have taken you with me. I'm sure if you leave, no other state will recognize your mother's claim to be your natural guardian. Is anyone at the house? Will you be alone when I come?"

"No one else is here now except my mother. *Please* come and get me."

I called Dr. West. He answered directly. I had mixed feelings about him because of the drugs he prescribed for Lucinda, but I needed to understand where he stood now that he'd been dismissed. When I mentioned Lucifer Henry, he lost his composure.

"That incompetent bastard quack! He's been suspended four times and always weasels back into the licensed profession. He *sells* medical opinions and prescription drugs."

"Do you think Lucinda's incompetent?" I asked.

"Not on your life. But this isn't good for her. Amnesia is strange; a new trauma could set her back months. I've tried to treat her as best I could."

"I don't want you in trouble with the courts. There's been a judicial order putting Lucinda under her mother's care. And a new order prohibiting me from having any contact with Lucinda."

"Neither of which is in her best interests, Mr. Brooks. Please don't repeat this but I'd rather see her leave Indiana in spite of the court orders than have her remain with her mother and her so-called legal and medical advisors."

"Do you think they will try to physically restrain Lucinda? She called me and said they plan to take her to some institution run by Dr. Henry tomorrow morning."

"She *can't* be taken to Henry's institution! It's gated and guarded. It would be very difficult to get her out. I don't know if she'd survive. You must act immediately."

"I don't think they want her to survive; they want her assets."

As I drove toward Lucinda's house, I called Dan Wilson in D.C. and told him about my problem. He took down the names of Jackson and Henry, said he'd check on them and get back to me.

Twenty minutes later he called with useful information. I called Lucinda on her cell phone. She was sobbing when she answered. "My mother's downstairs with Henry and Jackson. She's so confused. She's been asking questions about my best interests, and they aren't being fair with her. They want her to sign papers committing me immediately to a hospital Henry owns. Henry and Jackson said they'll take me there now, not tomorrow. If they take me there, I'm afraid I'll. . . . " Her voice choked and faded.

"I'll be at your house in fifteen minutes. Dr. West should be there sooner. Is there a back door?"

"Yes, to the kitchen. It's always open."

I called Dr. West and said, "I'm going in the back of the house; you knock on the front door and say you have Lucinda's records to turn over to Dr. Henry. Then, start an argument to keep things busy. Tell Mrs. Lang that Henry is unlicensed, *anything* to cause delay. If you have trouble, I'll intervene."

Getting into the kitchen proved easy. The door was ajar so Mrs. Lang's cat could go in and out. I listened as West entered the front. He immediately began to confront Henry and Jackson. They were arguing over taking Lucinda to Henry's institution. Jackson said he had the proper papers, but West refused to recognize them and wouldn't turn over Lucinda's medical records. Mrs. Lang was borderline hysteric. When I stepped into the room, Lucinda came down the stairs. Now there were six of us.

Loudly, I interrupted the argument. "Henry, give me your brief case—don't open it." When he started to reach in, I yanked it from his shaking hands. Inside was a small, loaded Smith & Wesson .32 caliber revolver. I handed it to West who pointed it at Henry. It wasn't a good time for a neighbor to drop by to borrow a cup of sugar.

Behind me stood Lucinda, waving her father's war prize German Luger. I hoped it wasn't loaded. In my jacket pocket was my Glock that didn't appear needed. When I do need one, it's usually in a zippered pocket or somewhere among my fishing gear.

"From the looks of it, we have the upper hand," I said to Jackson.

"You're in more trouble than you can imagine, Brooks," he responded. "Using weapons in the commission of a felony, assault, violating a court order, and—if Lucinda goes with you—kidnapping."

I looked at Jackson and added, "And quite possibly a double homicide."

The information Dan Wilson had given me might trump everything. "Jackson, the FBI has been looking for you for a Ponzi scheme you've been operating in Florida under a different name. Dr. West is going to hold you here until they arrive. I think Mrs. Lang will want the suit withdrawn when she hears more about you. And Henry, Indiana state police are right now on their way here and to your so-called institute. You're through with medicine. Lucinda, find some tape or rope for Henry and Jackson."

I turned to Mrs. Lang, who stood ashen and in disbelief at the scene before her. She hadn't uttered a word. I nodded at her. "I don't believe for a minute you're involved with these two in what they were planning, which surely ends with you institutionalized along with Lucinda.

"I'm certain they planned to have Lucinda conveniently die at Henry's institute. Then you'd be committed. They'd drain every dime you and Lucinda have. . . . I want your word that you'll follow Dr. West's orders and wait with him until the authorities arrive."

Calling me Macduff for the first time, Mrs. Lang said, weakly, "I don't know what to do. Dr. Henry and Attorney Jackson have been so nice to me. They told me awful things about you. Maybe what Lucinda has told me is true. I do know she has sparkled only when she's been with you here or was talking to you on the phone. She's a good girl. I should trust her judgment."

West nodded at her sudden understanding and said, "Jackson and Henry represent the worst of their professions. Hopefully they will never practice again. I've never liked seeing Jackson's face and ads on TV and billboards. . . .I'll help you get a new attorney, Mrs. Lang."

I talked to West quietly, out of hearing of the others. "We're heading south. I'll drive through the night. If the police ask, say you heard us mention we were on our way to Lucinda's apartment in Manhattan."

25

LUCINDA AND I WATCHED for flashing red lights in the rear-view mirror throughout the fourteen hour drive to Florida. Doing so at least kept our minds off the visual pollution provided by the billboard industry that infests the interstates, except in a very few scenic states. We didn't even discuss stopping at a motel, but during the night pulled in at a highway rest area when we entered Georgia, dozing fitfully for half-an-hour that didn't count as needed sleep.

Wuff ignored our antics; she sat in the rear, leaning up against the back of our seats, whining when her meals were due or when Lucinda returned with food and chased Wuff into the back seat.

Mid-morning welcomed us to the security of my cottage on the salt-marshes south of St. Augustine. I'd called ahead to my caretaker, Jen Jennings. The cottage was spotless when we walked in. We felt like we'd just gotten off an all-night flight to Europe and didn't know whether to go to bed in the morning daylight or stay up. We chose to stay up, fed Wuff, unloaded belongings, and drove to Crescent Beach's South Beach Grill for mid-afternoon bowls of Minorcan soup, a good re-introduction to Northeast Florida.

The Minorcans were southern European imports to the northeast Florida territory in the later part of the 18th century. They were viewed as better acclimated than the English to work in the heat, despite the latter's reputation for staying out in the noon-day sun, accompanied by their mad dogs.

My realtor Janet had not only discovered my cottage, but put me in touch with Jen, a piney-woods, skinny, four-foot eleven-and-maybe-a-half-inch Florida native. Jen has unruly short blond hair, clear hazel eyes, and the kind of high-muscle, low-fat body gals pay health clubs thousands to match—instead of giving much thought to exercise and diets. Jen's right out of a Marjorie Kinnan Rawlings novel. She checks on the cottage occasionally when I'm in Montana and gives it a cleaning before I arrive each fall.

Jen lives in a doublewide, expanded over the years by a screened porch, two carports, a barn, and a chicken coop, all guarded by a testy Rottweiler and four bickering macaws. It's two miles south of my place in the more accommodating Flagler County. She helps with the family earnings by keeping an eye on 5,000-plus-square-foot homes owned mostly by Canadian "snowbirds" who winter in Palm Coast, Florida. Mine's an exception . . . her smallest and most rustic charge.

Jen's husband Jimmy does finish carpentry and general repair work in the area. Their son, Tom, is a third-year 3.97-GPA President's Scholar at UF, headed in a couple of years to law school. I could tell him the country doesn't need any more lawyers. But he might ask, "How do you know? You're not a lawyer."

Jen dropped by the day after we arrived. "I left you guys stuff in the fridge yesterday—orange juice, milk, coffee—what I thought might be helpful. And a box of treats for Wuff."

"Thanks, the house looks great. I've got a couple of jobs for Jimmy. When he has some time. No rush."

"I'll tell him. Oh! . . . When I came by last week to check on your cottage there was a car parked outside the gate. Small, new, white. A sedan. With a sticker on the windshield—maybe a rental. I opened the gate, drove in, and locked it. When I got here to the house, a guy was sitting on the pine stump at the head of the path to your pier. Late thirties or early forties. Never seen him before. Scruffy . . . torn jeans and a tank top. Tattoos. I stayed in my car.

"In the glove compartment there's a pistol Jimmy makes me carry. I took it out and put it on the seat beside me, cocked. Staying in my car, I called to the guy and asked him what he wanted. Said he was looking for his friend, Macduff Brooks. I told him I didn't have any idea when you were coming and suggested he leave a note. He said he'd be back. I came up into the house, locked the door behind me, and looked out the window. He was gone. I didn't find a note."

"Thanks." Less than a dozen people in the area know me by name. A few locals helped do some work on the cottage when I bought it. It was probably one of them looking for more work. Some are a little rough around the edges. I worry when incidents like this happens, but I'll be damned if I'll submit to my circumstances.

≈

One January day, weeks later, when the morning sun was slanting through the swaying tops of the pines, causing shadows on the ground to flutter in a woodland's dance, Lucinda and I went down to my SUV. We paused and breathed deeply, like the doctor asks you to do to check your lungs at an annual physical. A light easterly breeze from the Atlantic, crossing the salt-water mud-flats, brought a pungency I welcomed, but would take getting accustomed to for Lucinda. It's an acquired smell, like the acquired taste we were soon to learn about.

After a couple of hours of errands, mainly the local wine shop and Publix, where at the register we combined all the nutritional necessities from Lucinda's cart with all the junk food in mine, we returned home convinced my cottage was set within the garden of the gods. The temperature was seventy-seven and might get a degree hotter, while in Montana it was heading south passing freezing and might get ten degrees colder.

Lucinda looked the picture of health in brick-red Bermuda shorts and a white linen short-sleeved blouse. If we were in Montana, I wouldn't be able to tell what she looked like under a hooded parka, face mask, and gloves. Of course, it would be a different story in August, when Montana was seventy-seven degrees and might get a degree cooler, while in Florida it was heading north passing boiling and might get ten degrees hotter.

≈

When we reached the cottage and I started up the outside stairs with a load of groceries, I heard what sounded like a few-dozen large round steel sinkers placed in an empty can being shaken in an automatic paint mixer. The noise is sometimes described as a buzz. Maybe that's for the *juveniles.* We were hearing the *adults'* noise.

Straight ahead an agitated, six-foot Eastern Diamondback was on the fourth step to the cottage. *Eye* level. Our approach had set off its rattle, a five-inch-long black coil of spirals rising up behind a body I *might* be able to get my hands around. The rattle was a blur in the background, attached to the end of a body that was not a neat coil, but a jumble of thick muscle that curved, looped, and slanted, leaving the head and first two feet of the snake *leaning* forward, suspended over its massive mid-section.

It was rigid in its fixation on me—a slight swaying made the head all the more ominous. Its chin was a dirty buff from where two white stripes slanted upwards, ending at the eyes. I was close enough to see the eyes—black vertical iris slits that affirmed: "Don't tread on me."

The top of the head had small scales that at first looked like soft, downy feathers, but were as hard as the body. While the snake held still, its black, four-inch forked tongue dropped, rose, and shifted from side-to-side—testing, feeling. I've seen rattlers before. But always on the ground; never eye-to-eye. And not five feet away measured nose-to-nose.

I *thought* I remembered a rattler can strike only two-thirds of its length. *Only*? That meant if it struck, it *should* be a foot short. Its hinged mouth would spread into an opening wide enough to swallow a rabbit, and the two curved, grooved fangs that usually lie hidden inside against the roof of its mouth, dripping with its poisonous fruit, would be targeted at my face. If it struck short, for an instant it would hang suspended, short of its goal, and then drop to the lower stair where I was about to step. Where it could take a second shot.

Staring into unblinking eyes, I froze, seeing behind the head the diamond pattern on its body shimmering in the morning mist. The snake was cornered in an open space. It couldn't go up the stairs without turning away from me. It wouldn't go down the stairs because it had calculated that I was already within range. Maybe. Space was fractionally on my side.

Jen was inside helping with some cleaning. I tried to emit a quiet scream of terror: "Jen, bring the shotgun. There's a rattler here. It's longer than you are!" She walked out carrying a six-foot-long pole with a squeegee on the end that she was using to clean my windows. She watched the snake for a moment. Its tail was almost silent, but the body remained stiffened with resentment over my intransigence.

In a motion too fast for me to follow, Jen calmly came down two steps and pinned the snake's head against a stair with the squeegee, reached down, and grabbed it in a tight pinch behind the head. She picked it up, held it out at arm's length—its tail dragging behind, walked down the stairs past me to her car, opened the trunk lid, pulled out a burlap bag, and dropped the snake in tail first. She twisted the top of the sack into a knot and tossed it on the front passenger's seat. Shutting the car door only partly muffled the buzzing. The rattler will be her companion when she finishes with the house and drives off.

I was incredulous. "That thing's alive! It's in your car! On the *front seat*! What are you doing?"

Jen calmly responded, "I got a neighbor who lives in a doublewide behind ours. He makes stuff outa gator and snake skins. Like belts, hat bands, knife cases. You name it; he can make it. They do stink up the car, but I'll get at least two-hundred bucks for the skin. Plus rattler meat makes *great* hush puppies. I'll bring you some. It's an acquired taste. A little like chicken."

"I like my chicken with legs and wings, not noisy tails."

The following day Jen brought us a dish with a half-dozen rattler hush puppies. They sat on a shelf in the refrigerator for three days. Every time we opened the door, we stood back and peeked in. When hunger and failure to do some needed shopping left us with a choice of canned tomato soup or Jen's hush puppies, we ate them.

Truthfully, *I* ate the hush puppies; Lucinda said she'd eat Wuff's food before she'd touch the snake. I admit I managed them only after two glasses of Gentleman Jack. The bourbon was delicious. The hush puppies did taste like chicken. I'm not ready for them to be part of my routine diet. If I encourage Jen she next may bring gator tail or possum. Or even armadillo or cooter.

When I bought the cottage, there were two dozen rattler skins stretched on Cyprus planks hanging on an outside wall. They ranged from four to nearly seven feet in length, adding an interesting geometric pattern to the cottage's side. But my skin crawled every time I walked up the stairs, only a foot away from them. I took them down and stored them under the cottage. Maybe when I'm more comfortable being around them and have built a garage, I'll hang them again. Or better, put them next to my entry gate, with a sign that says, "Rattlesnake Sanctuary." That ought to keep the St. Johns County Tax Assessor in his car.

≈

Now I worry about Lucinda and Wuff encountering a rattler outside. Lucinda scribbled "install more outdoor lights under the roof eaves" at the top of my chore list.

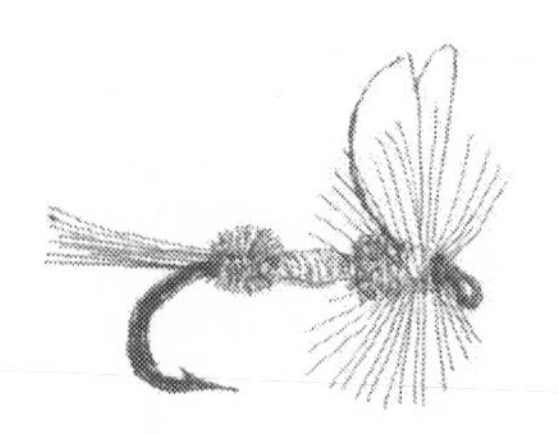

26

EVERY TIME I TALK WITH DAN WILSON in D.C., he pleads with me to stay away from Gainesville. But two decades are not so easily erased. The first ten years were bliss, the second too often obscured in a fog of grief, Gentleman Jack, and increasingly foolhardy travel for the CIA. But Dan's right: Gainesville is a town I should avoid. The UF soccer season was etched in the record books; I have no particular reason to go there this winter.

My reading about Herzog's visits to Gainesville, with his proposed four-million-dollar gift, convinced me he's secure believing that Maxwell Hunt didn't die of a stroke in D.C. How long it might take him to discover my new identity and location is a persistent thorn. But having Lucinda with me abates the worst of thoughts about both Herzog *and* Isfahani, however much it deepens my concern about her being brought into the umbrella target of these two fanatics.

Our days in Florida passed with Lucinda at least settled on the fringes of her former self. Only a day or so each month brings her flashes of memory loss or confusion. We talk openly about everything—except our future. We assume it will include being together, but we can't seem to confront who we'll be, where we'll live, or what we'll do.

I've come to enjoy guiding in Montana in the summer and spending a leisurely winter in Florida. Recurring flashbacks to teaching law grow increasingly infrequent. But not my recurring images of life with El. That's not something over which I have control. Such memories generally come in dreams that ultimately turn to our last float together, ending only with a trembling, sweating awakening. I can't get back to sleep without getting up and spending an hour or so recovering in the living room, reading in a genre far removed from mysteries or fly fishing.

Lucinda believes my night disturbances are related to my concern about Herzog and Isfahani. Their images do appear but are often obscured by bloody visions of the drift boat and shuttle murders, or El's last moments on the Snake. All versions hang heavily on my spirit and conscience. Nothing begins to reconcile the trauma I've caused Lucinda and the families of those so affected.

When Lucinda finally began to offer thoughts about her future, she's repeatedly stated little more than that she doesn't want to live in New York City. She has an injury-born dependency on me that must be cured if she's to blossom again as a productive individual. Perhaps her recent photographs, taken on the salt-marshes near my cottage, and anticipation of doing more when we return to Montana in early April, are a signal to me to give thought to how her photography might fit in with my life. . . . As unpredictable as it has become.

Applauding our good fit as a twosome is the way we often begin discussions, followed by failing to fully address anything more. Among the few possessions I've carried from Montana, stored in a back corner of a safe in the cottage, is that small, battered, black-velvet-covered box. Next to it is a similar but new box. The bullet that pierced the battered box during the shootout dislodged a two-carat, emerald-cut diamond from its now twisted platinum setting. That bullet has had more effect than those that left me with physical damage.

The thought of the diamond tumbling into the Snake River is something I can live with. If someone finds the diamond the century's first new "prospecting rush" may begin. Inside the new velvet box is a replacement diamond. I've not found the appropriate time and place that configured with my emotions to ask Lucinda if she'll have the ring. Maybe it's for my own selfish benefit; I haven't thought how I'd react if she rejected my offer. Nor have I planned how to proceed if she accepted. For now, our days together have sufficient quality to resemble what might be over the long term.

≈

My urge to pursue some contact with activities at the law college in Gainesville has been satisfied by compulsive reference to its website. If my departure voided the ultimate designation of Maxwell Hunt as an emeritus professor, reading about the professional activities of faculty I knew and admired implants on my psyche a role as surrogate emeritus. I often overlook that the law college is a far different place than it was when I arrived on a muggy August day a quarter-century ago. Among the fifty-four law faculty now listed, only seven were teaching when I joined. More than twenty have been added in the past six years.

≈

Nothing of consequence has arisen that might draw me to Gainesville this winter. Or so I thought until I went online in mid-February.

27

THE CALENDAR OF EVENTS at the law college included a late February dedication of a new wing, donated by a graduate of both the law and agricultural colleges. The donor, Catarina Paris, worked her way upward, crashing through a succession of glass ceilings, to become president of the largest sugar company in America. Amid much controversy, but with uncommon vision, she shifted all the company's South Florida sugar production out-of-state. The lands were sold to the federal government and added to the Everglades National Park. Sugar growing and refining were moved to three poor Caribbean nations.

Paris made millions by her decisions and donated the wing to be located at the law school because she had viewed her law degree as the primary reason for her success. To achieve that success, she had waged and won legal battle after legal battle against unions, counties, and both state and federal government agencies.

The dedication of the Catarina Paris Center for Agricultural Law Studies was merely a week away. Attending attracted me for one reason: Cat Paris was my best student and a superb research assistant in my first years on the faculty as Professor

Maxwell Hunt. I wouldn't be able to talk to her at the dedication—I have to remind myself repeatedly of the consequences of my death from a stroke six years ago. But as least I could sit and applaud her success.

≈

When I told Lucinda I *had* to go to Gainesville, she quietly asked, "Why? Dan Wilson has begged you year-after-year to avoid Gainesville."

"I'd like to go to a dedication of a new law building donated by a former student, Catarina Paris."

"What if she were to recognize you?"

"I'll sit in the last row and won't go near her. I haven't seen her in twenty years. Add to that my identity change, much less aging, plus my new name, and there's no lingering resemblance."

"Take me with you."

"I knew that was coming." Why waste time stepping into a losing argument? "OK. You've never seen Gainesville. We'll do a little 'Maxwell Hunt: This is Your Life' tour—like the celebrity tours in Beverly Hills. Where he lived, favorite bar, intersection where he got a ticket for going through a red light, favorite parking place at the law college, dentist's office where he had his cavities filled, doctor's office where he had his prostate probed—could your day be more exciting?"

"Do I get a personally autographed photo with the tour?"

"He no longer gives out autographed photos; you'll have to search on eBay."

"Since you're such a star, can I tag along as a groupie?"

"Or maybe like a Jackson girl."

"Let's forget the whole thing. *But I'm going.*"

≈

The celebrity tour started the Saturday morning of the dedication by driving through scenic Palatka on the way to Gainesville. The annual crab festival was in full swing. We had breakfast at Angel's Dining Car and stopped at Dunkin' Donuts for an old fashioned donut to take home to Wuff.

The front page of yesterday's Palatka newspaper on Angel's counter told about a Palatka High School senior, with a long record of drug selling and DUI's, who had shot three people in a local bank robbery. On the back page was an article about another Palatka High School senior, with a long record of community service and academic achievement, whose single-parent mom held down three jobs that would help supplement the Stanford scholarship the young man recently received. The two seniors were cousins.

Gainesville's abundant camellias and azaleas gave the city the impression of a small-town community. The city often made lists of the best places to retire, attend cultural or college sports events, or raise children. Usually among the top ten of those lists are seven or eight communities dominated by a university. Bozeman also made these lists. I wondered if Herzog might ever put that together.

Lucinda and I drove past the law buildings and angled down into Golf View, where El and I lived for ten years restoring an old stone house known locally as "the castle." The very house I languished in for another ten years after El died. By the time I "died" of the stroke, the house was in worse shape than when we bought it. It was apparent that in the last six years, under more appreciative ownership, it had been restored to a more glorious past than when I left.

We also drove past Roy Palladio's house. It must recently have been sold by his estate: a moving van suggested new people were moving in. The house had been repainted in garnet and gold, the colors of rival Florida State University, more cynically called Free Shoes University around Gainesville ever since the Tallahassee-based football team "acquired" considerable pairs of free shoes in a way that didn't seem to trouble the FSU administration, but didn't please the NCAA. The new owner of Roy's house was either an FSU graduate or had bet foolishly and lost.

Across the street was a house painted orange and blue, the University of Florida colors. It had been there for Roy's last ten years. Maybe Roy's will designated money to paint his house garnet and gold as postmortem revenge.

≈

An hour before the dedication, Lucinda and I drove back near the law buildings, and parked on the far side of the adjacent tennis courts. I didn't want to chance parking at the law school near where Cat Paris or a former colleague might park. Lucinda was aware, but not pleased, that I placed a Glock in a shoulder holster before we walked toward the law buildings. I was wearing jeans and a lightweight, gray, oversized hip-length jacket that nicely hid the pistol. There have been too many times when I needed a gun, but had left it out of reach, if not at home.

At the east side of the building, I led Lucinda up an ugly, moldy cement stairwell away from which visitors are directed. It emptied onto the third floor, a few dozen steps from my old office. It was no longer empty; a name I didn't recognize was on the door. There was no sign that said Professor Maxwell

Hunt once occupied this office. Walking further down the hall, a young woman in black, carrying a guitar case, crossed in front of us and went into the north stairwell. The program posted throughout the law buildings noted that a small chamber ensemble from the music department would play before the dedication. Strangely, the stairwell she went into was marked as an emergency exit leading down.

Otherwise unmarked, the stairs also led to the roof, where I had occasionally joined colleagues to watch distant Cape Canaveral shuttle launches. The young musician was in a hurry—I didn't have a chance to redirect her to where the musicians were assembling.

Lucinda and I used another set of stairs that descended to the courtyard where the dedication ceremony was already attracting guests. The seats were filling rapidly, but we found two on the side in the last row. We settled in our seats and listened to the chamber group, a quartet finishing the popular *allegro* to Vivaldi's *Four Seasons.* The program noted that next was Schubert's *Trout Quintet.* The quartet would eliminate one violin and add a piano and string bass to play Schubert. Something troubled me; I looked at the program, and noted that the two pieces were the only ones scheduled to be played.

"Lucinda," I said quietly, leaning toward her. "Come with me. *Please* don't ask questions." We slipped out the back area and I rushed her toward the third floor. The upper floors were deserted with the dedication underway.

"Mac, *what's wrong*?" she whispered when we were out of hearing of the assembled crowd.

"That young woman in black carrying the instrument case, who we saw heading toward the stairs to the roof, isn't playing in the chamber group. There's no guitar in the *Four Seasons* or the *Trout Quintet*, and she wasn't sitting with the chamber group."

"Why would she be going to the roof?" Lucinda questioned. "*Oh, my God!* The roof overlooks the courtyard where the dedication's taking place."

We crossed between the two main buildings, which embrace the courtyard north and south. Looking down on the assembled people, we heard the final passages of the musical introduction.

"*Oh, no!* Lucinda . . . count back to the sixth row. Two and three seats in. The person on our left is wearing a white Muslim kaftan. When he turned his head, his jaw looked badly disfigured. Next to him, with sunglasses and a Panama hat, is a man in a white suit."

"I see them. I've never seen them in person, but I'm afraid I know who they are . . . Herzog and Isfahani. Why are they here?"

"Both graduated from the agricultural college but took a law course. I don't think they're up to any good. The university may not know much about Isfahani's activities since graduation. Herzog, if that's him, is well-disguised. . . . We need to get on the roof."

I took her hand and pulled her up the stairs to the roof where the woman with the guitar case had disappeared. Fifteen stairs to the door at the top. *It was closed!* But the lock had been broken. I opened the door slightly. Fifty feet away, at the edge of the roof overlooking the courtyard, from where we could hear the president's voice drift upwards, the young woman was holding a black sniper rifle with a large scope and silencer.

Her guitar case lay open next to her, but there was no guitar in sight. She was beginning to point the rifle over the edge and downward. She hadn't heard us because of the amplified noise from the president's introduction.

I pulled my Glock from my jacket pocket and fitted a silencer. Running across the roof, I needed to cover thirty feet before I was confident of my accuracy. Halfway across I must have startled the woman—she looked around.

When she saw me she quickly turned her head back to the scope and got off three rapid shots toward the assembled group below before my first bullet hit her in the back, causing the weapon to fall into the assembled group below. Screams rose from the ceremony.

I fired three more times as I closed on her. When I reached her there was no doubt she was dead. I grabbed a small cloth bag that was in her open guitar case and ran back to the stairwell.

"Quick, Lucinda!" We flew down the stairs two at a time to the third floor, ran through the hall to the west stairs that took us to a little used door on the far side of the building. Mayhem had broken out at the dedication.

Lucinda and I walked quickly north across the street, passed through the parking area beside Wilbert's store, and were soon at University Avenue. We turned the corner as two screaming police cars approached, turned in behind us, and disappeared toward the law buildings.

"Walk normally, Lucinda. Don't look nervous. If more police cars pass, watch them as though we were out walking on a nice February morning, wondering what all the commotion's about."

In three blocks we reached the car, less than ten minutes after the shooting. We drove nervously at the posted speed through the middle of the campus, down University Avenue, passing at least five more police cars racing to the scene, and were soon east of Gainesville heading for our sanctuary near St. Augustine.

"Mac! What happened? Who was the shooter? Do you think she killed anyone? Could she have been CIA taking out Herzog and Isfahani?"

"*My God!* I never *thought* of that possibility. I may have killed a federal agent. Look in her bag. Any identification?"

"Yes, a passport and some other cards. . . . Her name's . . . Belinda Stamer. She has a Florida driver's license with a Miami address. Plus a U.S. passport. It's a *diplomatic* passport! Mac, could she be CIA? I was joking when I asked about the CIA sanctioning Herzog and Isfahani."

"Damn! I don't know. Turn on the radio. FM 89.1—local public radio. Or AM 850—but I doubt AM 850 interrupts sports for murders. Unless someone shot the football coach."

She turned on 89.1, catching the middle of a sentence: ". . . came from the roof. It isn't clear how many shots were fired. Witnesses have said the gunshots were quiet. The shooter must have used a silencer. There might have been anywhere from four to nine shots. One witness said he thought two different guns were fired. One, likely a rifle; the other, the last to be fired, a pistol."

"Can you see who was shot from where you are, Reynolds?" Apparently he was a reporter at the scene, interrupted by the question of a woman who was in the radio station studio.

Reynolds continued, "The police are moving people back from the stage area. There's an emergency crew placing someone on a stretcher. Two other emergency vehicles have arrived. There's at least one person being attended on the ground. I think that's all. The crew is lifting a stretcher into the back of the emergency vehicle. I can see the victim's face. It's President

Killingsworth! His eyes are shut. There's blood on the ground where they lifted him."

"Reynolds," came the voice again from the studio, "try to work your way toward the podium and see if there's anyone who seems to be in charge who you can interview."

"I'm there, Cynthia. There's a young woman with a name tag that says she's an assistant dean. . . . Miss Jones, Miss Jones! Can you tell our listeners what happened?"

Rebecca Jones was Assistant Dean for Student Services. She often helped with special programs. Sometimes she talked to the media, but never before under these circumstances. "I can't tell you very much. I was sitting on the stage three rows behind the provost and the deans of the two colleges. I saw the president fall forward from the podium and thought he'd had a heart attack. But when he landed on the floor, I saw he was bleeding. I don't know where he was hit, but the blood seemed to be around his shoulder. There was no sharp crack of a weapon. One other person—a guest whom I don't know—was hit in the cheek. It looked like a graze. Someone said there were four more quick shots that sounded a little higher in pitch, but like the first shots were muffled. We don't know much yet."

Ms. Jones began to move away, but Reynolds kept up with her and asked, "Where were the shots from?"

"We think the roof. The police are there now," she answered.

The station voice said, "Get up on the roof and see if you can find out any more."

Reynolds rushed to the roof, where he met a police deputy he knew from covering other crime scenes. Shoving the mike in front of the deputy, Reynolds asked, "Hey, Jimmy, can you answer a few questions for the radio?"

"I'll try, but you really need to talk to our public affairs people."

"Were the shots fired from here?"

"Yes, and look there," the deputy pointed to a body that was being covered. "It's a woman. Probably in her thirties. Four shots in her back. She apparently fired the first three shots. It was a .308 rifle that fell into the crowd. Three shells were ejected. I picked up the casings. We also found four 9 mm shells, twenty feet this side of her. Someone must have come through that door onto the roof, saw her shooting, ran toward her, and shot her four times on the run. Killed her. She has no identification. We'll take prints in a few minutes."

"Thanks Jimmy. I owe you."

"You always owe me, Reynolds. I'll collect someday."

The rest of Reynolds' commentary added little. The station announcer shifted to other news, with a promise to break-in with any new developments. We wouldn't hear them; we were quickly losing the station as we crossed the bridge over the R.R. tracks that divide the rural hamlet of Hawthorne. When we got back to the cottage, we'd go online.

"What do you think happened?" asked Lucinda, a thrilled look tempered by fear.

"Mostly speculation. We know who she is, but not who she's working for. It's fair to assume she was trying to kill the UF president, but our sudden appearance confused and rushed her. Given time, she would easily have killed Killingsworth and maybe others. The law dean? The ag college dean? I don't know. But it doesn't appear to have been a CIA attempt to kill Herzog or Isfahani."

"Do you think either Herzog or Isfahani were involved? They were in the audience."

"If they were, they set it up, and the shooter, Belinda Stamer, whoever she is, was working for them."

"Carrying a U.S. diplomatic passport, Mac?"

"We don't know whether it's forged. I'll send her bag to Dan Wilson. Let the CIA handle it rather than giving it to the local police."

"The police will be looking for the person who shot Stamer. Did *you* leave any prints?"

"I hope not. I didn't touch the door, nor did you. I pulled her bag out from the guitar case without touching anything."

"What about the shell casings from your Glock?"

"I never load a weapon without using gloves and first wiping the bullets clean."

Lucinda was calm, considering the circumstances. I'm pretty sure she thrived on the action. "Lucinda, how're you feeling? This is pretty stressful."

"I'm fine," she said quietly. Grabbing my arm, she added, "I'm an old hand at shootings when you're around. And this time I didn't even get one scratch!"

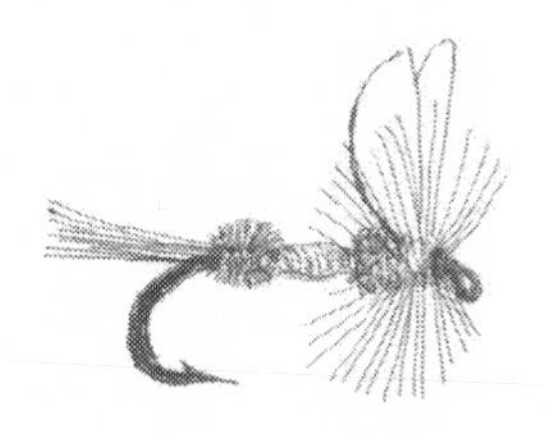

28

WE DIVERTED TO ST. AUGUSTINE for a mahi-mahi seafood dinner under the arbor of Kingfish Grill at Camachee Cove. Our rapid pulse rates diminished with the disappearing sun.

Driving home south paralleling the Intracoastal Waterway, windows down to absorb the pungent smell of the salt flats during a full-moon's expansive low tide, my cell phone rang. It was from D.C. "Hi, Dan."

"How did we *ever* get involved with you? You're in more shootouts than any of our own agents. It's on national news here."

"Why do you think *I* was involved? Lucinda and I are in Crescent Beach near my cottage. We just finished a relaxing dinner in St. Augustine."

"We *know* you went to Gainesville. Any time you're in Gainesville, there's likely to be trouble. I assume *you* killed the shooter?"

"I guess so. I didn't hang around to find out if she was dead. I picked up her bag. I'll overnight it to you in the morning. The shooter's name is Belinda Stamer. She carried a U.S. *diplomatic* passport. Her driver's license lists Miami as her residence. Is she one of yours?"

"You don't really believe that, do you? But we know a lot about Belinda Stamer. Any guesses?"

"Herzog and Isfahani were in the audience. My gut says she was working for Herzog."

"The passport and driver's license are forgeries. She's been using a false name while she's been in the U.S. the past two months. We tracked her until a week ago, when she left D.C. in a private plane. Her real name is María-Martina *Herzog*! She's Herzog's niece. Or she was. Herzog can't be happy; she was his favorite niece. One of the few members of the Herzog family who idolized him and didn't dispute his lifestyle."

"Meaning Juan Pablo's going to want to know who killed her."

"Yes . . . and seek revenge!"

"How long before he links her killing to Maxwell Hunt?"

"Herzog has to be careful. If his niece is correctly identified, the Florida police will want to pick him up. But I'll bet he's in flight right now, with Isfahani. Maybe already home in Guatemala."

"What do you suggest for Lucinda and me?"

"What I suggested to you last year, last month, and last week! What you ignored last year, last month, and last week. *Stay in your cottage.* I mean that. Let Lucinda, or even better your caretaker, do your food shopping. At least while we see how this plays out over the next few days."

≈

It played out strangely. The *Gainesville Gazette* had the most coverage, although many national papers carried at least a brief paragraph about the dramatic shootout. Several days after the shooting, the Gainesville paper printed an update:

The attempt on the life of UF President Alfred Killingsworth three days ago is thought by local police to have been an attempt to kill the president as well as the two deans, Hobart Perry of the law college and George Mudd of the agricultural college. If the assassin had not been killed before she could get off more accurate shots, she probably would have succeeded in her grisly mission.

Who was the hero of the day? That remains unknown. Man or woman, the hero apparently was running toward the assassin firing a silenced pistol. The shots were accurate—the first shot likely killed the assassin instantly.

There was no identification on the assassin. Finger prints were taken, but her prints had been surgically removed, suggesting a professional assassin. The FBI is investigating.

The "hero of the day" remained secluded, as Dan requested and Lucinda enforced.

"You *can* shoot after all!" Lucinda commented with faint praise. "Even on the run! The paper says the very first bullet killed Herzog's niece. How were you certain she wasn't a CIA assassin trying to take out Herzog and Isfahani?"

"I wasn't. But the CIA wouldn't do it that way. An agent could have sat down next to Juan Pablo, injected him with ricin-filled pellets, and walked away. It would have killed him in a few minutes. The same way Bulgarian dissident Georgi Markov was killed in London, the pellet injected by an umbrella tip.

"Using a high powered rifle in a crowd wasn't wise. I thought the assassin had to be shooting at someone on the speakers' platform, where the target was clear and the people weren't squeezed together. You and I know Herzog was angered by the president's rejection of his proposed gift. He has to be the main suspect."

"So he brings along his niece and throws her to the wolves?" Lucinda asked.

"I think he believed they'd get away with it. Now I wonder if he'll assume Maxwell Hunt was involved."

"No reason to think that," Lucinda responded encouragingly. "The president's office said he receives threats from cranks. Not often, but they come with the job. I'd like to see his office announce that they had university police on the roof who killed Herzog's niece. That would take the focus off you."

"I'll talk to Dan and see if he can put some pressure on the president."

≈

By mid-March, the president's office had responded. Official press releases stated that a university police force deputy shot the assassin, but would remain nameless to protect the deputy against any attempts at revenge by whoever was behind the attempted shooting of President Killingsworth. Who was behind the shooting, if the opinions of the president and law dean were made public, was without doubt Herzog. But because the president was recovering nicely and the shooter was dead, no one much cared about further inquiries. Spring football practice was starting. The annual Orange & Blue scrimmage was the next scheduled campus spectacle.

≈

Perhaps it wasn't fully true that no one cared about the identity of the shooter—Juan Pablo Herzog very much cared.

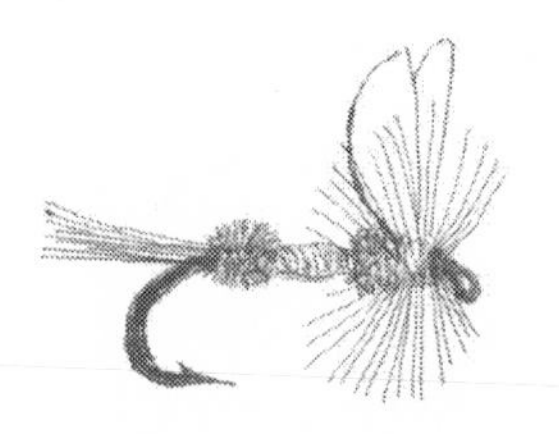

29

THE DEDICATION SHOOTING lasted less than thirty seconds. It sent an angry Herzog and Isfahani walking away quickly from the ceremony—discouraged but determined. They drove a car rented under the name Hernando Gomez to the Ocala airport where Herzog's private jet waited. Four hours later they were in Guatemala City, sitting in Herzog's elegant condo, sipping Guatemala's prized musty Limited Edition Ron Zacapa Centenario from glasses hand-blown in a tiny highland village. But the touches of fine living did not compensate for the loss of Herzog's niece.

"What went wrong?" asked Herzog emotionally.

"The police apparently had deputies on the roof. A product of our troubled times, Juan Pablo—excessive security. You know the UF president had received threatening calls. The police were likely hidden behind air-conditioning units. They waited until your niece María was ready to shoot and killed her. Actually, they were a little late, she got off three shots—it almost cost the university president his life."

"I don't believe that, Abdul. I think Maxwell Hunt had something to do with the killing."

"Aren't you letting your emotions and hatred for Hunt govern your thinking? He *died,* after you beat him in the hotel room here. Can't you accept that?"

"He didn't die from my beating, Abdul. It wasn't life threatening. And I don't believe he had a stroke. He was a healthy man in his early fifties. . . . I want to share something with you I learned yesterday from a member of our embassy in Washington. A person loyal to me. Do you believe *you* were shot by Israel's Ben Roth?"

"Yes, of course. My al-Qaeda colleagues have been searching for him since the shooting. Ben Roth is very elusive. But we will find him, and when we do, we will. . . ."

Herzog interrupted, "What would you say if I told you that Maxwell Hunt shot you?"

"Impossible! You are more delusional than I thought. Why would you even imagine that?"

"For the sake of my argument, Abdul, assume Maxwell Hunt didn't die of a stroke. How would he have felt after recovering in D.C. and returning to teach at Gainesville?"

"That he should frequently look over his shoulder for you. You promised to kill him if you discovered he was working for the CIA. He was rescued by them. That's probably enough proof for you."

"If the CIA were convinced I was determined to kill Hunt, how might they react?"

"Try to kill you first."

"Or?"

"Hide Professor Hunt!" Isfahani rose from his chair, and stared out the condo's window overlooking the mountains. His brow was as furrowed as his disfigured face allowed. He poured another drink, a habit he began during his recovery and which troubled him at prayer time.

"How could he teach, Abdul, or return to live in Gainesville? Or move to another law school, even as far as California or Maine? I could find him in any law faculty directory. I tell you this did not happen. I have searched."

"So what other choice did the CIA and Hunt have?"

"Perhaps a federal program like witness protection. A process that helps compromised agents by providing a new identity and a new location."

"Juan Pablo! It cannot be! You're suggesting that Maxwell Hunt is living somewhere in the United States under a different name and working as someone other than a teacher of law?"

"That's exactly what I'm suggesting. It has been on my mind a great deal the past few months."

Isfahani sat again. His brow was moist. He slowly ran his hand along the distorted, scarred pathways on his face. Both men took long sips from their glasses, seeking immediate pleasure in the sweetness of the rum.

Herzog told Isfahani more of the details and conversations about his proposed gift and request for a report on Maxwell Hunt's death, and how the UF President and dean had turned down the gift and persistently refused to disclose what they had discovered about the death.

"Juan Pablo, we *must* find out how he is now called. Where he lives. And what he does."

"Exactly, Abdul."

"What name do you think he would take?" Isfahani inquired.

"It's speculation to guess. Perhaps a similar name, so he would react when someone called his former name. But it would be more appropriate to take a different name— a name to which he would adapt when responding to a greeting."

"Maybe he would keep his initials?"

"Whatever benefits that might offer, Abdul, it would also increase the likelihood of being identified. I do not think he will have the initials MWH."

"Must he have three initials, Juan Pablo?"

"No, Abdul. Most Americans appear to have a middle name; it is more cultural than required. Persons of the Catholic faith nearly always adopt the name of a saint as a middle name. But he could have just two, or he could have four. I would expect it would be two or three."

"He has been called Maxwell, or Max, for many years. Would he not want something similar such as Matt, or Mac?"

"Again, Abdul, the trade-off in adopting something similar is the possible compromising of his new identity. For example, I think he wouldn't want to be called Mac Lunt; it's too close to Max Hunt. There are many variations. . . . I do not think we can come close by *guessing* how he might now be called. Maybe determining his place of residency will be easier. Do you think he would remain living in Gainesville?"

"No, Juan Pablo. He lived there for twenty years. He must know hundreds of people, within and outside the university community. But maybe he has remained in Florida—in some other city? You know how much he and his wife El loved living in the warm South."

"Didn't he come from the Northeast?" asked Herzog. "Might he have chosen to return there?"

"He came from Connecticut. But I recall him often saying he disliked cold weather. I think he lives somewhere in the South, but that could be from the Southeast to the Southwest."

"That covers many states, including large states like Texas."

"Juan Pablo, I once talked to him about boats. He said he could never live away from salt water. But he and his wife El also enjoyed annual fishing trips to Wyoming. Could Wyoming be a place he would choose to live?"

Herzog stood, took a sip of rum, set the glass down, and looked out the window, wondering whether he and Isfahani were on an endless track that led nowhere. "I don't think Wyoming held any attraction. After El died, he never went back to the West to fish. In fact, he never *fished* again. . . . Abdul, which do you think more affected his decision? Would he choose to live based on the kind of work that attracted him or choose where he wanted to live and find acceptable work?"

"That assumes he *wishes* to work, Juan Pablo, or that he must work to support himself."

"I think we need to investigate his Connecticut background thoroughly, including whether he inherited or saved enough to live on? If he did, he can live anywhere and work or not as he wishes. . . . Abdul, I wonder if he chose some position that makes use of his extensive legal training."

"I doubt that he's *teaching* law," said Isfahani. "At least not in the United States. There cannot be that many white, Anglo males who are in their early 50s and are teaching international law. Maybe a hundred."

"I agree. The same would be true of moving to Canada. But I doubt he would have done that because of the cold weather. If we are convinced he insisted on continuing to teach law at some level, it would have to be in the South. That narrows the search."

"Couldn't he teach law at an undergraduate school rather than at a law school? Perhaps foreign policy law in a political science department?"

"Yes, of course, Abdul, but I think he preferred the maturity of the students in law school. He once told me it was most enjoyable to teach in the *graduate* level law programs because so many of the JD law students were still immature and more interested in partying at their former fraternities and sororities than preparing for the following day's classes."

"What other jobs for law-trained people are there in the United States? He could *practice* law most anywhere."

"Abdul, I'm quite sure he was admitted to practice in Connecticut. He could take the bar exam in any state where he might want to practice. But there's one obstacle—he would have to provide a great deal of background information to any state bar admission process. He would not want to disclose any information about himself before he assumed his new identity. But he would have to explain his existence as Maxwell Hunt. Any job that required providing evidence of having a law degree would be difficult for him. . . . Of course, he might *work* in a court, but in a job that didn't require proof of a law degree.

"I believe that Maxwell Hunt is not engaged in any job related to law," concluded Isfahani. "And I eliminate anything to do with fishing, but include such work as teaching music or soccer. He played a woodwind—the clarinet or something. And he was an excellent soccer player in college. As to location, I believe he lives in one of the Southern states. But that hasn't gotten us very far. . . . It did make me think of something—do you imagine his *appearance* has been changed?"

"In one respect you may have answered that, Abdul. If people believe that Ben Roth shot you, but it was really Hunt, wouldn't he have had to pass as Roth?"

"But who actually saw him at the time I was shot?"

"Unfortunately, no one who knows Roth. The suspicion that he did the shooting may have been a CIA ruse to convince people he tried to kill you."

"It's possible, is it not," pondered Isfahani, "that Maxwell Hunt could have undergone minor cosmetic surgery that made him resemble Ben Roth?"

"Certainly. If he has reasonably similar facial characteristics. Also his hair style and color can be changed. Including sideburns, moustache, or a beard. Plus wearing eyeglasses or hearing aids. And, importantly, his skin could be darkened with makeup to give him the more Mediterranean complexion of Ben Roth."

"I assume it would have been possible to make some minor changes to Hunt's nose, ears, and maybe even his eyelids."

"You're right, Abdul. . . . I suggest we put together some composites as a start."

"But, let's be realistic. We have no idea how he calls himself. We have only some idea where he might live, based on eliminating a few places where he most likely would *not* live. We don't know what he might be doing, even whether he's working. Finally, we don't know what he looks like—Maxwell Hunt, Ben Roth, or someone entirely different."

"What we do agree about, Abdul, is that Maxwell Hunt *is alive.*"

"There are people who know the answers to these questions," Isfahani exclaimed excitedly. "CIA agents who worked with Maxwell Hunt in establishing his new identity. Do you think we can reach them?"

"I don't rule that out. Money causes people to betray the most sacred of trusts. I have one person who is loyal to me working in the American embassy in Guatemala. He's not part of the CIA mission. He's in cultural affairs. I'll talk to him."

"Meanwhile, Juan Pablo, it's to our advantage to visit Gainesville and talk to people around the law school and others in the community who knew Maxwell Hunt—neighbors, musician friends, church contacts, soccer booster-club members. You went to the funeral of Maxwell's friend, Professor Palladio, a year or so ago. That kind of presence is helpful. We also know Maxwell liked watching soccer. We might be wise to become soccer fans. . . . But remember—you are very likely wanted for questioning about the shooting of the UF president. You must be careful. And for me, no more wearing white kaftans when I visit the United States. To find Maxwell Hunt, I am more than willing to dress like an infidel!"

"I, too, am capable of disguises, Abdul. Your mentioning the funeral brought a thought to mind. At the cemetery, I watched someone kneeling by a grave, perhaps a hundred feet from the service for Professor Palladio. The figure was all in black, including a hat and sunglasses. Although he was kneeling at another grave, he seemed focused on Palladio's burial. I wonder if he might have been Maxwell Hunt?"

≈

"If he were, Juan Pablo, we will finally witness *his* funeral."

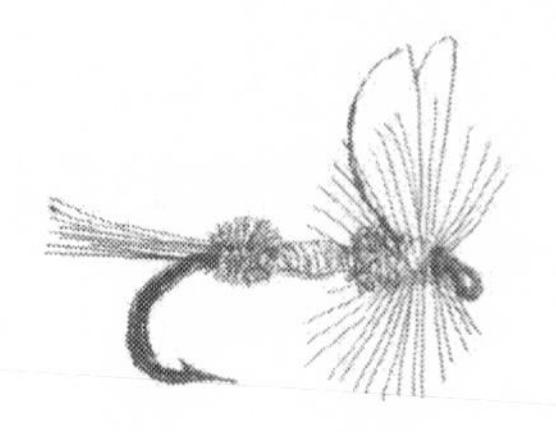

30

LUCINDA AND I passed the remainder of the winter in seclusion at my Florida cottage. We often rehashed the events at the dedication in Gainesville and speculated on how it affected our attempt to work out a life together.

The solitude was not unwelcome. We kayaked in the adjacent salt-marshes, silently paddling around bends to come upon scores of birds—our favorites the flocks of roseate spoonbills and occasional mated pairs of American oystercatchers. We caught spotted sea trout, redfish, flounder, and even snook near the northern limits of their migration. Lucinda cooked the fish in ways unimaginable to me. She learned that the greater danger to her than Herzog was allowing me in the kitchen. It slowly was renovated under her guidance, and I even bought a new oven.

Some very good days passed. Lucinda progressed in her health—most of the last vestiges of amnesia had disappeared—and in her photography, which continued to convince me that her instincts in composition were more God-given than learned. Less and less frequently our conversations included references to Herzog and Isfahani. But it was hard not to find a conversation, if long enough, that didn't ultimately introduce their omnipresence in our lives.

"Lucinda," I asked one evening when we were sitting on the cottage porch, watching the mauve sky in the east over the Atlantic that was generated from behind us by the setting sun, "are you convinced that Herzog believes Maxwell didn't die? At least not of a stroke as announced?"

"I am, but I'd rather talk about more pleasant topics."

"Me, too. About you. That's more pleasant than talking about Max, much less Herzog. Do you think he has any idea I'm living in sin with an investment banker?"

"I'm sure he thinks it's a sin you're still alive—a sin he must correct. I don't know about the investment banker part."

"What I'm getting at is risking *you*. Could he find me through you, which means he'd kill you as well?"

"I think he has to learn who *you* are before I come into the picture. You were alone at Roy Palladio's funeral, the only time he might have seen you. I don't believe he knows you were at the dedication. He was focused on his niece shooting the president. . . . Would he have thought you had any reason to be there?"

"I don't think so. I've never taught or consulted on international agriculture issues. There was no reason for me to go to the dedication. We went because Catarina Paris was my former student—long before Herzog was at UF. He would not have known about my feelings about Cat."

"He may not be as much of a threat as you believe, Mac. And he has to learn who and where you are before I'm possibly involved."

"I guess you're right. . . . How about a pact—not a word of Herzog or Isfahani for two months—through May?"

"Promise!. . . Are we going through Indiana on our way west?"

"I think we should. Your mother seems increasingly reconciled to your being with me. Why don't we drive directly to Indiana? I'll stay in the background and you visit your mother for a few days? Then we'll head west."

"You'll be impossible to be with if you have to hang around waiting while I do mother-daughter things. Why don't you stay as long as you don't fidget, then drive to Montana with Wuff. I'll get a flight a week or so later to Bozeman. Will you two come and meet me at the airport?"

"Sure, unless there's a good hatch on the Yellowstone."

"You'd leave me waiting because of some bugs?"

"Not for *Baetis tricaudatus* or *Ephemerella inermis.* But if there's a good *Tricorythodes minutus* hatch, the choice will be hard to make."

"Is this what I'm going to have to live with?"

"It gets worse when the stoneflies are out . . . I think your flight should get in around dinner time. I'll take you to the Montana Rib and Chop House in Livingston on the way home."

≈

Mrs. Elizabeth Parker-Smith Lang was a different person. Lucinda had kept in touch by frequent phone conversations from Florida. From what I overheard before I left, the relationship had turned a corner. Mrs. Lang had retained the lawyer who'd worked with Lucinda drafting the trusts she'd established a year ago to assure her mother and siblings were cared for if any tragedy befell Lucinda. Living with me has proven pretty hazardous.

When Wuff and I reached Paradise Valley the last week in April, it was sunny and mid-60s. Spring fishing was underway;

the day I faced with uncertainty was not far off—my first float of the season. *If* I had any scheduled. I'd avoided calling the outfitters I guide for.

Approaching Livingston I called Erin, wondering whether the Shuttle Gals were still in business. Erin suggested we ask Ken to join us and have lunch when I arrived.

31

ERIN AND KEN WERE WAITING for me in Livingston. We all ordered bison burgers, the bison likely freshly killed a few days earlier. Maybe shot wandering onto some cattle rancher's spread a mile or so north of the park in Paradise Valley.

"How's the winter been . . . too cold for crimes?" I asked.

"Montanans find a way," Ken answered. "No murders, but plenty of the usual drudgery—domestic violence, snowmobile DUIs, drunks fighting, game poaching, and countless moving violations."

"Anyone arrested for driving too *slowly* on 89?"

"We have only one Park County resident who does that, and he spends the winters in Florida."

Erin broke in. "Enough about Macduffy's strange driving habits. I'm sure he wants to hear about the investigations."

"Not solved yet! What have *you* two been doing all winter?" I asked.

"What law-abiding Montanans do," said Erin. "Shovel snow. Jump-start cars. Chop wood. Shovel more snow. Clean guns. Shoot moose. Shovel even more snow. Try to stay alive. Not many drift boats floating the Yellowstone. What did you two do while *you* were away?"

"Drank Gentleman Jack on the cottage porch in the salt marshes. Stood off rattlesnakes. Ate stone crabs and pompano. Walked on the beach in the moonlight. Slept late. Turned on the heat for two days in January when the temperature threatened to drop into the thirties. That's thirty *above*. It was a harsh winter. But we persevered and survived."

"I don't want to hear another word," mumbled Erin. "But about the investigations, there's been nothing new at all. Victoria Montoya is not at her ranch. We got a warrant and looked. Only two caretakers were living on the property. They looked about fourteen! Didn't speak a word of English. We didn't want to raise any immigration issues that might affect the murder investigation, so we never checked their papers. They weren't even plowing the place—it was snowed in. . . . As far as Markel is concerned, we haven't developed zilch! It's *damned* frustrating!"

Ken interrupted, sensing Erin was losing her usual composure. "I hate to admit it, but we're almost at the point of agreeing with Jimbo Shaw—that Victoria Montoya did *both* killings, fled to Mexico where she's out of reach—and that's the end of it."

"That's hard to accept, Ken. They were horrible killings. I hate to start floating the Yellowstone without knowing who killed Julie and Olga. Plus, worrying about the other Shuttle Gals. Maybe I should do wade guiding this season."

"I thought you'd have trouble hiring shuttle people this coming season," Ken replied, "but I was wrong. You'll be surprised—and pleased—to hear that the remaining three Shuttle Gals are not only going to work this season, but they're going to work for you! And–they've hired two new women."

"Great to hear . . . but intimidating. You can imagine how I'll feel on my first river float, wondering if there'll be a crucified, mutilated body on my trailer when I finish."

"There won't be," said Ken. "We're going to watch the shuttles. Shaw approved some funds to cover the extra expense. Where you may have some trouble is with a few outfitters. Word is some won't book you this year, at least until the murders are solved."

"I don't blame them, Ken. It's another reason to wade guide until the summer season on the Yellowstone is underway. I'd like to take some clients into the park early—work the Madison, the Gibbon, and the Firehole before that river heats up."

"There's a movement among some West Yellowstone guides to have the Park Service license guides in the park," noted Ken. "And to set territories. West Yellowstone guides are claiming exclusive rights on the three rivers you mentioned; Jackson guides responded demanding all the Grand Teton water, including the Wyoming portions of the Snake, the Lewis, and the upper Yellowstone; Paradise Valley and Livingston guides are claiming the Yellowstone from the park boundary north fifty miles to Livingston; and Cooke City guides want the Lamar River and Slough Creek. The rest of the park, including the Yellowstone from the lake to the canyon, would be open to any of the guides who've received one of the specific territory licenses."

"Won't happen," I responded. "Some of the West Yellowstone guides have tried this before. But the more prominent guides who rely on reputation rather than government protection have never liked the idea. They want to *compete* for clients. Not be told what they can do by state legislatures or county commissions. . . . I'm mainly concerned with the Paradise Valley guides. They're a good bunch. I don't want *my* problems to hurt their livelihoods."

"Macduffy," said Erin, annoyed at me for some reason I wouldn't attempt to fathom, "you've been here an hour, talked about everything on earth, but never said a word about you and Lucinda."

The rest of the lunch was about Lucinda. A little about Indiana. A lot about our time together in Florida.

≈

It was a welcome lunch; not a thought came to mind about Herzog or Isfahani.

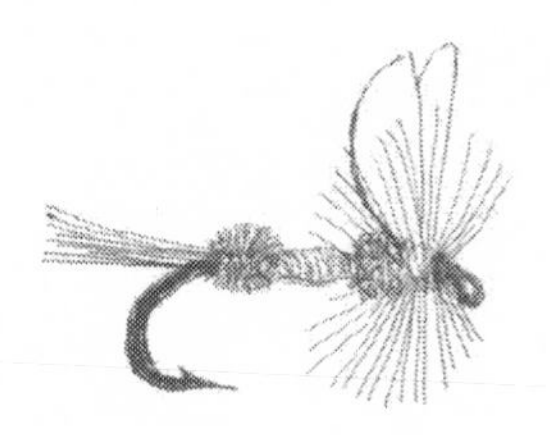

32

LATE SPRING AND EARLY SUMMER GUIDING, limited to wading some of the spring creeks, feeder streams of the Yellowstone, and portions of the Gallatin, kept me out of the news. I reduced stress by taking only one client at a time, or a twosome whom I knew fished together compatibly. I wanted no more Park Salisbury "three percenters," the more or less three in a hundred who convert a day of great expectations into an introduction to Dante's *Inferno.* On days without clients, I spent hours prepping my two drift boats, mostly the *Osprey*, whose mahogany, ash, and oak impose maintenance demands far more time consuming than the plastic version that plays at best second fiddle in my boat garage.

I couldn't control the dates of my first floats on the Yellowstone River in Paradise Valley. It's not decided by outfitters or guides or anxious clients calling to book floats. The gods of the Absaroka and Gallatin mountains mandate when they will begin the snow-melt and how long they'll send the water, rocks, and mud tumbling down to obscure the water's clarity and impose on the river's velocity. Sometimes the river isn't floatable until mid-July.

Financial needs chase most of the waiting guides elsewhere, west to float the Madison, south even beyond Big Sky as far as Henry's Fork . . . or even to the South Fork of the Snake in Idaho. Do the math on whether it's financially sensible to tow a drift boat from Paradise Valley to the Palisades Dam to float the South Fork for a few days.

Most guides drive a gas- or diesel-guzzling pickup, and the price of fuel hasn't been going down. Some outfitters and guides are adding fuel surcharges to the regular fee, which is about $475 for a full day. But a Paradise Valley based guide, taking a client on the Snake, can't add a surcharge that makes the total more than using a guide based in Jackson Hole. If he does add a surcharge, the client will book at an outfitter in Jackson, which he most likely did in the first place anyway. If I do go to help in Jackson Hole, I like to stay a few days—if I can arrange multiple bookings. So it's usually float the Madison or wade until the Yellowstone clears.

While I was pondering such worldly issues, my cell phone rang. I put down the wax buffer I was using on *Osprey*.

"Macduff here."

"Atwood *here*. This is Marge. Got a minute?"

"For you, of course." Marge is one of the original Shuttle Gals. She's taken over making the daily shuttle arrangements.

"You know I'm doing the scheduling. And I wanted to tell you, I'll do the shuttles for you personally this season. I don't want to risk the other gals."

"I don't want to risk *you*," I responded firmly. "Why so determined? Trying to be the canary in the mine?"

"You know my ex is now with the Helena police. He gave up guiding. One thing he did real good was teach me to shoot. Rifle, pistol, cross-bow, compound bow . . . even had me play paintball. I have a little .32 Smith & Wesson I'm going to carry. Where I can get to it real quick, in a shoulder holster, not in the bottom of a purse. Or like you, in the bottom of a guide bag in a closed compartment on the drift boat. If I am the canary, this canary is *carrying!*"

"That hurt. Just this morning, on each boat I rigged a holster to the inner the lid of the locker next to my rowing seat. I can get to the gun in a couple of seconds. I don't know how word spreads, but rumors of my being slow on the draw are greatly exaggerated." I wanted to tell her how good my shots were at Gainesville, but that opens a world unknown to my Montana friends.

"When do you think summer floats will start on the Yellowstone?" Marge inquired.

"I have a dozen unexpected bookings, beginning the third week of July. I'm a little surprised I have *any*, but I guess people feel the killings have run their course, and they probably want to talk about the murders during the float—gather good stories for cocktail parties. Maybe I'll sign autographs at the end of every float we survive."

≈

"Well . . . call me when you need me."

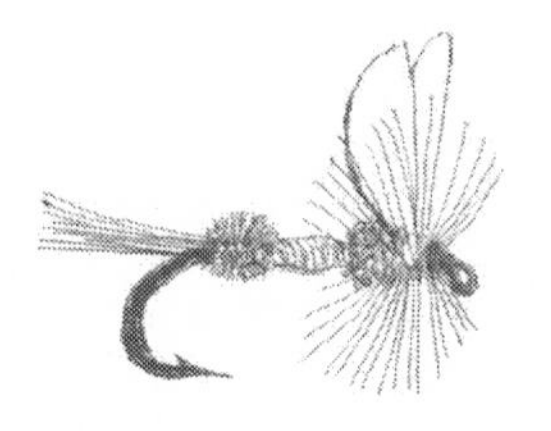

33

JULY ARRIVED PREMATURELY—at least more quickly than to my liking. I wasn't looking forward to being a fly fishing guide second and a tour guide of murder scenes first. But time affirmed I worried too much: late July and August passed composedly. My floats went smoothly. Ken and Erin said I was watched by deputies; I never saw any of them. One distraction was enjoying the best hopper season in years. The brown trout were waiting. The clients were thrilled. Hoppers jumped, lurched, catapulted, or just tumbled from the high grass banks to their death in the deceptively tranquil water.

By mid-September, I'd completed three dozen floats on the Yellowstone without incident. Marge provided the shuttle service for every float. I thought she seemed a little weary and needed some time off. I was right. She called me late one September evening while Lucinda and I were picnicking at Mallard's Rest campground amid the spectacular fall colors of Paradise Valley.

"I need a few days off," said Marge's tired voice. "A dozen shuttles a day, seven days a week, for two months. I'm bushed. But I'll probably help a little with the new gals."

"Take a break. Can someone else do a shuttle for me tomorrow? I have a friend from Jackson coming to stay with me tonight. He owns an outfitting shop and I owe him. I'll use *Osprey* . . . I haven't taken her on a float in a month."

"I'll have someone there. Where you floating?"

One of the best—to Carter Bridge. Probably from Loch Leven, maybe even Mill Creek."

"You're kidding. Or compulsive. Your friend must be special. Mill Creek to Carter is nearly twenty miles."

"I want to show him a lot of the river. We'll start at daybreak and swap time at the oars. He doesn't know this valley. We're wading some creeks upstream off Mill Creek when he gets here today."

"Good luck. See you early."

≈

John Kirby arrived from Jackson with a couple of hours of sunlight to spare. We immediately headed up Mill Creek to one of the feeder streams.

"How's the Snake in Grand Teton fishing this year?" I asked.

"Slow start this season. But terrific now. Until late July, we all had to fish from Wilson Bridge down or drive to the Salt River in Star Valley. Sometimes over to Idaho to the South Fork. Too much driving. But since the Snake between Jackson Lake and Moose finally cleared, I've floated the river almost every other day. Including your favorite section—Deadman's Bar to Moose. I'm beginning to think that section was named after you. . . . It's a difficult row this year. There are huge strainers and some formidable sweepers. It's an obstacle course. And the strainers aren't only along the banks. Many of them have piled up in the middle of the river. But the view floating along the foot of the Grand Tetons is the best."

"We're at a good spot on this creek to start. If you get in the creek here and wade close to the edge, you can fish the bends upstream for twenty yards. Then you'll come to a pool where some trees have piled up. Around the trunks there're usually some small cutthroats—at most about eight inches. I've seen Moose and bear here recently, so watch more than your fly."

As he disappeared behind some brush and stepped into the creek, I called, "No nymphs. Dry flies only."

"House rule? Montana rule?" he called back.

"*Your* rule," I said. "The last time we fished, I put on a Copper John I'd tied and showed it to you. You bit it off and threw it overboard."

"I have nothing against nymphs. I just prefer them about 5'3" with brown hair."

"Catch and release?"

"Allowed to keep one. And I've kept the best."

≈

I walked a quarter-mile further up the road to a usually productive run that parallels the road—a fifteen yard long, straight section that broadens and has a few drops. I'm always amazed I catch fish almost anywhere along this section, but not always in the same runs or pools. There are small cutthroats in the riffles, the inner and outer bends, and hanging in front and behind the few large boulders. I haven't talked much about this brief stretch with friends or clients. I usually don't bring clients here, unless they're from out of the area.

Over the next hour, John closed the distance between us and joined me with a half-hour of light left. The first thing I did when I saw him coming toward me was check to make sure I didn't have a nymph on. I didn't need to check; I hadn't touched a nymph fishing with him since he tossed my Copper John. At least it had a barbless hook. It has probably attracted a hundred cutthroats as it rolled along the bottom of the Snake with the current, maybe all the way from where he threw it in close to Deadman's Bar downstream to the Palisades Reservoir.

≈

When we returned to my cabin, there was some kind of ad tacked on my front door. I thought it was a note from Lucinda, who went to Bozeman for lunch with Wanda Groves and Judge Amy Becker. Wanda's my attorney who's become a friend of Lucinda; Amy's the judge who asked me to rescue Wuff—more like coerced me by conspiring with Wuff to find her a home. But the note on my door wasn't from Lucinda. I wondered who went on my porch and tacked it to the door.

I'm amazed that so many Montanans can't read—there are clear signs at my gate and along the road politely informing visitors they aren't welcome unless specifically invited. I've come home to find flyers advertising free delivery of pizza, roof-gutter leaf-cleaning, and church fundraising events stuck in the door or even stapled to a porch support.

Closer to my front door, I could see it didn't read like a sales or solicitation pitch:

NO FISHING ON THE YELLOWSTONE RIVER. ANYONE FOUND FISHING WILL FACE SERIOUS CONSEQUENCES.

REMEMBER THE DRIFT BOAT SHUTTLE SERVICE MURDERS. YOU COULD BE NEXT. PEOPLE AGAINST RECREATIONAL ANGLING (PARA)

I called the Park County Sheriff's office and asked for Ken or Erin, or, if they weren't in, Jimbo Shaw. I got Shaw.

"Chief Detective James W. Shaw speaking."

"Hey, Jimbo. It's Macduff. Sorry for calling late. I've just come back from fishing Mill Creek with a friend and found a poster on my door." I read it to him. "You heard of any others?"

"Yep. Marge Atwood called me a half hour ago. One was left on her gate. More in the mail boxes of Pam Synder and Lucy Denver. They're the three remaining original Shuttle Gals. The two new gals got them as well. And other shuttle services also. The outfitter you do some floats for in Emigrant had one taped on his door—he never saw the person who put it there."

"It says PARA , Jimbo. With a pretty clear threat. Is Helga Markel back in our area?"

"Don't know. But we have to think PARA may be active. This is a threat to fishing, directed not only to the Shuttle Gals. I'm trying to track down Helga Markel and the professor she ran off with. I hadn't followed up on her before because I'm convinced Victoria Montoya did the two murders. Think you better cancel your trip tomorrow?"

"No, I know you're watching the shuttles. I carry a Glock in the boat. I'll loan one to my friend who's here from Jackson to fish. . . . Oh! By the way, Marge Atwood is bushed and called to say another Shuttle Gal will be doing my shuttle tomorrow.

Could be Pam or Lucy or one of the two new gals they've added."

When Shaw hung up, I called Marge. "Jimbo Shaw said you received one of the notices from PARA. Want to cancel tomorrow?"

"The hell I do," Marge responded. "No one's going to drive us out of business. Pam or her new partner, Jilly Conner, will do your float. I'll drive with them in the morning to talk to Jilly."

"See you tomorrow at Mill Creek if you're there early. I'll tell you then or leave a note about how long a stretch we plan to float. It depends on the weather."

34

JOHN AND I ROSE EARLY, tried unsuccessfully not to wake Lucinda or Wuff, downed coffee on the porch while watching the sunlight unfold along the creek, ate a light breakfast, left the cabin pulling *Osprey* behind my SUV, and stopped for gas at Emigrant just as Marge, Pam, and one of the new gals, Jilly, arrived with a similar fueling urgency. Refueling is neither a subsidized entitlement nor an act wisely allowed to linger very long after the fuel gauge warning light has blinked on. Compared to Florida, Montana gas stations are few and far between.

"Hey, meet Jilly," Marge said to us.

"You're a brave woman to work with this group," I said, hoping my sense of humor was shared.

"You armed and ready?" asked Pam. "We're doing *your* shuttle. Jilly's driving the van. I'm riding shotgun while Marge drives your SUV with the trailer." From her van Pam pulled a 12 gauge Remington pump that held five shells and had seen lots of use in the field. "Marge has her S&W. What've you two got?"

"I have a Glock. John has my new .40 Sig P226. We're ready for PARA."

"You really floating as far as Carter Bridge?" Marge asked.

"It's nice weather. I think we'll make it to Carter from Mill Creek. Maybe dawn to dusk! A long run—we won't stop and wade."

"Your SUV and trailer will be waiting," said Marge. "I'm buying Pam and Jilly breakfast at Howlin' Hounds—we'll be along in a while. Jilly's doing a few other shuttles."

"We're off," I said. "We need to be on the river quickly if we expect to make Carter Bridge by dark."

35

AN HOUR EARLIER and ten miles south of Emigrant, five Mexican boys, ranging from eleven to fifteen, were gathered around a dimly lit ranch table, talking to an older woman they both worshipped and dreaded. She had brought them from Mexico to help her deal with a festering problem. They bore no piercings laced with metal, but they were heavily tattooed with religious panderings and grotesque renditions of scorpions. Blessedly, most of the tattoos were covered, thanks to Nike knockoff shirts.

The boys were all members of a Ciudad Juarez gang called the *Alacránes*—the scorpions. Three months ago they gained the woman's respect by murdering nine members of a rival cartel's youth gang. They were anxious to undertake their next job. This was their first trip to any part of the United States except for frequent, unchallenged crossings into El Paso. Five days ago they had easily crossed illegally into New Mexico and worked their way to Paradise Valley by bus and an occasional ride from someone sympathetic to the network of illegal Mexican migrant workers.

Although none of the youths evidenced the least familiarity with table manners, when the woman entered the ranch room, they all stood and remained so until she seated herself.

"Hombres," said the woman, giving them respect they would not have by calling them "jovenes" or "muchachos," "we gone over what you do lot a times. I plan real good. You gotta do what I says. Old truck here for you. Drive truck behind gringas from place called Mill Creek ramp. Easy find, near bridge. One gringa drive red SUV with trailer that no got boat. Other gringa drive white van. Hector, you boss man. You know what you gotta do. OK have fun with pretty gringas. *After* fun do your job. All can have gringas before they dead."

The smiling boys rose respectfully and waited until the woman left. Hector, the oldest, bore a face of innocence that masked his starring role in several brutal killings in Mexico. His youthful skin bore no scars, nor did his spirit, which was too undeveloped for him to comprehend the extent of his wrongdoings.

Hector led the other boys into an outbuilding where the truck was stored. They lifted beams onto the truck and then boxes containing rope and nails. They did not plan to use these items with the Shuttle Gals, but to place them to cast blame on others. Several tools followed, including a small wooden box carried by Carlos containing a razor-sharp scalpel, whetstone, and several Ziploc bags. He was the newest member of the gang and was determined to prove his toughness. His hawk-like nose looked as sharp as the scalpel.

The truck was driven by José, who appeared older than his fourteen years and less Mexican than the others. When he left home at twelve to join the gang, his Mexican mother confessed to him that his father had been a U.S. marine attached to the consulate in Ciudad Juarez. After his mother became pregnant with José, the marine was transferred to Iraq and never again saw or contacted José's mother. The boy looked nearly as Irish as his father including his red hair and saturnine expression.

When the truck reached Emigrant, José parked behind the general store and bought coffee for five. It was made from beans grown near Jalapa, Mexico, on terraced slopes that rose to the west of Veracruz. Jalapa remains a peaceful and relatively safe city, far from the drug traffic and youth gangs that terrorize the border cities.

The four high-fived José for the coffee, sipping along the edges of their Styrofoam cups as the truck crossed the river at Emigrant, turned left on the East River Road—ignoring the stop sign—and again left on the road that sloped down to the river and the Mill Creek ramp. Hector told José to park away from the ramp, but where Hector had a good view of the parking area. A red SUV, with its empty trailer, was the only rig in the parking area.

Not long after the Mexicans parked, a white van pulled into the launching area, marked "Shuttle Gals" on the side, along with a telephone number and e-mail address. Three women were in the van, clearly visible through the windows along each side.

José turned to Hector, "Why *three* gringas, Hector? No supposed to be two?"

"No problem, José. One gringa drive guide's SUV and trailer to place where fishermen take boat out. That one we follow. Another gringa drive van to pick up first gringa, who leaves SUV for when guide arrives with boat. Third gringa probably gonna be dropped somewhere for more shuttles."

"How you know they come *here,* Hector?"

"José, the gringas use e-mail to make shuttles. Boss lady hacks e-mail every day—why we not know before last night we gonna come here today."

"But Hector. . . . " José didn't have a chance to answer when Hector interrupted.

"Person getting out of van, José."

José and Hector watched as Pam Synder opened the gas cap to the SUV. They thought she might be going to steal gas, but she took some keys. Hector thought to himself: "This how they work shuttle business. Leave keys for gringa by gas cap. Maybe good way for me steal cars. Sometime."

Pam and Marge took the red SUV, followed by Jilly driving the white van. They were followed at a distance by the truck with the five Mexicans. Soon the white van, but not the SUV, turned off at a sign that said "Loch Leven Ramp." It confused Hector for a moment, but he assumed the van was going off to do another shuttle.

The truck followed the red SUV and trailer north for nearly twenty miles on the East River Road until it made a sweeping curve to the west to cross the river at Carter Bridge. The SUV and trailer turned off and parked near the only other vehicle at the ramp, a small silver RAV4 SUV parked by the toilets. José drove across the bridge and continued a few hundred yards, where he turned around and parked so he and Hector could watch the vehicles at the ramp on the far side of the river.

"Hector, there trouble? A car is by outhouse."

"That must be car owned by woman driving red SUV. They gonna leave SUV and trailer and take little silver SUV. We follow them. She either be doing other shuttles or go home."

After the gals left the ramp area, the five youths unloaded two 4x6 beams and partially hid them behind the bathrooms.

36

THE YELLOWSTONE RIVER EXITING THE PARK surges north past Gardiner and tumbles raucously through Yankee Jim Canyon, a narrow drift boat slalom with depths to sixty feet. The canyon stretch is left largely to rafters. The main road, U.S. 89, hugs the east side of the Yellowstone River for a dozen miles north from Gardiner, where it bridges and remains west of the river through the heartland of Paradise Valley.

East River Road breaks off from 89 a few hundred yards south of the bridge, remaining east of the river to and beyond Carter Bridge, which is ten miles short of Livingston and effectively the end of Paradise Valley.

At Carter Bridge, the Absaroka and Gallatin mountain ranges pinch together, never touching but leaving a narrow neck that for decades has provoked the adrenalin of dam builders. A floater's dream, the river between Gardiner and Livingston has nearly a dozen access ramps for small craft. Even better, it's rowing only—drift boats, kayaks, canoes, and rafts. Motorized vessels need not apply.

"Launching at Mill Creek adds nearly five miles to our float, John, but we have all day. Some good runs line this first stretch. We'll pass through less publicized parts of the valley, where deteriorating trailers and junkyards vie with trophy homes. Sometimes it's hard to distinguish them. There's a lot of bland architecture along the river. New McMansions sprout up every year like invasive weeds, built on the flood plain too close to the river and begging a record spring flood to float them to the Dakotas. Just because the valley is naturally spectacular doesn't mean that it's been enhanced by man's touch."

"Is the river braided like the Snake above Jackson?" John asked.

"Not as much. We have very few channel choices to decide. The river's filled with deep holes below grassy banks that serve as hopper launching ramps in this section."

"What are you fixin' to tie on to start?" John asked.

"You like Elk Hair Caddis. Try one. The browns here seem to like it. They confuse it with a real adult caddis."

"OK. It's simple to make—I've tied a bunch."

By noon John had enticed several browns out of the holes under the banks.

He was right; the fly is easy to tie. Wrap hare's fur dubbed on the tying thread from the turn of the hook to the eye and back down with hackle; add gold wire back to the eye again and finish with a tuft of the signature elk hair tied tightly with the front protrusion trimmed leaving a short stub—like a bristly crew cut. Every guide carries a bunch of these caddis imitations, usually with variations that cross the line from being imitations.

Passing Mallard's Rest, John set his rod aside and said, "My turn to row. I want to see if you're raising your rod tip when you have a hit, like I've been trying to get you to do for four years."

I conceded without argument, even about raising my rod tip part. Mainly because he's right. We entered a fairly straight run for two miles to the first decisive split in the river.

"Try the right channel, John. We'll pass where Macdonald's Creek sends Absaroka mountain water spilling into the river." It proved a good suggestion and soon delivered a nice sixteen-inch rainbow to my net.

"What fly?" asked John.

"A #14 yellow stimulator."

"Why that one?"

"Pure intelligence. . . . The truth is I opened and closed a dozen fly boxes and finally decided to put *something* in the water from the next box. Maybe it attracted a homeless rainbow trout from Macdonald's Creek, anxious to grab the first piece of food floating by."

"When it jumped on the first run," said John, "I thought you were in for a good fight. But it just seemed to give up."

"Maybe it'd been hooked yesterday," I suggested, "and knew the sooner it succumbed the sooner it'd be released."

"Like a homeless vagrant on Jackson Square," John quipped.

"I got my fish, John. Let me row; this is your first time on the river. There's good water a little ahead where the two channels rejoin."

I took over and watched John skillfully work the banks.

"Damn, you're in double figures, and we're maybe halfway to Carter Bridge," I said. "Lunch in about a hundred yards. Over to the left there's a good bar."

"Does that bar serve beer?"

"Even better—South Australian *chardonnay*!"

"Who does your lunches?" John asked.

"Howlin' Hounds in Emigrant. I added the wine from deep in the wine caves under my cabin."

"I know you don't drink at lunch, Mac—do I get the whole bottle?"

"I'd like to watch you cast after lunch if you drink the whole bottle. I don't drink when I have paying clients. And you've never paid me a dime to fish. So we share the wine."

John's company assures a good day on the river. There's a bonus—I learn more about guiding every time we're together.

While we were sitting sipping the last of the *chardonnay* he asked, "Worried about reaching the takeout?"

"A little. Well . . . more than that. I sure hope the killings are over. I'll be happy to see my SUV without a body crucified to a wooden cross tied on the trailer. I'm not sure how long I can guide if I can't keep my floats from churning out cadavers."

"How come *you* seem to draw trouble when you get in a drift boat? I never taught you that."

"It isn't taught. It comes with attracting the wrong clients like Park Salisbury. Or talking to the wrong people like Victoria Montoya and Helga Markel."

"*You* chose me. . . . You asked me to come and float the Yellowstone. And then handed me a pistol when we started. Do I have to come on every float and protect your rear?"

"I couldn't afford you, and your wife won't let you float with me that often. I'm too much of a hazard."

"Look at the bright side. Park Salisbury's dead. You believe Montoya and Markel have both left the state. Montoya's probably in Mexico. *You* weren't the target when the women running the shuttle service were killed. It was some psychotic scumbag after *women*. Or possibly some guy or gal who hates gays. Anyway, be thankful he or she wasn't fixin' to kill *guides*."

I wondered what John would say if he knew about Herzog and Isfahani. John's from Georgia—graduated from the state university at Athens—and may have read about the attempted killing of the UF president. But if that shooting's linked to anyone, it's Maxwell Hunt, not Macduff Brooks.

Herzog and Isfahani are becoming more and more a threat every time I hear about them. If John knew El was my wife when she died on the Snake a decade and a half ago—a float he was scheduled to guide before a family illness called him back East—I think he'd see me more certainly as someone who draws trouble. And possibly someone to avoid.

"How far to Carter Bridge?" John asked after we packed up the lunch remains and pushed off.

"We're two-thirds of the way, passing a bend strangely called 'bend' on my river map. I think we have about six miles. Tired from catching so many fish?"

"No complaints. You know we don't get many days like this—going with a friend who can fish—at least when he keeps his rod tip up. Not having to row the whole way. Gorgeous weather. We could stay on this river and float to New Orleans."

"Not enough wine. And the river gets warm. The trout run out long before we reach the Mississippi."

When we turned the bend where the river and road nearly touch, a mile before Carter Bridge at the end of DePuy Spring Creek, I began to panic over what we might find at the ramp. It became the longest mile of the float. But as we closed on the ramp, I saw my SUV parked off to the side of the restrooms. My trailer was where it should be, not backed into the water. There was no body crucified on beams strapped to the trailer.

"You look a lot better, Mac. Your deaths per drift ratio has dropped a little."

"My pulse has dropped a lot more."

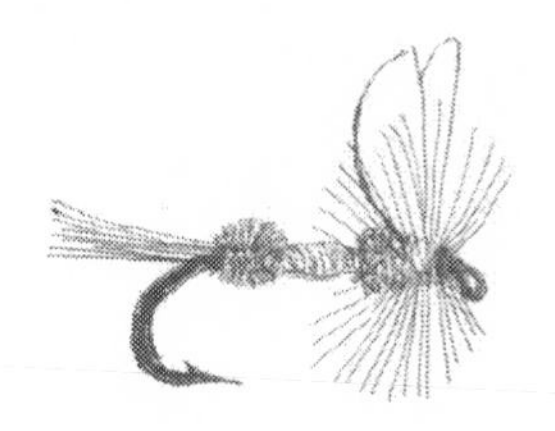

37

MARGE ATWOOD AND PAM SNYDER arrived at Carter Bridge with the SUV and trailer about an hour after the Mill Creek float had begun. Marge parked the rig under cottonwoods beside the restrooms; within five minutes she and Pam drove off in Marge's RAV4, which she'd left at Carter Bridge earlier.

Marge turned to Pam and said, "That's enough for the day, Pam. Lucy, Jilly, and our other new gal, Deb, are taking care of all the other shuttles today. I'm bushed from the past two weeks. Need anything on our way to my place to pick up your car?"

Her place is a restored 1920s cabin on a secluded thirty acres ten miles west of Livingston off I-90. She kept the place after her amicable divorce four years earlier. She had invited Pam for a lunch of leftovers. But Pam was still struggling from the emotions of Olga's death. Jilly seemed inclined to fill that gap in Pam's life, but Pam thought it was too soon.

"I think I'll rain check the lunch offer, Marge. I'll pick up my car from your place, but I won't stay. Thanks for asking."

Neither noticed the truck that began to follow them after they had dropped off the rig and headed north toward Livingston. José hung far enough behind to avoid detection, but not miss any turns by Marge. He nearly missed the turn when she exited I-90 suddenly—occupied with talking to Pam—but José saw her and cut to the right in front of an eighteen-wheeler driver who blew his horn in anger and yelled something about "wetbacks."

Ten minutes later Marge turned into her quarter-mile crushed gravel driveway, beneath two lofting cottonwoods that merged above in a gothic arch. José had closed the gap so quickly he couldn't halt. He drove past, glancing to see Marge disappear down her drive, turned around, and returned more slowly, just in time to see a dust cloud far down the driveway. José followed quickly, as though he were a UPS truck making a delivery.

Approaching the house, José watched Marge and Pam get out of the SUV. Pam unlocked her car, slipped into the front seat, started the engine and glanced at Marge who leaned over to say goodbye. They both looked up as the truck drove up and skidded to a stop a few feet in front of them. Hector stepped down from the passenger's side of the truck's cab, smiling and trying to look lost.

"Can I help you?" Marge asked cautiously. A single woman living alone, she was always suspicious when unmarked vehicles drove in. But the S&W pistol she began carrying the morning after Julie was murdered lay under a scarf in a light leather carrying bag that had been given to her. It was hanging from her shoulder, and she placed her hand slowly inside far enough to feel the walnut pistol grips. They were reassuring to a small woman unskilled in any martial arts. Julie had been a brown belt, but it proved of no help to her.

"I got delivery for some guy named Roberto Jones," said Hector. "This his house, or you know where he live?"

"There's no Roberto Jones *anywhere* near here," Julie responded, with an edge to her voice. "I know *everyone* around here. What's his *address*?"

José had slid down from the driver's seat on the far side and walked around to join Hector. Marge was becoming more concerned. The first boy clearly appeared to be Mexican. The other, the red-haired driver, didn't look at all Mexican but spoke Spanish.

Pam opened her car door, got out, closed the door, and stood by her car. She wasn't comfortable with the two—whom she judged to be mid-teens at most. She could see some tattoos showing on their necks and wrists. Neither male looked like someone a reputable business would hire to deliver packages; neither wore either a shirt or a hat bearing a company name.

She doubted the red-haired youth was old enough to have a driver's license. Before she could speak, the rear canvas cover on the truck was pulled back. Two more young Mexican-appearing males jumped down and walked around the truck to join the first two. A wolf-pack: the singular roughness of each was enhanced as a group. The one who had inquired about Roberto Jones was clearly the alpha male.

Marge and Pam didn't understand Spanish, and only the first youth had yet spoken any English. The appearance and mannerisms of the four were disconcerting. They were dressed startlingly similar. All wore black shirts with long sleeves bearing the Nike swoosh. Their dark, faded black jeans were baggy and dirty. New Nike sneaks spoke big bucks. Earned from doing what?

The two who had jumped down from the back of the truck had shaved heads that were covered with tattoos. Both wore a matching forest-green head band. Each bore the same scorpion symbol. The first two reached into pockets, pulled out, and tied on similar head bands.

"Hector, Marco take *this* one," said the third youth, pointing at Pam. Not waiting for a response by Hector, Marco walked up to her, grabbed her pony-tail and, spraying garlic overwhelmed breath, exclaimed, "I want this gringa—*now*." Marco grabbed Pam and thrust her against her car so hard she lost her breath and dropped to her knees. He took a step toward her, then unbuckled and dropped his pants. Pam's head was close enough to read the washing instructions on the Jockey label.

Marge watched anger spread across her friend's face. Pam rose quickly and, with her pointed Western boots, kicked Marco squarely in his vulnerable groin. He screamed and tumbled to the ground, writhing in pain. He got up with effort and started toward Pam, yelling in Spanish what she couldn't understand, but knew wasn't foreplay talk. Then he shifted to English: "You gringa whore, you dead meat. But first. . . . " He got no further.

Pam had turned around, reached into her car, and pulled out the shotgun from the rear seat. In one sweep she turned, pointed it at the Mexican and fired point blank as he was reaching forward to grab her. The foremost pellets of 12 gauge buckshot hit the youth in the nose. The pellets following close alongside made a pattern that mapped his head and left his youthful features scrambled.

His head jerked back so quickly from the impact that it lifted his body off the ground. An instant later it tumbled to the ground, his blood emptying onto the gravel drive. Pam turned, pumped the gun, and pointed it at Hector.

"One step, you slime ball. One hand movement. One eye blink. And you follow your friend to hell," she said, as calmly as she would order a cup of coffee. She didn't know whether Hector understood her every word, but she did know the gun spoke more strongly than the Mexican's words, whatever the language.

Marge stepped back next to Pam. "You OK, Pam?"

"I will be when I shoot three more damn illegal wetbacks."

"Don't shoot, Pam. I don't think the rest are anxious to look down your gun barrel."

"*You shoot me little brother Marco!* Nobody does that to Ruben's hermano," the fourth one yelled. He had been standing quietly in the background. Now his emotions disregarded Pam's advantage in holding the shotgun.

Pam and Marge knew both that he was called Ruben and at least knew a little English. They also knew he now had a *dead* brother named Marco. Ruben began screaming in Spanish but, realizing the women didn't understand him, returned to broken English.

"Marco not doing *nothing,* just playing," Ruben yelled, ignoring Pam and kneeling to hold Marco's body. Ruben's face was contorted with rage; he looked up at Pam and slowly rose. "Give me gun, gringa bitch."

Pam took a step back and tripped. As she fell, Ruben leaped at her. When she hit the ground on her back, she had the shotgun pointed at Ruben's middle and pulled the trigger. The shot did horrendous damage. Ruben had spoken his last words, Spanish or English. Pam was pinned on the ground under another dying Scorpions gang member.

José and Hector saw their chance. José ripped the shotgun from between Pam and Reuben. "I got this one, take other muchacha, Hector." José was so anxious to have Pam he foolishly tossed the shotgun aside. Pam spat at him. His backhand across her mouth drew blood and stunned her. He grabbed the collar of her blouse and dragged her away from Ruben's body. Blood flowed from the corners of Ruben's mouth in unison with his diminishing pulse.

Marge had frozen in terror, unable to pull out the S&W she was still touching. Hector turned to her. Staring at her, he called out, "Carlos, get out here. We got two gringas to kill." The fifth gang member, motion-sick from the drive, was not ready to assault the women.

Something jelled in Marge's brain. She recalled the horrors of Mexican youth gangs from a news program she'd seen a few days earlier. Her fingers curled around the Smith & Wesson as she pulled it from her bag and pushed the barrel against Hector's forehead. A single shot sent a third Scorpion to hell. She turned and fired two more shots that hit Carlos in the air on his jump down from the truck, a scalpel glistening in his hand ready for its work. Carlos was dead on arrival as he tumbled into a heap and lay silent.

Marge turned toward the only one left—José, who had stripped the semiconscious body of Pam. He backed away from Pam, started toward the shotgun, and tripped when his unbuckled pants caught his ankles. Marge walked toward him with the pistol pointed at him.

"Don't shoot me! I no hurt you. Hector made us do this." José pleaded with an unforgiving Marge.

"I'm not going to shoot you, you loco bastard. Not with this," Marge said as she tucked the pistol in her belt.

She picked up the shotgun and pointed it at José. Sweat slid through his red hair mingling with his tears.

"Please let me go. I no tell nobody."

Marge stared at José without a sign of sympathy or remorse at adding him to the pile of dead scum in her yard.

"There should be five shells left in this, you bastard. Where do you want the first one?"

José was screeching in Spanish something Marge didn't care to understand. She took three steps toward José. He was standing, his pants around his ankles, urine running down his legs."

"That's your last pee, José." She aimed the shotgun at his white shorts and when the dribbling stopped pulled the trigger. "Rot in hell with your four friends," she said. José wasn't dead, but the shot had thrown him back onto the ground. His eyes were pleading for a mercy he had never given his enemies, including the little children he'd slaughtered back in Mexico.

Marge aimed and sent the second load of shot into José's left knee. The third evened off the right knee, and the fourth destroyed a wooden crucifix hanging in the middle of his chest. Feeling the last shell slide into the chamber, she placed the end of the barrel on the cleft of José's chin and fired. Then she threw the gun aside and turned to Pam, who was sitting staring wide-eyed. The blood of the first to die, Marco, was already drying on his clothing next to her.

"He never got to me," Pam cried, hugging Marge.

"He never will." Marge walked away from the carnage and threw up the zucchini quiche she had so relished a few hours earlier before she left to do the shuttle.

38

AT CARTER BRIDGE John and I finished loading *Osprey* on the trailer.

"Thank God, John! No cross and no dead body on the trailer. You can't imagine how relieved I feel. Maybe we saw the last of it with the second murder."

While we loaded our gear into the back of my SUV, I pulled out my cell phone and turned it on. I don't like interruptions on a float and I wanted a quiet, private day with John. I had six calls in the past thirty minutes, all from Erin. I tapped on the last to call her.

"Macduff! When will you learn to keep your phone on? I'm at Marge Atwood's place. It's chaos. State police are here. Jimbo, Ken, and I arrived ten minutes ago. The FBI is on their way. The press is here demanding answers to questions they don't know how to ask. I just shoved a TV camera out of my face."

"What's happened? Is Marge OK?"

"All I know so far is dead bodies are all over in front of her barn. It looks like a slaughter house. Are you finished floating?"

"Marge is dead? What about Pam and the others?"

"Marge and Pam are alive! Pam's beaten up a little. But there are five dead Mexicans. They look to be teens. Gang members. Same dress. Same headbands. Same tattoos. You won't believe how bad they look. Three are unrecognizable. Marge and Pam together *destroyed* them."

"Are Marge and Pam OK?"

"Covered with blood, but not a drop of their own. Marge is giving interviews to the press. She and Pam are being treated like heroines."

"We're finished. . . . At Carter Bridge. Want me there?"

"Right now! Sooner! Bring your friend. We'll show him what happens when you mess with women in Park County!"

John and I arrived at Marge's thirty-five minutes later, close behind a Bozeman TV van with a rooftop satellite. Five covered bodies lay in discordant arrangement in Marge's yard. Ken noticed us park, came over, and gave us a nutshell description of what Marge and Pam had told him.

"Pam's clothes are torn. Were either raped?" I asked.

"No, but it was close. One of them was on top of her. Marge saw him, and he took the worst of it. Five shotgun blasts, each from no more than a few inches away. Four shots while he was lying on the ground. Keep that to yourself—I don't want to encourage the press to ask why self-defense required five shots. The guy looks like he was run over by a grain thresher. . . . They never touched Marge. When she first saw one of the Mexican youths on Pam, whose clothing had been stripped off, Marge went wild. She first shot one guy point blank when he headed toward her, and a moment later shot a second in the air while he was jumping down from their truck. When she turned to the one on Pam, she put her pistol aside, picked up the shotgun, and emptied it at him."

"Anyone talking about self-defense?"

"Not yet. But you know the press will raise it. Even Montana has its bleeding hearts. Pam said one of the Mexicans—apparently their leader—started it by going after her. She pulled her shotgun out of the car and shot him point blank."

"But what about the one Marge shot five times; you said he was on the ground. Did she need to shoot him?"

"She sure needed to shoot him. She thought he'd raped Pam, and she'd be next—the kid rolled off Pam as he saw Marge. Hey, you're not a lawyer. Why the doubt?"

"I don't want to see Marge or Pam charged. I think it might be wise to get Wanda Groves here before they make *any* statements—to *anyone*."

"Agreed. The FBI and state police will be here soon. Will you call Wanda? It'd look strange for a Park County deputy to call in a defense attorney. Shaw would pull my badge."

"Right now. With pleasure." I walked a few steps away from the carnage, pulled out my cell phone, and tapped on Wanda's name. I looked up and watched the last rays of a blood-red sun disappear beyond the Gallatin Range. Hopefully, it mirrored the end of the murders of Shuttle Gals.

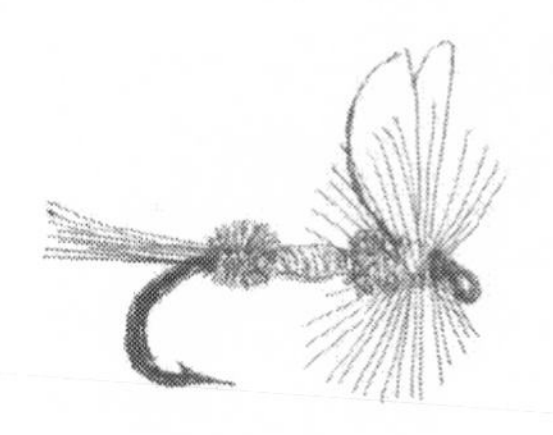

39

WHEN WE REACHED MY MILL CREEK CABIN, I was relieved to find Lucinda sitting quietly on the porch, putting her camera gear away. She had been along the creek photographing reflections from the same blood-red sunset I'd watched forming from Marge's yard. She looked so at ease I thought I might not tell her about Marge and Pam. But she would know sooner or later, probably sooner because I was likely showing anxiety over the killings.

"Good float with John?"

"Perfect day on the water. But trouble while we were floating—not with us, with two Shuttle Gals at Marge Atwood's."

"What happened? They weren't. . . ."

"They're OK," I interrupted, "but they went through a few terrifying minutes. John's putting his gear in his truck; he wants to drive home to Jackson Hole, even if it means night driving through the park. I couldn't talk him into another night's stay. When I've said goodbye to him, I'll fix us a couple of drinks and tell you what I know. It's been on the radio and TV. I'm glad you didn't hear . . . or see it."

When John had left and I handed Lucinda a glass of Montana Whiskey, she asked, "Are they mentioning *you* on the news?"

"Not a word I've heard and I listened carefully on the drive home."

"Tell me what happened."

I replayed the day between sips of the fluid smoothness of Gentleman Jack. Most of my references to blood described the sunset. My version of the killings was mild enough to make the Disney Channel.

"I think it was worse than you described. I wish I thought I could be as brave as Marge and Pam if anyone came after me—or you."

"I think your amnesia's back. You're not remembering saving my life on the Snake."

A soft bark of support came from Wuff, who was curled at Lucinda's feet.

"And you saved Wuff," I added. "She remembers better than you."

"That was all instinctive reaction. I never had time to think. You said once the law calls it 'irresistible impulse.' That describes it."

"That was true today with Marge and Pam. . . . I'm surrounded by a great bunch of women. You. The Shuttle Gals. Erin. Wanda. Amy."

"Don't forget Jen—the rattlesnake catcher!"

"At the mere mention of Jen, I smell the stench of that snake on the stairs. But you're right."

"We're taking over the world."

"I'm all too aware of that," I said sipping my bourbon. "And maybe just as appreciative at the mere thought." That comment may have been influenced by the Gentleman Jack, but it surely scored points with Lucinda.

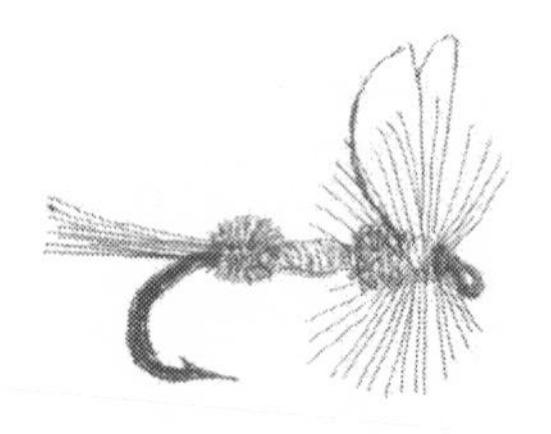

40

THE SHOOTINGS MADE NATIONAL NEWS. They were described in a Denver paper as the most dramatic shootout since the OK Corral. The Mexican teens were portrayed as evil as the Clanton gang when the Earp brothers and Doc Holliday shot them.

A San Francisco paper called Marge and Pam the *Butch Cassidy and Sundance Kid* of this century. *The New York Times* and *Washington Post*, on their editorial pages, made brief reference to the killings and called for more gun control. Fox News immediately responded and replayed the scene, imagining how it might have ended with the women facing the gang *unarmed.*

Marge and Pam were flown to N.Y. and did the rounds of the talk shows, from *Good Morning America* to the *Late Show.* Viewership that day, especially among women, went ballistic.

There was strong objection by the Hispanic caucus in Congress for singling out Mexicans, who the caucus members said were only representative of disadvantaged kids worldwide seeking better opportunities in America. That version didn't sell in Middle America.

In an Iowa newspaper the five who were intent on raping and killing Marge and Pam were identified at length as Mexican youth gang members illegally in the United States. They were estimated to have been involved in a half-dozen mass killings in Ciudad Juarez.

Marge and Pam hadn't seen them as Mexicans—the red-headed half-Irish youth didn't look Mexican. They saw five scroungy thugs intent on raping and killing. The women's caucus in Congress, despite a couple of California and Maryland representatives' abstentions, overwhelmingly voted Marge and Pam most qualified to be Women of the Year on the cover of *Time.*

Only one newspaper article I could find even made reference to me—and not by name—in a passing statement about Marge and Pam having earlier that day done a shuttle for "that Montana guide who was in the news a year ago when his trailer was twice found after a float with a crucified body of one of Ms. Atwood's partners." I *have* been mentioned by name in e-mails among outfitters and guides, not very kindly by a few. How bookings might play out will have to wait. Clients may be more interested in who's doing the *shuttle* than who's guiding. Whatever happens, I'm content to have the spotlight off me for once.

≈

Jimbo Shaw called me the following day.

"Macduff, I may try to hire Marge and Pam away from working as Shuttle Gals. I think they'd make great deputies. Maybe we could start a women's swat team with them."

"They were *spectacular.* . . . Have you traced the Mexicans to Victoria Montoya?"

"We went to her ranch late last evening after the killings. The ranch was deserted. We forced entry into one of the outbuildings and found a bunkroom we think they must have used."

"Did they leave anything that identified them?"

"No. It was spotless. But we know Victoria Montoya runs a teen gang in Ciudad Juarez that's been violent during the past year. A *lot* of killings."

"Rapes? Mutilations? Are they members of *her* youth gang?"

"Don't know details about her gang. No reported mutilations, like with Julie and Olga. But one of the dead Mexicans at Marge's place had a razor-sharp scalpel with him. He was the one who was sick from the driving and stayed in the back of the truck until shots were fired. He was apparently sharpening the scalpel; we found a whetstone in the back of the truck. We think we know his intentions. He jumped out to join the action with the scalpel in his hand. He was probably dead when he hit the ground, still holding the knife. At least I'm now *convinced* that *all* the attacks are traceable to the Montoya woman."

"Let's hope this page of Paradise Valley history isn't just turned, but ripped out, and the book is closed. I'd like the rest of the season to be quiet. I have a bunch of floats scheduled. But first I'm taking some time to spend with Lucinda. A trip to Missoula and on to Glacier. I've never been beyond Missoula; Lucinda hasn't been beyond Bozeman."

"You deserve some time together. You'll be close to Canada; you could drive up into Alberta and fish the Bow near Calgary. There's a magnificent historic hotel in Banff in the mountains."

"What Lucinda and I want is a big room with a big view and a big bed and a big duvet and a big 'Do Not Disturb' sign on the door."

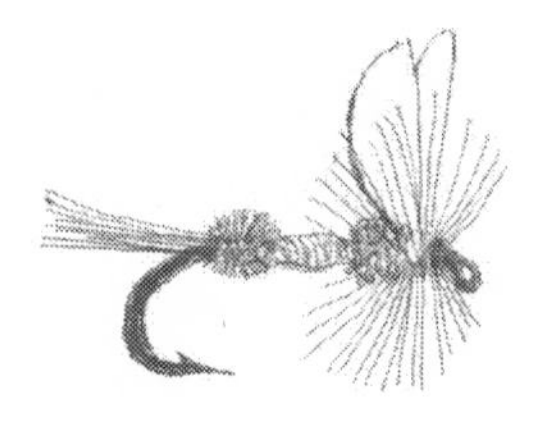

41

LUCINDA AND I DROVE TO MISSOULA, Glacier and on to Calgary and Banff, promising not to talk about "who did it." We were gone two weeks. It seemed like two days. Understanding friends took my scheduled floats. We found the big bed and the big duvet. Plus the sign on the door.

The no-talking-about-"who-did-it" rule ended abruptly as we arrived home. When I unlocked my gate, I found a note tucked under the lock:

I knew you two would turn off your cell phones. Good for you! Give me a call when you get back. It must have been a wonderful trip, or you would have been back sooner. Erin

Mavis brought Wuff to us at 5:10 p.m. Wuff ignored us, walked straight to her food bowl, saw it was empty, turned, sat, and whined. So much for "welcome home!"

Lucinda opened a dense inky purple Spanish Manso de Velasco *Cabernet.* I put on a Buena Vista Social Club CD and we sat on the rear porch hearing the strains of the classic *Dos Gardenias* drift up from the music room, Ibrahim Ferrer singing that the two flowers: *will live beside you and talk to you as I do and you will even believe, that you hear them say: "I love you."* Lucinda moved close to me. A time to be with loved ones and friends.

An hour later, we called Erin, leaving the speaker phone on.

"Hey, Kendoka, all quiet in Park County?"

"Lucinda there with you?"

"I'm here," Lucinda called out. "Did you think I wouldn't be?"

"I thought you might have run off with some handsome Mountie in Alberta. Would have served Macduffy right."

"Never found the right Mountie, but I looked. . . . Quiet trip! Nobody shot at us. No bodies spread across our car. Macduff offered to rent a drift boat in Calgary and take me floating on the Bow River, but I opted out. We waded some beautiful creeks and streams in the mountains southwest of Calgary. All-in-all, it was an unexpectedly uneventful time for being with Macduff. Can you imagine that? . . . Was it uneventful here?"

"The shootout at Marge's has quieted down. Jimbo's closed the file on Julie's and Olga's killings. He's *positive* Victoria Montoya did them and was also behind the attempt to kill Marge and Pam. Marge continues to run the shuttles. She agreed to Jimbo's suggestion that all her bookings be done online, and she granted Jimbo access. He wants to occasionally check for clues Marge might not notice. I think it's a good idea. Jimbo's actually bright. Granted he's hard to get along with most of the time. He's been a pain in the ass the last week. Ken and I stay out of his way."

"What are you going to do without Macduff around stirring up work for you? Tag double-parked cars?"

"Jimbo may believe that the matter's closed. *I'm* not. A hunch maybe. Some loose ends I can't resolve. I'm not going to let the file be buried away. Now that you're back, are you guiding again, Macduffy?"

"Sure am. Starting in another few days. I want to get back to work. Some outfitters must feel sorry for me. Season's about over. The color on the river's beautiful this year."

"Can I ask you a strange question, Macduffy?"

"Everything you ask is strange. But ask away."

"You wear glasses. All the time. Right?"

"Yeah. You've seen me enough to know that."

"Why do you wear glasses that have *no* prescription? You set your glasses down on Pam's car after the shootings. They slid off. I picked them up, cleaned the dust off the lenses, and looked through them. I was curious how bad your eyes were. They're not bad at all. In fact, I suspect they're *perfect*."

I didn't want to lie to Erin. She already knows a lot about me.

"All I can really say is that I *have* to wear them. They were *prescribed*, but you're right—they aren't prescription."

"I think I understand. In the same way that the moustache is something you *have to wear*."

I paused, but finally said in nearly a whisper, "Yes."

When Erin hung up, I turned to Lucinda and said, "So much for intelligent women. See what kind of trouble you stir up?"

"Erin's on your side. Ever thought how it would be if she weren't?"

"It makes me thankful Herzog and Isfahani aren't women!"

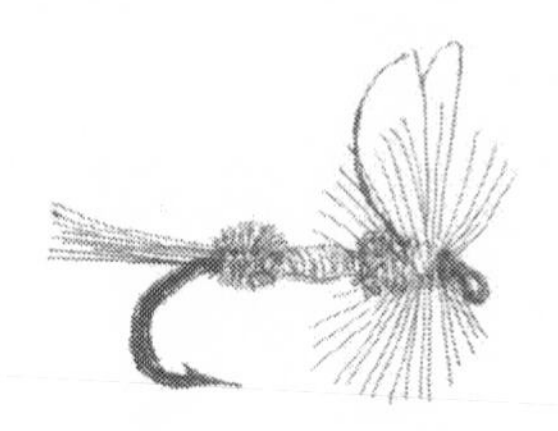

42

THE NEXT DAY THE MONTANA SKY looked more cerulean than ever, but it may have been my attempt to view bottles as half-filled. Several late season bookings had come in. I wondered if the clients really wanted to fish. Half first asked if the Shuttle Gals were doing my shuttles and if they could meet the women and take some photographs before floating.

Lucinda was busy photographing; a professional studio in Bozeman asked her to help with a state historical research project, establishing a photographic record of Paradise Valley. The purpose is largely to counter any new demands to build a dam. I worry about her taking on too much. Her amnesia shows up when she's under stress; the time in Canada had quelled any stress I had caused with the floats. If only life could continue so uninterrupted. But Herzog and Isfahani would not have it so.

≈

A call came from D.C. "It's Dan. Got a few minutes?" I was preparing my drift boats for the last floats of the season.

"If I said 'I'm busy. I'll call back,' I wouldn't sleep tonight, wondering what you wanted."

"With good reason. Since the attempted killing in Gainesville, we've tried to keep track of Herzog and Isfahani. You know they flew directly back to Guatemala in Herzog's private plane. We don't know why Isfahani remains with Herzog, but assume it must be that they're planning something. It could be legitimate business between Guatemala and some Arab nations.

"We have our mission at the embassy in Guatemala trying to track trade, but Herzog is increasingly getting cronies placed in government positions. They won't cooperate with us. Another reason Herzog and Isfahani could be together is they're looking for you. The FBI and the police in Gainesville would like to question them, but there's been no indication they've tried to slip back into the U.S. They may have others doing their work, like Herzog's niece who tried to kill someone at the dedication. There are currently two students with Guatemalan citizenship studying at the law school."

"Are there any Arab students at the law school who might be under Isfahani's control?"

"There is one we're watching carefully. He's a graduate tax student from the University of Khartoum. You know the Sudan and you know Khartoum. That's also where Isfahani's from."

"Don't remind me. Years ago I got out of Khartoum through Omdurman—and down the Nile—just ahead of the group who tried to kill the U.S. ambassador at a reception at his residence."

"I don't think Isfahani knows about your activities in Khartoum. In any event, you were acting as Maxwell Hunt, and he's dead."

"You and I want to think that, but I'm certain Juan Pablo and Abdul Khaliq believe otherwise. Is there anything we could do to make Maxwell's death more believable?"

"What we released at the time," Dan explained, "was that Maxwell was cremated and his ashes scattered on the Snake River in Wyoming."

"Who scattered them?" I asked.

"I guess I should tell you. It might help you think how we might reaffirm Maxwell's death. Remember the heavy-set agent who asked you about what work you'd do in Montana? You were a bit testy?"

"I remember him; he seemed bored with being there. Still with you?"

"He's not. He left government service two years ago. He was unhappy about not being promoted to a position he thought he had a lock on."

"Any reason to worry about him?"

"Developing. He's written a book about his decade in the CIA. As required, he gave us the manuscript to review. We're in a debate now with his lawyer over some items. One is a section on agents who have been protected under the IIPA. There haven't been that many—you're still the only outsider, and the only professor, who's gone through the program.

"He mentioned that fact in the book without naming names, but we're challenging it. He also mentioned how we dispose of a person's original identity and routinely report cremation and scattering ashes. He wrote that he scattered the 'ashes' of a compromised agent on a Wyoming river. And added that they weren't actually the agent's ashes, but the ashes of the *Times* he'd read on the plane. Obviously, we're challenging that."

"If that book comes out, assuming Herzog or Isfahani read it, it will confirm I'm alive. Is your agent going to pull what Philip Agee did?"

"I don't think so. When Agee left the CIA and wrote *Inside the Company,* we think he compromised several agents and may have caused at least one death. I hope we won't let that happen again. If we don't get the material redacted, there will be an accident some dark night here in D.C. that solves the problem. By the way—Agee died in 2008 in his beloved Castro-led Cuba."

"I know about Agee. I've always thought he should have been taken out. I guess he made himself so public it would have been too obvious if anything happened to him."

"You're right, Mac. Agee fled to Cuba, the U.K., the Netherlands, France, Germany, and Italy. Then Grenada gave him citizenship, which became useless when the leftist government collapsed. Next Nicaragua allowed him in, until that government changed. He spent most of his remaining years in Cuba and Germany—his wife was German. We'll act sooner if that kind of activity compromising our agents happens again."

"What about having another agent sign an affidavit stating that he was the one who actually scattered the ashes in Wyoming, that they *were* the ashes of an agent, and that what your agent has written is self-serving and obviously a lie? If you can discredit him enough with the lawyers and publisher, the book may never come out."

"You should have stayed in D.C. and worked for us. . . . We're doing something along those lines. I doubt the book will ever be published."

"I hope not."

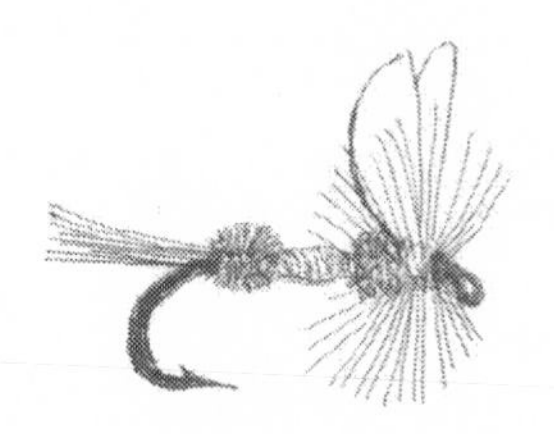

43

FALL SEMESTER LAW CLASSES IN GAINESVILLE commenced the third week of August, a week after the rest of the university opened.

Among the fall term registrants for the graduate tax law program was a twenty-two-year-old from Guatemala. He stood out from the other entering law students because he was impeccably dressed in dark, chalk-striped suits, white shirts and ties bearing the pale blue and white of the Guatemalan flag.

He was tall and thin with the light complexion of his ancestors. Not a trace of Maya blood flowed in his veins; indeed he always introduced himself saying, "I'm Guatemalan of *German* ancestry."

Encroaching on his narrow nose, his dark eyes were his most distinguishing feature, appearing as polished ebony and bearing an intensity that caused one talking to the young man to think of a falcon that had targeted its prey and was about to strike. That intensity was disconcerting to one newly introduced to the young man, until he opened his mouth and in any one of three languages—English, French, or his native Spanish—and his soft, baritone voice placated any hesitation to converse with him.

The young man made friends easily as he registered for classes and met law faculty and fellow students from both the law college and Center for Latin American Studies. At a reception for new students from Latin American countries, he introduced himself to the retired head of the Center—Terrance MacElroy. The seventy-two-year-old MacElroy had a legendary but recently faltering gift of remembering faces and names.

Reading the young man's nametag, McElroy said, "Martín Paz. From Guatemala! Are you studying agriculture?"

"What made you think that, Professor? I am here to study tax law."

"You remind me of a student here some years ago from Guatemala, who was in our agriculture graduate program. I participated in teaching a seminar in which he was enrolled, a general one on contemporary issues in Latin America that was also taught by two members of the law faculty."

"That was my uncle," said the young man, offering nothing more. He turned away, took a drink from a tray being passed through the crowd of guests, and didn't turn back. But as Paz was leaving the reception an hour later and stepped into the elevator, Professor MacElroy appeared behind him. They were crowded together facing each other with no room to turn for the short two-floor ride down.

MacElroy looked at Paz with an inquiring stare, and as they walked out the door into the lingering humidity of an August day, MacElroy turned and said to Paz with the pleasure of a sudden revival of his fading memory: "Herzog! The student's name was Herzog. José Herzog? José Pablo Herzog?"

"Professor, his name is Juan Pablo Herzog. I call him Tío Juan."

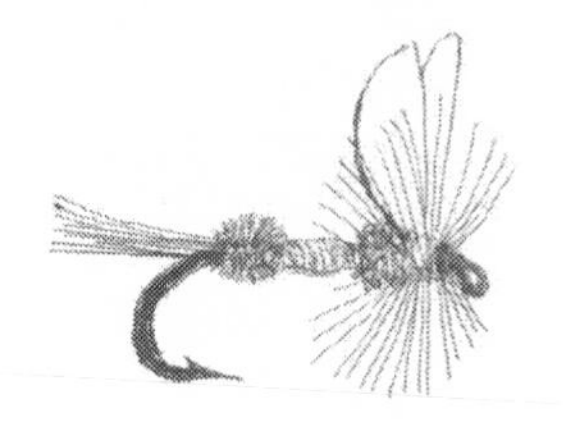

44

MARTÍN PAZ WAS THE SON OF GLORIA HERZOG PAZ, an older sister of Juan Pablo. She had once loved her little brother, but not for very long. By the time he was nine or ten, he scared her.

As a young woman she had prayed nightly that she had been spared the "bad genes" passed to Juan Pablo, and when Martín was born years later, she prayed those genes had not lain dormant within her body only to be passed to her son. That prayer was not answered.

Martín adored his uncle, one of few of the family to do so. Tío Juan reciprocated. Martín drove the only Ferrari in Guatemala during his vacations home from prep school and the university in the United States.

Another who also had been drawn into Tío Juan's sphere of indecency was María-Martina Herzog, the niece of Juan Pablo and cousin of Martín, who had been killed on the law school roof only a few months earlier. Paz's mother had turned to the solace of alcohol and drugs. She was now kept secluded and sedated by the family so she could not besmear the name of Herzog—and diminish the presidential ambitions of Juan Pablo.

An accomplished student, Martín had a business degree *cum laude* from Notre Dame and a JD *magna cum laude* from George Washington in D.C. Accepted to study tax law at NYU, he chose instead the University of Florida's tax law program for one reason—he was instructed to attend by his Tío Juan after his cousin María was killed. Martín applied late but was accepted. Nothing in his application made reference to the name Juan Pablo Herzog.

≈

Martín settled comfortably in the large Gainesville house Juan Pablo had recently purchased in the name of a Panamanian corporation. Close to the law school in the small neighborhood called Golf View, the house was known as the "castle" because of the three-story turret entrance. But more significantly, for some twenty years the house had been the home of Professor Maxwell Hunt!

After returning from the reception, Martín phoned his uncle, whom he and only he had always called Tío Juan.

"Tío Juan, I'm at your house in Golf View. It is a very nice house and has a library where I will do my studying. I've been reading the file you gave me about Professor Maxwell Hunt. Last evening, before the sun set, I walked through this neighborhood and saw the house where Hunt's close friend, Professor Roy Palladio, lived until his death."

"Good, Martín. I want you to know the places Maxwell Hunt, however he is now known, might want to see if he revisits Gainesville. I should say *when* he visits because I believe he compulsively returns each year."

"I don't blame him, Tío Juan; it is a pleasant university town. I will enjoy studying here, although the August heat and humidity are not inspiring. No one seems to mind, especially after the cooling afternoon rains. Most everyone is less interested in academics than in the opening of the season for what they call football. I went to one of these games when I was at Notre Dame. It was a game displaying more pageantry than skill. The newspapers often have extensive accountings of the latest arrests of players caught using drugs, abusing coeds, or fighting in the local bars."

"Forget that silly game they call football, Martín. When you have finished in Gainesville and have your LL.M., there will be a place for you as head of legal affairs for my businesses. And when I become President of Guatemala, there will be a special place for you as Procuradora General of the country. But first you have important work for me in Gainesville."

"You know how much I enjoy fútbol, Tío Juan, or soccer as they call it here. Strangely in this southeastern part of the country most of the universities with large football programs do not have men's soccer. They did at Notre Dame and it's played in most other parts of the country. They say here that it is because of something called Title IX; they can't have men's soccer because it would be impossible to do so and comply with Title IX. But many fine universities—the Ivy League, Stanford, Michigan, the Atlantic Coast Conference, except for the members in Florida and Georgia, have men's soccer.

"I think the athletic department people and alumni worry about football competing in the fall with the much more popular sport—fútbol. Perhaps when we Hispanics are the majority in this country it will all change.

"As we agreed, Tío Juan, I will attend all the *women's* soccer games this fall, sit in the highest row, and look for any lone man who is about fifty and close to appearing anything like the composite face of Maxwell Hunt that you and Señor Isfahani put together."

"I knew you would help me, Martín. We *must* find Maxwell Hunt and repay him for the loss of your cousin. Call me often, dear nephew."

≈

That Friday evening, at the women's soccer team's opening game, Martín was among the first to enter Pressley Stadium. He sat high in the last row on the hard metal benches and placed two items beside him. One was a leather bag containing a small camera with a powerful telephoto lens. The other was a plastic cup of Pepsi he bought on the way into the stadium. He emptied the contents of a Ziploc bag into the Pepsi. The bag contained Ron Zacapa Centenario he had bought at the duty-free shop at the airport before departing Guatemala City.

Martín watched the crowd carefully during the game, rarely following the action on the field. He never saw anyone who bore any resemblance to the penciled image of Maxwell Hunt that was folded and kept in his shirt pocket. But he would return for the next game Sunday afternoon and every home game thereafter. Until he found Maxwell Hunt.

≈

While Martín was enjoying his first weeks in Gainesville, I remained ignorant of the fact that Juan Pablo's nephew had enrolled at the UF law school and was residing in the house that I lived in for ten years with El. I remained another ten years as a widower—until Martín's Tío Juan started the events that caused the "death" of Maxwell Hunt and the creation of Macduff Brooks.

≈

Lucinda and I didn't plan to depart Mill Creek for Florida for at least another month. I wanted to fish hoppers into early October; she planned to photograph the fall colors along Mill Creek and in Paradise Valley. For the moment life seemed idyllic. But when it had seemed so before El's death, that simplicity hadn't lasted.

45

"MACDUFF, TAKE ME ON A FLOAT with you," pleaded Lucinda. She had joined me soon after daybreak, sitting in front of the windows overlooking Mill Creek. "Thanks for the coffee," she added, as she lifted the cup from my hand, took a long smell, and a longer sip.

"That's *my* coffee. It has sugar and non-fat milk. You like yours black!"

"Unless *you* make it," she said, sipping it again as she sat smiling across from me at the small table. "What's for breakfast?"

"Oh, I'll put a chunk of lard in a pan. Fry up some pork jowl. Maybe cook pig's fee. . . . "

"You wouldn't feed that to Wuff! But you would to me?"

"Of course I wouldn't give it to Wuff. She has a special balanced diet of duck, salmon, and turkey, plus a little added fruit and topped off with applesauce. She loves it."

"And *I* get pork jowl? How about some haggis? You're a Scot."

"I draw the line at sheep's heart, liver, and lungs all boiled in the sheep's own stomach, Lucinda—haggis is not part of my food chain. . . . I'm trying to fatten you up after your injuries. The best of intentions."

"By lining my insides with lard? . . . *I'll cook.*"

"That's what I hoped to hear."

"One condition. If I cook, I also get to be the household nutritionist."

"That's not what I hoped to hear. But I guess success lies in the art of compromise. OK, Miss Nutritionist. What are we having for breakfast?"

"Pan-seared asparagus with frisée and fried egg."

"Hold the asparagus," I pleaded.

"No! You need the vegetables."

"Hold the frisée."

"Not a chance. You don't even know what it is."

"Sounds leafy," I said.

"It is. It's lettuce. You need that, too. . . . Now, are you *going* to take me on a float?"

I didn't answer for a long minute. I was lost in the joy of seeing her so recovered. She hadn't shown the slightest sign of amnesia for a week.

"Float? Right now? In the middle of coffee on an early October morning, sitting looking out at our part of Mill Creek?"

"*Macduff*, I don't mean *now*. It's awful outside. The sky's not Montana blue; it's New England lead-gray."

Uninvited storm clouds were scuttling in from the southwest, from where weather changes arrive unannounced over the Gallatins. Sporadic rain showers slanted under the roof eaves and ricocheted off the windows. But it was clean water unadulterated by industrial smog or nature's testy fires. The weather report said it should turn to sleet by mid-afternoon. I didn't care. Lucinda was across from me, her Cheshire cat grin above the rim of *my* coffee cup, held by both hands, her elbows on the table, a few loose hair strands awry. She was leaning toward me across the table with an intensity of happiness that countered my weather-born grumpiness.

"You haven't been on a float since the shootout on the Snake when Park was killed. Are you sure you want to float with *me*?" I asked.

"I don't know how to row if I go alone. I'm dependent on you."

"I'll give you my book on drift boat rowing and the keys to my SUV. Go have fun."

"What if I hit a rock in some rapids and the boat turns over?"

"You swim. Actually, you float downstream. On your back, feet out in front, protecting you from rocks." I turned back to the book in my lap.

"Are we getting too complacent together? Do you have another iron in the fire?"

"Three or four. All Jackson girls. Real western cowgirls—leather, buckskin, and silicon."

"How did I get here? Who are you? I think my amnesia is back!"

"*You* invited me to Thanksgiving dinner five years ago, made me slip and fall and kill my butt on the ice, then took me in and seduced me. I've been a captive to your charms ever since."

"That part is OK. But I want to float with *you*."

"Are you *that* bored?"

"Bored on *your* boat? How many notches now. . . . Oh, that's awful to mention. All I want is to photograph along the Yellowstone River. Are there places we can anchor?"

"Lots. What time of day do you want to be on the river?"

"At least during the late afternoon sun. The last hour of sunlight when the rich colors come alive and then so quickly succumb to dusk. The days are getting shorter. If we start around noon, and have lunch about two, we could finish at sunset."

"I have a float scheduled tomorrow and another on Thursday. I'm lucky they haven't canceled. Friday's weather is supposed to be clear."

"Do I get a special rate?"

"Are you going to fish?"

"Of course, when I'm not photographing."

"Then I have to charge you for both fishing and photographing. It'll be double the usual rate."

"But we're not beginning the float until half the day is gone."

"But we're not *finishing* until dark. That means overtime," I added. "That doubles the rate again."

"Is this how you charge other clients?"

"No, only beautiful wealthy women. Then I can calculate how much they're willing to pay to spend the day with me."

"How many of those have you taken this season?"

"One. She was the most beautiful of all . . . But she was shot."

"You're so sweet. I think."

"She was shot in the butt by a glancing bullet."

"That wasn't *me*. It was Wuff! Why her?"

"Because she doesn't whine as much as you."

"I *don't* whine. Why do you think I do?"

"So I'll feed you on time and take you out to pee."

"Can you recommend some other guide?" she asked.

"No one else will take you in their drift boat," I commented. "You're a danger. Remember, the last time you floated one person was killed, and three more, if we include Wuff, were shot. Neither humans nor dogs will float with you."

"But it was *your* boat," she replied. For another moment her face showed the old fun we had with each other. But I had taken her a float too far. Her composure crumbled, and the memory of that day caught up. She broke into convulsive sobs. Her body trembled, and I grabbed her and held her so tight there was no room for shivering. She was a long time settling down.

"Lucinda, I should have remembered that you still have some memories you'd like to put to rest. I threw them right at you. I'm sorr. . . "

"No regrets, Macduff. There'll be more tears. But they're submerged in the joy of being here. Right now." She got up from the sofa and stood looking at me.

"You want to walk?" I asked.

"No, I want another hug."

Lucinda slept soundly that night. I didn't. I slipped out of bed at midnight after tossing about and sat in a chair in the corner of the room, watching and listening to her discontented breathing. I fell asleep only as the first shreds of light crept over the Absaroka Range.

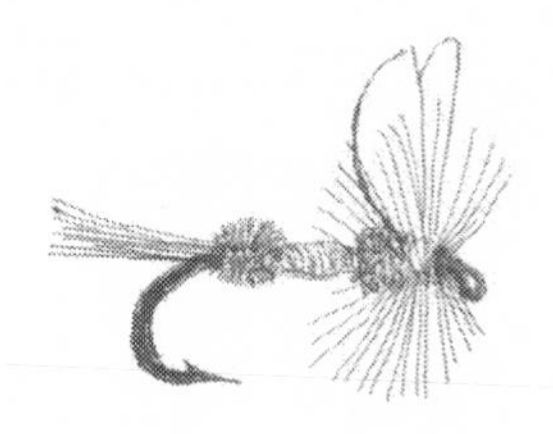

46

THE SOLAR GLOW OF A PROMISING FRIDAY flooded the valley as we breakfasted at the cabin.

"You're not saying much," commented Lucinda.

"I don't want to say the wrong things," I answered. "You're not saying much either," I added.

"I don't want to make you answer me and say the wrong things," she said.

We were inclined to be open with each other in relating feelings. But it often backfired because we had shared some anxious moments over the past few years which, when brought into a conversation even obliquely, struck sensitive nerves.

I had uneasy feelings about the float and decided not to say anything. The last image I have of Lucinda on *Osprey* is her hanging over the transom, bleeding from Park Salisbury's bullets. Without much conversation we spent the morning on chores and at noon hooked up *Osprey* and hopped in the SUV. To our surprise Wuff was sitting on the top of the compartment dividing the front seats, ignoring us and staring out the front window.

As we started out the drive, I commented to Lucinda, "I didn't know you invited Wuff."

"I didn't. I assumed you did."

"Shall we take her back? It's a long day for her."

"Do you think she wants to stay home? You know she'll lie by the front door all day and wait for us."

"What about her dinner?"

"She'll wait. And I know you keep a bag of treats for her in the compartment she's sitting on."

"You pamper my dog."

"She's my dog, too. Look how she's leaning against *me*, not you."

"That's called alienation of affections. I could get a restraining order against you."

"You don't have an attorney. Wanda told me if you ever mistreat me she'll dump you and represent me."

"That's sex discrimination. . . . I suspect I'm in trouble. Erin will side with you. I know Mavis will. And Amy as well if it ever goes to court. Damn!"

"Also Jen, if you escape from me and try to hide in Florida. I told you we're taking over the world. Better get used to it."

"If you are, I think I'll become a fishing bum."

"You already are. Maybe you could be a photographer's assistant."

"Matthew Brady's dead. He doesn't need an assistant any longer."

"But I do."

"What would I have to do?"

"Maybe pose nude. I could do a guide calendar. I'll sell hundreds."

"My photo will be on every single female's refrigerator, locker, and office cubicle. I'll be as famous as Goya's *Naked Maja*. They'll even put me on a postage stamp."

"OK, that's *not* such a good idea. But you could spend a lot of time with me in the darkroom."

"You don't need a darkroom. You use a digital camera and Photoshop."

"I'd think of something we could do in a darkroom."

"I accept."

≈

We launched *Osprey* at Pine Creek around noon. I thought we'd float to Carter Bridge, an easy seven miles. I'd called Marge Atwood the night before. She scheduled Pam Snyder to do our shuttle. Poor weather during the week had kept people home. It was better today, and there would be other boats floating. But we were starting late so that other boats would be off the river when we reached the places Lucinda wanted to photograph.

She turned toward me from the front seat, and said, "You like the channels and islands and all the bends on the mile-and-a-half upriver from here. Why didn't we put in at Mallard's Rest, so you could fish that upper section?"

"I thought being near Carter Bridge for the last of the sunlight would be good for your photography. My shoulders are a little sore from the past few days guiding. I don't plan to row hard."

"And you don't mind ending at Carter Bridge? That was the float you did the day Marge and Pam were attacked."

"It *was* the day they were attacked, but not at Carter Bridge. *Osprey* and my trailer weren't touched. I asked Pam last night how she felt about doing the shuttle for us. She said she isn't worried. She carries her loaded shotgun on the seat beside her."

I wasn't intent on putting a fly on the water. Wuff was curled up and snoring on *Osprey's* floor behind me. Lucinda was casting from the front seat, but turning around often to talk. We weren't afloat more than twenty minutes when, on the first tight bend to the left, a rainbow ripped into a Royal Wulff on Lucinda's line.

The sun was enough past its noon high to build a haven of shadows along the western bank. The fly had rotated through an eddy, and as soon as it passed into the shade, the trout struck. Lucinda hadn't been looking when the rainbow gulped her fly. In an instant the fish understood its mistake, rushing to get away from all that was artificial.

A Royal Wulff is clothed as no respectable bug would be seen dressed. A good suggestion from a guide friend said, "Look at your fly from the bottom, the way a fish does." I did. A Royal Wulff looks a bit like an ant. The wing on top, whether feather or tuft of hair or modern, synthetic clump, is there more for the person fishing, than for the fish being stalked.

"The fish is still on," cried Lucinda. "What do I do?"

"Tip up! Keep some tautness in the line and try to reel in the pile of line at your feet."

"My foot's caught in the line! It's caught in my boot laces. Help me!"

"I don't do boot laces. . . . Fortunately, the trout's hooked pretty good. It's staying near the boat, not running. It's hanging around to watch you demonstrate how to land a trout."

"You're *no* help. How do you ever guide for a living?"

"If you'd paid me in advance, I'd be helping you more."

"Look! Now it's running."

"That's because your show is over."

"I'm calling John and ask if he'll guide for me."

"He won't. He's scared of you being in his boat. Like I'm scared of you driving my SUV. And John doesn't like having to carrying a gun on a float."

"It's time to take some photographs," she said. "*You* fish."

"I'll watch. You might get caught in your camera strap. . . . We'll have lunch in a few minutes. There are a couple of islands ahead. Lunch on our own island. . . . I do pamper you."

"I deserve it. Will you set up the table and chairs? And serve some wine?"

"I thought I was employed as your photographer's assistant, not a waiter."

Because it was a special day—Lucinda's first float since the shooting on the Snake—I had bought some French *brut*, a Philippe Foreau *Vouvray*. Lucinda had made lunch. I set up the table, added a foulard print tablecloth, plus crystal and china—carried in a reed-woven old English picnic basket.

"If it's French and sparkles, Macduff, it should be called *champagne*, not *brut—n'est-ce pas*?"

"Only if it's made in the Champagne *region*. The *brut* we're having is made much the same way as champagne—grapes fermented into a still wine and bottled. Then *another* fermentation induced inside the bottle. It produces carbon dioxide that can't escape, so instead it carbonates the wine. There are different ways to make it."

"Is this part of your duties as my assistant?"

"I have to remind you wine is a *health* food. It's part of my duties as your caregiver."

"Does it help me forget my amnesia?"

"At the rate you're sipping, it will help you forget everything."

Lucinda began to photograph. I sat quietly, rowing carefully to keep the boat steady. She became increasingly engrossed in her work. I sensed that she was in a world that didn't include me, her intensity was so focused. She continued until the orange sun went peacefully behind where the mountains to the west were fast closing in upon us.

"Thanks," she said, putting down her camera. "It's enchanting water. Are we close to Carter Bridge?"

"You'll see it when we turn a little to the right in another thirty yards."

Dusk was erasing our vision as we drifted right and passed beneath the bridge. I looked toward shore—and froze—my hands tightening on the oars as we glided along the last bit of the east side toward my trailer—*backed into the water*. It lay deeper than the previous times, but not so deep I couldn't see a lone foot bobbing in the current, visible in a final shaft of the day's light.

"What's wrong?" Lucinda, sitting in front, had turned to face me and couldn't see the trailer.

"Don't look. Call Erin's number on your cell phone. Tell her we're just coming ashore at Carter Bridge. But please don't look. Get out of the boat when we land and go sit in the SUV."

She didn't move. "Who is it?"

"Pam Snyder."

The body was nailed to a wooden cross that was in turn tied to my trailer. A green, red, and white sash was tied around her waist. A mirror image of Julie and Olga. Pam's left foot had come free of the nails and her leg was drawn upward by the current. Her foot lifted above the surface and dropped down like a sweeper in the spring runoff.

Lucinda turned, looked, and screamed, "Her breasts are gone!"

Pam's body had been mutilated in the same way as Julie's and Olga's.

"It's awful!"

"Worse," I said.

I walked Lucinda to my SUV. Wuff climbed in front and put her head against Lucinda's shoulder. Lucinda's eyes were glazed. Her face had lost its glow from the sun and breeze of our afternoon. The Cheshire cat smile had vanished. I must have looked like hell—and didn't particularly care.

47

ERIN, JIMBO SHAW, AND TWO OTHER DEPUTIES arrived within minutes. Battery powered light stands were set up. Reporters and TV camera crews began to fill the parking lot. Within thirty minutes, two dozen vehicles crowded the area. Erin went to my SUV and sat in the front with Lucinda. The two other deputies took photos of the area before they asked me to pull out the trailer.

"We need to talk," Shaw suggested calmly. "Walk over on the bridge with me for a minute."

As we walked, Shaw put his hand on my shoulder and said, "This isn't something I expected. I was *sure* the Montoya woman was finished with her killing. She's obviously been back. But I'm also sure she's on her way to Mexico as we speak."

"Maybe it wasn't her," I offered, in as unchallenging a manner as I could muster.

"It *was,*" Shaw replied.

"How do you know?" I asked.

"I'm the chief detective," he declared, without the least awareness that the position was not a *source* of intelligence.

"Anything more?" I asked.

"Experience. Intuition."

"That ought to be enough," I responded, not interested in a debate.

We stood on the bridge, Detective James Shaw proud in his efficiency in solving crimes. I thought, "Maybe I'm in the wrong profession if it's that easy."

"Do you think she'll strike again?" I asked him. "Two old and two new Shuttle Gals could be targets."

"That's why I'm going to close the river to floating."

"Can you do that?"

"I can."

"A lot of people make their living from the river. This is past the peak season, but I know a lot of guides with scheduled floats this fall."

"Breaks of the game."

"Let me suggest something else. *I'll* stay off the river. In fact, I'll leave for Florida early—within the week. Every death has involved me in some way—though we don't know what the intentions of the Mexican boys were."

"Are you sure? You make a living from guiding."

"It helps. I have a few floats booked. I'll get some friends to take them. They'll be glad to see me go."

"Don't blame yourself. But . . . OK. I won't close the river."

"Thanks. . . . You'll need to keep the trailer. I'll borrow one to take *Osprey* home. Can I tow my trailer to your office?"

"No thanks. I've called for a pickup with a hitch. Maybe you ought to take Lucinda home."

After we transferred the trailer to the county truck that soon arrived, Shaw asked, "When did you contact the Shuttle Gals and make your arrangements?"

"Only yesterday. I sent Marge an e-mail around five, telling her I wanted to take Lucinda out for the first time since her injuries and asking if Marge could do the shuttle. She said she wanted to check with Pam. She called her and got right back to me. Pam was going to finish with some shuttles by noon or a little later, and since we were floating late, Pam said she'd do the shuttle. Marge uses e-mail for scheduling more than Julie did. She did it mostly by phone and making notes."

"Would you forward me the e-mails you sent and Marge's replies?"

"As soon as I get to my cabin."

Shaw didn't ask me much, other than about booking the shuttle. It must be nice to be so self-assured—especially when solving murders. I could think of no reason to stay after Lucinda talked to Shaw briefly and confirmed the shuttle arrangement. We drove home in silence, neither of us able to formulate sentences that helped sort out the day.

Wuff whined a bit until I prepared her late dinner. Setting it down on her small Oriental rug, I noticed Lucinda shivering.

"Make a fire, please," she asked. "I'm chilled. Probably more from the events than the temperature. I'm going to make us a couple of drinks. I want to sit with you on the couch in front of the fireplace and feel your warmth."

She brought the drinks and curled up on my left. Wuff had gulped down her dinner and curled up on my right. It seemed like paradise—in the heart of Paradise Valley. But it wasn't. Pam's body was on the way to the morgue.

Lucinda sipped her Montana Whiskey, turned to me with a look that told of a troubling day, and asked, "When can we leave for Florida?"

"In a couple of days. We'll start to close up the cabin in the morning and make winter arrangements with Mavis. You in a rush to get to Florida? Or get away from here?"

"We both need a change of scenery. Let's divert a bit and go to Connecticut so I can continue the tour of Maxwell Hunt's life before you were created," Lucinda said.

"Like where Maxwell was born in Farmington? Where he had a paper route? Where he beat up a bully in kindergarten? Where he kissed his first girl—and second and third and fourth and. . . . "

"*Enough*!" Lucinda interrupted. "I want the PG-13 tour. No sex. No violence."

"Then there's not much to tell." I could sense the punch coming. Wuff let out a bark of approval.

Changing the subject, I said, "I haven't been in New England in years. That *would* put us close to New York City. We haven't talked about your apartment or your job. I wanted you to raise them only when you were ready."

"I'd like to stay in the apartment—if you're with me. You saw it when the attempt was made on the Chrysler and Empire State buildings. By the time I left for Montana—the visit that ended with the shooting—the apartment had taken on a 'Macduff' appearance. Our photos together are everywhere, but don't get any ideas."

"The only time we were there together I was sleeping on your couch when I was seduced by a beautiful ghost who drifted in to the living room in a long, flimsy nightgown. I wonder if she still lives there."

≈

"Wait and see."

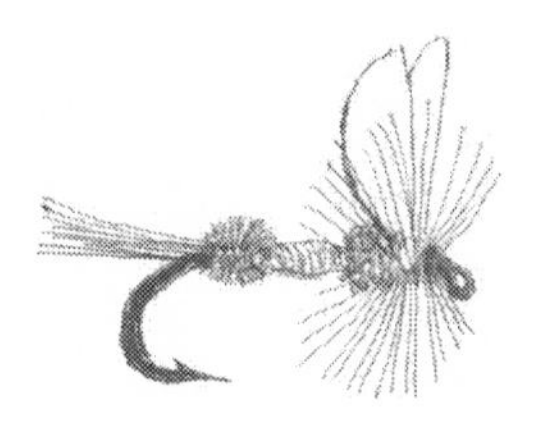

48

DETERMINATION DROVE US BOTH to tie up loose ends and with Mavis' help clean our lodgings. We left with Wuff in four days, drove leisurely as we'd planned to Commenticut, and two days before Halloween unlocked the door to Lucinda's Manhattan apartment. That began two weeks of whirlwind walking around the Big Apple. On the very first night, the seductress returned. And revisited nightly.

We decided to have Thanksgiving at my Florida cottage and departed the Northeast three days before, joining the crowds on the interstates heading for a few days of uncertain sunshine and warmth over the holiday. Jen Jennings, my Florida caretaker, had prepared the cabin and left a small turkey in the refrigerator.

Thanksgiving dinner was a quiet, private affair. It was five years from our first meeting at Thanksgiving at Lucinda's Mill Creek ranch.

"When most couples sit down for Thanksgiving dinner," I commented, "their previous five years were probably much like the five before and the five to follow. That's not been typical of our time together. I pray the shuttle killings are over. But Herzog and Isfahani remain a threat. It's been six-and-a-half years since I became Macduff, following Herzog's attack on me in Guatemala. Those two haven't faded away accepting that I died of a stroke. They assuredly know Maxwell Hunt didn't die. . . . We have maybe 20-25 years ahead together. I don't know how you feel about living under my cloud. It may not have a silver lining."

"I'm no prize. . . . An old maid settling into her forties. Amnesia that may reoccur. Probably abandoning a high paying job. Not sure I can make it as a photographer. Three bullet holes. How's that for damaged goods? . . . But one thing I agonize over—if we stay together, would you be doing so because you feel responsible for my injuries?"

"If I convince you otherwise, would it make a difference?"

"Very much."

I stepped over to a small wall-safe behind a large John Moran photo of a Florida marsh. Opening the door, I removed two small boxes, took them to the table, and placed one in front of Lucinda. It looked like it had been in one of the machines that crush derelict cars.

"This has seen better days," Lucinda said curiously. "You keep this in a safe? You are strange. There's a scrap of black velvet hanging from one side. There's a hole in that side . . . No—in both sides! It looks like it was shot."

"It was," I said. "A year-and-a-half ago on the Snake River. Jackson Hole deputy Huntly Byng found it on the bank of the river two days after the Park Salisbury incident. But part of it was missing."

"It looks like an intended engagement decades ago that went astray. Maybe she didn't like the ring and shot him."

"I'd like to think of it more like an engagement put on hold for a year-and-a-half."

"Does the box open?"

"Try it."

"Look at this! It *was* a ring. You collect the strangest things. Why is the setting twisted and missing a prong? As well as missing the diamond!"

"The box was in my pocket on that last float on the Snake. You remember our plans for that evening?"

"You planned dinner on the deck at Moose."

"I was going to propose at that dinner, with the sun setting over the Grand Teton. But I spent that evening on life support. You spent it in a coma. When Huntly recovered the box, the diamond was gone. The bullet had knocked it from the setting. I saved what was left of the setting, even if it bears some scars."

"Like me?" she asked in a whisper.

"And me," I responded. "And Wuff."

"It fits perfectly," she said as she slipped it on.

"Shouldn't I do that?" I asked.

"Too late. We're engaged!"

"But there's no diamond in the ring."

"That's OK."

"And I haven't actually asked you if you'll marry me."

"Too late!" she repeated.

"Is this how it's supposed to be done? Giving someone a battered ring with no diamond?"

"Have we ever done *anything* the way it's *supposed* to be done?"

I handed Lucinda another similar but new box. Soft, black velvet. With no bullet holes.

"I get two rings? One for each hand?" She opened the new box. "You found the diamond!"

"Not exactly. I bought another. We'll have it set tomorrow. I can't have people thinking I'm proposing in stages, first the box and setting and later the diamond. People suspect I'm odd enough as it is. But remember, you asked if I want to marry you because I feel responsible for the shooting. I'd already decided to ask, months ago. But you know I'm a little slow about these things."

"Not slow, Macduff—different. . . . Different's often good."

When Jen Jennings learned from Lucinda the next day that we were engaged, she brought us a celebration dinner of frog's legs, smoked mullet, black-eyed peas, grits, and rattlesnake hush-puppies. Jen and her husband Jimmy gave us beautiful matching belts their neighbor had made from a deceased rattlesnake. Not just any rattler—the one we'd found coiled on my stairs last year.

49

THE WOMEN'S REGULAR SOCCER SEASON at the University of Florida was in the record books with mostly wins. Once again the team would play in the NCAA tournament. The first two rounds were scheduled at home in Gainesville; the first, Friday evening, was only two days away.

"Shall we go to Gainesville and see the game Friday night?" I asked while we sat on the porch with the morning newspapers.

"Aren't you worried about being seen in Gainesville? Dan hates to hear you've gone there."

"I have a hunch that if Herzog is searching for me he's looking for a *single* person. He knew me at the depths of my despair over El's death. I think he was persuaded by my comments that I'd never remarry. *Maxwell Hunt* never did remarry. Shouldn't Macduff get one shot at it?"

"One *shot!* You mean one *marriage;* you've already received enough shots for a lifetime. . . . Do we wear disguises to the game?"

"Florida's playing Florida State. We'll stop at the Goodwill warehouse in Palatka on the way. They usually have a lot of FSU hats and jackets people are too embarrassed to wear. We'll sit among the obnoxious FSU fans. Herzog would never believe I'd stoop so low."

≈

I hadn't talked to Dan Wilson since we left Montana. I called him . . . not intending to tell him we were going to Gainesville . . . just to check in and see if he knows anything new about Herzog's whereabouts and activities.

"Hope you had a nice Thanksgiving, Dan. Lucinda and I are in Florida until April or May."

"I know you're in Florida. I talked to our Bozeman agent, Paula Pajioli, yesterday. She said I should call and remind you to stay away from Gainesville. . . . Sticking close to your cottage?"

"Yeah. Not hard to do with Lucinda here."

"She's good for you. When are you going to come to your senses and propose?"

The cell phone's speaker was on, and Lucinda heard. She called from the other side of the room. "He came to his senses last night."

"What a relief! You're far safer with Lucinda around—to keep you from doing dumb things."

"I can't deny that. Any news of Herzog? Or Isfahani?"

"Yes. Herzog's nephew, Martín Paz, is enrolled for a year of law study *in Gainesville*. He's living in a house in Golf View. Not *any* house—the house you owned and lived in. The title is now in the name of a Panamanian corporation we believe is a front for Herzog. We know Martín has frequent contact with his Tío Juan. We're watching him. One pattern we know about—he's been to *every* home soccer game all season. He always wears an orange Gator sweatshirt and blue UF cap. He has dark hair, light complexion, about six feet, and thin. He's a good looking young man. Black, deep-set, hawk-like eyes. Wears eyeglasses. He sits near the top of the bleachers and spends much of each game with a camera with a telephoto lens or with small binoculars, scanning the crowd. He's armed, which violates university policy. But we prefer not to challenge him about carrying a weapon without a license. All the more reason for you to *stay away*."

"You . . . call's break . . . up, Dan. I'll cal . . . gain . . . oon." I was shaking the phone.

"Do we still go to the game?" Lucinda asked.

"Even more so. We know Herzog's looking for Maxwell Hunt, thinking he lives in or near Gainesville. We know how to identify his nephew Martín—he doesn't know how to identify us. . . . And Dan apparently has an agent watching Paz. Presumably hoping he will lead Dan to Herzog."

≈

We drove to Gainesville Friday afternoon and parked in the law school lot, a three-minute walk to the soccer stadium. I splurged on dinner for Lucinda at the stadium—two allegedly all-beef hotdogs and we shared a Mountain Dew.

"Where should we sit?" Lucinda asked as we entered the stadium."

"We want to search for Paz, but not have to turn around obviously in doing so. Let's sit with any group of FSU fans and high enough so we can try to learn where Paz sits. We know he's near the top row; not many sit that far up."

≈

Five minutes before the game started, while the players were being introduced, Martín Paz entered the stadium and climbed to the third row from the top. He was wearing his Gator orange and blue. He sat on a cushion he'd brought and laid small binoculars on a game program next to him. Paz looked over the crowd until the national anthem was over and the referee blew his whistle to begin the first half. Then Paz took up the binoculars and began to focus on the different sections.

Lucinda and I were in a mix of fans several sections away, wearing FSU gold and garnet. Paz wasn't concentrating on where we sat.

"I'm sure I've spotted Paz," I said to Lucinda just before half-time. "I won't look while you try to locate him. To our left, over two sections. Look up near the last row, above the UF fans. He's using binoculars to scan the crowd. The few times he's looked this way, it was a quick glance."

"I see him. He's put the binoculars down. He's eating something, probably some of that same gourmet food you bought me."

Lucinda watched the game while I tried to keep an eye on Paz without being obvious. This surveillance continued until the last fifteen minutes of regulation play, when I noticed that Paz was no longer scanning—he was transfixed on someone I couldn't see sitting two dozen rows below him. Lucinda and I moved up a few rows to where we could see who Paz was watching.

"You won't believe this. Paz is certain he's spotted Maxwell Hunt. There's a man in his fifties sitting below Paz. When the man turned this way, I was *sure* I was looking at Maxwell Hunt. He's a dead ringer—even wearing khaki pants, brown walking shoes, an orange gator shirt, and a windbreaker. He must have bought my old clothes at a garage sale."

It was surreal sitting and watching Paz watch the man he thought his uncle Juan Pablo had sought for over a decade.

"The man's leaving," Lucinda exclaimed. "Is Paz still sitting?"

"Yes . . . *No*, he's up and going down the stairs two at a time. He's following the guy. Come on."

We went out a different exit, thirty yards from where the man walked out. He was oblivious to Paz following ten yards behind. Paz was oblivious to us. The man had no reason to believe he was being followed. Nor did Paz—he had his prey in front of him. He would avenge María and surely please Tío Juan, except that he was instructed only to locate Maxwell Hunt and inform Tío Juan, not to harm Hunt. Juan Pablo would take care of that. But Martín Paz intended otherwise. He had decided *he* would kill Maxwell Hunt.

The sun was long down and the campus lighting marginally protective. Lucinda and I walked quickly across the parking lot and west beyond a student housing complex. We were paralleling Paz and his unknowing prey. They were both to the north of the housing, we were to the south.

When we turned right and rounded the building, hoping to come up well behind them, we ran directly into the man Paz was following, nearly knocking him to the ground. My apology was mixed with confusion from looking at a face so like the one I saw in the mirror for many years.

"We're really sorry," I said to the man. "We should have looked where we were go-. . . . "

The man was looking beyond us. Paz had closed the gap and pulled what looked like a small revolver from a shoulder holster under his Gator jacket. He was screwing on a silencer. He pointed the gun directly at the confused and terrified man we had run into.

Paz's eyes spoke a hatred that couldn't be expressed in words. He ignored us as he sent three quick shots into the man's chest. I never knew if the man's voice sounded like Maxwell's; he never got to speak a single word. By the time the man hit the sidewalk, Paz had turned his gun to us.

"I have no choice," Paz said. "You two can identify me." My Glock was where it always seemed to be when it was needed, this time in a zippered side pocket of my ragged FSU jacket. I looked at Lucinda for one last remembrance. But six more silenced shots came from behind us, and Paz crumpled, dead before he landed in his own blood, which began to merge with that of the man whose only wrong was to look like Maxwell Hunt.

"Get out of here you two, quickly." Firm words came from the shooter, clad in black, his face in deep shadow.

I froze. Lucinda grabbed my elbow, "Quickly, come!" We walked as fast as we could past the law school buildings to my SUV, hearing the first sirens as we drove off.

"What on earth happened?" I asked Lucinda.

"We both just used up another life. We were a finger squeeze away from joining Maxwell's look-alike on the cement, life draining into the grass. I couldn't see who saved us, but I have a good idea we'll know more about it by morning. He had a slight limp as he rushed away. We need to get back to the cottage. I was wrong to let you bring us here."

≈

In fewer than two hours we were at the cottage. The eleven o'clock news came on the UF FM station five minutes after we walked in. The unsteady voice of a student announcer said two people had been shot to death near the law school and tennis courts. The announcer said the police had arrived at the scene, only to be told by two federal agents that the matter was under their jurisdiction because the shootings involved an assassination of an American by a foreign agent. Someone was making things up. The campus and local Gainesville police were angry they were excluded from investigating. It was the first shooting on campus since the attempt to kill the university president a year earlier.

"We've had front row seats for both the shootings," Lucinda commented. "I'd prefer the back of the balcony the next time. But I think we better stay away from Gainesville altogether."

"Even if the women win again Sunday and the next round is here next weekend?" I asked, like a kid about to lose a plea to his mom.

"*Even if!* We don't *move* from the cottage until we go to Montana."

"What will we ever do?" I asked.

"Consummate our engagement."

"You don't consummate engagements; that's for marriages."

≈

"Whatever. Call it practice."

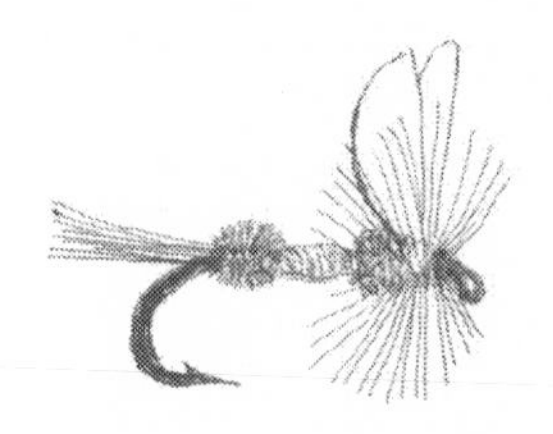

50

LUCINDA LEFT THE COTTAGE AT DAWN, while I was rolling about in restless sleep. She returned with the *St. Augustine Legend* and *New York Times*. The killings were too late to make the *Times* and not local enough for the *Legend*. She made coffee while I went online for the *Gainesville Gazette* and found the shooting was the lead article on the front page::

Two killings occurred last night on the University of Florida campus while the final minutes of a UF women's NCAA first-round soccer game played out no more than two-hundred yards away. UF and Gainesville police were unable to provide much information because federal agents were on the scene and assumed control.

What is known is that a UF graduate law student, Martín Paz, was killed by federal agents after Paz had shot and killed a reclusive, former law professor. The professor, Maxwell Hunt, was reported to have died of a stroke seven years ago in D.C. while attending a law meeting.

It's now known that he left that meeting and flew to Guatemala purportedly to give lectures, but was engaged in some unspecified activity for the CIA. He was attacked and nearly killed in his hotel room by assailants who have never been positively identified. CIA agents saved him and transported him by private jet to Washington where he received medical treatment.

His cover compromised, he was placed in a special federal agent protection program. He refused to have minor surgery that would provide him a different appearance and insisted on returning to live in Gainesville. He did assume a new name, Richard Potter. As Potter, he always wore a hat with a long bill, usually wore dark glasses, occasionally grew a beard, and dressed in what might be described as homeless chic.

Potter lived in a small house in Newberry and had become a reasonably successful novelist writing the increasingly popular saga about a family who first came to Florida with the Spanish in 1565.

Potter's assailant was at first unknown. He was carrying no identification. But a law student returning from studying late at the law library and passing the crime scene identified Potter's killer as a fellow law student, Martín Paz. Because of the continuing investigation the university has not released any further information.

"Who was Richard Potter?" Lucinda asked. "He obviously *wasn't* Maxwell Hunt."

"I'll know when I talk to Dan. I don't know why the person who saved us was on the campus. He must have been trailing Martín Paz. He might have been trailing us. Dan will tell us, maybe."

"I think you're wrong," offered Lucinda. "He wasn't FBI or CIA."

"How can you say that?"

"Did you see him?"

"It was dark; he was in shadows and wearing black."

"Which hand did he shoot with?" she inquired as though she were interrogating.

"I don't know. Does that matter?"

"He shot Paz with a pistol in his left hand. He couldn't do it with his right hand. He didn't have a right hand."

"What are you saying?"

"One more thing. When the man walked away, he was limping; something was wrong with his right leg."

"You can't be thinking that it was . . . "

"I *do* think . . . it was Juan Santander, the wounded and disabled vet you've taken fishing in Jackson Hole. Remember telling me about him?"

"I remember. But that's impossible! It *had* to be one of Dan's men."

"Why would Paz shoot the man he thought was Maxwell Hunt? Wouldn't he have informed Juan Pablo and let *him* do it?"

"Juan Pablo wants me dead. I don't think he cares who does it anymore. Remember, he sent his niece to kill the UF president. Why wouldn't he send Paz to kill me?"

"You're probably right. I thought he hated you so much, as does Isfahani, that one of those two would have insisted on doing the killing."

"Juan Santander doesn't know much about me. Not enough to intercede in the Herzog matter."

"Don't short change Santander. He was a Rhodes. He's a brilliant young man. He respects you. You helped him a lot. You've taken him floating a couple of times and talked to him off-and-on on the phone. Did you tell him much about your background?"

"No. Well . . . I don't think so. . . . But I'm *sure* it was one of *Dan's* people."

≈

We would soon find out. My cell phone told me Dan was calling.

"You cause more trouble than you're worth. You're *engaged.* You need to settle down. Raise a family. What normal people do. What the hell happened last night?"

"I thought you'd tell me. At least tell me who you sent to track me. He saved my life."

"I sent *no one* to track you. I don't have the faintest idea who shot Martín Paz."

I looked at Lucinda. She was smiling and nodding.

"I'm confused. I'll call you back. Lucinda wants to tell me something." I hung up, looked at her, and said, "You were right."

"Did you see Santander during the game?"

"No."

"What happens now? What will Herzog think? How will he react?"

"That's not pleasant to think about. Herzog's lost a niece *and* a nephew trying to get to me. He isn't going to blindly accept newspaper reports about what happened. I think Dan will do everything he can to make Herzog believe Potter was Maxwell Hunt in disguise."

≈

For two days we didn't move from the cottage, having nightmares and conjuring the most horrific consequences Herzog might plan. Lucinda and I both carried pistols. Wuff was aware that something was up and spent much of her time behind our bed. There was no whining when dinner was late.

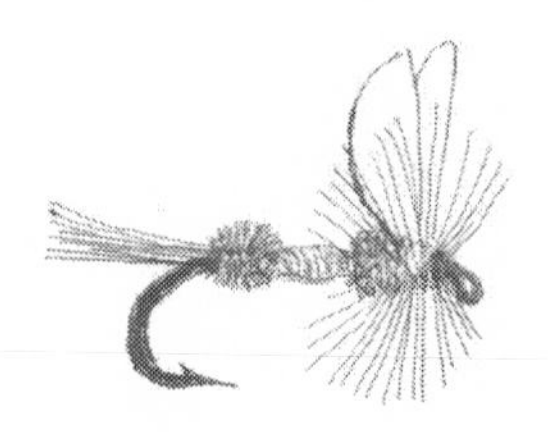

51

TWO DAYS LATER DAN CALLED again in late afternoon. Lucinda and I were doing make-work projects at the cottage. We were edgy and tried not to get in each other's way.

"I knew you'd want to be updated about Martín Paz," Dan offered.

"And about *your* agent who shot Paz. And who the hell is the person the newspapers call Richard Potter?" I demanded.

"Listen! We gave the newspapers his background info. Potter was an innocent bystander we *adapted* to be Maxwell Hunt. He was a reclusive man who looked like Maxwell Hunt and lived on about fifty acres outside Gainesville, where he moved about the time Maxwell 'died' of a stroke. Neighbors didn't know Potter. He stayed by himself. He was *not* an author. We made that up, also.

"And, of course, he was not Maxwell Hunt. I can tell you who he really *was*. He was the *consigliore*—a kind of in-house legal advisor—for the New Jersey Giovanni mafia family. He was in the witness protection program! Richard Potter was the name the folks at the DOJ gave him. Gainesville was where he chose to live. He loved sports. Pretty ironic, using an assumed name he unknowingly gave his life to save another person in *our* protection program who was also using an assumed name. A little unfair—Justice no longer has to pay for *his* protection. But we still have to pay for *your's!* . . . It'll be impossible for Herzog to get information about Potter. Like you, his history suddenly vanishes. But Herzog will try, especially with his nephew killed. He'll want to confirm that Potter was Hunt, and he'll want to know who shot Paz. Does that answer your other question? The shooter *wasn't* one of ours—period.

"We're investigating. We aren't going to play a public role in any of this. We'll blame the newspapers for any errors that arise about the incident. We're content that the newspapers took the bait and incorrectly identified Potter as Hunt. But the university's going to stick to its belief that Hunt died in D.C. of a stroke. If the university is proven wrong, the end result is the same—Hunt died—one way or another. If Herzog believes that Potter was Hunt, it should put to rest his search for you."

"What about identification from Potter's DNA?"

"There won't be any. The undertaking firm that took the body from the FBI cremated it—'accidentally.'"

"Herzog won't accept that. Where's the body of Martín Paz?"

"It's being delivered to the Guatemalan consulate in Miami for return to Guatemala."

"And Lucinda and me? We were at the scene of the killings. Did anybody see us?"

"Yes, unfortunately. But we've taken care of it."

"Meaning?"

"There was a university student standing by a window of his third-floor apartment in student housing. He could see figures in the shadows of the lights along the sidewalk between the buildings. He told an FBI investigator that he saw *five* people. He didn't see the face of the person who shot Martín Paz.

And he couldn't identify the two who weren't shot—you and Lucinda. Your backs were to him."

"Did he say *anything* about us?"

"Only that there were two figures who stood next to the man who was first shot. The shooter turned the gun on the two persons, but before he could fire again, he fell from shots by a fifth person who the student couldn't see. We've told him he's not to further discuss the matter with anyone. He was so scared we doubt he's a problem. In any event, he couldn't even tell if you and Lucinda were male or female."

"Has the Guatemalan government responded?"

"Only expressing regrets that Paz was killed. He was described as a 'promising young Guatemalan and nephew of a presidential aspirant.' They didn't comment on the fact that Paz murdered an innocent, unarmed man, by walking up to him and shooting him with an unregistered pistol fitted with an illegal silencer. The student in the apartment saw the man who shot Paz pick up Paz's pistol and remove and pocket the silencer. We think that shooter wanted the killing to look like a random robbery that ended with a shooting, not an assassination."

"I don't buy your 'not our agent' part, Dan. Your agent was watching us. He shot Paz because he was about to shoot us. He told us he had to kill us because we were there. Your agent intervened and saved our lives."

"Not true, even if I wanted to take credit for saving you two. We're mystified about the fifth person. But let's leave it with the fifth person being unidentified. That's the way it would be if we admitted it *were* our man."

"OK. Lucinda and I can't complain about surviving. Any recommendations for us?"

"Enjoy your engagement somewhere other than Gainesville. Go back to Montana."

"Montana's beginning its winter!"

"Go to Cancun or somewhere warm."

"Guatemala City?"

"If you do, it'll be one way, and we'll be relieved of you. Leave Lucinda with me."

"Not a chance. We'll talk about it and call before we do anything. . . . If we decide to go abroad I hate to go on airlines and through security using our names. Can you get us a couple of 'special' passports?"

"Send me photos. You'll be man and wife. Like you should be. Sorry they can't be diplomatic passports."

"Crosses to bear, Dan. Thanks."

52

JUAN PABLO HERZOG WAS IN HIS PENTHOUSE in Guatemala City overlooking the majestic volcanic mountains to the west. He sat at an antique German desk he "inherited" when his "dear brother" Padre Bueno mysteriously was killed years ago. Herzog was twisting a bronze letter opener in his hand, looking as though he was about to use it other than to open letters. He was berating his driver, who had dented Herzog's new, armored Mercedes SUV.

"Get out of my sight!' Herzog screamed at his driver. "I'll deal with you lat. . . . " His cell phone rang and postponed the coming retribution.

"Señor Herzog, I do not wish to interrupt you at home, but this is important. I am First Secretary with the U.S. embassy here in Guatemala City. We have just received sad news that your nephew Martín Paz died in Gainesville, Florida."

Herzog's hands were shaking—he dropped the letter opener and set the phone on his desk, turning on the speaker

"How did my nephew die?" he asked demandingly.

"There was a shooting near the soccer stadium. Martín was shot by a yet unidentified person."

"*When* did this happen?" he asked more gently, his voice losing its contentious anger and assuming a more calculating tone.

"Last night about nine, Señor Herzog."

"Why wasn't the killer apprehended immediately?"

"It was dark, along a dimly lighted walkway by the tennis courts. There is more. Your nephew apparently had shot a man before he, in turn, was shot."

"Do you know who Martín shot?"

"The newspaper this morning identified the man as one Richard Potter. But apparently he was actually a professor who taught at the law school until about six years ago when he was reported to have died from a severe stroke in Washington, D.C."

"What was this professor's real name?"

"His name was Maxwell Hunt."

"Thank you for informing me. Please let me know about obtaining my nephew's body for burial here in Guatemala."

"There will be an autopsy. The body will be released to your consulate in Miami as soon as allowed."

"Thank you." Herzog closed the cell phone, poured some rum and walked out onto his balcony. The moon illuminated a landscape that he loved and was positive he was destined to govern. He thought about Martín and María. It was hard to accept their untimely deaths, but he concluded it was a fair exchange for the life of Maxwell Hunt. He would call Abdul Khaliq in the morning.

What he didn't yet know was that Martín had unknowingly exchanged his life for that of a New Jersey mob thug who Herzog now joyfully believed was Maxwell Hunt.

53

AFTER TALKING TO DAN, I poured drinks while Lucinda created tapas. We carried them down to the boat dock and sat on a double swing with shoulders and ankles touching—sipping in silence. The sun behind us added its final hour's glow to the marsh grasses.

Lucinda broke the silence. "You think Dan will send us passports as an alias couple?"

"We'll soon know. But I think he will. The agency works in mysterious ways."

"Let's use them. I have a Sterling account in London with Barclays I've used for personal expenses when I traveled on business. I haven't touched it since before Isfahani's attempt in Manhattan. We could go anywhere in Europe; I'd like to stay in small, secluded private hotels."

"Where do you want to go?"

"Rent a car. Drive until we've seen enough. Jen will take Wuff. . . . Are you wanted by anyone in Europe?"

"By scores of beautiful women who flocked to my lectures in many countries."

"I didn't know law lecturers had teeny-bopper groupies follow them."

"It was hard. But part of fame."

"Didn't you have a bodyguard?"

"No. I loved being admired—and groped—in every port."

"This time you have a bodyguard. Armed. With scars to prove her ferocity."

"Spoil sport."

≈

We idled in London for two weeks and on the Continent for two months, pushed slowly further and further south by winter's frigid surges.

Three months later, on a repetitious sunny morning at the Posada in Rhonda in southern Spain, Lucinda was standing with coffee on our balcony, high above the surrounding plains, looking more relaxed than I could remember. We were about to drive to Seville for the day.

"I'm rested," Lucinda commented. "I haven't thought about Juan Pablo, Abdul Khaliq, Victoria Montoya, or Martín Paz in a month."

"Ready to go home, Mrs. Collins?" I asked, using her now familiar passport name.

"I am. I miss Montana, my ranch, and your cabin and cottage. And especially Wuff."

≈

Two days later April Fools' Day returned us to my Florida cottage where we picked up Wuff from Jen and packed for Montana. The drive west included a week with Lucinda's mother in Indiana. I was now on a "Liz" and "Mac" basis with her, far better than "Mrs. Elizabeth Parker-Smith Lang" and "you wretched person." She even invited Wuff to stay inside the house and, by the time we left, wanted to keep her. No one has ever asked to keep me after a week's stay. Liz learned of our engagement and for the first time introduced me to her closest friends. I was as nervous as facing Herzog. Well . . . not really.

Montana never looked better as we ended our drive west, stopping at Dan Bailey's and Albertson's in Livingston. Truthfully, Lucinda dropped me off at Dan Bailey's and went to Albertson's. She came back with a dozen grocery bags. I hadn't bought quite that much at Dan's.

≈

But I had tried.

54

MAY WAS IN BLOOM to the extent that vestiges of a Montana winter allow the full arrival of any spring. Lucinda was spending time on the phone re-establishing contact with a few loyal clients in Manhattan. I immersed myself in trying to sort out loose ends to the murders that may be the reason for my trouble sleeping. I couldn't bring myself to share Detective Shaw's certainty that all three Shuttle Gals deaths and the attempt against Marge and Pam at Marge's home were the work of Victoria Montoya.

Wanting to explore Shaw's conclusions with Erin, I called her. We agreed to meet for dinner at Chico Hot Springs. Erin preferred not to choose a restaurant in Livingston. She was having some personal difficulties with Shaw she didn't explain further.

I made another call, arranging to meet with Dr. Herman Ross, the Park County medical examiner. He performed the autopsies on each of the three women.

Ross's office was clean and neatly organized and looked like other professional offices—diplomas on the wall noting only that his profession was medicine.

I don't know what I expected, but there wasn't a sign of his being the ME. He didn't greet me wearing a blood-stained apron, holding a scalpel in one hand and a damaged liver in the other. He wore a well-fitted dark blue suit and a rep tie that may have expressed his college colors.

"I'm Herman Ross. I understand you want to talk about the three murders. I know your somewhat tenuous relation to the killings and your obvious concern. I'm happy to assist."

"Thanks, I wake at night wondering about what may be trivia unrelated to the killings. That bothers me. I appreciate your patience." I wasted no time on small talk and asked Ross directly, "Were each of the women dead before they were crucified on the beams?"

"Yes, they never felt the nails, or rather spikes, used by whoever impaled them on the wooden crosses. The women weren't killed by being crucified. That was done to make a statement."

"*How* were they killed?"

"Julie was attacked and raped. We have DNA from three persons who raped her. But she didn't die because of the rapes. She was strangled, possibly during one of the rapes, perhaps before."

"When was she mutilated by the removal of her breasts?"

"Almost certainly *after* she was killed. Possibly after she was nailed on the cross. She never knew. That outrageous act may have been part of the statement the killer was trying to make."

"Was there anything unusual, considering your autopsy on all three? Anything that might assist determining whether each woman was killed by the same person?"

"Perhaps. Olga was burned by a cigarette. Likely at about the time her breasts were removed. The burns appeared on each shoulder. And, of course, Olga wasn't raped."

"Was she beaten or abused?"

"No. She was strangled; the cigarette burns were made, and her breasts were removed."

"No cigarette burns on Julie?"

"No."

"Anything different with Pam?"

"Yes, Pam was first beaten. She was hit in the face several times with something club-like. Baseball bat? Axe handle? Something smooth. Not a piece with corners, such as a 2x4. After the beating, she was raped several times by the same person. She may have died from the combination of the beating and rapes. No sign of strangulation. And no cigarette burns."

"In your opinion, were all three murdered by the same person?"

"I don't think that's likely, but Detective Shaw believes they were and has closed the case. Indeed, I suspect he's never read my reports."

"Couldn't the killer have used a slightly different method of killing each woman to throw off the police investigation?"

"Yes, but there are significant differences. Julie was raped by three men. Olga wasn't raped. Pam was raped by one man, who was not involved in the rape of Julie. Different DNA."

"But, assuming Victoria Montoya was responsible for more than Julie's death, she may have used illegal workers or youth gang members she brought from Mexico. We know there were at least three people involved in killing Julie, one who killed Olga, five who tried to kill both Marge and Pam, and the one who later killed Pam. . . . We have DNA from eight of the ten, but not from Olga's or Pam's killer. The five Mexicans killed by Marge and Pam were not the ones who raped Julie. They were dead before Pam was killed, so they were obviously not involved. And the DNA was different with Pam. They might have been the ones who killed Olga, but since she wasn't raped . . . no DNA . . . we don't know. There were no traces of DNA other than those we obtained from the raped women. Except, of course, from the five killed by Marge and Pam."

"Nothing else to distinguish one case from another?"

"One unusual item I didn't include in my report on Pam. I didn't realize it when I made my report, but I recently went back to look at Pam's body and my previous reports. Pam's breasts were removed by someone who is *left handed*."

"How could you tell?"

"A person who stands over a body and removes a breast with a sharp instrument makes an incision and cuts at the flesh clockwise if the person is right handed. But if they are left handed, they would most likely cut counterclockwise. In Pam's case her breasts were removed with a counterclockwise cutting around them. That convinces me that a different, left handed person removed Pam's breasts. The cuts on Julie and Olga were clockwise."

≈

Erin was late arriving at Chico's that evening. I ordered a Heiniken's Light when I sat down alone at a reserved table by a window in a quiet corner. My affair with Moose Drool wasn't over; I just was slow in readjusting from our time in Europe, where "moose drool" is what it says. I'd finished one beer and was about to order a second when Erin arrived. She lighted up the room as she walked to my window table. I stood and hugged her, longer than might have been taken by some patrons as a gesture of platonic friendship.

"Wow!" Erin exclaimed.

"Sorry, Kendoka. It was a tough winter. It's good to be back among the people who count most."

"I want to hear about your winter. I'll take a hug like that *every* spring. . . . Work will take your mind off of whatever's bothering you. . . . You booked up pretty good for the season?"

"So-so. I've checked with several outfitters. The response was mixed. Some talked around the edges for twenty minutes before they made it clear I wasn't going to guide for them this season. One flat out said I was through, period! But enough seemed satisfied with Shaw's closure of the cases to book me. My weeks aren't filled with floats and wade trips; it looks like two-to-three days a week at most. I've rationalized that it's OK. I'll keep busy."

"How's Lucinda doing?"

I didn't think it was the time to tell Erin about our engagement. Lucinda and I would do that together.

"Little evidence of her amnesia. But I've put her into some difficult situations. I'll tell you more. First, I'd like to clear up some issues about the Shuttle Gals murders. OK?"

"Sure. Are you comfortable with Jimbo's views on the killings? You know he's closed the cases. The evidence is boxed and stored somewhere in the basement of our offices."

"I don't share Shaw's view at all. There are questions I want answered. . . . I met with the ME today." I told Erin all about the meeting. "Dr. Ross's autopsies made me more certain than ever that there were different protagonists."

"But, all ten could have been engaged in the killings and attempts following orders of Victoria Montoya."

"True, but why would she use so many different killers? One or two reliable gang members would be less likely to talk than one."

"They're back in Mexico. They may be talking. It's not as though one of them could brag about a killing in some local bar around here."

"What would you say if I told you that the five Mexicans Marge and Pam killed were not from Victoria Montoya's youth gang—the *Cascabelas?* They were part of a *rival* youth gang in Ciudad Juarez—the *Alacranes.* Montoya had nothing to do with the *Alacranes.*"

"Interesting! . . . How do you know about that? Our sources haven't led to finding that out."

"I have some friends in Washington in the DEA. One owed me a favor. I collected. The information's accurate . . . Erin, why did Detective Shaw close the cases so quickly, if he knew all that Dr. Ross told me?"

"Tell me. . . . You obviously have an idea."

"I think it has to do with Shaw's short attention span and his preoccupation with catering to the whims of the sheriff, especially at election time. . . . Another thought, the three women who were killed were all lesbians. If Mexican youth gang members did the killings, were they anti-gays? That doesn't make sense to me."

"That might be important," Erin replied, "*if* we were dealing with a serial killer after gay women. But when Olga was killed, she was *substituting* for Marge, who wasn't gay. The killer was probably after any one of the Shuttle Gals, not any one of the three gay Shuttle Gals."

"A lot to think about. Thanks."

I drove home to my cabin as dusk was settling in. There were lights on in Victoria Montoya's house as I passed her ranch gate. My preoccupation with the killings and wondering who was at the house distracted me. When I later turned off East River Road, I'd been driving for the last ten minutes at no more than thirty mph. I'm glad Ken Rangley wasn't patrolling this evening.

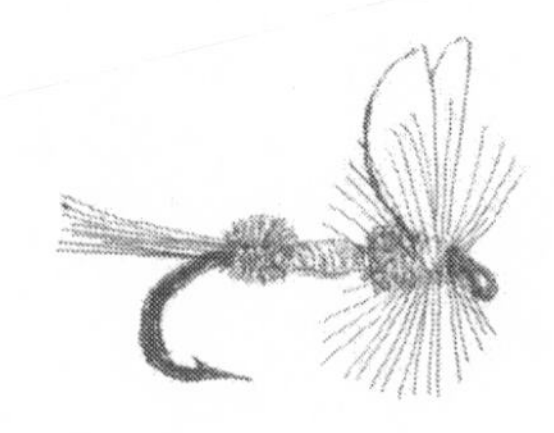

55

NIGHT FAILED TO BRING THE SLEEP I craved. I tossed until two, got up, threw on a robe, poured a Gentleman Jack, and went and sat on the sofa in the front living room. A few embers remained from a fire I'd made when I returned from dinner, more to keep occupied than for warmth.

I missed Lucinda. She had been alone working at her ranch for a week. We had not talked by phone. Wuff went back to my bed, hopped up, and curled up on my warm pillow. Looking at the dying glow of the fireplace, I started thinking about the three deaths, working through every detail I could remember. Then I refilled my glass and thought them through again. Sleep came finally as the first morning glow rose over the Absarokas.

At eight I woke, but not from the usually distressing news on the morning radio. I felt a warm sensation on my mouth—a pulse that wasn't mine. And thankfully it wasn't Wuff's. Lucinda had let herself in, crawled quietly into my bed and found only Wuff. She then discovered me on the sofa and sat for an hour on the edge quietly waiting for me to stir.

"Good morning. Miss me the past week?" she asked.

"What a surprise! To feel the softness of another presence waking me. . . . Warmth. . . . Fragrance. . . . I thought it was Wuff."

"Think I'll *ever* show up again like this?" She shoved me off the sofa onto an old Oriental carpet covering the stone area in front of the fireplace."

I rolled over, looked up at her, and said quietly, "I know who killed the Shuttle Gals."

"Did you just hit your head on the fireplace stone and have a revelation? . . . Who killed them?"

"You may not believe it. We need to get Erin here. I had dinner with her last night at Chico's after talking with the ME in Livingston. Erin was suspicious about some of the details of the deaths."

"Get shaved and showered. I'll call Erin and give you the phone."

Erin was arriving at her office when Lucinda reached her twenty minutes later. I'd finished dressing, the details of my theory rebounding inside my brain like a ball in a squash court. Lucinda handed me her cell phone. "Erin, I know how the three murders were committed."

"*And* who committed them?"

"Yes."

"Can you tell me?"

"I'd prefer to have you, Ken, and Jimbo all together. Easier to tell you all at one time. I think we can work out a few missing links if we all talk together. Can you arrange for us to meet tomorrow?"

"Of course. Do we need the County Attorney or anyone else present?"

"Good idea. Invite the County Prosecutor: Will Collins."

"Call you back."

She called back in fifteen minutes. "We'll be at your cabin tomorrow morning at ten."

"*You* don't have to be here," I said, turning to Lucinda. "I know you're in the middle of getting back to working with some clients. Come down from your lodge when you can."

"You sure you don't need me? I have my dad's old Luger."

"We won't be needing guns."

≈

Erin, Ken, and Jimbo arrived a few minutes before ten, followed by Will Collins a few minutes later. I'd moved enough chairs to seat six in my front living room. I asked the four to pour their own coffee and relax.

"Someone else will join us in a few minutes. I think I hear his car." Moments later a Mercedes 500 sedan pulled up in front, its polished body gathering dust from my driveway. Two tall, husky Hispanic men got out from the front and stood surveying the area. I could see bulges by the left armpits of their suit coats. Not from steroids, but from weapons ready to foment or suppress violence as the occasion demanded. One man opened a rear door and another man stepped out, wearing a black suit and white shirt; a red, white, and green tie; and sunglasses.

The group differed from three CIA agents only in their finely fitted suits and the green rather than blue in their ties. Plus, they didn't have little American flag pins in their lapels. Instead, they showed flags of Mexico—in the center a tiny eagle held a snake in its mouth. The man from the rear seat . . . logically the leader . . . stretched in the morning sun and walked alone to the cabin.

"Who is *he*?" asked Collins.

I turned to Collins and said loud enough for Erin, Ken, and Shaw to hear, "That is Roberto Montoya, head of the most ruthless drug gang in Ciudad Juarez, Mexico. He's Victoria Montoya's brother."

"He's not getting out of *here*," Shaw asserted. "He's going straight to *my* jail!"

"Don't even dream of that," I stated firmly. "He's never been directly linked to the murders, other than being Vicky's brother. . . . Be patient. He has some things to tell us."

I introduced Montoya to the group and asked him to sit. "Senor Montoya, would you restate what you told me the evening before last at your sister's ranch?" My curiosity on the way home from having dinner with Erin, when I saw lights on at the Montoya house, had caused me to turn back, open the gate, and drive in. Roberto Montoya was there alone. We talked for over an hour.

Montoya began: "As you all know, I am the brother of Victoria. My sister is not a well person. She is currently in an institution near Chihuahua, Mexico. She has excellent care, but I am convinced she will never be well enough to be discharged. She had a massive stroke recently, which left her unable to speak or walk without assistance. I have been here in the valley at her ranch the past week, preparing the property for sale. I intended to call Mr. Brooks, but fate brought him to my door two nights ago."

"We've closed the cases of the three murders, Montoya," said Shaw. "We know your sister was responsible for all of them and the attack on the two women as well. I doubt you have anything to add."

"I do have something to add, Detective. Victoria confessed to me before her stroke that she arranged for Julie Conyers' murder. She used three men who were part of a youth group she advised in Ciudad Juarez. I am extremely distressed that she did this. I have no intention of jeopardizing my good relations with the United States."

"She will have to be brought here to stand trial for the murders," said County Prosecutor Collins.

"Don't patronize me, Mr. Collins," said Montoya. "Victoria will never stand trial."

"But we have an extradition treaty with Mexico," responded Collins.

"That treaty is so much paper. You know my influence in Mexico. No request for extradition will ever even be considered."

"But we have you, Mr. Montoya. You *are* an accessory," interjected Shaw.

Montoya moved very slowly to extract a leather passport case from his suit-coat inside pocket. He opened the case and placed a passport on the table in front of him. "Detective Shaw, this is my Mexican passport. Please notice what it says on the cover."

Shaw leaned over and read: "Passaporte de la Republica Mexicana – DIPLOMATICO."

"You can't have a diplomatic passport," Shaw replied. "You're not a Mexican government official."

"But I am, Mr. Shaw. I am entitled to full immunity, even for a charge of murder made against me, much less against my sister."

"But aren't you also a U.S. citizen?" asked Erin.

"I am not. I am the only child of my mother who was born in Mexico. Victoria is both a U.S. and Mexican citizen. She was born in El Paso."

I interrupted. "Senor Montoya is correct. He is entitled to diplomatic protection. For a traffic violation. An assault. Even a murder. Shaw, you can do nothing to stop him from travelling home without creating an international incident. It would surely cost you your job."

"What do you think you are, Brooks, a damn attorney?" For the first time in months, Shaw showed the old anger I confronted when I first met him, but which had seemed to end abruptly the day after Olga Smits' murder.

"No, I'm not an attorney," I said. Erin looked at me and raised an eyebrow. She knew I was law trained, but also realized that I was not a member of the Montana bar, and, if I were licensed by any state in the past, it was likely no longer as an active attorney." I was *technically* correct.

Collins interrupted, "As much as you and I don't like it, Jimbo, Mr. Brooks is right. Roberto Montoya has full protection. But, as an American citizen, Victoria is subject to our law and will have to be extradited from Mexico."

"No, Mr. Collins," said Roberto. "Her Mexican citizenship will trump her U.S. citizenship in any Mexican court. Mexico does not extradite any of its citizens to any state or country where there is capital punishment. Montana has capital punishment."

"But Victoria is a *serial* killer; she's killed three women. And tried to kill another. It's outrageous!" Shaw was losing his composure.

"Detective Shaw," responded Montoya, "I have been speaking only to the matter of the killing of Julie Conyers. Victoria did not murder either of the other two women. Nor did she have any role in the attack by the five Mexican youth gang members. Furthermore, when the second killing occurred, she was here at *this* cabin. She was trying to burn it down, but was scared away by what she said was an attack dog."

I looked at Wuff curled and sound asleep with her head on Erin's foot. Some attack dog!

"Do you know anything about Victoria trying to burn the cabin, Mr. Brooks?" Collins asked.

"This is news to me, I. . . ."

Erin interrupted, "Señor Montoya speaks truthfully. I went to the Montoya house at midnight after Olga was killed, well before Marge and Pam were attacked. I wanted to look in the outbuildings, including the workshop. I took a listening device with me and overheard Victoria and Roberto talking in the house. While she denied killing either Julie or Olga, she admitted that she had come here to burn the cabin the very day that Olga Smits was killed. I found enough evidence to arrest Victoria, but she, with you, Senor Montoya, left that night to return to Mexico."

"That is exactly correct," Montoya confirmed.

"What evidence did you find, Erin?" asked Shaw.

"I found a small piece of wood in the workshop that hadn't been swept up," Erin continued. "Lodged in the foot of the table saw, it was a thin piece cut off the end of a 4x6 beam. Stapled onto it was a small tag with a bar code. I had it analyzed. It matched the end of a beam on which Julie Conyers was crucified. But more incriminating, when I was watching the house, Victoria and Roberto came out to the workshop to put some tools away. Both were carrying a bottle of Negro Modelo—a Mexican beer.

"When they finished replacing the tools, they walked back to the house, but Victoria left her beer bottle. I went in and took it and bagged it. There were some unusual keys, but I left them. Tests showed DNA on the beer bottle matched some DNA on the beams and rope used when Julie was crucified. We've since confirmed that DNA as Victoria's. None of her

DNA, or anyone else's, was found at the scene of Olga's murder, and nothing was found at the home that links Victoria to Olga's death. I'm convinced that she committed only one of the killings: Julie Conyers."

"May I interrupt," broke in Montoya. "Detective Giffin speaks the truth. Forty minutes after Victoria and I left the workshop and were about to board my plane at Gardiner, I realized I had left my airplane keys in the workshop where I had set down my bottle.

"I asked Victoria if she had them. She said she had started to pick them up, but left both the keys and her beer on the workbench. We went back. The keys were there. The bottle was gone. I knew someone had been there. So it was you, Detective Giffin."

County Prosecutor Collins had listened carefully and now spoke. "We have enough evidence to try Victoria, but likely no way to bring her to Montana for trial. What I've heard convinces me Olga was not killed by Victoria. That should re-open the investigation of Markel. But what about the murder of Pam Synder?"

"When Pam was murdered, Victoria already had been institutionalized." Montoya sat back, as though he had just made a move and declared "Checkmate."

"Even if this settles Julie Conyers' murder, what about the other two?" inquired Collins.

Roberto rose and walked to me and embraced me in the typical warm *abrazo* of two close friends in Mexico. I was embarrassed and awkwardly withdrew. "Thank you, Senor Montoya. We have little in common, but I admire your coming here."

Montoya turned to Erin and said, "You're an extraordinary woman. There were two armed men on duty the night you visited Victoria's. They would have shot you on sight if they had seen you. But they were far from the ranch house along the river netting trout and drinking. . . . I must leave. I think you have enough information to proceed." He rose to leave, looked carefully at Collins and Shaw to be assured that they would make no move to stop him, and departed quickly.

Shaw rose and said, "I don't believe one word about Victoria not being involved in *all* the murders. As far as I'm concerned, the whole matter is over. Closed!"

"Wait a minute please, Detective Shaw," I said. "Erin and I have more. Erin?"

"We do know more. Shaw, you never believed Helga Merkel was involved in the killings. We now know that she was."

"That's ridiculous. The matter is *over*. Besides, a scarf was wrapped around Olga Smits' waist. It was red, green, and white—Mexico's colors. It confirms that Victoria killed Smits."

"Helga Markel murdered Olga," declared Erin forcefully. "However much you think otherwise, we have proof. The scarf does not confirm Montoya's participation in Olga's murder."

"What proof?" Shaw asked, hesitating a moment.

"Helga is dead. Killed instantly last February in an accident in Venice Beach, California. She was with Professor Henry Plaxler, who died three days later in a hospital. Their car was totaled by a fire engine they couldn't hear because they were drunk and their radio was on loud."

"So how does that prove Markel killed Smits?"

"Markel left a letter. She was a troubled young woman with a conscience. What she wrote confirmed what Ken and I had discovered. We kept investigating; even after you told us not to because you were convinced Victoria did all the killings."

"What did you and Rangley discover?"

"You know, Shaw, that we never located either Markel or Plaxler immediately after Julie was murdered. You would never authorize an APB on them. We had no way to have them sought by police in other jurisdictions. Ken and I pulled a few strings and called in some favors. We learned that Markel and Plaxler drove to Venice Beach, California, and rented an apartment.

"Markel fit right in with the locals; Plaxler stayed pretty much out of sight. Mostly in a gym working out. After a few months, he began to ridicule her and humiliate her in front of what few friends they developed. She sought help but was increasingly depressed. Finally, she wrote a 'to whom it may concern' letter telling how Olga was killed. Two weeks later the fatal accident occurred."

"And how did Markel kill Olga?" Shaw asked. "She wasn't a big woman. Those beams are awkward and heavy. And Olga wasn't going to give up easily."

"Markel wanted to kill Julie," Erin continued. "She tried to convince one of her friends who were thrown out of the PETA conference to help. He refused. When she got to Missoula, a couple of hours after Julie had been found on Macduff's trailer, she convinced Professor Plaxler to help. Much of that convincing took place between bed sheets.

"They decided to duplicate Julie's murder, figuring that if it followed the same pattern, we would assume the same person, Victoria Montoya, organized the killing. Thus, it couldn't have been Markel. She knew about the matching colors of the Mexican flag *and* of PARA, but she used her own scarf, which had some of her DNA on the label. Shaw, you fell for that. You were *adamant* that Victoria was the killer of both women."

"How did Markel know about the details of Julie's death, so she and Plaxler could repeat them with Olga?" asked Collins.

"That wasn't too hard. The papers covered Julie's death in detail, down to mentioning the size of the timbers, describing the nails, the rope, and the scarf. Even how the cross had been tied to the trailer. And, of course, the removal of her breasts. There wasn't a rape in Olga's murder. Markel may not have read about that. . . . It was omitted from a lot of papers. And she apparently was not inclined to go so far as to arrange to have someone rape Olga."

"Erin," Collins again inquired, "how did Markel work out the actual killing of Olga?"

"She borrowed a small, enclosed trailer from Professor Plaxler. He refused to do the dirty work, but he provided help in planning. Markel drove the trailer from Missoula to Paradise Valley four days before the killing. She camped out at Pine Creek. She left her tent and locked trailer at the campground and, having temporarily exchanged her black dress and most of her body metal for jeans, a denim shirt, and a baseball cap, she hung around Emigrant talking to people about fishing—who was doing what."

"I didn't arrange to fish with Macduff until the day before we floated. How could she have known we were going to do the float?" Ken asked.

I interrupted and nodded at Ken. "The evening you and I decided to float the following day, I called Marge Atwood about a shuttle. She said she'd have someone there. Marge called Lucy Denver, who, if you remember, asked Olga to do the float when Lucy woke up with the flu the next morning."

"That doesn't tell us how Helga knew Olga would be floating the next day," said Ken.

"No, it doesn't," I answered. "Markel learned only that there would be a float the next day and one of the Shuttle Gals would be doing the float."

"How did she know that?"

"Helga Markel called Marge Atwood each day," Erin began, "arranging a shuttle and then calling to cancel because of something urgent. Marge is pretty patient; after all clients don't grow on trees when the economy is down. Markel played dumb—asked all about how the shuttle arrangement works. Marge is a talker and proud of what she does.

"The third day Markel called, she struck gold. Marge told her she had only one booking the following day—for Ken and Macduff. She mentioned them by name. Their booking the shuttle was a bonus. Markel hated them both for the way they treated her the morning of Julie's death outside the Howlin' Hounds Café. She decided to strike.

"The next day, she abandoned her campsite pulling the trailer. She watched from a distance as Ken and Macduff set off at Mallard's Rest. She drove there and waited for the shuttle van to arrive. When it did, she followed it closely to the Pine Creek ramp, where she placed several stolen orange cones at the entrance. That left Markel and Olga the only ones at the ramp. Olga never suspected trouble when Markel walked up and chloroformed her. Olga wasn't very big. Markel beat her to death with a club used to kill fish and dragged her into her trailer.

"Then Markel moved the orange cones so anyone could use the ramp. It turned out that no one did. If you recall, the weather was threatening. Next, it all turns grisly. Markel had cut the beams to the right size. She tied them to the trailer. The ropes and nails were ready. With effort, Markel moved Olga's body. She got her onto the cross. The last thing was to tie her own scarf to Olga's waist. It was red, green, and white. Markel bought it from PARA. She also wore one of those colored PA-

RA bracelets—red, green, and white. She knew the colors of Mexico and PARA were the same. . . ."

Erin nodded at Shaw. "You apparently didn't know about PARA's colors and assumed that the scarf meant Mexico. And that meant Montoya. . . .Blows to the head caused Olga's death, not unlike how Julie had been killed. But there was no rape of Olga. The final act was cutting off Olga's breasts. That was done the same way as it had been done to Julie—the newspapers were quite explicit describing the process. Finally, she backed the trailer into the river and removed the orange cones. Then she drove to Missoula. She and Professor Plaxler left the next day for California."

"That's incredible, Erin," I said, in awe of Erin's and Ken's investigation. "I still wonder if Julie, Olga, and Pam all being gay influenced the killings. Victoria may not have known Julie was doing the first float. Julie's being a lesbian seems to have had no part in her killing."

"Olga," I added, "who also was gay, wasn't originally going to do the float. She substituted at the last minute. The fact that she was gay doesn't seem relevant if Markel did the killing. Markel hated anglers, not gays."

"It wasn't relevant," Ken noted. "Victoria killed Julie not because she was gay but because she hated all the Shuttle Gals and Julie was their leader. Being gay had absolutely nothing to do with it. Helga Markel didn't care *who* she killed. Your float was *convenient,* Macduff. She would have gone after any shuttle person associated with any service. But she liked the fact that it was one of your shuttles; she was furious when she thought you ridiculed her in front of Howlin' Hounds. And she obviously disliked me."

"That leaves the attack on Marge and Pam and later the killing of Pam," I said. "Ironically, Pam's murder was the third killing of a *gay* woman. But we seem to agree that Julie and Olga being gay had nothing to do with their murders. Victoria hated the whole Shuttle Gals group for snubbing her. Helga hated anyone who was involved with recreational angling."

"But, Erin and Ken," Collins inquired, "do you two believe that that the third killing wasn't related to the first two? Who killed Pam Snyder?"

"We don't know yet," said Erin and Ken, simultaneously.

"*I* know," I said. All eyes turned to me. "In our case we have multiple killers, actually ten, if we include the five would-be killers. There were three victims. Or four or five counting the attempt on Marge and Pam, depending on whether you count Pam as a victim twice. We're all agreed that Victoria and her three Mexicans killed Julie. Roberto has just confirmed that.

"I hope also that we all now agree that Markel and Plaxler killed Olga. We of course all know *how* the five Mexican youths tried to kill Marge and Pam. That was done under orders from someone who wanted to challenge Montoya.

"But it wasn't Victoria Montoya. It was her main nemesis in Ciudad Juarez, Teresa Tormenta, the woman who leads the *Alacranes* youth gang. Erin has located the ranch Tormenta rented to house the five youths. Finally, I believe only one person killed Pam. And it wasn't arranged by someone else—it was a solo effort."

Slowly a left hand lifted a pistol from a leather holster and pointed it at me. We all turned to face the person.

"*Why, Jimbo? Why did you kill Pam Snyder?*" Erin screamed.

"I was completing a hat-trick on the three homos. And I didn't even have to kill Julie and Olga; others did it for me. All three were lesbians. Olga Smits and Pam Snyder had even gone to California and been married. *Married!* We're better off without them."

I didn't like sitting facing the round opening at the end of a barrel. I've been there before, and the ending didn't come out right. Just as on *Osprey*, when I confronted Park Salisbury, I faced a gun in the hands of a madman while my own gun was deep and inaccessible in my jacket pocket. "Shaw, we're not better off without them. They were fine members of the community. Give up the gun."

"Do as Macduff asks," Erin pleaded. "You can't get away with this. How could you have so much hate?"

"I would have been *sheriff* if it hadn't been for the damn *Corcoran* case."

Shaw had been publically rebuked by a judge for tampering with evidence in the case involving a gay bar that Shaw was trying to close. The bar's owner was George Corcoran

"Why did you kill Pam?" asked Ken. "She had nothing to do with the *Corcoran* case."

"Synder's older brother was the judge who rebuked me in *Corcoran.* I've been waiting for years to get even. I didn't want to try to kill the judge because it would have been linked to me. Pam was easy. And she was gay. Lots of people had motives that provided a cover. Montoya wanted all the Shuttle Gals dead. Markel wanted anyone associated with fishing on the river dead. They did two of the killings for me. I took advantage of Julie's and Olga's deaths. No one would link me to them.

"I could make Pam's killing look like a third strike arranged by the same person. I had access. I convinced Marge to copy me with all her shuttle schedules, allegedly so our office could protect them. The killing was easy—a copycat murder with a whole bunch of people with motives. No one cared when I closed the case, except you three, because it was just another bunch of Mexican thugs who must have done it, regardless of who actually was behind the killing."

"You raped Pam, you bastard," said Erin.

"Just as many times as the three wetbacks raped Julie," Shaw laughed.

"You cut her breasts off?" asked Ken, incredulously.

"He did," I interceded. "It was his downfall. Notice that Shaw's holding the gun with his left hand. I knew he was left-handed from when we talked about his experience playing football. The person who removed Pam's breasts was left handed according to the ME." I repeated what Dr. Ross had explained.

"So *that's* why you knew it was me, Brooks," yelled Shaw, pulling the slide back on the gun. I was a finger tremor away from one more episode with a sadistic killer.

"Partly, Shaw. I knew from Erin and Ken about your homophobic past. The *Corcoran* case. Your strong arm tactics with gays. But it really happened when you changed your attitude toward me right after Olga was killed. I didn't buy your friendly, patronizing manner."

"Was Shaw at all involved in the attacks on Marge and Pam?" asked Ken.

"No. Roberto Montoya told me about that attack. I didn't want to raise it when he was here. I knew the five Mexicans weren't part of his gangs. He told me they were a rival gang in Ciudad Juarez; Roberto had killed the brother of the cartel leader—Teresa Tormenta's husband. Tormenta wanted to get even and blame the murder on Montoya or his sister Victoria. It was horribly executed. Victoria was already back in Mexico and institutionalized.

"The five kids wore their signature headbands as *Alacranes*. They had gang tattoos. When the cartel leader learned what happened here, he went on a rampage on Roberto's turf in Ciudad Juarez. But Roberto killed him as he had his brother."

Erin turned to Shaw, who had the gun pointed at me. He was no more than ten feet away. "Don't be foolish, Jimbo. You can't get away. You can't kill all four of us. If you could, you'd be on the run until you were caught. Killing two deputies and the County Prosecutor doesn't go well with other police. Or with the FBI. Give up the gun."

"I have nothing to lose," Shaw said. "I'll take as many of you as I can. Macduff first. Then whoever makes the first. . . ."

A shot rang out, deafening and shaking glasses and dishes within the confines of the cabin room. Detective Shaw's hand that was holding his gun effectively exploded, parts of his gun and hand scattering in the room, leaving little more than a bleeding stub where his hand had been. Shaw screamed and grabbed at the bloody stump. It would never be used again. But he wouldn't have much use for it in a Montana jail, sitting on death row for the far too many years before he did the slow, final shuffle to the death chamber.

Slowly, the door to Macduff's darkened bedroom opened, and a figure stepped out of the shadows. The figure had opened the rear cabin door and slipped into the bedroom by its back door, carrying the .44 magnum Henry rifle that Mac had earlier been cleaning on the rear porch.

As the figure stepped into the light, the left hand was raised in front. The sun's rays streamed into the window and flashed against a bright, emerald-cut diamond, mounted slightly crooked, in a ring that had once deflected its own bullet.

≈

It was an incredulous way for Lucinda to announce our engagement.

EPILOGUE

Elsbeth Brooks set down the manuscript on the table beside her. She had not moved for the hours it had taken to read the second of her father's handwritten memories of his life. It was the first she knew of the details leading to his offering Lucinda Lang a diamond. The very same diamond that now hung from Elsbeth's neck. Elsbeth went to the small, walnut writing desk in her library.

The desk, once in the old Talbot Island hotel near the mouth of the St. John's River, had been in her dad's cottage south of St. Augustine along beautiful Pellicer Creek. That land had been donated to the Nature Conservancy. The cottage had been disassembled by Elsbeth a decade ago when her father decided he would no longer travel twice a year back and forth between Florida and Montana.

The parts of the cottage were stored until a few years ago when Elsbeth had it rebuilt on her small lot on Captiva Island. She had read the manuscript sitting on the same porch that once faced the salt-marshes behind the Atlantic dunes.

Elsbeth took a pen and piece of paper and began a letter to her dad:

Mr. Macduff Brooks
Mill Creek Road
Pray, Montana 59065

Dearest Father,

I have finished the second manuscript and now know the events of your life as Macduff Brooks up to the time you admitted you were engaged to Lucinda. You needed her; she saved you once again when your life was about to end and your guns were stored away.

Will the saga of Juan Pablo Herzog and Abdul Khaliq Isfahani ever end? They had sought you for seven years without success. You had both eluded them and further angered Juan Pablo by killing his niece María and by evading death at the hands of his nephew Martín, who lost his life trying to kill you.

I assume there are no further manuscripts, but I have more questions. You carefully kept Juan Pablo and Abdul Khaliq out of my life—I never learned much other than Herzog nearly beat you to death in Guatemala, and Lucinda once told me about Isfahani's attempt to destroy her office building in New York City. Whatever happened to them? They seemed to be closing in on learning your identity and location and cannot have been a pleasant part of your life.

Your loving daughter,

Elsbeth Hunt Brooks
14 Seahorse Way
Captiva Island, Florida 33924

AUTHOR'S NOTE

I enjoy hearing from readers. You may reach me at:

macbrooks.mwgordon@gmail.com.

Or through my website:

www.mwgordonnovels.com.

E-mail will be answered within the week received, unless I am on a book signing tour or towing *Osprey* to fish somewhere.

Because of viruses, I do not download attachments sent with your e-mails. And please do not add my e-mail to any lists suggesting for whom I should vote, to whom I should give money, what I should buy, what I should read or especially what I should write next about Macduff Brooks.

My website lists coming appearances for readings, talk programs, and signings.

Made in the USA
Middletown, DE
18 February 2021